Emma Davison's career began ignominiously when she was asked to leave her public school in Kent. A modelling course at the London College of Fashion led to her successful debut on the Paris catwalk as Dior's bride. She worked for top designers across the globe, and once caught Prince Charles nodding off in the front row of a fashion show as she pirouetted inelegantly in Vivienne Westwood's platform shoes.

In Sydney, she ran her own courses in self-development skills and communication before writing her first novel *Catwalk* in 1994. Her second book, *The Game*, set in the international world of tennis, followed in 1996.

Emma lives in London with her husband and their recently arrived first child.

Also by Emma Davison

CATWALK
THE GAME

WHO'S BEEN SLEEPING
IN MY BED?

—

Emma Davison

ORIEL

An Oriel Paperback

First published in Great Britain in 1998 by
Oriel
a division of Orion Books Ltd
Orion House, 5 Upper St Martin's Lane,
London WC2H 9EA

Copyright © Emma Davison 1998

A CIP catalogue record for this book
is available from the British Library

ISBN 0 75281 441 9

Typeset by Deltatype Ltd, Birkenhead, Merseyside
Printed and bound in Great Britain by
Clays Ltd, St Ives plc

To my mother and sister Harriet-Laura

ACKNOWLEDGEMENTS

My thanks to Sandy Webster at NORCAP; to Paul (he knows who he is) for his insight into police matters and that most precious of commodities – time; to Mark Cullens, Lucy Crawford, and Elaine Dobson for being frank and allowing me to peak behind a few closed doors; to my friend Vanessa for her encouragement and unfailing honesty when it was needed; and to my agent Luigi Bonomi – I'm *so* glad I found you – for turning this book around and making me feel I could do it! Special thanks also to my editor Jane Wood for taking me on, who, together with the inimitable help of Selina Walker, has made this a much stronger book.

Finally to my husband Greg for always being there and for teaching me the real meaning of unconditional love.

Home, home, sweet, sweet home!
There's no place like home! there's no place like
home!
John Howard Payne

ONE

It had been dark for three hours by the time he reached the house. There was a half-moon but most of its cold light was obscured by low, fast-moving clouds. The keys to the flat were warm, almost illicit, in his free hand as he walked swiftly across the quiet, residential road and up the front steps, two carrier bags jostling at his side. A car drove past as he reached the door, its headlights sweeping his form. He tensed, waited for it to pass, keeping it in his sight as it carried on into the night, then slipped the key into the lock and stepped inside.

The house was divided into two parts, access to each level from separate internal doors. He let himself into the garden flat on the ground floor, carefully wiping his shoes before stepping on to the polished pine-stripped floor. For a moment he allowed the morgue-like hush to sweep over him, poised, alert, as if he didn't trust what his ears conveyed, then gently closed the door. Immediately, the faint high-pitched bleep of the alarm broke the silence. The hall was lit only by a shaft of orange street-light and in the semi-darkness he stumbled and almost fell over a chair. 'Shit,' he whispered, quickly rubbing his knee, but pressing forward – urgently – until he had reached the small panel box concealed in a cupboard, and punched in the code. Instantly the shrill noise ceased and he stood there in the darkness, conscious of a tingling sensation spreading across the back of his shoulders.

All week he had been looking forward to this evening. All week he had been adding meticulous details to his plan, bound up by feelings of excitement, anticipation. But now he was sweating and nervous. This was insane. He hardly knew anything about her. They had only met once – at a pub – and spoken twice on the telephone. All kinds of things could go wrong. Some of them ran through his mind and he thought, God, is it really worth the risk? He contemplated calling her at home, but one glance at the luminous dial face of his watch told him it was too late to cancel. Nicole would already be on her way. With an almost fatalistic shrug, he decided he was worrying unnecessarily. He had come this far without any mishaps. Perhaps luck really was on his side. Gathering up the shopping bags, he carried them through to the kitchen and started unpacking. He would have to act quickly.

Twenty minutes later when Nicole arrived, he had everything under control. 'Wow,' she exclaimed, as he drew her into the drawing room. 'Oh, *wow*.'

Soft amber rays fell from the recessed downlights, and a coal-effect fire flickering blue flames from a cast-iron grate lent the room an added grandeur. 'This is so –'

'Unexpected?' he suggested, pleased by the transparent look of surprise, delight, on her face. Pleased too with the evident care she had taken with her appearance. A good sign.

'God, I had no idea. When you told me the other night –' she gave a playful shrug of apology, 'well, to be honest, I thought it was a wind-up.'

He smiled to show he understood, that the misunderstanding was something he was used to, then followed her gaze proudly around the room as each detail was absorbed: the classical furniture, the bold black-and-charcoal Regency stripe wallpaper, an elaborate band of cornice moulding just below the ceiling. Finally, as a touch of drama, the crimson-and-grey scallop design silk curtains, drawn to afford maximum privacy.

'Come on through to the kitchen and I'll get you a drink.'

She followed him along the brightly lit sunflower-yellow hall, pausing to admire a beautiful tapestry hanging, then past the master bedroom, the stripped, panelled door to which was partially open. As he had anticipated, the Napoleonic-style bed dominating the

2

room, caught her attention. She poked her head round the door to get a better look.

'What do you do on this,' she asked, eyes wide as she ran an admiring hand along the bed's blond wood. 'Play tennis?'

Several corny puns sprang to mind, but he resisted the temptation to voice them. He didn't want to create the wrong impression – not yet, at least.

They wandered into the kitchen with its range of French maple units, chrome appliances, the blue-pearl granite work surface gleaming like a slab of ice. French doors opened on to a wooden deck patio with large tropical plants, a silver-grey eucalyptus, and an Italian-style classical garden beyond. 'I *do* like your taste.' Nicole was unable to disguise the envy in her voice. 'Did you do much of the work yourself?'

'I had some help,' he said evasively.

'Guess in your job you've got all the right contacts. Perhaps I could lure you round to my place and get a few tips from you. I've no eye for that sort of thing.' She cast a surreptitious glance at her appearance in the huge circular wall mirror and teased a few blonde strands of fringe with her fingers, before settling on to a zebra print chair.

'God I'd love a place like this. You're so lucky. But then you've worked for it – gone for the big ideas. That's always been part of Barry's problem. He's not a forward thinker. Doesn't push himself. I keep telling him you've got to take risks if you want to get anywhere these days.'

He checked the food heating up in the oven, then pulled a bottle of champagne from the otherwise empty fridge. 'Barry?'

'My boyfriend,' she began, then realising her mistake quickly corrected herself. 'My ex. We split up last month,' she said, stressing her current availability.

'Because of his job?'

'Because of mine. He couldn't handle all the attention I was getting. Saw every man who crossed my path as a threat.'

Looking at her – golden legs, hair waterfalling over her shoulders, her opulent figure straining against her clothes – he could see Barry's point. He wound a tea towel round the neck of the champagne bottle and eased off the cork. It popped open with little more than a sigh, fine smoke escaping from the top.

'What does Barry do?'

'He's a gym instructor. Good at his job but won't push for promotion. To be honest, I think he's happy as he is. More fool him.'

Nicole was a model with ambitions. Not the kind usually found prowling the Paris catwalks. Although extremely pretty, she lacked the height demanded by the designers of haute couture. With her generous curves and perennial tan she was more at home sprayed across the bonnet of a McLaren F1 at the Earls Court Motor Show. There was no shortage of work and it paid well, but as she told him later over dinner, between sips of an exceptionally good Bordeaux he'd unearthed from the wine rack, what she really wanted was to save up enough and start her own PR company.

'I mean, you're already there,' she sighed, spooling egg noodles on to her fork. 'What's your secret? How did you manage to get so far so young?'

'I'm a quick learner,' he said.

She liked that. 'I imagine you are.' All the same he could see her struggling to understand how someone in their mid-twenties could be in possession of a four hundred thousand pound two-bed flat with priceless antiques littered about the place like betting slips at the Grand National. It was time to iron out a few of the question marks.

'Look,' he began hesitantly, so that it would sound like a reluctant confession. 'It's not something I normally talk about, but I have a trust fund I can draw from.' She stopped eating, fork paused mid-air. 'Some of it helped me to get started. The furniture, for example, most of it came from my grandmother.'

'Cool grandmother.' She said it lightly, but her eyes

were like blue ponds. He could see he was going up in her estimation by the minute. 'My gran's not very fond of people,' she complained. 'Makes a point of telling us whenever we visit that she plans on leaving everything – such as it is – to the RSPCA. What is it they say? You can change your friends but not your relatives.'

'Unfortunately not.'

She washed down a mouthful of pasta with some wine. 'Not that *your* relatives are anything to complain about.'

He smiled. 'I suppose not.'

They ate for a moment in silence, listening to the wind whistling up a storm outside. Suddenly she put down her fork. 'Who's Sophie Muir?'

He looked blank.

'I'm afraid I couldn't help noticing. There was a letter addressed to her in the bedroom.'

'Sophie?' On the wall behind Nicole were several photographs and postcards stuck to a pin-board. He hadn't been happy about leaving it up but the hinges were fixed to the wall with drill screws. It would have taken him too much time to dismantle. One of the pictures was of two teenage girls pulling faces at the camera.

'Sophie's my sister,' he said, after a pause. 'I let her stay here last week.'

'But I thought your surname was Leak?'

His brain slipped into gear. 'Muir's her married name.'

'Are you a big family?'

'No. Just the two of us.'

They drank their coffee in front of the drawing-room fire. Nicole was in the middle of telling him about an Arab who had tried to buy her during a recent trip to Abu Dhabi when the phone rang. There was an extension on a little Swedish table by the sofa, within easy reach, but he let it ring. Through the doorway in the hall he could see the black answering machine on a console table. Come *on*, he thought, glaring at it. Intercept the call.

'Someone wanting to make sure you have pleasant

5

dreams?' Nicole asked sweetly. Her voice was laced with curiosity.

'Work hassles. I'm always telling them not to call me so late. Here,' he reached for the bottle, 'let me top up your glass.' His smile was strained as the phone continued to ring.

She was watching him strangely as she held out her glass. 'Yes please,' she said, 'but aren't you going to pick that up? It might be important.'

'The machine's on.' He hoped to God it was – he was a bloody fool for not having checked it when he'd arrived. That was what came of giving himself so little time. 'I didn't want us to have any interruptions tonight.'

She seemed to accept his explanation and nudged closer towards him. 'Sounds promising.'

Just as he was beginning to get seriously worried, the machine clicked on. With a tight smile, he listened to the playing message, then relaxed when he realised the recording was too indistinct for either of them to hear what was being said. Nicole was leaning back against the cushions with one arm thrown above her head, a dreamy expression on her face. Earlier he remembered noticing that only one of her shirt buttons had been left open. Now four of them had come undone, leaving a large expanse of bare skin. Accidental or a surreptitious green-light move? He couldn't tell, but he wasn't about to complain. The view from where he was sitting was pretty bloody wonderful. Encouraged, he put a hand up to the edge of her jaw and ran a finger along her bottom lip. 'You have a beautiful mouth. Very sexy.'

She giggled. 'I was thinking the same thing about yours.'

Conscious of a delicious, anticipatory thrill rushing through him, his hand inched downwards. 'You know what I'd like to do right now?' He could feel himself growing hard at the thought of taking her in that incredible bed.

Her gaze was bold. 'I know what I'd *like* you to do.'

They started kissing, him stroking and murmuring as

6

his fingers teased free the rest of Nicole's buttons. She held his gaze boldly, but he could tell by the frequent rise and fall of her chest that she was wildly excited. With increasing haste, they grappled with each other's clothing until most of it was on the floor and they had become a frenzy of half-naked limbs. He had just found the fastener at the front of Nicole's bra – an unbelievably complicated design – when she pulled herself free from his grasp. Misunderstanding her intentions he tried to pull her back down.

'Loo,' she mumbled, stumbling from the room in her knickers – what little there was of them.

She was no more than a few minutes but he was waiting impatiently for her outside the bathroom door when she surfaced. She gave a half-squeak, half-giggle as he pushed her back inside and pinned her against the marble sink. 'You're keen.'

'I'm easily led.'

Their lips met. He could feel her fingers skilfully undoing his flies. '*Very* keen,' she drawled, as the last button gave way and her hand found his bulging erection. His trousers dropped to his ankles. 'How about in the shower?' she invited.

For a fraction of a second he hesitated. But then she took off her bra, liberating those warm, wonderful breasts he had been fantasising about all week, and he thought: To hell with the risks. Wasn't that what tonight was all about?

Needles of hot water steamed down on their heads as they fucked. He had to keep his feet evenly spread on the enamel floor to stop himself from slipping. Nicole's legs were wrapped around his waist, her head forced forward by a hanging chrome soap-basket. His knees were getting bashed against the glass partition wall and his legs were beginning to protest and tremble from the exertion, but she kept urging him on. 'Yes!' she kept crying. 'Oh, yes, oh yes!' And he was so close to coming that an entire party of Japanese sightseers could have wandered into the room and he wouldn't, couldn't have stopped. She was begging now, pleading in his ear to keep going. As he moved faster, shampoo bottles from the chrome basket hurtled to the tiled floor; a bar of soap landed on his foot – which hurt, but he kept pumping away, faster and faster. And then, just when he thought he couldn't stand it any longer, when he thought his cock would actually catch fire – she felt so hot inside – her hand made contact with his balls and the orgasm swept over him, Nicole gripping him, biting into his shoulder and making tiny mouse-like squeaks, until the spasms brought them both to a shuddering halt.

'A girl could get used to this,' she purred later, after they had done it again in the Jacuzzi. They had returned to the drawing room and were lying on the floor together in front of the coal-effect fire.

He looked at her thoughtfully. 'Me or the surroundings?'

'Both,' she said, gently nibbling his shoulder. 'I'd like to see you again.'

'What about Bruce?'

'Barry,' she admonished, frowning slightly, 'is history. I don't want to talk about him.'

'Fine by me.' He pulled her naked body back down against his and ran a hand up the inside of her thigh. 'In fact I don't want to talk at all.'

By the time Nicole left it was three in the morning. His main concern had been that she might want to stay the night. But as it turned out she was leaving for Munich first thing to make a commercial, so the matter never arose. The bathroom was a tip and it took him a while to get it clean. On the floor of the shower was a tortoiseshell soap dish with a large crack in it. Then there was the problem of the towel. It was hanging over the side of the Jacuzzi, sopping wet, and looking a little the worse for wear. But he found an identical one in the airing cupboard. He swapped them over, placing the used one in the laundry basket. The basket was already half full so it was unlikely that anyone would notice. In the kitchen he chucked all the take-away food containers into the empty carrier bags, including the remnants from their plates. Then he washed and dried everything, carefully returning each item of crockery and cutlery to its home. When he had finished, he went twice round the flat until he was satisfied that all traces of their presence had been eradicated, then gathered together the bags and his things, switched off the heating and reactivated the alarm.

Outside he was hit by the contrast in temperature. The freezing night air bit into his cheeks. The wind was up and its icy breath sent brown leaves chattering along the pavement. A furtive look round told him the road was deserted. He descended the steps to the basement where the dustbins were kept, and was about to offload the bags when he saw that they were all empty. If he dumped his rubbish here it might lead to suspicion; he was thinking of the tenants in the flat upstairs. Better not risk it. A few yards up the road, past a row of parked Audis, Mercedes and BMWs, he remembered having seen a skip. He climbed back up the basement steps, walked along to the skip and threw in the bags.

The inside of his car wasn't much warmer. He shivered, yawning mist into the air as he slipped on his seat belt. Minutes later, speeding along a deserted Ladbroke Grove towards North Kensington, the imposing façades of W11 began to give way to stuccoed terraces, some peeling and shabby. Soon he crossed the Grand Union Canal, passing bus depots and council estates. Litter danced in the wind. In a doorway the lone figure of a tramp lay hunched protectively over a bottle. As he turned left into Harrow Road, he gave way to the tiredness he had been storing all evening. The effects of the alcohol had worn off and he could feel a headache trying to assert itself. With only three-and-a-half hours to go before he had to be up for work, sleep had suddenly become an urgent priority.

He parked opposite the walled cemetery by a pub. It

had long since closed for the night so he wasn't too concerned about anyone vandalising his car. On the pavement someone had been sick. The pool of Tango-orange vomit was inches from his right shoe and gave off an ominously fresh odour – the remains of a curry if the colour was anything to go by. Inside the house an ever-present pile of minicab cards and free pizza delivery coupons had collected on the mat. He dragged himself upstairs to the top floor – cheap but cheerful carpet, white paint on the banisters, fading pastel wallpaper. The flat was a mess, with washing-up stacked by the sink and enough ironing to keep Irene, his mother, busy for a year.

He walked through the small, cluttered sitting room and into the bedroom where he collapsed on the bed, the smell of Nicole's perfume still on his skin. Within minutes he was asleep. He hadn't even taken off his jacket.

Two

Nick Hammerton, branch manager of Carlyle Estate Agents, faced his team, sitting in a fan around his desk, and sighed. Ruddy-faced and foxy-haired, with a propensity for loud double-cuffed striped shirts, Hammers – as he was known – looked as though he had spent his thirty-four years outdoors. In fact he was a confirmed Londoner who, when away from the office, was happiest socialising in pubs and noisy restaurants. This cheerful sixteen-stone Goliath who smelled of baby powder and loved German beer, was popular with his staff, but his temper was fierce and he had been known to roar as impressively as the MGM lion. This morning he was trying to sort out a crisis left to him by his senior lettings manager, Rupert. For months Rupert had been indulging in an affair with a married man – one of his clients. When his wife eventually found out, the two men had decided to run away together. With only an assistant lettings manager left to run Rentals, Hammers' main concern was finding a quick replacement.

He glanced at the small wooden sign on his desk which read, *You don't have to be crazy to work here – but it helps!*, then looked up and assessed the impact Rupert's departure was having on his staff.

'Always was a selfish bloody toad!' Oliver Sinclair grumbled in his public-school voice. 'Uphill bloody gardener.'

'He never liked you either,' snapped Roger Hymn, the assistant lettings manager from Leeds, an intense, whippet-like man.

Eve Scott, Carlyle's only female negotiator, frowned. 'Uphill what?'

'Fudge packers,' Oliver reiterated. 'Turd burglars, jobby jabbers, up-your-bum.'

'He means gay,' Roger muttered, his jaws working a piece of gum.

'Cut it out.' Hammers glared at his senior negotiator through fine, steel-rimmed specs.

Unperturbed, Oliver flicked a mop of fine blond hair off his handsome face, ignoring Roger's angry scowl. It was strongly rumoured that Roger and the former senior lettings manager had been more than just colleagues.

'I'll take over Rupert's workload,' Hammers went on, 'until we can get his position filled. Roger cannot be expected to carry the burden alone. And for God's sake handle the clients sympathetically.' Oliver yawned. 'Don't make unreasonable promises either. I'd rather you asked them to be patient; delay booking valuations until the end of the week. Try to buy us some time.'

The door to the agency opened, then closed. Martin Leak, twenty minutes late and rubbing sleep from his eyes, pulled up a seat and sat down. Eve, sitting on Oliver's left, leaned over and whispered in his ear, 'Hope your excuse is good. He's in a foul mood.'

11

Just my luck, Martin thought, catching Hammers' reproachful glance.

'Contact the recruitment agency, Eve,' Hammers instructed, as Eve doodled a Hermès bracelet on a notepad, 'and I'll get an ad placed in *The Negotiator*.'

'Why don't we just poach Dan Hills back from Foxtons?' Oliver suggested. 'I know for a fact he's looking to move.'

'We wouldn't get him. And after the fiasco he caused us last year, I wouldn't bloody have him.'

'At least he's straight,' Oliver hissed.

Eve glanced at her watch and Martin, watching her, knew that she was thinking about her fix, her hit of nicotine, the cigarette she would smoke as soon as the meeting was over – her first of the day. He had studied her closely over the months they had been working together and the slightest shift in her expression told him what she was thinking.

The first time he saw her was the day he had applied to Carlyle for a job. Eve, manning the office alone, had just secured a deal on a large house in Holland Park. Her eyes, an intoxicating shade of watered-down mint, had shone as she replaced the phone. She had seemed to him hopelessly beautiful, a star emanating gold tentacles of light, her laughter like music piercing his bones. It was a really big sale and because she was so excited, and he was the only person around with whom to share her success, she had kissed him. Even now, he could feel the surprise of the soft, warm pressure of her lips. The memory was like one of those precious shells he used to collect on holiday as a boy and bring back home; to be taken out once in a while and admired. At the time the agency hadn't been looking to recruit new staff, but some of Eve's good fortune must have attached itself to Martin because a week later Carlyle had taken him on.

Watching her now, the small hairs stirred along his neck and he wondered, as he always did in her presence, if she was aware of her effect on him. She looked up, and smiled sweetly at him. A smile without guile. Probably not, he thought ruefully, turning his head away to concentrate on the flickering blue flames of the gas-fire. He grinned all the same when he heard her say to Oliver, 'I'd kill for a smoke.'

At nine o'clock the meeting came to an end. As if on cue the phones sprang into life and everyone shuffled back to their desks. Martin was about to do the same when Hammers stopped him. 'A word, please.'

'"There may be trouble ahead,"' Oliver sang, reaching for the nearest ringing phone.

'I know what you're going to say,' Martin began, 'but it was unavoidable.'

Hammers removed his glasses and rubbed his eyes, which looked vulnerable without the optical frames to shape them. 'Look, chum, you're a great negotiator and I like having you on the team,' Martin could sense a 'but' coming – 'but Tracy's been off sick for three days and now I've lost Rupert. I can't afford to have my negotiators turning up whenever it suits them. For crying out loud, get a new alarm clock or something but don't let me down like this again.'

'Two red flags, Leak.' Oliver waggled a finger at him once he was back at his desk. 'Better watch your back.'

Martin ignored him and picked up an incoming call. It was Russell from Fairfax Hill, a rival estate agent. A deafening sound of drilling could be heard in the background which made it hard to make out what he was saying. 'Road works!' Russell shouted down the line. 'All bloody morning. Can't even hear myself think. I'm trying to track down the keys to Bedford Gardens for a ten-thirty viewing. Any ideas?'

'Er ... I think we showed someone round there yesterday.' An image of Nicole's lush, naked body spread out in the flat's marble Jacuzzi swam into his mind. He felt for the keys in his jacket pocket. 'I'll have a root round and get them over to you.'

'Get up to anything exciting last night?' Oliver asked, after Martin had hung up the phone. 'I only ask because you look a trifle pale this morning. Worth it, was it?'

'You, Ollie,' Martin said with a ghost of a smile, 'wouldn't know the half of it.'

His eleven o'clock appointment, an American couple in their forties, arrived twenty minutes early carrying several shopping bags and complaining of the traffic. The man bore an uncanny resemblance to Rupert Bear, both in nature and appearance. His wife was more formidable and wore a fur coat with sleeves that appeared to have been inflated with a bicycle pump.

It was a bitter morning with a hard blue sky, the ground mulchy with leaves, but at least the sun was out and for that Martin was grateful; properties invariably viewed more favourably on a bright day. From Kensington Park Road, he turned left into Arundel Gardens and parked his car outside a six-storey Victorian building. The large and airy maisonette had been taken on by Carlyle as sole agency a week ago. Given its price all the negotiators were champing at the bit to find a buyer.

'Which floor is this on?' the woman asked, glancing at the particulars he had given her earlier. 'Only Bill here's not keen on stairs.' She patted her husband as though he were a pet dog.

They climbed the concrete steps and, while the Americans waited, he wrestled with the lock, which was stiff and awkward to open until you had acquired the knack. It was a question of teasing in the key two-thirds of the way, then gently jiggling it clockwise. Inside, the heating blazed. As they passed through a door immediately to the right of the hall, a high-pitched insistent sound started to bleep, reminding him of last night's little hiccup. Automatically his hand shot out to deactivate the alarm. The code number was inside his breast pocket, but he didn't bother to consult it because he had it memorised already.

It struck him, as it had on each of his previous visits, that he had never lived in a place where light as a presence so dominated. He hovered in the hallway on a Persian runner, allowing the Americans to take the initiative. He watched them wander into the first of two drawing rooms, huge and book-crammed, which boasted a subdued, informal grandeur and looked out on to the communal gardens at the back of the house. There was a smell of lemon polish which he found both comforting and stimulating.

'All the fireplaces, cornices, mouldings and ceiling rosettes are original,' he said automatically.

'We'd have to carpet in here, dear,' the woman said, her narrow heels tap-tapping across the faultless oak floor. 'What about AC?' Martin blinked. 'Air conditioning.' The slight edge to her voice implied irritation in having to explain herself. She consulted the particulars again. 'I don't see any mention of it here.'

'No,' he said, thinking back to the three miserable weeks of good weather they'd had last summer. 'On the whole there's not much call for it.' She gave an unimpressed sniff and wrote something down.

The owners of the house, the Fitzherberts, whom he had never met, were obviously keen antique collectors. The rooms were full of carefully chosen pieces. Martin ran a hand along a nineteenth-century fruitwood desk by the window, and stopped for a moment to gaze at the gardens beyond. The only view his own rented home afforded him was of Kensal Rise Cemetery. He thought about the asking price on this place and wondered what it felt like to have half-a-million quid to spend on a flat. The things he could do with all that money – pay off his sizeable overdraft for a start. What a mistake it had been to take out that loan to buy a second-hand car for his ex-girlfriend – he was still paying off the finance company.

The Americans had emerged from the kitchen and were in the front drawing room which doubled as a dining room. 'Which direction are we?' The question came from Rupert Bear. It was the first time he had spoken to Martin. His wife was busy opening cupboard doors.

'West facing. You get the sun in here in the afternoons although, as you can see, all the rooms are very light.'

'*Aah.*' The man managed to draw three syllables out of the word as though he'd been told something of grave importance. Idly, he ran a stocky hand along the keys of an upright piano.

'Our present house was featured in the *Architectural Digest* last year,' the woman told him, 'a five-page spread.' She stopped and frowned. 'Oh, honey, now this would have to go,' she waved a manicured finger at the marble mantelpiece. 'It's not us at all.'

Martin had been admiring the fireplace – grand with a garland of flowers and fruit carved into the mantel – so kept his mouth shut. But he felt anger at the woman's insensitivity. What the hell did she want exactly – Buckingham Palace?

Five minutes later they were out in the street again. The Americans declined his offer to drive them back to the office. Instead they agreed to speak again in the morning and flagged down a taxi. After they had gone, he sat for a few moments in his car with the engine running. Laughter rang out near by and, as he looked out of his side window, three teenage girls walked by. One of them, a pretty redhead with large blue eyes, briefly caught his gaze. She continued on with her friends but just before they rounded the corner she glanced back at him with a curious half-smile.

A leaf landed on the windscreen and he watched it trembling, before it was swept away by the wind. He glanced up at the trees – almost bare now – and blinked as an image of his father, Frank nudged his memory: Frank sitting in the garden with a copy of the *Mirror* open in his lap, smoking one of those mild cigars that, as Irene used to say, gave you a mild form of cancer. Martin was six years old when Frank suffered his first heart attack. They were alone together in the shop and Frank was stocking shelves when suddenly he dropped to the floor, one hand pressing against the left side of his chest, the way he sometimes did when he got indigestion. Martin gazed at his father's inert form, sticks of Cadbury's Flake fanning his head like a yellow halo, until something seemed to snap inside him and he ran next door for help. His quick thinking saved Frank's life and got his picture in the local paper. They even had his name read out in school assembly. He could remember vividly the handshakes from the ambulancemen, the whispers, the curious looks in his direction in church, the free bag of chocolate brownies Mrs Brines at the bakers had given him. He had worn his pride like a badge, living off it for months, trading on it whenever he felt his prestige fading. Irene had kept all his press cuttings, just as she had from that other time, the time that neither of them spoke of, but lingered in the air like a bad smell that no one wants to mention.

A van pulled up behind him. On the side was written: *Curry's Constructions. You've tried the cowboys, now give the Indians a go*. Two men jumped out and opened up the back with a clang. Together they unloaded a boiler tank wrapped in plastic. Martin's hand hovered over the ignition, an internal voice nagging at him about the pile of messages waiting on his desk, the risks he had already taken by bringing a woman to a client's home. But the temptation was too great. He got out of the car, locked it and returned to the Fitzherberts' maisonette.

Without his clients, a sense of peace had been restored to the rooms. Intoxicated by the dazzle of beautiful things around him, he dropped his bunch of keys and mobile phone on to a sofa and drifted over to the recessed bookshelves which flanked the fireplace on either side. High up in a corner of the room, a small red light blinked on with a tiny clinking noise. He ignored the sensor, having already deactivated the alarm for the second time that day.

His fingertips skimmed the titles while he tried to assemble clues about the owners: Dickens' complete works, a leather-bound copy of *The Whitsun Weddings* with the author's signature inside, novels with French titles he couldn't understand, several weighty books on law and history. Among the many animal and hunting scenes on the walls were four small Victorian prints of an ethereal woman with bow lips and clouds of PreRaphaelite hair. He drew closer, hungrily taking in every detail.

On a nearby coffee table sat several framed photographs. One was of a young man who looked as if he had not yet learned how to fit into his tall lanky frame. A crop of acne skirted his forehead, and the slight scowl around his mouth suggested he had been an unwilling subject. But neither detail detracted from his undeniable good looks. A second photograph showed a girl whose features enabled him to identify her as a younger sister. In a larger frame was a picture of them, with their parents, at younger age. The father had the same broad jaw as his daughter and bore the look of a man in command. But it was the mother whom Martin studied with real interest, for he recognised a striking resemblance to himself; fine, straight hair shaped, in her case, into a pageboy, strong eyebrows arching large cinnamon-brown eyes, a wide, generous mouth. The parity was so striking that they might have been related. A protective arm was placed around each child and she was laughing as though one of them had just told a joke. She had the air of someone who was utterly happy. Quite suddenly he wanted to know her, to be the recipient of that smile. The image of the woman still in his mind, he looked up and caught his reflection in the large mirror over the fireplace. For a moment the two images fused and he considered the life he might have had if this woman had been his mother.

Upstairs in the master bedroom another wall sensor glowed red like a tiny heart. He examined a pair of ivory hairbrushes in a leather case on the dressing-table, in one of which a few grey hairs were trapped. In a side drawer he found a set of studs and solid gold cuff-links, a pile of white linen handkerchiefs – each monogrammed and carefully ironed. The suits hanging in the cupboard bore the mark of a Savile Row tailor. He fingered the cloth with envy. A wardrobe like that would cost him a year's salary. He drifted into the ensuite bathroom – with yet another telephone extension, he'd already counted four – and found a pile of books and magazines stacked haphazardly on a stool next to the lavatory: the *Spectator*, *Country Life*, the *Field*, several Christie's catalogues.

The third bedroom – somewhat smaller than the others and facing the back of the house – was his least favourite, but his attention was caught by the cricketing memorabilia that dominated the small space. Even as a small boy he had been passionate about the game. He took in every detail: a bat signed by the 1986 county team of Middlesex propped against the wall; several biographies of cricketing heroes; an enlarged, framed photo of a dozen young men in school blazers and peaked caps, each of them gazing seriously at the unseen photographer. Immediately he recognised a more mature version of the young man he had seen downstairs: his brooding, slightly arrogant stance, arms folded and with a hint of a smile as if he had just thought of something amusing. This was obviously his room. But despite the many personal belongings, Martin got the distinct impression that it wasn't used much. It was too neat and tidy. He opened a drawer. What he found inside contradicted his initial impression. Nestled in the underwear – male – was a carton of cigarettes, a silver cigarette lighter – reassuringly heavy with the initials C.F.H. inscribed on one side – and a collection of pills, mostly amphetamines, with labels from a number of pharmacists.

He returned downstairs. The lid of the Steinway piano in the front room had been left up. It had been years since he had played but he sat down on the piano stool, unable to resist the ivory keys. Gradually the music took him over, clear, exquisite chords of notes, slow and rather soulful. The piano would have been his second choice of instrument if things hadn't worked out but, from the very beginning, a saxophone in his hands had felt so absolutely right that playing it was as natural at breathing. Eve came into his mind, as she so often did when his emotions were stirred – usually through music. He imagined that they had just waved off their dinner guests, happy and rather sleepy, Eve leaning across the top of the piano with a dreamy expression on her face as he played.

Eve, voluptuously spilling out of black velvet, blonde hair loose around her bare, creamy shoulders, watching him, only him. And after a while, when neither of them could wait any longer, he would take her hand and lead her up to the bedroom. Just thinking about it made him hard.

Somewhere a machine whirred into life. The noise froze his fingers and for one fearful moment he imagined someone else was with him in the flat. Shit! They had heard him playing and had come to investigate. Then he realised he was being ridiculous. He closed the lid of the piano and followed the clicking sounds to a fax machine regurgitating paper in the adjoining room. It was from a hotel in Scotland confirming a six-day booking made by the Fitzherberts. The letter-case on a nearby desk proved more interesting. Amongst the envelopes, the personalised cards and sheets of notepaper, he found a folder of photographs and a crested letter written in a huddled, sloping hand, not without character. From the *Dearest one* at the top he assumed it was from Mr Fitzherbert to his wife, but after reading it he concluded, with some surprise given the uninhibited affection, that the letter was from her son. Dated two months earlier, it had been sent from America where he had apparently spent the summer, with relatives. He wrote at length about what he'd done, who he'd seen, how good the break had been for him. He was, he said, finally able to put what had happened behind him. Reading between the lines, Martin gathered he was referring to an affair that had ended badly.

It has been over a year now, yet if it hadn't been for your unshakeable love and support, I think I might have given up altogether. Even now, I can't think of them without feeling a terrible rage, a burning desire to get back at them for what they've done. And to think I once thought of him as a friend. How wrong I was, how horribly misguided I was about him.

Martin put back the letter and sifted through the photographs which showed various aspects of a pretty Queen Anne house in the country. In one of them was a figure, the same woman he had earlier admired, older this time and with a rather severe haircut but still wearing that captivating smile. Already he felt that he knew her.

It had begun to rain. Martin remembered Irene telling him that rain was God weeping on the world. He thought about the letter he'd just read, and found himself resenting the writer. Resenting and envying him at the same time, for having a loving family, a place like this to come home to, for having so much to take for granted.

A clock chimed. He had lost all track of time. His watch told him it was twelve o'clock and that he should have been back at the office half an hour ago. Hammers' earlier threat had been cause for alarm, but he knew that it had more to do with Rupert's sudden departure than Martin's time-keeping. Obeying a sudden impulse, he slipped the photograph of the woman inside his breast pocket. He collected his mobile and keys from the front room, reactivated the alarm and hurried back to his car.

THREE

Wednesdays were hailed with a degree of wariness by the staff at Carlyle. A great age seemed to have passed since Monday morning and yet the end of the week seemed a long way off. For those whose turn it was to work the Saturday shift it seemed even longer. The office was spacious with recessed lighting, and framed pictures of Notting Hill at the turn of the century were suspended below the picture rail. In the front lobby two green sofas faced each other, separated by a vase of fresh flowers and a low glass-topped table adorned with property magazines and agency literature. Off to one side was the financial room where clients were given privacy to discuss mortgages. Downstairs was the kitchen, known as the shit pit, and the administration room from where the office secretary worked. Dog-eared signs beginning to peel off the wall read: *The only place you'll find success before work is in the dictionary*, and *Losers let it happen, winners make it happen*, a hangover from the eighties.

At their desks with Martin were Oliver, Roger and Eve. Oliver was on the phone and a fraught Roger who was now doing the work of two people, was registering a new client. Eve, eating chocolate, sat slumped in her chair, green eyes gazing vacuously out of the window as if she had given up on the day. Because of her beauty clients often underestimated her skill as a negotiator, but she took her job seriously and was often the last to leave the office. Only last year she had earned the accolade of Carlyle's top sales person; the certificate hung on the wall behind her desk. Eve. Classy, beautiful, elusive, with a jackpot body; golden skin, a bell-like laugh, citrus curves that had grown men squabbling around her like attention-seeking children. The mere sight of her evoked in Martin an almost infinite range of fantasies, from the conviction that they would one day marry and raise a family, to the hopeless reality that he had about as much chance of securing her interest as a pre-pubescent smitten by a screen goddess.

'I'll be glad to have today over with,' she sighed, well-developed breasts straining against her pea-green twin set. 'I hate it when it's so quiet.'

'Any plans for the weekend?' Martin asked. The tasteful little Cartier watch on her wrist glinted expensively. There were rumours that a wealthy client had given it to her as a bribe to secure the purchase of one of Carlyle's properties.

'Spend Friday night in Cirencester then drive on over to Partridge Manor, probably. You?'

He shrugged. He would be with the boys playing his sax in Pike's insulated garage as he did most Saturdays he wasn't working. The band (four blokes and a girl who occasionally sang with them) had rough edges and lacked tightness – they were never going to succeed professionally, but that wasn't why they played. They played out of a love for music, a mutual appreciation of jazz and, in spite of a few technical flaws, when they got going they produced a sound that was fluid, effortless and natural. Only Hammers knew about this side venture of Martin's, and that was the way he liked it.

Eve took an incoming call and, while she was talking, Martin conjured up an image of her parents' Georgian mansion a few miles outside Bath. Oliver, who had seen photographs of it, used to wax lyrical about its infinite charm and beauty. Descriptions of the surrounding countryside unfolding like the soft lush contours of a woman's body, the grass tennis court on which it was said Max Carter, an ex-Wimbledon champion, had played, the impressive list of celebrities who had been to stay there . . . it all compounded his attraction for Eve. He knew she had a boyfriend – girls like Eve didn't stay single for long, but he hoped it wasn't serious. Oliver, who knew the man had again provided Martin with the sobering details: a title, money, the only son of a lord who would one day inherit a three-hundred-acre Cotswold estate worth millions, along with a mile-long island in Invernessshire, who was into shooting, flying and fishing and who threw himself down the Cresta Run every year. What bloody chance did he have against that kind of competition?

'By the way,' Eve said, hanging up and taking the note she had scribbled over to Hammers' desk, 'did you get the message about your mother?'

'Irene?' His voice was instantly wary. 'What did she say?'

She gave a little shrug. 'Ollie spoke to her.'

'You mean she was *here*?'

Oliver had just come off the phone. In one of his more flamboyant moods, he was wearing a newsroom blue shirt and a salmon-pink tie. 'Don't suppose either of you could sub me a fiver?' They both knew what he wanted the money for – a quick trip down to the bookies. In spite of this, Eve opened her bag obligingly.

Martin looked at his childishly full face. 'What did you say to my mother?'

'Ah, ye-es. Now let me see.' Maddeningly, Oliver stopped to help himself to some of Eve's chocolate. 'If memory serves me right, she popped by yesterday lunchtime. In London to do a spot of shopping and hoping to catch you before getting the coach home – Bury St Edmunds, I believe she said.' His left eyebrow looped slyly. 'I didn't know you were from Suffolk.'

'Any message?'

'Just that she was sorry to miss you. She didn't stay long.'

Irene – in London. More to the point, here, at the office. He lifted a pencil from his desk and started gnawing the end. She hardly ever came up to town. Why hadn't she phoned in advance?

He was aware of Oliver watching him curiously. 'Don't take this the wrong way, Leak, but I thought she was your grandmother at first. I got the impression you don't see the old girl much. Not close to the folks, then?'

Martin flushed at this perceptive deduction. 'It's difficult finding the time,' he mumbled, busying himself with paperwork.

'Indeed,' Oliver looked delighted at his colleague's evident discomfort, 'I should imagine it is.'

Martin looked away. He was assailed by a sudden image of his elderly mother hovering in the office doorway, hands – gnarled and veined like the bark from a tree – clutching a Bhs shopping bag, smiling sweetly but eyes anxiously searching out a familiar face. He pictured the tiny council house with its cardboard-thin walls, the cramped rooms groaning with knick-knacks and ill-advised furniture. Upstairs, after years of talking about it, she had finally redecorated the spare bedroom. With its flock wallpaper, lavender bedspread reflecting a slight sheen, peach curtains competing busily with the matching fitted carpet. Martin hated the room, hated it for its cheap vulgarity, for failing to rise above the menacing familiarity of mediocrity. It made him cringe and yet, when his approval was sought, he had refrained from saying anything. How could he have done? Irene and her soft, generous heart, transparent as glass. The room was her pride and joy. His opinion meant everything to her – he knew that. To admit the truth would have meant hurting her, and that was something he wasn't prepared to do.

He shot Oliver, who was taking a call, a wary sideways glance and thought: How much did you wheedle out of her, you devious snake? How heavily did you turn on the charm? He could imagine all too well the sort of things he must have asked Irene. It appeared to needle Oliver that, of everyone at the agency, Martin was the only one he couldn't quite figure out. So Irene's unexpected visit would have provided him with a real source of amusement. Even now he was probably having a good laugh at his expense. Martin felt a pang of dislike towards the sulky ex-public-school boy who thought the world owed him a living. What the hell gave him the right to sit in judgement?

Martin's afternoon was taken up with viewings. He got back to the office just as it was getting dark and, in the time he had been away, a transformation had taken place in Eve. The restlessness had been erased. Eyes shining, she looked a vision of loveliness and, as he walked through the door, she turned laughingly towards him. For a moment his heart melted. It was as though she was offering him her golden smile as a gift. Dazed, wondering if he were perhaps dreaming, he sailed towards her on a wave of emotion. A man's laughter, not his own, penetrated his blurred senses. He turned towards the source and found a stranger sitting at his desk, rocking back his chair.

'Piers, you are outrageous. However did you get away with it? If it had been me I'd have *murdered* you. Oh, hello, Martin,' Eve wiped tears of mirth from her eyes. 'You've just missed the funniest thing.'

He smiled uneasily at the four happy faces in the room, one of them unknown to him. In the corner, Roger Hymn was shaking his head in helpless laughter. Oliver was looking on with a foxy expression. Eve, giggling, made the introductions.

'This is Piers Hunt – a friend of mine,' she said. The man raised an amused eyebrow as though her choice of the word 'friend' didn't quite convey the quality of their relationship. 'And I'm afraid he's rather taken over your desk. Oh, honestly, Piers,' for a moment she attempted to look serious, 'look at the mess you've made.'

The man gave a disconcerting roar of laughter which was followed by more howls from everyone else. It was as though they had just shared the punch-line of a joke in which Martin had no part. Beginning to feel a climbing apprehension, he studied the tanned stranger lounging in his chair. He looked so much at home there that Martin half expected him to put his feet up on the desk. He was taller and broader than Martin, with thick crow-black hair and eyes like blue headlights dominating his face. He radiated a powerful sexual athleticism. Not even the layered swank of his clothes could hide the physical strength of his body. He was the sort of man women swooned over. Martin disliked him instantly.

Without making any effort to relinquish Martin's seat, Piers held out a china mug. 'Here,' he said amiably, bringing the front legs of the wooden chair down with a thump. 'Have some champagne before it goes flat.'

Martin's desk was in a terrible mess. Mugs brought up from the kitchen, and an assortment of glasses, which during the course of time had made their way over from the pub across the road, rested precariously on top of his paperwork. One had been knocked over, leaving his phone floundering in an alcoholic pool. Martin accepted the cup which was chipped and had a picture of the Spice Girls on one side. 'Just what are we celebrating?'

'Piers coming back from a trip to the States and New

South Wales,' said Eve, leaning provocatively towards the stranger so that she had his full attention. 'And next time you can damn well take me with you.'

He saluted her with his glass.

'Lucky sod,' said Oliver in his flat, arrogant drawl. 'What I wouldn't give to spend two months scuba-diving in the Barrier Reef.'

Piers eyed Oliver in amusement. 'I did find time to do a *bit* of work.'

'Where are you off to next?

Piers was looking at Eve not Oliver when he spoke. 'I fancy I'll stay here for a while. England's grown rather more attractive than I remember.'

Martin didn't like the direction the conversation was taking. 'Where'd Hammers get to?' he asked abruptly.

Eve answered. 'Went over to the solicitor's office. Some query over a client's fee.'

Oliver drained his glass. 'He did mention something about having found a replacement for lettings.'

'It had better happen soon,' Roger muttered. 'My patience is fast running out.' As he grabbed his coat, Martin noticed Piers's bored glance lingering casually over the papers on his desk. 'Right then,' Roger said, 'I'm off. Someone be nice and man my calls.' He threw Piers a look of melancholy desire as he left. 'Nice meeting you.'

A gust of cold air breathed into the room as he opened the door. Eve caught sight of the office clock and wailed, 'Oh, God! I should have been at Mr Ash's ten minutes ago.' She sprang up, rifling through papers strewn on her desk.

'Who have you got?' Martin kept Piers in the corner of his eye.

'The Wilkinsons. They rang again this morning.'

'I thought they wanted to avoid basement flats?'

'They do, but they're getting so desperate to find something they'll look at anything.'

Mr Ash's flat was a new instruction, taken on that morning by Hammers. Martin, on the lookout for a garden flat for one of his clients, had read the details

27

while Tracy the office secretary, typed them up.

Eve's searching took on a new urgency. 'Where the hell did I put those particulars? I've just photocopied them.'

Casually, Piers held up two stapled sheets of A4 which had been lying on Martin's desk. 'This what you're looking for?' Stuck next to the address on the front page was a yellow Post-it on to which she had scribbled: *Mr Ash away until next Tuesday. Wilkinsons 4pm with key.*

She shot him a grateful smile. 'I'll just grab the keys and we can leave.'

'Guess you want your desk back,' Piers said to Martin. He put down his empty glass and stood up. His movements had a vaguely feral quality so that, even in the apparently innocent ritual of smiles and eye contact, there lurked a hint of the predatory. 'Sorry about the mess,' he said, not looking sorry at all. 'Got a bit carried away.' Then to Eve who had returned, coat in hand, 'I don't have to be at Harry's until six. Why don't I give you a lift?'

'If you don't mind dropping me back here afterwards – save me losing my parking spot.'

He tossed his keys in the air and caught them with a jangle. 'Let's go.'

Martin, who remembered seeing the alarm code on the instructions, said as they reached the door, 'Don't forget: 8434.'

Eve turned round. 'Sorry?'

'The security code to Mr Ash's flat. 8434.' A few weeks ago she had summoned half of the Notting Hill police force to a client's house in Holland Park after forgetting to write down the alarm number. From the sudden look of relief on her face, it was clear she had been about to do the same thing.

Piers glanced at him curiously over his shoulder. 'That's a good memory you have.'

Martin shrugged. 'Some things stick. 1978: Botham bowled eight for thirty-four against Pakistan at Lord's.'

He drove to work the following Monday in the dark. The

sky pressed downwards with a gloomy foreboding, leaving commuters stumbling from their homes towards work unable to distinguish night from day.

With the gas-fire already flickering, the brightly lit office offered a welcome respite. Roger, holding a cup of steaming coffee in his hands and chewing gum, was sitting at his desk already on the phone. He was wearing the pleasantly grim expression usually associated with an operating surgeon. Hammers was talking to a woman with her back to Martin.

'Ah, Martin.' Hammers had spotted him. 'Over here, chum. I want you to meet Celia Fallow. This is Martin Leak, one of my negotiators.'

The woman turned to look at him. She was tall; tall enough to meet his eyes levelly, and pale. She wore her nutmeg cap of hair with an air of severity, the sharp fringe and sides which obscured most of her features reminding him of a cloche hat. On her feet were pretty, low-heeled pumps and she was wearing one of those long military navy-blue coats that had recently been in vogue.

'Celia's agreed to be our new lettings manager. We were just saying,' Hammers explained, 'how much easier it's going to be for her to get to work. She only lives up the road.'

'Bayswater,' she disclosed, smiling guardedly at Martin.

'Walking distance,' Martin said. 'I'm envious.'

The door to the office opened again and Oliver swept in complaining about the weather. Behind him emerged Eve, a striking flash of red cashmere. They both eyed Celia curiously as the introductions were made.

'You'll certainly make Roger happy,' Oliver said, removing a packet of Rothmans and a disposable cigarette lighter from the inside pocket of his jacket, ready to smoke in the kitchen later. 'He hasn't been himself at all since Rupert left.' Hammers shot him a look of warning.

During the meeting there were appraising glances all round as Hammers told them about Celia. He gave her quite a build-up and it became clear how pleased he was to have her on the team – obviously she had been head-hunted. Her back ruler-straight, she kept her face averted, a posture that could easily have been construed as arrogance, although Martin was more inclined to think it was because she found the overt praise uncomfortable. From time to time she smoothed the right side of her glossy slab of hair with her palm, coaxing it back into place against her cheek like a silken curtain. But it wasn't until the meeting was over that he discovered the reason for the nervous gesture. It happened in a moment: the two of them colliding in a doorway – her going out, him coming in – but during that brief interlude she looked at him properly and he drank in the huge slate-coloured eyes slanting gently upwards, full of seriousness but rather wonderful, he thought, none the less. And then he saw it. Under a film of foundation the scar ran from the right edge of her mouth up to her cheek-bone. The tissue appeared even more white than the skin around it. It looked as if someone had used a thin blade to slice it open. He thought he had arranged his expression casually enough, but evidently he hadn't. The surprise, the shock, must have been smeared all over his face because she flinched and, with a stricken look, turned away.

'They found a baby at Gatwick,' Eve announced later.

In Hammers' absence, Roger was flicking through a copy of *Hello!* 'Inside a bin in one of the loos, I heard.'

'Ideal place for it, in my opinion,' Oliver quipped, stapling particulars together. 'Snivelling brats.'

'Wearing your charitable hat today, are we?' Roger smiled thinly.

'Try living with them,' Oliver complained. 'My sister came to stay last week with all three of hers. I'd have got more peace if I'd pitched a tent on the Portobello Road.'

'But to carry it for nine months,' Eve mused. 'And only *then* get rid of it?'

Oliver eyed her sceptically. 'God, don't tell me you're

getting broody.'

'Don't be ridiculous. I only meant that for a mother to go and dump her baby in a public loo, she must have been half out of her mind.'

Oliver's retort was blunt. 'Makes perfect sense to me. It simply means she didn't want the damn thing.'

'There speaks the great expert.' They turned in surprise to find Martin at the top of the stairs. In one hand he held a cup of coffee. 'As usual, Oliver,' he said coldly, 'you're talking out of your arse!'

Martin's day had started with a blank diary, but by ten it was full of appointments. He was so busy trying to keep up with himself, responding to calls, dashing in and out of the office, that he hardly gave the new recruit a thought. Just occasionally he would glance up and find her in his vision: head bent over her desk; recessed lighting catching the polish of her helmet of hair as she arranged a small vase of flowers on her desk; running through the management files with Hammers. He felt bad about his earlier tactlessness, conscious that he had conveyed the wrong message, so as a gesture of goodwill he suggested they go for a drink after work. To his surprise she accepted.

At six thirty he was shrugging on his coat to leave when Oliver surfaced from the basement.

'God help us. You're not *still* wearing that old rag,' he sighed, eyeing up Martin's elderly duffle-coat in despair. 'Frankly, you want to get yourself something snazzier, something with a bit of zip.'

'I appreciate the concern, Ollie, but I happen to like the way my coat looks. Besides,' he peered down at Oliver's luminous socks screaming at him, 'since when did you become such an authority on fashion?'

Oliver ignored the sarcasm. 'That's the difference between you and me, Leak. Whether you like it or not, appearance is the name of the game – something I take very seriously and you unfortunately don't, which is why I make three times as much money as you.'

*

Martin decided on the Beach Blanket Babylon which was perhaps an unwise choice as it was already packed with noisy drinkers. They both took cars, but whereas Celia had to park round the corner, he managed to get a parking space directly outside after spotting a Mercedes pulling away. The packed interior was like walking into a sauna. He carried their drinks over to the table Celia had secured by the fire, the wide-open jaws of a lion's mouth carved in bleached stone.

He set down a gin and tonic and a pint of Guinness. 'How was your first day? Still reeling from the shock?'

'To be honest I wasn't expecting such a smooth start. Everyone's been great.'

'Maybe you just have the knack.' She raised an eyebrow. 'Of first days. Mine was an unequivocal disaster. I managed to get myself and an important client stuck in a lift between two floors. There was an alarm but the building was a new conversion with all fourteen flats empty so there was no one around to hear our cries of help. Couldn't even get a signal on my mobile. When I failed to turn up at the office they eventually sent one of the negotiators to find me. You can imagine the ribbing I took when I got back.'

She leaned back against the wall and smiled, taking in her surroundings in a seemingly relaxed manner but, to Martin, her movements were studied and shy. He took a quick pull of his pint, eyeing her over the white-peaked rim. Out in the street she had looked grey with cold, but the warmth of the bar had brought the colour back to her cheeks. He noticed that she kept the damaged side of her face turned away from him.

'How long have you been at Carlyle?' she asked.

'Almost fifteen months. They're a nice enough bunch once you get to know them. Ollie's the only thorn.'

'Doesn't seem to enjoy his job much.'

Martin shrugged. 'The truth is he's in the wrong profession. I reckon he'd be much happier lording it up in a country manor somewhere. He resents having to earn a living.'

His eyes were smarting from the fog of smoke around them. He tried to work out how old she was but, unlike some people who wear their age like an accessory, hers was somehow indefinable. She could have been anywhere from her mid-twenties to early thirties. She wasn't beautiful in the conventional sense. Her features were too strong, big nose, eyes too far apart, but her face had an arresting, unsettling quality. When she smiled – which she didn't do enough of – it glowed with a quiet radiance, erasing all trace of its defects. He became aware that he was staring so he asked her about her family.

'I'm an only child. Why do you ask?'

Because he took a vested interest in other people's families. No. He couldn't say that. 'I'm an only child too.'

'Mum and Dad were always too committed to their work to extend our family,' she said reflectively, 'I think after me they said, that's it. No more babies. But I've always regretted not having a brother or a sister, someone to grow up with.'

He imagined an ambitious couple running a small but affluent restaurant tucked away in a leafy suburb. 'Are you close to your parents?'

'Used to be, but our lives have taken different paths.'

'Inevitable, I suppose,' he said, thinking of himself. 'What do they do?'

She avoided the question. 'Nothing very glamorous.'

'So they're not cabaret singers.'

'No,' she smiled, then looked at him challengingly. 'They're missionaries.'

He picked up his pint to cover his surprise but, as he brought the glass to his mouth, something hard jolted him in the back and he lurched forward. Some of the contents spilled on to the table, catching Celia's pleated skirt.

'God! Sorry, Celia.'

'Don't worry,' she said gracefully, dabbing at the mess with a tissue she'd retrieved from her bag. 'Most of it

33

went on the floor.'

Angrily, he swivelled round to see the vaguely familiar figure of a man walking away from him. It wasn't until the man joined a rowdy mob at the bar that Martin identified him as Piers Hunt.

As far as he could make out they were a group of five. Piers was propped against the bar on one elbow, inclining towards one of the two women. Why wasn't Eve with him? Then Martin remembered her saying something about having dinner with her mother in Chiswick. The woman, perched on a stool, leaned towards Piers and whispered something in his ear. Her top was cut so low that her nipples were almost exposed. What would Eve have to say about that? Martin wondered. Suddenly, Piers threw back his handsome head and roared with delight: a reckless, hungry sort of laugh that reeked of sinister undercurrents. The gesture struck a chord in Martin. He had heard it before, from someone he used to know. But who?

The door to the bar opened with an abrupt jerk and a short, stocky man in a leather jacket appeared. He had a baseball cap pushed low over his head, but a few dark-blond strands of hair had escaped through the gap at the back. After a quick scan of the room he advanced to the bar and, to Martin's surprise, tapped Piers on the shoulder. He had just bent to whisper something when Martin heard a cough and realised that Celia had stopped talking. She was looking at him expectantly, waiting for a reply.

'Sorry?' he said, dragging his attention back.

'I was just wondering if they were friends of yours?' She was looking at Piers and his companions who were laughing again.

Martin shook his head. 'I've only met one of them once.' He stifled a sudden yawn. 'You were telling me about your parents.'

But she must have interpreted the yawn as a hint to go and began to gather up her belongings. 'Perhaps another time. I could do with an early one. Didn't get much sleep

34

last night.'

After they had parted and Martin was getting into his car, he noticed two shadowy figures huddled together outside the entrance of the bar. One was the stocky man with the baseball cap he had seen earlier. He was lighting a cigarette, one hand cupped around the flame to shield it from the wind. The other man was Piers. They were too far away for Martin to pick up strands of the conversation, but they appeared to be arguing. Piers turned away in disgust as if he were about to return to the pub, then he suddenly turned back again and thrust something – Martin couldn't see what – into his hands.

Piers glanced over his shoulder and, instinctively, Martin shrank in his seat, ducking his head. But Piers didn't appear to have seen him. Two girls with messy hair wearing ludicrously high-heeled shoes, appeared from the bar and tottered into the road. With a brief nod which seemed to suggest some sort of command, Piers and the stranger broke away, the stranger heading off in the opposite direction to the girls, Piers back inside the bar no doubt to rejoin his circle of friends.

What was that all about? Martin wondered as he started the engine and pulled away from the kerb.

FOUR

Hammers had found a buyer for the Fitzherberts'. The maisonette far exceeded his vendor's price range, but the couple – who were in the throes of selling their own place – had been so enchanted by it that they were prepared to beg, borrow or steal to raise the necessary funds. In their favour the Fitzherberts had yet to find somewhere to move to, so they had a bit of breathing space. Martin, who felt a particular attachment to the maisonette and had wanted to secure its sale, was disappointed that his American clients had failed to come through with an offer.

He was in the office basement an hour later, still mulling over the situation while he made himself some coffee, when his eyes were drawn to a grey sheet of paper lying in the hallway just beyond the kitchen door. He bent down to retrieve it and would have given it no further consideration had his eye not been caught by a name at the top of the page. It was a legal document – a decree nisi – drawn up by a firm of lawyers in Kent between Celia Jane Fallow and Richard Catford. She must have dropped it by mistake. Not the sort of thing you left lying around – particularly someone like Celia whose pleasant but detached manner conveyed a clear desire to keep her professional and private lives entirely separate.

Uncomfortable suddenly, Martin glanced furtively towards the stairs. The prospect of learning more about the elusive Miss Fallow (or was it Mrs Catford?), was too much of a temptation, and he speed-read the contents. The divorce became effective on the twenty-third of December, just two days before Christmas. What a miserable way to end the year.

He was trying to imagine what kind of man Richard Catford was when a high-pitched Essex cadence jolted him from his musing. It was Tracy, the office secretary, teetering on three-inch heels.

'Oh, Martin,' she said, self-consciously hitching her lycra skirt over meaty thighs. Her hair, a sort of shaggy-dog look, matched the pumpkin orange of her nails, 'I'm glad it's you. I've been meaning to ask you about something.' He waited obligingly. 'A mate of mine's organised this gig at the Banshee Basement and I was wondering if you'd like to come.'

Tracy was always inviting him to things; finding excuses to stay on at the office when he had to work late. 'When is it?'

'Friday week.'

'Tracy, I think I've already got something planned,' he lied.

'Oh, go on,' she urged coquettishly. 'You *never* go out with me.'

It was true. Refusing her invitations had become a reflex so ingrained that he said no automatically. 'Let me check my diary.'

'OK,' she looked appeased. 'And seeing as you're on your way up, be a love and give this to Celia.' She passed him a lengthy fax. 'She's been waiting for it all morning.'

Back upstairs Celia was nowhere in sight. He placed both documents on her desk, ensuring that the fax was on top. For the rest of the morning, interspersed with phone calls and registering new applicants, he watched for her return. When, just before lunch, she finally materialised, she took a seat at her desk and reached eagerly for the fax. At first he thought she must have missed the decree nisi because, after a quick scan, she put it down, apparently satisfied with the contents. But then she picked it up again, more slowly this time. When she saw what was underneath colour seeped into her pale cheeks. She glanced up sharply and looked around the room almost as if she expected to find herself the butt of a joke.

Feeling ashamed, Martin bent his head over a client's file in feigned concentration. During the ten minutes that followed he didn't take in a single word.

Lambton Place Health Club was tucked away in a tiny cul-de-sac off Westbourne Grove and as a bonus for coming in as last month's highest performer, Hammers had given him a week's membership. Martin had been about to suggest trading it in for dinner for two at the Halcyon Hotel when he remembered that Eve belonged to the club and worked out there most days. It was an ideal opportunity to spend time with her away from work.

During his first visit, he was taken in hand by a female instructor with a gorilla handshake and muscles normally seen on Sylvester Stalone. The woman was a masochist and put him through a gruelling workout. By the time the session ended he was bathed in sweat, shattered, but exhilarated and feeling better than he had done for a long while.

The next day he was given an exercise programme and left to get on with it. At first he poured all his concentration into what he was doing, but as the minutes ticked by and the time for him to leave drew closer, he grew impatient. Whenever someone new entered the room he looked towards the door. Once, two attractive blondes appeared, but his flicker of hope quickly turned to dismay when he saw that Eve wasn't one of them. For someone who treated the club like a second home, she was proving remarkably hard to track down.

By his third visit – a Saturday this time – he had all but given up hope of her appearing. He had stopped watching the door, and instead had adopted a habit popular with many of the other gym members, which was to flick through magazines while working out on the bikes. His legs burned as he peddled, but it was a gratifying pain and he gave in to it. He had found an out-of-date issue of *Tatler* and was drawn – as he invariably was on the rare occasions he read that sort of magazine – to the society pages. One featured the marriage of a top model to the American tycoon Steve McInerney. Lavish pictures of the groom's fifty-six-acre ranch in Aspen, Colorado, with its own landing pad and private lake that cost him six hundred dollars a day to heat could only be drooled over. There were various shots of the glamorous-looking guests and bridesmaids surrounding the happy couple, with references made to the six-course banquet and firework display which followed the ceremony. He skimmed through the details but one small photograph demanded closer attention. He peered at the three men immortalised on film: the groom in the centre, in a somewhat drunken manner, had thrown his arms around the shoulder of his two companions. The man on the left, brandishing a fat cigar and acknowledging the unseen photographer with an elaborate thumbs-up, was clearly joining in with the spirit of the occasion. By contrast, the man on the right had his handsome face half turned away from the camera, as if someone had called out his name at the very moment the photograph had been taken.

Martin read the caption underneath:

Hot property: fellow architects Ed Williams and groom Steve McInerney are joined by friend the Hon. Piers Hunt for some light-hearted banter.

Obviously, Piers had friends in high places. Martin scoured the rest of the photographs looking for Eve but, if she had accompanied him, she was one of the few to have eluded the camera's eye.

'Are you going to be long?' He looked at the sinewy girl hovering next to his bike and realised that she was waiting for a turn. In the last twenty minutes the gym had become almost full and there were several people waiting to use the machines.

'Go for it,' he said good-naturedly. 'I was almost done anyway.'

He had a quick shower and was on his way out, his kitbag slung over one shoulder, when he spotted Eve in the bar. Her face was glowing and her wonderful hair hung around her shoulders in damp curls. Best of all she was alone. He approached her table.

'Hello, stranger,' he said. An empty glass lay abandoned before her. 'I didn't see you in the gym.'

Eve looked up and smiled. 'Oh, hello, Martin. No, I went for a swim. Seem to have done something to my right knee so I thought I'd give the gym a rest for a few days.'

It hadn't occurred to him to check the pool area. He pointed to her glass. 'Can I get you another one of those?'

She glanced at her watch as if undecided, then smiled. 'I'd love some tea.'

He returned with a pot of Earl Grey and a bottle of mineral water for himself and sat down in the opposite seat. It was the first time he had been in the bar and he cast a cursory eye over his surroundings: the striped floor and the blue-green murals of dancing figures. The fluorescently lit counter which ran along one wall rather spoilt the overall effect of the room. They began talking about a luxury house Oliver had just taken on – four bedrooms all with ensuite bathrooms, a sauna, Nautilus gym, swimming pool in the basement – and calculated how much commission he would make on its sale. Then they discussed work more generally – ground on which Martin felt comfortable – until they were getting on so well that he decided to say what was really on his mind.

'Eve, I was wondering –' he cleared his throat '– if you'd like to have dinner with me?' She was pulling gently at her hair, running fingers through the heavy dark-gold strands to see how damp it still was. The gesture made it hard for him to concentrate. 'Tonight,' he suggested, imagining a candlelit supper for two, a romantic stroll along the Embankment, then later, well – he'd have to be made out of stone not to at least imagine what that might bring.

'Dinner?' she echoed. 'I –' Now it was her turn to sound awkward. 'I'd love to, only I'm not sure what my plans are. I'm still recovering from last night. We didn't get to bed until four.' She looked down at her watch so she missed the crushing effect her words had on him. 'Where did you have in mind? I mean,' she went on, 'not that I'm promising or anything. I'll have to check something first.' From her bag she took out her cigarettes then put them back again with a little sigh of exasperation. 'They don't let you smoke in this place and I'm desperate for a –' she broke off, the soft folds of her mouth curving into an enormous smile.

'At last!' Her face softened as Piers, gleaming like a thoroughbred stallion, strolled across the room. Martin scowled. The bloke had only been back in the country a matter of days and suddenly he was everywhere.

'Sorry, darling,' said Piers joining them. 'The traffic was hell.'

'How did it go?'

He grinned broadly. 'I'm on a winning streak.'

'You thrashed him,' she cooed. 'Oh, well *done*.' She caught his enquiring glance. 'You remember Martin, don't you? We work together at Carlyle.'

'Oh, yes. The numbers man.' Piers shook his hand briefly. 'Do you play squash?'

Martin – aware of Piers's fingers stroking Eve's shoulder through the thin fabric of her T-shirt, an unthinking gesture – smiled as sincerely as he could. 'I used to. Don't get much time for it these days.'

'Martin was just suggesting we all go out later for supper.'

'Well, I –' Martin began, appalled at the idea of Piers tagging along, with him as piggy-in-the-middle.

'That's very good of you,' the inflection in Piers's voice was a little less warm, 'but I'm afraid we're already committed elsewhere. And if we're going to make that auction, angel . . .'

Eve shrugged resignedly at Martin, but it seemed to him she actually enjoyed having Piers boss her about. 'We'll do it another time,' she said appeasingly.

'Sure, It was just a thought.'

They left soon after, filing back out to the reception lobby where Eve stopped to talk to someone at the desk. Mumbling farewells, Martin wandered disconsolately towards the main entrance.

'Martin?' He turned on hearing his name. 'It *is* you. I thought as much when I saw you in the gym earlier.'

Oh shit! 'Hello Nicole.'

'How have you been?'

'Fine. You?'

'I tried your number a couple of times but I kept getting the machine.' She scolded him with her eyes. 'I was beginning to think you were avoiding me.'

'My answerphone's been playing up,' he replied lamely. 'I really should buy a new one.'

Piers, waiting for Eve, did exactly what Martin had been afraid of. He came over to join them.

'Aren't you going to introduce us?' he said to Martin, directing the full blue beam of his gaze at Nicole. 'I don't think I've seen you here before.'

'I'm not a member. Actually, I just popped by to see an old friend.' She threw Martin a half-guilty look. 'He – er – usually finishes his shift round about now.' Martin remembered the blond instructor built like an Olympic shot-put thrower on duty in the gym upstairs. Had that been Barry?

'And is Martin an old friend too?' An apparently innocent remark from Piers but full of dangerous implications. Martin's apprehension mounted.

'We met recently. Martin gave me a few useful interior-decorating tips. In case you don't already know it, he's got the most amazing taste.'

'Has he indeed.' Piers's bright eyes were intent and the force of his attention was on Martin.

This was getting out of hand. 'How was your trip to Munich?' Martin cut in.

'Cool. It rained throughout the first week which pissed everyone off except me. The delay meant we had to reshoot so I came away with double my fee.'

'You're a model?' said Piers.

She smiled at him delightedly. 'How did you guess?'

The bloke made you want to throw up. How could she fall for such an obvious line? Infuriatingly, Martin's mobile chose that moment to ring. It was a solicitor he had been trying to track down all week so he couldn't risk calling him back later. The line was so bad that he was forced to take the call outside. Through the front window he could see Piers and Nicole, Piers's head bent slightly as he listened to something she said. Martin hoped that Nicole would find some excuse to extricate herself, that Barry would finish his shift and cart her off somewhere far away, but she seemed to be hanging on to Piers's every word. Smooth bastard! He was forced to look away from them in order to note some information the solicitor was giving him, and there followed the usual scramble for a pen and something to write on – he used the back of one of his business cards. By the time he hung up, Nicole was gone and Eve and Piers were leaving.

'Sorry again about tonight,' said Eve, as they left the club. Both she and Piers were smoking. 'Enjoy the rest of the weekend.'

He watched them walking off together and was about to follow suit, when Piers broke away from Eve.

'I must get the name of your plumber from you some time,' he said with a nasty gleam in his eye. 'I hear your bathroom's quite something!'

FIVE

On Sunday morning Martin woke in a panic. In his dream he had been in his mother's kitchen on a bright, sun-packed day: a ten-year-old boy rummaging around in the drawers of an old dresser pockmarked with woodworm. He didn't know what he was looking for, only that he had done this before – many times – and that he would do so again. Some part of his dreaming mind urged him to stay clear, move away, but he *had* to find it. And then the noise. A stricken, guilty look filled his face as he heard the footsteps of his mother coming downstairs, her sharp cry of alarm as she walked into the kitchen and caught sight of him. Numbly he followed the direction of her shocked gaze and watched, as if from far away, a thin stream of blood seeping like sap from his hand to collect in a crimson pool on the linoleum floor.

The clock next to his bed showed that it was ten past nine and, without stopping to shave or change his clothes from the day before, he was halfway down the stairs, his tie at half-mast, before he remembered that it was Sunday. He hated Sundays. Everything that had ever turned sour and gone bad in his life had happened on that day.

Although the office was closed on Sundays, he decided to go in anyway and put in a few hours' work. He sometimes did this if a good property had come in on Saturday and he thought he could make a quick sale, or if a Carlyle ad had featured in *The Times*. People would often respond, half expecting the office to be open anyway, and it was a good opportunity to get a head start with new applicants. He was able to wade through a backlog of paperwork until around eleven when there was a brief burst of activity. An hour later the phones went dead and he decided to call it a day. Pike had organised a practice session that afternoon after which he had invited the band to a dinner-party hosted by his girlfriend.

On Hammers' desk the details of Mr Ash's property off the Portobello Road – with '*Awaiting photo*' stamped across the centre – caught his eye. Eve had been to see it the day Piers had stopped off at the office, and on her return had talked about the tiny flat's unusual use of space, the eclectic mix of fabrics and furniture, urging him to take a look. His curiosity was further aroused when Hammers mentioned the owner having shown him a saxophone which apparently had once belonged to the great John Coltrane. Ever since, he had yearned to take a look, but the chance had never arisen. However, with Mr Ash in Paris until Tuesday, there was nothing to stop him from going round now.

He opened the index box and flicked through Hammers' filed application cards until he found the one he wanted. At the top of the left-hand corner was a code number. Making a mental note of the digits, he went to the cupboard and pulled out a set of keys from which hung a tag with a matching number. He left the spare set on the little hook. Then he slipped the keys into his pocket, switched on the office answering machine and let himself out. He would return them first thing in the morning. No one would even know they had been missing.

The first time he had done it – lingering by himself in a

client's property – was just after he had moved to London and got himself a job at an estate agency in Ealing. The artist's studio, with its raw pistachio walls and theatrical overtones – the painted *trompe l'œil* ceiling that made you feel as if you were gazing up at a real sky – provoked feelings of irrepressible curiosity. A vast work-table with sketches and drawing instruments dominated the main part of the room, and beautifully constructed models of set designs filled every shelf. For Martin, who had never seen anything like it before, the temptation to explore on his own had been too great to resist.

His job would give him access to many grander and more unusual houses in the future, but that first time was like landing on another planet. He had only ever seen places like it on the big screen. Of course, after he'd had a good root around, he swore to himself that he would never do it again, but the noble intentions didn't last. Other people's homes attracted him, hooked him like the pull of a fisherman's bait. The more he saw, the more curious he became, the more he wanted to nibble. And why not? It wasn't as if he had sinister designs. A career as an estate agent hadn't at first held much allure but, his fate had been sealed at the age of six when he was given his first Christmas calendar. The thrilling, quivering excitement in, first, the anticipation, then discovering what lay behind all those closed doors, was to remain with him for ever.

He entered the flat from the side steps which led down to the basement then he stepped into the sulky, emerald green corridor, shutting out the flimsy rays of sunlight as he closed the door. It was a mild day, but the flat was stuffy and felt very warm. Leaving his coat on a chair, he followed the short hall into an opulent drawing room decorated in dark reds and warm mustards, relics from Africa and the Middle East. It was cramped but full of a rich mix of embroidered fabrics and fabulous antiques. He opened a few drawers which yielded little, then sat down on a velvet damask sofa strewn with cushions in silk and paisley prints, listening to a clock striking the hour, the intermittent creaking of floorboards above his head as somebody moved around in the flat upstairs.

A lavish glass chandelier, which overwhelmed the small room, hung from the ceiling while, all around him, glittering ornaments, fruit bowls and lamps crowded the surfaces. The walls were covered in paintings, mostly Victorian watercolours – in Martin's opinion rather tame, until a closer inspection revealed the subject-matter: all of them were erotic. On a table next to an African mask spotlighted in an alcove stood a Kama Sutra chess set, each marble piece the size of a man's fist. He ran a finger over the polished head of a Knight. The man had some kinky stuff.

He found the saxophone in its hard case behind one of the chairs near the fireplace. Opening it up, he got his first view of the silver instrument, flashy and covered in an elaborate, swirling Deco design.

What he was looking at had once belonged to the leading practitioner of free-form jazz in the sixties, probably the most celebrated tenor sax of them all: John Coltrane. Wow! He felt his fingers tingle in anticipation as he reached out to pick it up, handling it reverently, lovingly, marvelling at the craftsmanship, its history. Yet the experience was a humbling one. In spite of the Selmer hallmark which told him it was one of the finest on the market, it was still only a piece of metal. It intimidated him because he knew that no matter how hard he practised, how accomplished he became, he would never, ever be able to do it justice. Only great musicians like Coltrane, Stan Getz or Dexter Gordon had the gift of bringing real warmth and life to such a hard, cold instrument, of producing a sound that was both sultry and melancholy. Oh, but to own something so prized!

He put the saxophone back as he had found it and left the room to explore further. The mint-coloured walls of the bedroom struck a cooler note with its calico-embroidered curtains, wicker footstools piled high with books on art, a wood-stained pedestal supporting a statue of a goddess which he briefly stopped to examine. Mr Ash was a menswear designer who had found sudden fame and wanted to move closer to the shop he'd just opened in Knightsbridge. The location was good – Portobello was always popular – and the unusual decor of the flat meant that it would attract interest. But because the building faced a pub and had such small rooms, it was overvalued. Martin made a bet with himself that within six weeks Hammers would drop the price by ten grand.

In the kitchen he thumbed idly through an out-of-date newspaper with the TV playing gently in the background, and stopped to read an article about a middle-aged man who had just won nine million pounds on the Lottery. A staggering sum for someone who had worked all his life in a sawmill and was coming up for his pension. Martin checked his own numbers but found that only two had come up. With more than a twinge of jealousy, he examined the photograph of the man, his misshapen, jowly face slightly bewildered as, all around him, representatives of Camelot and employees in drab uniforms and fake smiles toasted his good fortune with champagne. His father would have been about the man's age, if life had only been a little kinder.

Martin had just celebrated his twenty-first birthday when Frank suffered his third heart attack. It had happened on a Sunday afternoon. Irene was in the kitchen making his tea when Frank exhaled sharply, put a hand to his chest and, with a terrible look on his face as though the devil himself had whispered in his ear, crashed to the floor. There he remained until the ambulance carried him off, wailing through the roads towards the hospital. He regained consciousness once, just long enough to see Irene, white and frightened, in the chair next to his bed. By the time Martin arrived from Aberystwyth, Frank had been dead for two hours. His eyes were closed and his already cooling brow was slightly furrowed as if in puzzlement. A great expanse of orchid-white belly was exposed where his shirt buttons had given way. Irene kept muttering about how they should be fastened. She didn't want people to think he hadn't been cared for properly.

Events were going on around Martin in a fog as he looked at his father's body: the suction of doors opening and closing; the loud rattle of trolleys shivering with metal instruments; the slow, manufactured movements of nurses going about their tasks, anxious glances cast in his direction. It seemed inconceivable that this gentle silver-haired giant, made humble by the machines and tubes around him, was never again going to be part of his life. He looked at the man who had held his hand through infancy and adolescence, and willed him to open his trustful blue eyes one last time, to tell him the truth, to set free the albatross he had burdened his son with for so many years.

Time lost all significance while they waited with Frank's body. Someone had put a clear plastic bracelet around his wrist with the bare details with which Frank had entered the world – his name and date of birth. The sight made Martin profoundly sad. Irene had withdrawn into a cave of silence and when finally he had suggested taking her home, she stiffened as if to protect herself from another wave of pain. She looked down at her husband's meaty hand in her own small one, the stain of newspaper print still on his fingers, and raised it to her cheek. Then, drawing in her breath as if about to lift something of great weight, she rose to her feet and allowed Martin to lead her away from the man whose life she had shared for thirty-five years.

Martin returned slowly to the present and, responding to his stomach which was rumbling with hunger, helped himself to a handful of sugared almonds in a glazed bowl near his hand. He was just debating whether or not to cut himself a slab of the Parmesan cheese he had found in the fridge, when a noise disturbed him. At first he thought that someone in the upstairs flat had dropped something. But the sound was unfamiliar. And it was growing louder. His ears picked up muffled voices, footsteps.

Someone laughing – a woman.

Abandoning the nuts, he turned off the television and followed the noise to the little bay window in the front bedroom. He peered out. From the top of the steps, he saw first one, then two pairs of shoes appear. Christ, he thought, his pulse spiralling out of control. Someone was coming down. Who the hell could it be? The skin on his forehead began to prickle as he risked taking a second peak. By now the two pairs of shoes, one belonging to a man, the other to a woman, had become legs. Martin looked wildly around the room for a place to hide as he started to panic, but he could find nowhere remotely suitable. The bed had one of those boxy divan bases which meant there was no space underneath. He contemplated standing behind the curtains, but the fabric was too flimsy and it was a stupid idea anyway. The way he was shaking they would see him immediately. Then he remembered the utility cupboard.

Keeping his head down, he scampered on hands and knees towards the hall. As he reached the doorway his shoulder clipped the edge of the pedestal. It rocked precariously, toppling the statue which fell towards the fake hardwood floor. His hands shot out just in time to catch it. Shoving the wooden goddess back on to her plinth, he heard the sound of a key in the lock – startlingly close – and crawled hurriedly across the hall; a mole scurrying towards the dark. Somehow he got himself inside the cupboard, cursing as he stumbled into things he couldn't see. He had just managed to shut himself in when he heard the front door open. Something sharp was digging into his back, and the head of what he guessed to be a vacuum cleaner was uncomfortably pinned to one ear. As he crouched there in the dusty blackness hardly daring to breathe, he recalled another occasion when he had found himself in a similar situation . . .

There was a boy at his school who used to work in his father's shop doing the paper rounds. His name was

Andrew Hillsborough but everyone called him Slug. Cocky, wilful and undeniably good-looking – the sort of looks that in another life, another set of circumstances, might have put him up on the big screen – the resident school bully had been trouble from the age of three. He lived by his street credibility and physical strength and the few stupid enough to cross him often spent long spells in Ipswich Hospital. An uneasy friendship was struck up with Martin – even though he was four years younger – an attachment which endured even after Frank had caught Slug stealing cigarettes and batteries from the shop. Afraid that Slug's corrupt behaviour might rub off on their son, Frank and Irene had used their influence to discourage the relationship. But Slug fascinated Martin; an instinct for survival told him that it was wise to have the strongest and most feared boy in town on his side.

Martin was fourteen when they broke into a neighbouring house. Slug had found out that the owners were going away when they had cancelled their paper for ten days, and thought it would be a laugh to 'look things over'. They went round after dark and found a side window which had been left open. Martin was debating how they were going to reach it when Slug returned with a ladder.

'Where did you find that?'

'In the garage. Not very security conscious. That's gotta be asking for trouble.'

'We're not going to take anything,' Martin whispered, reminding Slug of their earlier agreement.

It was almost eight o'clock on a mild October evening but the moon was so full and round that they had no need for the torch that Martin had brought along as a precaution. Slug, already possessing the build and attitude of someone in his late teens, tucked the top of the ladder under the window-sill and began to climb.

'What if it's bolted with security locks?'

'Then I'll find another way,' Slug called down. 'Stop worrying, will ya. I know what I'm doing.'

But Martin *was* worrying. Waiting below in the dark,

his hands holding on to the ladder to keep it steady, he was beginning to regret his rash consent to Slug's plan. He had never broken the law before. Why on earth was he hanging around with a troublemaker? The truth was that he found Slug exciting. Dangerously so.

Slug was at the top of the ladder and had one leg and half his body through the window which he'd managed to open more fully.

'I'm in,' he called down triumphantly, with no attempt to lower his high, scratchy voice. 'Give us a sec and I'll let you in round the front.'

After Slug had gone, Martin's ears stretched to every sound. He could hear rustling coming from the bushes as he made his way to the front of the house. Alarmed, he tucked himself into a corner and fixed his eyes on the indefinite procession of shadows. But it was only a cat. It skipped neatly out into the moonlight then stopped to lick its hind leg. All day Martin had acted out in the film-set of his mind what they were going to do. But the bravado had gone the moment they had arrived. He should have known Slug couldn't be trusted to do the right thing.

Slug was leaning against the front-door frame as if he'd been waiting for Martin for some time. In his left hand was a cigarette. 'Found these lying around.' Casually he offered the pack to Martin. 'Want one?'

Martin swore aloud. 'Are you mad! Someone will see us. Get inside. Quick.'

Once they were inside the house, however, Martin's fear of getting caught abated. Every day on his paper rounds before school, he had walked up Constitution Hill past this big detached house with its two-car garage and sweeping front lawn. People in this neighbourhood owned their houses. They had au pairs to look after their children and bought clothes with designer labels on the outside. Irene, who used to clean for one of the owners while Martin was at school, was full of stories: about holidays in the Canaries, drinks parties held in the back garden, the money spent on a weekly trip to the supermarket – enough for the three of them to live off for a month. Now at last was his chance to see for himself.

It took a moment for Martin's eyes to adjust to the murky dark. The house smelt fresh and expensive, and for a second his head swam. He stood listening to the rhythmic tick-tock of a clock, and watched Slug in his frayed red shell-suit, sucking on a cigarette like a starving infant as he moved around the living room.

'Not bad,' he declared, whistling through his teeth. Slug's tone was casual, as if he were used to grander things, but Martin could tell that his friend was as impressed as he was. Through the gloom he was able to make out a heavy glass-topped coffee table with sturdy chrome legs, a large sheepskin rug, floral curtains topped with a wavy pelmet, a brown leather three-piece suite. At closer range – on the mantelpiece – was a large owl with a fierce gaze stuffed and mounted in a glass jar.

Slug had turned on the television which resembled a small cinema and was flicking channels. Unable to find anything of interest he investigated a pile of videos stacked underneath and slipped one of them into the machine. A naked man appeared on the screen, his ankles and wrists tied to a bed with red ribbon. He was being fondled by two large-breasted women with lots of blonde hair and kohl-ringed eyes.

Martin had seen a naked woman twice in his life: the one and only time Irene had forgotten to lock the bathroom door; and when he had crept behind the back of the school's changing room and watched as the girls wriggled out of their swimming costumes. As one of the women eased herself on to the man like a giant nesting bird his blood started to pound and Martin could feel his erection swell and strain against the fabric of his trousers. 'Dirty old man,' he said to hide his embarrassment.

Grinning, Slug settled himself into a chair and unzipped his flies. 'Go and see what they've got in the fridge,' he commanded, as though Martin were some meek little wife. His eyes were fixed to the screen. 'I've had nothing to eat all day.'

'Get it yourself,' Martin sulked, but returned to the hall where it was cooler and after groping his way past two doors that turned out to be cupboards, found he had come to the kitchen. He could see the eye-level digital clock on the oven, the numbers lime green and shining like cat's eyes. The blinds were down and because the light switch was a dimmer, he risked turning it on low. The room, spotlessly clean and fitted with mahogany units, was about the size of his parents' entire flat. Irene would have given her right arm to own a kitchen like this: shiny pots and pans, a dresser crammed with matching china, various gadgets he didn't even know the names of. He pushed the microwave on-button just to see what would happen.

The fridge was disappointing: potatoes sprouting green tentacles, a lettuce going bad in a skin of plastic, cheese in a circular tub that reeked of garlic. But the freezer yielded more. He dug out some ice cream and from a cupboard took some roasted peanuts and an economy-sized bag of mixed crisps. He took his hoard back to the living room but when he got there the television had been switched off and Slug was nowhere to be seen. His denim jacket lay abandoned on the floor next to the video box. Martin's penis stirred. He was about to switch the television back on when something thumped overhead. Irritated, he glanced up at the ceiling. What the hell was Slug up to now? Pooling the torch beam in front of his feet he trekked upstairs. He found Slug in what appeared to be an office, glued to the screen of a ZX Spectrum. A bottle of whisky – opened – was parked next to the keyboard.

'They've got Frogger on here.' Slug was jogging the joystick furiously from side to side, sending the frog leaping into the air as logs and crocodiles came hurtling across the computer screen. Frogger was the latest fad in computer games at school. Slug swore as it came to an end. 'Fuck. And I almost had it. Here, give us some of that.' He took a swig from the bottle then passed it to Martin. 'It's good stuff.'

The whisky swelled hotly as it travelled down Martin's throat. He gagged, not liking it, but drank some more under Slug's approving gaze and started to feel better. He shone the torch around the room. Rows and rows of industrial files filled one wall, each grey spine carefully marked with a coded number.

'What's this man do?'

'Some kind of an accountant.' Another programme appeared on the screen. 'And organised. A bit too tidy for my liking. I've been checking out his files. The bloke's gotta be making six figures.'

Martin peered over Slug's shoulder at the screen full of names and figures. Suddenly they started to disappear. The flickering cursor was eating up the print. 'Hey! What are you doing?'

'Having some fun.'

'But you're erasing his work,' Martin protested. 'You can't do that.'

'The wanker's probably got it all saved on disk somewhere. And if he hasn't, then this'll teach him to do so in the future. Silly sod.'

Martin recognised the viciousness in Slug's voice. He liked to destroy anything beyond his grasp or comprehension, and to witness this ugly side to his character brought out in Martin a quiet shame. 'How come you know so much about computers?' he asked, trying to distract him.

'A mate nicked me one from his work. I'm always messing about with it at home. These babies are the way of the future. Take it from me. One day I'm going to start up my own company and make a fortune selling these little hot cakes.'

Suddenly bored, Slug switched off the machine and bent his fingers backwards until the joints cracked. His gaze settled on the tub of chocolate-chip ice cream in Martin's hand and he took it from him, scooping bits into his mouth. 'I could die happy eating this stuff.'

A small gold crucifix glimmered against his throat. Ten minutes ago it hadn't been there. Martin contemplated asking him where it had come from, then decided against it. Slug took things because he felt it was his right. This was the difference between them. Martin just wanted to see what he was missing.

For the next half-hour they raided drawers and cupboards, in their mounting alcoholic excitement heedless of the mess they were making. Martin found a Polaroid camera and they used up an entire film of each other trampolining on the double bed. They made random, anonymous phone calls, cramming fists into their chocolate-chip-rimmed mouths to stifle laughter, poured Bailey's Irish Cream into the cat's saucer, switched the contents of a bottle of mineral water with one of vodka. Slug found a marker pen and daubed on the wallpaper up the stairs; *I fucked your wife.*

They ended up in the upstairs bathroom which had a mirrored flush-fitting wardrobe along one wall. Clothes littered the floor. Martin – in a panama hat – was admiring his reflection. Slug, who had been filling a plastic carrier bag with whatever happened to take his fancy, suddenly put it down as though the contents had become too heavy.

'Hey, Martin? Would you say you like living dangerously?' Martin's bemused reflection found Slug's in the wardrobe mirror. 'Taking risks, I mean?'

The alcohol had blurred Martin's senses. A risk taker. He liked the sound of that. 'I like to live on the edge,' he said carelessly, without consideration.

'Exactly how far would you go?'

Slug was challenging him to something. He didn't know what but, propelled by a rare charge of affection and daredevilry, Martin tilted his head to one side, pulled the hat over one eye and, Superman-like, speared the air with his hand. 'The sky's the limit.'

'You mean that?'

Martin crossed his heart and giggled. 'I'm a man of my word.'

Slug smiled evilly. 'Then now's your chance to prove it to me.'

In what seemed like one movement, no more than the blink of an eye, Slug picked up the carrier bag and walked out of the room, closing the door behind him. Martin heard a click, then the sound of diminishing footsteps. Inside the small room, his body very still, he waited for Slug to open the door. When nothing happened he began wrestling with it to see if it was operable. The door remained firmly closed. Slug must have removed the key and locked it from the outside.

Martin called out, 'Come on, Slug, you've had your laugh. Open up.' No response. He started pounding the door, losing the Panama hat which slipped from his head into the bath. 'This isn't funny. Let me out. Let me out or I'll kick it down!'

Somewhere in the lower half of the house he heard a door slam.

'SLUG!' he shouted, anger overriding caution. Scraping sounds coming from outside sent him scurrying to the window. He got it open in time to see Slug disappearing round a corner, armed with the ladder. Bastard! He would kill him when he caught up with him. He would bloody *kill* him. An ominous sensation replaced the numbed, pleasurable effects of the whisky. Martin's intestines began to erupt and fold inwards as he realised that Slug must have planned this all along. He peered down at the ground and judged the distance to be about twenty feet. Too far for him to jump. How the fucking hell was he going to get out?

The sound of Mr Ash's front door slamming propelled Martin abruptly back to the present. He kept quite still, blinking in the darkness. He could hear footsteps moving around, and muffled voices – how many he couldn't be sure but it sounded as if there were more than two of them. Frantically he tried to remember what state he'd left the kitchen in and what he'd done with the newspaper – he had a horrible feeling that in his haste it had been left open.

The footsteps began to fade away until he could no longer hear them, but that was almost worse than having them right outside the cupboard door. At least then he had known where they were. The thing poking into his back was really starting to hurt. Very gingerly, he risked bringing one arm behind him in an attempt to dislodge whatever was there. His hand made contact with a shelf and a long metal tube which was causing the problem. The tube seemed to be stuck. He gave it a gentle tug, careful not to make any big movements – he could hear the footsteps returning – and it sprang free in his hand. Unfortunately, in so doing, it knocked several things off the shelf which made a terrible racket as they fell to the floor. Fuck! The footsteps stopped somewhere near by and he held his breath. Any second now the door would be wrenched open and he would be revealed, cowering like an idiotic prat.

But the moment never arrived. Thankfully the callers – whoever they were – left soon afterwards. Martin waited ten minutes before he dared crawl out from his black cubbyhole, pushing the long metal tube, which turned out to be part of a vacuum cleaner, back into the cupboard. Quickly he scoured each room to check that everything was as he had found it, rescued his coat and left the flat. Back out on the pavement, he took a greedy gulp of air to steady his nerves and promised himself that he would never, *ever*, be so stupid as to put himself, or indeed his job, at risk like that again. He was halfway back to the car, parked at the end of the street, when he felt a hand land heavily on his shoulder.

'Game's up!' Jumping out of his skin, he swivelled round.

'*Christ!* Ollie,' he swore, half-angrily, half in relief. 'You almost gave me a heart attack. What the hell do you think you're doing creeping around like that?'

'Shouldn't I be asking you the same thing?'

Martin tried to look baffled. 'You've lost me.'

'That old fleapit of a thing you call a coat. It's what gave you away.' His heart sank. 'You were stupid enough to leave it on the hall chair. It was the first thing I noticed.' Oliver folded his arms and studied him curiously. 'Just what are you up to, Leak?'

Martin had saved up a hundred different excuses in case a situation like this arose, but now that he had been caught he couldn't think of a single one.

'I suppose you're going to tell me you're into bondage or something equally unimaginative?'

'So you knew it was me in the cupboard?'

'Well, you were hardly quiet about it. I had a frightful time trying to distract my clients. She was the type who likes opening doors.'

'I was getting cramp,' Martin said feebly. 'Then something went and fell off the shelf.'

Oliver grinned. 'I can just picture it.'

'Pretty bloody funny, eh?' Martin said bitterly. He looked down the road at a woman struggling up some steps with a pram. 'Look, I had a viewing this morning and left my coat behind. The flat felt like an inferno and I didn't realise I'd forgotten it until I was back at the office. It was a stupid thing to do, but when I heard you arrive I was having a slash and just panicked.'

He could see Oliver weighing up whether to believe him or not.

'I've spent more comfortable half-hours,' he added ruefully, rubbing the bruised area in his back which made Oliver smile again.

'Oh, this is bloody *brilliant*. Just wait till I tell the others. I'll be able to dine out on this for a week.'

Martin looked alarmed. 'I'd rather we kept it between ourselves.'

Quick as a flash, Oliver said, 'That depends.'

'On what?'

'On how you demonstrate your gratitude.'

'OK,' Martin conceded, 'I'll buy you a pint? Two?'

Oliver looked unimpressed. He rubbed his hands and held one out.

'Hard currency would taste better and save me a trip to the bank. I lost a packet on the gee-gees yesterday.'

'How much?'

'A tenner should cover it. I've a good tip for the three forty-five.'

Martin was tempted to tell him where to shove his bribe but faced with the grim alternative, he wasn't in a position to argue. Reluctantly, he pulled a note from his wallet and handed it over.

'Good man,' said Oliver, the money quickly disappearing into his back pocket. 'I'll buy *you* that drink if my horse wins. By the way,' he added, as he started off down the road, 'how did you get on earlier?'

Martin frowned, not understanding.

'Your client, Leak. What did they think of the flat?'

'Oh, a bit of a dead end that one. You?'

'They loved it. In fact I wouldn't be at all surprised if they ring through tomorrow with an offer.'

Six

Nick Hammerton chose the popular brasserie 192 to take his staff for their annual Christmas meal. By eight o'clock both the blue-and-orange rooms of the Kensington Park Road restaurant were full, with a large and noisy birthday party well under way. Their boisterous Friday-night mood echoed around the interior and, in a rare display of extravagance, Hammers ordered two bottles of champagne; the last quarter had been a highly profitable period for Carlyle.

Despite the vast amount they ate, they drank even more. Two further bottles of champagne were consumed, followed by an ever-flowing supply of wine so that by the time the food – which was slow in coming – arrived, there was an air of alcoholic merriment. For all his arrogance, Oliver, with his truant eyes and killer smile, could be very amusing and he regaled them with stories of some of the more bizarre events in his life, including hilarious anecdotes about his family who sounded disastrous. Even Celia found herself smiling into her glass. But Martin wasn't deceived by her apparent lightness of mood. She had done little more than play with her food – most of it lay untouched on her plate. Like the inflamed colour in her cheeks, there was a falsehood to her gaiety. Instinct told him that behind the smiles lurked someone who was far from happy.

The main course was cleared away and, after sloshing more wine in everyone's glasses, a flushed Hammers rose from the table, mopping his brow with a handkerchief. His braces made a large maroon cross on his back as he descended the frosted glass stairs to the Gents. Conscious of Eve on his other side, Martin realised that here was a chance to talk to her on her own. A waiter hovered, ready to take orders for dessert. Martin declined and while Roger dithered between the white chocolate truffle cake and the ginger and sticky toffee pudding, he made his move. 'How was your steak?' he asked.

'A little overcooked. What did you have?'

'Argentinian Ribeye. It was delicious.'

She swirled wine in her glass, looking at him affectionately. 'What have you planned for Christmas? A quiet spell with the parents or something more romantic? I can't remember if you have a girlfriend?'

A brief struggle. 'No,' he said, then corrected himself, 'We split up.'

'I'm sorry.' She brought the rim of the glass to her lips and toyed with its edge. He felt a strong desire to be the glass she held. 'Were you in love with her?'

He shrugged. 'We never spent enough time together for it to get to that stage. She was a nurse with a lot of night-shifts.'

'Passing ships?'

'Something like that. Besides,' he admitted, feeling a rush of wine-infused blood rush to his heart, 'my interest lay elsewhere.'

Eve leaned slightly forward to stub out her cigarette

and glanced at him. 'I'd never have pegged you as the two-timing sort.'

'You make me sound so dull.'

'No.' Her voice was slightly lower, a little more measured than it had been. 'You're not that. This girl –'

He could feel her interest and was compelled by some mad impulse to confide in her. 'I've been in love with her from the start.'

'We've never seen her in the office.'

He thought of Piers. 'There are – complications.'

'Does she live abroad?'

'No,' he said, after a pause.

She nodded understandingly. 'She's married. I got caught up in something like that; never being able to see one another when you wanted too, feeling fretful and insecure the whole time. It was torture.'

'Nothing's happened,' he said gravely, 'because I haven't told her how I feel.'

Her eyes widened slightly. 'Why?'

Why? His mind echoed the word and he thought about the two worlds which divided them, hers a place of power and wealth, his of much more humble origins.

'After all, what have you got to lose?' she persevered encouragingly. 'You might be throwing away the romance of the decade.' She leaned nearer and put a hand on his arm, perfectly formed nails like tiny pink half-moons. He could feel the heat of her skin against his. It was all he could do to stop his lips from trembling. 'If it's rejection that concerns you, then you're worrying unnecessarily.' She lowered her voice further so that they couldn't be overheard. 'She'd be a fool to turn you down.'

Martin decided that there was nothing he wouldn't do for her. Feelings of love rushed through him with such force that he knew he wouldn't be able to resist declaring himself. 'So you think I should tell her?'

She lit another cigarette. 'If it was me, I'd want to know.'

He could see Hammers coming back from the loo.

Seize the moment, said a voice. Take the initiative. Be bold. He looked down at the spoon in his hand and for a moment words shaped themselves in his mouth. Then, as a sudden gust of cold air whirled around his ankles, he murmured, 'It's you, Eve. It's always been you. I –'

She nodded vaguely, glancing over his shoulder, and then back at him again. There was nothing in her expression to suggest she had registered what he had said. He swivelled round in his seat and followed her gaze, which went beyond him, towards the restaurant door. Oh, for Christ's sake. Not *again*. Was he to be haunted by him indefinitely? The unmistakable figure of Piers Hunt, in a sharp Italian suit, was bearing down on them.

'I'm late.' Unapologetically, he bent down to kiss Eve. The gesture was casual but territorial. 'The fucking car broke down.'

'Not the Aston Martin?' Eve's tone was sympathetic but she was unable to contain her pleasure at seeing him. Martin caught the glimmer of a platinum American Express as Piers stuffed a fifty, one of many, into his wallet. 'But darling, that's the second time in less than six months.'

'I've left it with Harry to sort out. Damned if I'm going to. The man's made enough money out of me to retire on.' Impatiently he swept a wave of treacle-black hair to one side. Then, from his jacket pocket, he took out a packet of cigarettes and lit one. 'Did you get the message I left on your machine?'

Eve looked blank. 'I haven't checked it since lunch.' She rested her cigarette in the ashtray. Martin stared at the burning tip.

'Dad's organised a hunt for Sunday and wants us to go down. I said we'd be there.' His eyes wandered round the table as he drew on his cigarette and paused at Celia who was listening carefully to something Roger was saying.

'Pull up a chair and join us for a drink, chum.' Hammers, who was back from the loo, shifted his seat to make a space between him and Eve. 'You look as though you could do with one.'

'Good of you, Nick, but I've got a taxi waiting outside. We're meeting someone at Annabel's and we should have been there –' Piers consulted his watch '– an hour ago. You're welcome to join us after your meal – all of you,' he added as an afterthought to the others. He nodded briefly to Martin, then bent his mouth to Eve's ear and murmured, 'You look wonderful, baby.'

There were conflicting murmurs around the table. Martin watched Piers's hand gently massaging the back of Eve's neck. What was it about the man that evoked in him such a strong sense of the past – niggling away at the back of his brain, as if they had known one another before? What was it that seemed so familiar and, at the same time, so unsettling? The hand had made its way round to her collar-bone, and he was stricken to see that the gentle glow of her face, which only moments ago had seemed to him so encouraging, had changed completely. Under Piers's gaze, she bloomed like a sunflower, enlarged pupils dominant against the background of her adder-green eyes. What had happened to their conversation, so intimate, so full of promise? It was as if he had ceased to exist. A cold, childlike despondency settled inside him, a bitter sense of rejection and yearning. To hide his dismay he picked up his wineglass.

'We should go,' Piers said to Eve. A command. He was a sleek but very dangerous Doberman, guarding what he clearly thought belonged to him.

Eve was putting on her coat. 'Have we got time to stop off at my place first? I'd really like to get out of these clothes.'

A look passed between them. 'I think we could squeeze in a little detour.'

Half an hour later, after Hammers had paid the bill, the party convened outside on the pavement. Above them a black, impenetrable sky grumbled. Rain, which had threatened all day, now seemed imminent. While Hammers and Oliver sorted out car arrangements, Martin went over to join Celia. She was standing slightly apart, arms clasped around her shivering body. 'Are you going on to the club with the others?'

'No. I think I'll go home.'

'Want to come for a drink with me?' he suggested, digging his hands into his pockets. He didn't feel like going to a nightclub – particularly as Eve would be there with Piers – but he couldn't bear the thought of going back to his flat, not in his present state of mind.

'Some other time perhaps. It's getting late.'

'Fair enough,' he said. They'd probably have nothing much to talk about. He started back towards his car.

'On the other hand,' she said, impulsively turning back to him, 'I don't have to be at work until nine. I suppose one quick one wouldn't hurt.'

'You're sure?'

She laughed at their mutual indecisiveness. 'Absolutely.'

He felt a rush of gratitude. 'The Market Bar's just around the corner. If we hurry we could catch last orders.'

They walked together in silence and turned into Blenheim Crescent past the Hogshead Pub, Grifoni Café with its insipid lilac façade, Books for Cooks where he sometimes went for lunch on his days off. The small streets running off Portobello Road were bustling with the advent of the weekend; music and animated voices seeped from restaurants and bars, and the occasional whiff of perfume was diluted by the cold air but still assaulted Martin's nostrils whenever a woman walked past. Just before they reached the pub, a car swooped from the opposite side of the road and ground to a stop beside them. Oliver, at the wheel, rolled down his window. Martin could see Hammers sitting in the passenger seat, with Roger and a redhead whom he didn't know in the back.

'You two off somewhere?' Oliver asked, eyeing them curiously.

'I said I'd give Celia a lift back to her car.'

'Where'd you park?'

'Further on up.' Martin waved vaguely to his right.

Oliver looked at him slyly. 'I thought you'd left the car in Elgin Crescent?' Elgin Crescent was in the other direction.

'I'd get your eyes tested,' Martin said smoothly.

Oliver revved the engine impatiently. 'Suit yourself. Have a good one.' And the car roared off up the road.

'Why did you lie to him?' Celia asked, when they were alone again.

'I didn't lie. I just misled him. Oliver has an uncanny knack of distorting the facts. The less he knows the better.'

Celia lived on the ground floor of a substantial cream-bricked Victorian house. The flat was much bigger than it looked from outside: two large rooms with a bathroom, and a quarry-tiled kitchen which looked out on to a well-tended back garden. The living room was not what he had expected. It was bright and imaginatively decorated, with high ceilings and fresh flowers everywhere. Their scent hung in the air, mingling with the remnant smells of ground coffee beans and newly washed clothes.

Martin bent his head towards a winter jasmine plant. 'These must cost you a fortune.'

'My fetish,' she confided, slipping out of her coat. 'I absolutely adore flowers.'

On a coffee table was a copy of the *Radio Times* and a glossy brochure. He edged forward and tilted the cover towards him. It was a programme of a West End show, starring London's current heartthrob, Rory Calf.

'I hear it's very good,' he said, flicking through it with lazy interest. 'Although I don't understand this obsession half the female population seem to have with this Rory bloke. What did you think of him?'

She looked at the programme in his hand, and for a

split second hesitated before answering. 'I haven't seen it. A friend sent me that because she knows I'm a theatre fan, but lately I've just been too busy to get to plays.' If he hadn't known better, he could have sworn he saw her blush.

Two young cats trotted into the room and wound themselves around her ankles. She bent down to stroke them. 'Kent and Captain Haddock,' she smiled fondly. 'Like all men a law unto themselves except when it comes to food. Which reminds me,' she disappeared into the kitchen, trailed hungrily by the cats. 'What can I get you?' she called. 'I'm afraid the alcoholic choice isn't very extensive. There's some red wine,' a pause, 'whisky, herbal tea – hell,' he could hear her rummaging through the fridge, 'or coffee. It'll have to be black. The cats had the rest of the milk this morning.'

'Wine will do me.'

He sat in an armchair by the bay window, loosened his tie and undid the top button of his shirt which had threatened to choke him all evening. The feeling of space seemed due to the sparse use of furniture in the room. Whether this was out of choice or necessity, he could only guess, but he was intrigued by her unexpected sense of style and colour: saffron, crimson, and midnight blue with splashes of cream thrown in. A far cry from the conservative blues and browns she wore to work. Photographs on top of a chest of drawers tempted him out of his seat; a small, serious-looking child dressed in a sailor suit – unmistakably her; an older couple whom he took to be her parents; a rather intense-looking man who looked vaguely familiar; another of Celia, smiling this time, in her teens with long hair – and here he stopped because it was such wonderful hair, thick and heavy with an almost oriental quality. He wondered what had possessed her to cut it off.

She returned with their drinks. 'You always this tidy?' he asked, putting back the picture.

Her smile was rueful. 'I'm afraid I don't like mess,

which probably carries with it all sorts of awful connotations.' She passed him his drink. 'I hope the wine's all right. The bottle's been open since Monday.'

'Cheers.' He raised his glass. 'You've got a really nice place. How long have you been here?'

'Over a year now. I moved in last August.'

'Nice neighbours?'

'A gay couple have the top flat – they're in the throes of trying to adopt a baby.' He raised an eyebrow. 'At least they're settled,' she said in their defence. 'They've been together now for eleven years. Then there's Robin on the ground floor. He's an actor – mostly out of work, except for the odd commercial he lands, and jobs I pay him to do for me here. He's turned his flat into a miniature cinema haven. You have to see it to believe it. Everything is authentic right down to the smallest detail: velvet seats, posters on the wall, buttered popcorn during the intermission. I've been invited along to a few screenings and needless to say Robin's in most of them.' She grinned. 'He's forever hopeful I'll introduce him to one of my girlfriends but I don't think any of them would put up with him. Actors have very large and very sensitive egos.'

'Do you know many of them?'

Her response was offhand. 'I used to live with one. How's the wine?'

'Fine. Although, to be honest, after the amount I've packed away tonight I doubt if I could tell the difference between a vintage Bordeaux and Ribena.'

He pointed to the picture of the middle-aged couple who looked stiff and awkward together. 'Your parents?'

'That was taken on their silver wedding anniversary,' she said briefly. 'It's not a very good shot of either of them.'

He saw her stiffen slightly. 'Celia,' he said delicately. 'you haven't been yourself all evening. What's wrong?'

She sank heavily into the sofa. 'Has it been that obvious?'

'I noticed it.'

'You might as well know.' She sighed. 'My divorce came through this morning.'

In his mind's eyes he saw the decree nisi which he had rescued from the office floor three weeks earlier. At the time he had registered how closely the divorce date had been set to Christmas. 'How long were you married?'

'Five years.' She shook her head as if she couldn't quite believe it had been so long. 'I should have walked away ages ago.'

'Hindsight is very overrated,' he said tactfully.

'So is love. At least I think so. Whoever said that it conquered everything was a fool.' She looked at her drink, and he looked at the floor.

'Tonight can't have been easy for you,' he said and, as he uttered the words, he acknowledged his own pain. He saw now that he had been deluding himself. Eve's interest in him stretched no further than that of an affectionate colleague. He cringed when he thought how close he had come to disclosing his feelings. What a clot he'd been. Had she been paying attention, had Piers not walked in when he had, who knows what sort of embarrassing outcome he might have had to face. He groaned inwardly. Working in such close proximity with her knowing how he felt – well, it would have been unbearable.

He glanced up at Celia. 'Do you want to talk about it – about what happened?'

She took a large gulp of her drink and shrugged. 'It's all in the past now. My husband,' she corrected herself, 'my ex has a demanding and high-profile job which often took him away from me and our home. Those long separations put a tremendous strain on our marriage. If you keep up that length of separation for long enough you end up becoming strangers to each other.' She brooded for a while over her glass before she spoke again. 'I began to feel like two different people, each pulling in different directions. The result was I went nowhere which was exhausting. If I'm completely honest, a small part of me isn't yet ready to let go, even now that

68

we're divorced. I can see that surprises you – but I believe we're all guilty of holding on to the past in some form or other.'

He wasn't used to her being so candid and suspected the influence of alcohol at work, but the truth of her words struck him forcibly. Yes. He was guilty of that, too, perhaps more so for not being honest about it.

'Sometimes we do it to protect others,' he said, thinking of himself. 'What I mean is, it isn't always easy to deal with the truth when there are other people involved.' That was a little close to the bone. Afraid he might be digging himself into a hole, he shifted the subject back to her. 'Do you still see much of him?'

'Infrequently. Our meetings are always painful and unresolved. I don't think we'll ever be able to come out of this as friends, but I'm prepared for that. It *is* possible to move on and forget.'

'I wonder,' he answered gravely, wandering off again in his mind.

They had gone further than either of them had intended, and for what seemed like an age they each waited for the other to introduce another topic. He thought about making some excuse and leaving. It was after midnight, after all, and he had been up since five. Instead he joined her on the sofa. Her hair looked darker now, almost black. Within its severe frame her eyes seemed to take up most of her face. Imperceptibly they filled with tears, tiny rivers of water spilling over and running down her cheeks.

'Stupid,' she whispered, biting down hard on her lip. 'I shouldn't drink. Wine always makes me horribly emotional.'

'Shhh,' he murmured, moved by her sudden frailty. 'Let it go if it helps.'

'I just need someone to . . . I'm just going through . . . Oh, it's no good.' She shook her head, dismissing whatever she had been about to explain.

He could see her struggling unsuccessfully to gain control over her emotions. But she made no attempt to wipe the tears away, her body stiff and proud as she held his gaze, almost defiantly. He put a hand out to touch her arm and – as if he had released a switch inside her – she seemed to slump towards him, her head finding a place on his shoulder. Her hands stayed in her lap as he held her and for a long time they sat there, him listening to the shuddering flow and ebb of her breath, the wind gathering force outside. Instinctively, he had lowered his mouth to her head. He could smell the bittersweet perfume of her hair, feel the warmth of her nearness. He felt suddenly so physically aware of her that when the knee of his trousers brushed against her skirt he felt the electric shock of contact. She stirred against him and before he had time to think about what he was doing, he put up a hand and traced the scar with a fingertip.

'Don't,' she gasped, pulling away.

He gazed into her eyes. 'I want to.'

'But you –'

'Nothing's going to happen unless you let it.'

'I can't,' she sobbed. 'Oh God, it's too soon.'

'Shush,' he soothed, 'I'm not going to hurt you.' Very gently he leaned forward and began licking her tears. She made a tiny strangled sound in her throat and shut her eyes. When he kissed her she didn't pull away, but he felt her rigidity. She was trembling like a kitten. His thoughts were in turmoil. Part of him knew that he should take things no further and just keep on holding her, give her what she needed. But a more driven side – swept away by a strange and powerful force of chemistry that had emerged – urged him forward.

He moved his lips along the slender column of her neck. Tiny goose bumps appeared. Celia moaned and tried to turn away, but less convincingly. This time when he kissed her he met no resistance. Her lips seemed to swell and soften, something deep within her responding to his pressing need to comfort her. She moaned as he gently pushed her back against the sofa. He took her head in his hands, kissing her face with more urgency – he couldn't have stopped now – her eyes, her cheeks, her brow, the tiny hollow at the base of her throat, then down further. Impatiently, he pulled her blouse over her head but, as he released her bra and ran his hands over her small, neat breasts, she stopped their exploration with her own hands, covering herself, and looked at him imploring.

'Please,' she said, her voice uneven as though she had been running.

They were both breathing heavily. Martin – trying to get a grip on himself – saw that she was fighting herself as much as him.

'You want this to happen as much as I do.'

She swallowed. 'Yes,' she confessed, eyes closed as if resigned to her fate.

He lowered his mouth to a nipple and tugged on it greedily. As he shifted into a more comfortable position, her hands slid round him, inside his trousers, and grasped his buttocks, pulling him aggressively against her. All the coolness about her now seemed no more than an elaborate fraud. Her gestures were urgent, almost angry as they threw off each other's clothes and wrestled together among the soft debris of cushions and clothes. Once inside her, feeling the movement of muscles shift in her belly as she allowed him to thrust deeper, he forgot about Eve and his own suffering. He no longer cared. Skin on skin, he was lost in a moment of touch and smell – his body suffused in a giddy, spiralling heat. The last thing he remembered as he fell backwards into the exquisite black hole of sleep was the sound of someone sobbing.

When he opened his eyes he was lying on Celia's bed, under a duvet. The first thing he saw was a cat curled up like a giant snail by his feet. He had no idea what time it was, only that he felt cold and vaguely nauseous. There was a faint, sweet smell of herbs which made him think of incense and added to his feeling of disquiet. The bed was an old brass one that had been painted black, above which, suspended from the wall, were two silver-plated

71

candle-holders. Underneath the window were three old-fashioned leather trunks in various sizes stacked on top of each other, posing as a table, and curtains made out of a diaphanous fabric which diffused and softened the light. From behind the closed door to the bathroom he could hear the clapping spray of running water. He felt like a beached fish; disorientated, thirsty and ready to swim back to the safe, familiar waters of his flat. He could smell Celia on the white sheets and pillowcases, the edges trimmed in royal blue. Last night reran itself in his mind. What had he been thinking of? They worked in the same office, for God's sake. Oh, shit, this wasn't good. He should never have let it happen.

Wearily, he sank back against the bank of pillows, angry yet, in spite of himself, triumphant too. The warm feel of a body in his arms – not just to fuck, but to hold, to stroke, to feel tender towards had become a dim memory, something almost forgotten. His skin was marked with angry little indentations where she had bitten him and in spite of himself, he smiled at the memory. Who would have thought her capable of so much – passion? Such savagery in her love-making, almost as if she had wanted to hurt him. A wave of incense struck his senses, reminding him of his nausea. As the bathroom was occupied he closed his eyes, trying to shut off his brain. Thank God today was his day off. Very quickly he drifted back to sleep.

When he next opened his eyes she was standing at the side of the bed looking down at him. She was dressed and her hair fell like a sleek bell around her face as if it had just been blow-dried. Her grey watchful eyes, which matched the colour of her pleated skirt, looked tired.

'Morning,' he said, gently – testingly.

'I brought you some coffee.' She indicated the steaming cup next to the bed. Alongside he noticed two bottles of aromatherapy oil: neroli and rosemary. Perhaps they accounted for the smell.

He stretched and yawned. 'Thank you. What time is it?'

'Nine thirty and I'm late for work,' she spoke formally. 'But don't feel you have to leave immediately. I've left you some breakfast on the kitchen table –' an awkward hesitation. 'I wasn't sure what you liked. And there's a fresh pint of milk in the fridge. I popped out earlier to buy some.'

He pulled himself up into a sitting position and took her hand. It was cool and unresponsive. 'Don't go. Call the office and tell them you're sick.'

'I can't. I've a lot to do.'

'Can we at least talk?'

She sighed, carefully withdrawing her hand. 'I'd rather we just forgot about last night.'

'What was wrong with it?'

His question caught her off-guard. 'Nothing. It's just that I . . . We both know it was a mistake. A lot was said, we'd had too much to drink.'

'Celia –'

'I'm not blaming you at all. I was upset and – well . . .' She trailed off. 'I only hope it doesn't affect our working relationship. My job means a great deal to me and I don't want to lose it because we couldn't resolve this sensibly.'

'No one's going to hear about it from me.'

'Oh,' her voice was hesitant – tightening fractionally. 'Right. Well, good. Then I take it we can put this behind us?'

He looked down at his hands, the old familiar feeling of rejection tugging at his insides. 'If that's what you want.'

She chewed her bottom lip. 'I think it's best.'

Her bag was hanging on the back of the door. Deftly, as if she couldn't be shot of him quick enough, she removed it and hooked the strap over her shoulder.

'I really must go. Help yourself to whatever you need. There's plenty of hot water if you want to take a shower. Just make sure the cats are in when you leave.'

After she had gone, he lay gazing up at the ceiling for

some time listening to the early-morning hum of traffic outside, a tap dripping in the bathroom: drip, drip, drip. He contemplated turning it off as he knew the sound would irritate him, but he didn't have the energy to get out of bed. Instead he folded his arms across his face like a shield.

'Fuck,' he said, then closed his eyes and went back to sleep.

SEVEN

It was a bitter Christmas. Havoc reigned with snow storms bringing down power lines, stranding motorists, thousands of homes without power, and a flu epidemic which had surgeries straining to accommodate the demand. Temperatures, not experienced in thirty years, plummeted to Siberian depths as the new year woke up from its drunken stupor. Snow fell in big, silent crumbs for days, relentless waves burying the ugliness of the city until the light seemed to come not from the sky but from the thick, powdery ground. Dazed by the hypnotic effect of the surreal landscape, dark wool-wrapped figures glided like ghosts through the white-carpeted streets of London.

Martin spent Christmas with Irene. For some of that time he had thought about Celia, of their strange night together, and had written to her – a Christmas card rather than a letter which felt safer and couldn't be misconstrued. Returning from a drunken spree on New Year's Day, he had called at her flat. It was late at night and he could see a light burning from her window, but if she was in – and he felt certain that she was – she refused to answer her door. He had wandered home with snowflakes whirling around his head, feeling like a cuckolded husband ejected from his wife's bedroom.

The icy spell continued into February, putting a depressing restraint on property sales. Those brave, or foolhardy enough, negotiated the hazardous conditions with mindful caution, and only then for essentials: getting to and from work, petrol stops, a quick trip to the local supermarket. Invitations to see friends who lived across London were rejected. Martin was without heating for eight days after his boiler packed up. The flat was so cold that he went to bed in two sweaters on top of his pyjamas, thick socks and thermal long johns purchased in desperation from a camping shop. After leaving umpteen messages – all fruitless – for his landlord to rectify the situation, he finally coughed up the money himself to have a new boiler installed. It could come off his rent.

In the third week of March, Hammers' sale of the Fitzherberts' maisonette collapsed when his clients – hours before they were due to exchange contracts – were forced to pull out after their own vendor's sale fell through. No doubt lamenting his fat commission fee, Hammers looked as glum as a bloodhound as he announced – during the staff meeting – that the maisonette was back on the market. But Martin was secretly delighted as it gave him a second chance to sell what had been one of his favourite properties. After the meeting was over, he returned to his desk to see what interest he could drum up. While he was flicking through his client file box he overheard Hammers say to Oliver, 'You still off the booze?'

'A temporary measure. I've been to three stag-do's this year already but last week will take some beating: we drank enough to sink the *QE2*. I think it was the effect of paint-balling – you know, all that macho stuff when you go to a forest and try and shoot your opponent with a paint gun. Piers arranged it all. Didn't think I'd enjoy it but it turned out to be a hoot.'

'Hear you had a stripper too. Any good?'

'The best man seemed to think so – he went home with her.'

Hammers laughed. 'I gather the groom didn't fare so well.'

Oliver grinned toothily. 'Passed out cold halfway through the evening. Some of the other chaps put him on the overnight sleeper to Edinburgh, took all his cash and plastic, leaving him with only a phone card. The poor sod rang me the next morning in an awful state. Didn't know where the hell he was.'

'Woe betide anyone who did that to the man I marry,' warned Eve who was in earshot.

'Angel,' said Oliver with a wink, 'no one would *dare*.'

It had been weeks since Martin's last visit to the Fitzherberts' pad, but he didn't have to wait long before he saw it again. He got his chance later that afternoon when he took a call from a new applicant keen to see anything they had in. He arrived at the house on time and waited in the frigid air, stamping his feet against the pavement to keep the circulation going. At the time of the conversation – which was brief – he was already running late, so there wasn't time to record the appointment details in the office diary. But now, having hung around for fifteen minutes with still no sign of the man, he was regretting not having taken a note of his name and number. He thought about leaving; indeed he would have done, had his next client not called to put back their appointment to the afternoon.

He watched a woman in a business suit flag down a passing taxi. The taxi, which made a neat U-turn to her side of the road, idled in a cloud of fumes as the woman opened the door and disappeared into the vehicle's dark interior. A pale yellow shaft of sunshine appeared briefly, but soon disappeared, leaving the air feeling colder than ever. He blew on his hands and vowed to invest in a pair of gloves as he observed a man in blue overalls up a ladder, cleaning windows with brisk efficiency on a house opposite. As time ticked by he grew increasingly restless. And after standing there a further five minutes, decided to wait inside. No point in catching hypothermia.

A pile of letters clogged the door. He picked them up and had just deposited them on the hall table when he became aware that things were not as they should be. The feeling was instinctive, hairs standing up on the back of his neck. He turned round and saw that the internal door to the Fitzherberts' maisonette was ajar. His first thought was that the owners had returned early; Hammers had explained earlier that they had gone skiing in Meribel with friends and weren't due back until the middle of the following week. Perhaps he should have called first and let them know he was bringing someone round? His hand found the light switch and he edged towards the door, listening out for signs of life. He was about to knock when his eye caught sight of a thin split in the door-frame and muddy markings around the dented lock. As he leaned forward to inspect it more closely, an ominous thought struck him: someone had used their foot to force an entry. His voice sounded artificially loud as he called out: 'Anyone home?' No response. He raised a hand to nudge open the door, stepped inside and came to an abrupt halt. The heat hit him first, cloying and powerful, bringing an immediate warmth to his cheeks. In spite of his fears, he was unprepared for what awaited him. 'Jesus!' he exclaimed. The front room had been savagely taken apart. He couldn't believe his eyes.

Somewhere amongst the confusion was the thin echo of a computerised voice. As he moved further into the room he could hear it chant over and over again: *'Please replace the handset and try again'*. He slipped the receiver back into its metallic cradle, restoring an eerie silence to the room. The shade of a floor lamp was askew, casting an irregular light over everything. As his eyes roved slowly around the room he saw that the stereo, TV set and video were all missing. Also gone were the four little Victorian prints he had so admired. He could just make out the outlines of where they had hung. He stepped gingerly around a photo frame – a glass hairline fracture running across the grinning bride and groom – and a vase lying on its side. The spilt contents had left a large stain on the carpet. Who had done this? In a trance, Martin wandered through the ground-floor rooms, righting an upturned chair, slotting drawers back into the wooden body of the walnut writing-table, returning to book-shelves first editions left clumsily strewn across the floor.

In the kitchen, the freezer door was open and around the base of the fridge were tiny pools of water. He put out his hand and felt the radiator. It was boiling hot. Strangely, there was an untouched sandwich on the table and a bowl of soggy cornflakes with a cigarette butt floating on top of the souring milk. Why hadn't the alarm gone off? he kept wondering. Mr Fitzherbert was a stickler for security – as Oliver had found to his peril on the one occasion he'd brought a client round and had forgotten to reset it. He eyed two used glasses and a half-empty bottle of some rather fine whisky perched next to the sink. With a trembling hand he helped himself to a clean mug and into it poured some of the amber liquid. It wasn't something he normally did – drinking this early – but right now he needed it.

There was further carnage upstairs. As he climbed towards the first floor, glass in hand, he grimaced as a sickening odour reached his nostrils. He followed it into the master bedroom where it grew in strength, a putrid richness that made him hold his breath. Someone had vomited on the bed; part of the spray had caught the edge of the counterpane which, in the heat, had solidified, and there was a distinct, ripe smell of urine where someone had pissed against a wall. He stepped further into the room and something snapped underfoot. It was a plastic syringe. Careful not to touch the needle from which leaked a tiny ball of clear liquid, he squatted down to get a better look. Insulin, he wondered, or had it been used for more hedonistic purposes? And then he remembered the prescribed drugs he'd found in the underwear drawer. A half-eaten packet of shortbread biscuits and one empty beer bottle had been left on the floor near the bed – a sign that the thief had been alone? They must have had nerves of steel to have taken time out to eat and drink. He left the room in disgust.

In the front bedroom – seemingly unscathed – he sank on to a little chesterfield sofa and put his head in his hands. What shocked him most was the extreme brutality of the break-in. He thought about the mindless destruction of such beautiful things and felt outraged, personally violated. It was as though the object belonged, not to a stranger, but to him.

Through the sash window he could see the window cleaner across the road moving his ladder along to the adjacent house. A large grubby cloth stuck out of his back pocket and the white stick of a cigarette burned from his lips. It occurred to Martin again that the owners would be back shortly. Christ, he thought, what a thing to come home to.

With a start his mind went back to the night Slug had left him locked inside the bathroom, his terror at being caught in a stranger's house such that he'd vomited into the sink. For over an hour he had waited for his friend to return, but when it became clear he had gone for good his search for an escape began in earnest. The door to the bathroom stood firm, so his only hope was the window. It was very small but he knew it would accommodate his skinny frame. The only thing he had to worry about was the twenty-foot drop to the ground.

He gathered together the strewn clothes on the floor; silk, piqué cotton, linen, and began tying the arms and legs together. Then he threaded one end behind the enamel sink pedestal and brought it back on itself, knotting it. Satisfied the knot would hold, he lowered the free end outside the window. Not wanting to attract attention he turned off the bathroom light, then climbed on to the sink which was in front of the window. The drop from the window-ledge looked terrifying. Gingerly, he climbed out and inch by inch lowered himself down, a horrible, erratic thumping in his chest. Any moment he expected to be exposed by the harsh light of a police-man's torch.

When he was a third of the way down his fear abated. He began to think he was going to make it. Just as he looked down, trying to judge how much further he had to go, the twisted silk shirt in his hands split and gave way. He fell like a stone, one hand clawing at the bricks in panicky hope, and felt a sickening jolt as his body made contact with the ground. For a while he lay very still, trying to assess the damage. His left arm had taken the full brunt of the fall and lay awkwardly under his body and he could taste blood on his lips. The pain didn't strike immediately. It came later, in a sudden nauseating wave. For what seemed like for ever he lay on the cold, damp ground, the wind blowing fine strands of hair in his eyes, waiting for the pain to become bearable. Once he heard a sound and, for a single moment, he thought that Slug's conscience had guided him back.

It was two in the morning by the time he staggered home – to be confronted by Frank and Irene's shocked faces and a barrage of questions. His arm, when they took him to Casualty the next day, turned out not to be broken but to have a green-stick fracture. Later Irene, making warm fussing noises, tucked him up in bed with painkillers and a mug of Horlicks. His story of having fallen out of a tree after a dare seemed to have satisfied her. Even Frank seemed prepared to take him at his word. But when, three days later, Martin caught his father reading about a mysterious break-in on Constitution Hill, their eyes met for a long, uncomfortable moment. Frank never said anything, but with a horrible sense of remorse, a crushing red-faced shame, Martin knew that he had guessed the truth.

The empty memory of Frank was shattered by a shrill ringing, and with a start he remembered where he was. He stared at the phone by the bed, but after a few rings it stopped. A blanket of silence settled over the room, so still that he could hear the erratic thumping of his heart. Was he *insane*? The flat had been bloody well ransacked and he was sitting around waiting to be caught. There was still no sign of his client – the guy must have changed his mind. How the hell would it look if someone were to walk in now and find him here? He sprang up from the sofa and, forgetting the mug of whisky he had brought with him, raced back downstairs and grabbed his keys.

He had just stepped into the main hall, closing the door after him, when the light went on and a voice behind him said: 'Excuse me, young man.'

He whirled round to find an elderly woman in a dressing gown hovering at the base of the stairs. 'Jesus!'

'Oh, dear me, I didn't mean to startle you. No, indeed,' the woman said apologetically, mistaking his frozen look of alarm. 'It's just that I heard a noise and thought I'd better come down and investigate.' Her small, beady eyes darted cautiously from his face to the door he had been about to lock. Fortunately, his body blocked the damaged framework.

'Are you a friend of the Fitzherberts?'

'No, I'm –' he cleared his throat, 'with Carlyle. We're representing the sale of their flat. I just popped round to check on fixtures and fittings, for the particulars.'

The woman's face cleared. 'Oh. Oh, I *see*.' She looked very relieved. 'Only I knew they were away so when I heard – well, I thought for a horrible moment we had an intruder.' She laughed. 'You can't be too careful, can you?'

'No,' he agreed, laughing uneasily with her as he eyed the main door. 'I wish my neighbours were as diligent as you.'

The woman drew her dressing gown closer across her thin chest. 'I didn't sleep very well last night – nerves,' she explained, blinking rapidly. 'I've got a plane to catch later today and there's still so much to do. I loathe flying, don't you? My son keeps trying to reassure me that it's the safest form of travel, but it makes no difference. I'm only happy when I can feel soil underfoot.'

'Mmm.' Martin edged towards the door to show that he wanted to go.

'He lives in Florida – my son, that is, with his wife and three children. I'm told they're enjoying a bit of a heat

81

wave. Not that the climate makes the slightest bit of difference to me. I go because they're all I have left. The same time every year for a month.' She cast him a curious look. 'Will that other man be coming back today?'

'What man?'

'The one who was here earlier. He was another estate agent, like you. I must say I found him very charming.'

She was probably talking about Oliver. He'd had a viewing booked for that morning. Although he could be a cantankerous sod, Oliver was a surprising hit with middle-aged women. Almost without exception, they responded instinctively to his beguiling baby face, the ready quips, his penchant for gossip. Martin surmised that the burglary must have taken place some time between the two appointments. Otherwise Oliver – always one with a sense of drama – would have mentioned it.

'Well,' he said, making a production of checking his watch, 'if we're to get these particulars out today I really should get my skates on.'

'Oh, yes indeed. Well, I'm glad I've met you now, Mr –?'

He pretended he hadn't heard and opened the front door. 'Don't catch cold,' he advised, as a chilly gust of air blew into the hall.

The old woman gave a little shudder. 'No, indeed. Now that you've put my mind at rest I shall go back to my fire. I can see the Fitzherberts are in very good hands. Good day to you,' and she turned to retrace her steps upstairs.

Stay calm, Martin told himself as he made his way back to his car. Just keep your head. Nothing's going to happen. She didn't see anything untoward. She's just going to go back up to her nice cosy flat, do her packing and get herself a taxi to Heathrow. She'll be too busy worrying about her journey to give the matter a second thought. But another, more urgent voice in his head kept asking: What if she didn't? What if she'd seen through him all along and had gone back to have another look?

All it would take was for her to spot the Fitzherberts' splintered door-frame and she would get straight on to the police. Shit! She might even be calling them this very minute.

As he ground the gearbox into first and pulled out into the road – narrowly missing an oncoming cyclist – he glanced over his shoulder to take one last look at the house, guilt smeared all over his face.

EIGHT

By the time Martin reached the office he had made up his mind to tell Hammers what had happened, and then report it to the police. It was the only solution. But Hammers was out on a number of valuations and, according to Tracy, wasn't expected back until late afternoon. As the clock ticked by his resolve to do the right thing weakened. He began to reconsider whether keeping his mouth shut might not be the smarter option. Why complicate matters? All he could think about was what would happen to him when the police found out he had been there alone.

Whenever the phone rang he looked at it in dread. Who was it? The Fitzherberts? The police? One of his colleagues calling from the maisonette on their mobile? The chances of that were slim; he'd already checked the office diary three times and nothing had been booked in for that address. But this failed to alleviate his fears. He felt he should do something but he couldn't think what without incriminating himself. He tried telling himself that he was overreacting; that he hadn't done anything to be ashamed of; that a few hours' delay before finding out about the burglary wouldn't bring any comfort to the unlucky victims. Only the old lady knew he'd been at the flat and she was probably halfway across the Atlantic by now. He had nothing to worry about. So why did it keep coming back to haunt him? Why was it all he could think about? Because he should have reported it right away. Because he'd put his own interests before a client's and it had left a nasty taste in his mouth.

Thoughts of the Fitzherberts' break-in continued to plague him for the rest of the day even though there had been no mention of it from the others. But that evening Eve announced something which put all concerns of the maisonette to the back of his mind and turned his world upside down. He was downstairs in the fax room, pulling on his coat to leave, when she popped her head round the door.

'*Here* you are,' she said brightly. 'Roger thought you might already have left.'

He glanced at the clock on the wall. 'I should have, only I had to wait for a call from a client's solicitor. They've been pushing for an exchange on their property since ten this morning.'

'Do you have to rush off now?'

He calculated how long it would take him to reach his dentist's surgery in the rush hour and looked at her face. It was full of expectation and something else – joy. 'Not if it's important.'

'Only there's something I want to tell you. I've been dying to ever since we got back to work but we've all been so busy there hasn't been the right moment.'

His heart leapt. 'I'm all ears,' he said with studied calm.

'Piers and I are going to get married.'

He blinked at her. '*What?*'

'I know,' she beamed, 'I still can't quite believe it myself.'

He swallowed. 'I hadn't realised things between you had become so – serious.'

She gave him a funny, half-regretful smile. 'Oh, *Martin*. Be happy for me. I realise things haven't exactly gone your way with this woman you told me about. If I could wave a magic wand and make it right for you I would. But, if it's any consolation, Piers and I went through a terrible patch last year. Him being away so much. Well, at one point I didn't think we would make it. But look at us now.'

He ran a hand through his hair. This was turning out to be a very bad day. 'Eve, I – this is all so sudden.'

'That's Piers for you. Life in the fast lane.'

'When's the wedding?'

'August. We're already arguing about the exact date.' She giggled. 'Can you imagine – me, a married woman. I'm *so* excited! Anyway, I just came down to get you. The others want to celebrate.'

'Yes.' He experienced a sudden drain of energy from his head, as if someone had just turned off the lights.

'Martin?' Her voice seemed far away. 'Are you coming?'

'No,' he said, pulling himself together. 'Look, you go. I've got a dental appointment to keep.'

'You can be ten minutes late for me, can't you?' She used her most beguiling voice.

'The traffic –'

'Come on.' She reached for his hand and gently pulled him towards her.

'Just one glass. I'd really like you to be there.'

Upstairs Eve's news had caused a flurry of excitement. Everyone clustered around her, admiring the ring which Martin hadn't noticed: an exquisite knot of sapphires and yellow diamonds. Hammers popped open a bottle of champagne from the agency stock normally reserved for clients and raised his glass for a toast. Martin joined in along with all the other cheers, and even managed a smile. Any thought of admitting to Hammers what he had discovered at Arundel Gardens had evaporated. If he was going to tell him it needed to have been said immediately. Besides, now wasn't the time. Devastated as he was by Eve's engagement, he didn't want to spoil her celebrations.

There was talk of going on to the pub, but Martin managed to slip away undetected. He set off with a headache too mild to bother taking anything for, but it weighed on him throughout the stop-start journey to Baker Street, gaining strength by the minute. He had never been a sickly child but, from a young age, he had suffered from headaches – often quite bad ones. Sent home from school, he would lie in his darkened back room trying to keep still until the longed-for sleep put him out of his misery. Now, they came much more infrequently, no more than once or twice a year. But, when they did strike, they seemed to do so with increased ferocity.

At the dentist, where he learned that he needed a filling, he lay back in the chair, his eyes avoiding the long pointed instruments laid out on a circular tray. The dentist, a forgettable face bearing down on him, became a beard, then a nose, its proximity so close that he could see the tiny hairs sprouting from the end. Music played quietly from a tape-deck. A hooked implement and a tiny circular mirror on a metal stem was inserted into his mouth, then the sharp prick of an anaesthetic needle, his taste buds aroused by the peculiar, bitter taste, and the insidious brain-grinding noise of the drill. Hands clenched, he was almost grateful for the pain in his head because, for a moment, it stopped him from thinking about Eve or the break-in.

He reached his flat shortly after eight. Where he lived had never conjured up feelings of pleasure, but tonight the sight of the walled-off cemetery on the other side of the road particularly depressed him. The dustbin men had been that morning and, in their usual, careless haste, had left a trail of rotting food and rubbish along the ground. Behind him, cars whooshed past in a rush of exhaust as he put his key in the lock and let himself in. The hall was dark and smelt faintly of cooked cabbage as he climbed the stairs, something Mrs Wingate, his widowed neighbour, had a particular fondness for. Her flat faced his on the top floor. A nice enough old bat, she lived such an uneventful life that she made it her business to involve herself with everyone else's: a member of the net-twitching society who could talk without drawing breath for minutes at a time.

Martin closed the door to his own flat which felt cold, and went shivering along the corridor to the bathroom and ran a bath. He definitely felt unwell. Perhaps he was coming down with flu? Yanking off his tie, he ignored the blinking button on his answering machine and began surfing through the television channels. But Thursday was a bad night for viewing and watching it only aggravated his headache so he turned the machine off and wandered into the kitchen. The contents of the fridge proved uninviting – there never seemed enough time to do a proper shop – but as he wasn't hungry enough to cook, he decided not to bother. Instead, he took two painkillers. Still in his coat, he flopped on to the sofa and stared at the opposite wall. Under the bald, fierce overhead light, the flat seemed unfriendly. A crack had appeared, weaving its way along the opposite wall like an unsightly scar. Subsidence probably. He must remember to mention it to the landlord.

Through the living-room window, on the other side of the road, he could just make out the dark, shadowy forms of gravestones. Sometimes the cemetery offered him a strange comfort. Tonight, however, it seemed only to heighten his sense of isolation, of being displaced in the world.

He had left the water running for too long so that when he eased his body into the tub it was tepid. Under the water his skin looked magnified. Bubbles were trapped in his pubic hair – a reddish colour in the artificial light – which he dispersed with his fingers. Feeling sick, he lay back against the enamel tub's curved end, shut his eyes and tried to still the familiar pounding in his head. If he got an early night he might catch the migraine in time. Mrs Wingate's radio, on very loud – she was deaf in one ear – echoed through the thin partition wall of his flat. She was listening to some kind of folk music which made him think of dancing and rituals, ceremonies – wedding ceremonies – Eve and Piers together . . .

Someone was shouting in the back garden, and he opened his eyes. 'Oh Christ, Mikel,' he groaned. 'Not tonight.' Mikel was a Polish immigrant who had lived in the ground-floor flat for almost twenty years. Most of the time he was neither seen nor heard. But when he had been drinking he would appear at the front of the house – just inside the gate – like a ghostly apparition with his white Father Christmas beard and boozy smile, delivering loud, garbled monologues through the night.

'*Let me tell you something,*' he yelled now. 'When I die I don't want no bloody coffin. Just drop me in a hole and let the coffin to another one. Yes. That's right. Hmm.' A long pause. 'Or put me in a fire. You think I don't know what they're doing on this island? English, English, *English* bigots who take your money. I tell you I'm old man but I know. I *know*. These bloody stinky people. Coffin is *ve*-ry expensive. If you want to die you must do it in another country. Hmm. That's right.'

This lasted for fifteen, then thirty minutes, by which time Martin had towelled himself down and got into his unmade bed. He could feel the migraine start to take hold: blurred vision, nausea, a tightening band of pressure across his brain. He gazed at the ceiling for a long time, listening to Mikel's mad ramblings, wishing he would give it a rest, as a bleak melancholy, swelled into a great wave of loneliness. He felt as depressed as he had ever been in his life. He had lost Eve and it was his own stupid fault for not having got his act together, for allowing her lifestyle to intimidate him. Deep down he had always felt that there was something wrong with him. Memories flashed through his mind: sports day, Frank and Irene cheering him on as he ran the two-hundred metres and took first place, his moment of triumph squashed by one throwaway remark from a boy in his class: *You can run as fast as you like, boffhead, they still didn't want you. Not even your own mother!*

Words that had left him floundering in a pool of self-doubt. He felt as if he was floundering now, clutching at moving objects that floated by in a blur – too far away to grab hold of, always just beyond his reach. An image of the Fitzherberts' wrecked master bedroom swirled into his mind but was quickly rejected. He didn't want to think about that. He didn't want to think at all. The pain in his head was too great. Finally, he rolled on to his side, reached for the bedside light, and drifted into an exhausted sleep.

The migraine endured for three days. There wasn't much he could do other than stay in bed with the curtains drawn, taking Migraleve every four hours for his crashing head, trying to stay still, quiet. On day one, he managed to summon up enough energy to call the agency and let them know he wasn't coming in. Eve, of all people, answered, sympathetic but distracted and busy – he could tell by the noise in the background – him talking like some halfwit while small explosions went off in front of his eyes. The hours passed in grindingly slow tedium. He could hardly move his head without his brain reverberating like the sound waves of a ringing church-bell. In and out of consciousness he swung, barely aware of whether it was day or night. Until gradually the pain started to recede, and he was finally able to pull back the curtains and take a look at the late-afternoon light without flinching.

Hungry for the first time in days he was about to make himself a sandwich, then remembered the empty fridge. He had nothing to eat. Still too weak to face going out, he went back to bed and was wondering when he might feel well enough to return to work, when there was a knock on his door. He opened the door a crack and was astonished to find Celia standing outside.

'Hello,' she said. 'The front door was open so I came straight on up.'

'This is a surprise,' he said, taken aback. 'Shouldn't you be at work?'

She smiled gently. 'Martin, it's Sunday.'

'Oh.' He ran a confused hand across his brow. Had he been out of it for that long?

'I was on my way back from a lunch party. As it was only round the corner I thought I'd stop by.' She hesitated. 'How are you?'

'Better, thanks.'

'Feel up to some company? I brought you a newspaper.'

He stepped aside. 'Come on in.'

He was getting dressed when the phone rang. By the time he reached the living room Celia had already got to it.

'It's Roger,' she mouthed, holding out the receiver.

'Was that Celia I was just talking to?' said Roger.

'Yup.'

'You kept that one quiet, you jammy sod. How long's this been going on?'

Martin could feel Celia's gaze and said carefully, 'Roger, what do you want?'

'To borrow your car. Just for a couple of hours. Only mine's got a flat and I said I'd help a mate move some stuff into his new flat. I can't let him down.'

'You'll need to put in petrol. Last time I looked it was running low.'

'I owe you one. By the way,' he said, as an afterthought, 'how are you feeling?'

'I've had better weekends.'

'Oh, I don't know,' Roger chuckled. 'Sounds to me like you're in pretty good hands.'

'Did he mention anything about what's happened?' Celia said, after he had replaced the receiver.

He threw her an edgy glance as an image of the wrecked maisonette came flooding back to him. 'No.'

'Nick and Oliver have had a falling-out.' She was the only one who referred to Hammers by his Christian name.

He gave a little snort of relief. Was *that* all. 'I thought you were going to tell me something serious.'

Outside it had grown dark. Since she had arrived an hour and a half ago, she had been down to the shops, restocked his fridge, made him something to eat, and, with a deft hand, restored order to his flat. She had even brought aromatherapy oils which she used to massage into his feet and temples. He wasn't used to having so much done for him, but he was feeling too bloody feeble to make more than a mild protest and, if he was honest, it was nice having her around. A vase of flowers now cheered up the living room, and the remains of the chicken soup she had made had been set aside for his supper.

'Oliver's as good as handed in his notice,' she told him.

He set down his mug of tea. 'He does that about once a month but it's just hot air. Ollie seeking attention.' All the same, he asked her what had led to the row.

'Nick found out that Oliver had been taking bribes from an applicant he was trying to find a house for and confronted him with it. Oliver reacted badly, got all defensive – you know how he can be. The argument escalated into a God almighty row, and ended with Oliver storming out of the agency vowing never to return.'

They were all guilty of taking the occasional handouts from clients. The monthly pay-cheque never quite met the demands of living expenses and bills, so every little helped. Whether it was from a builder looking for a bit of extra business, or a purchaser in a hurry to buy and wanting to be made a priority, there was nothing like an under-the-table cash incentive to get a negotiator on your side. The only rule was not to get caught – or, if it was a retainer and it was going to take up a great deal of the broker's time, to pay the agency a percentage. If Ollie had found his client a property at Carlyle's expense but through another agency (*and* in the time for which Carlyle was paying him), then that was a sackable offence.

'What was the bribe?' he asked.

'An all-expenses-paid trip to Barbados – for two.'

He whistled. 'Who tied up the deal?'

She paused to take a sip of her drink. 'We did.'

One redeeming point to Ollie. He looked at Celia in her jeans and crisp white shirt, amber beads like tiny suns swinging from her earlobes as she talked. It seemed funny them being together in his flat, chatting about work as though nothing had taken place between them. Since the night they'd slept together they had gone about their jobs as before, but with an awkwardness injected into their conversation, smiling uncertainly whenever they happened to catch the other's eye. Seeing her now, however, he could detect no such unease. In fact she looked quite at home in his small flat, as though she had been installed for some months instead of paying her first visit. He hoped it wouldn't be her last.

'I'm glad you came,' he said, meaning it.

Her voice was conciliatory. 'We got off to a rather bad start, didn't we?'

'But making up for it now. That head massage you gave me was incredible. Where did you learn to do that?'

'I've always been interested in alternative medicine. My father used to get shocking migraines so I'd practise on him.'

'Did it help?'

'If I caught the signs early enough I could stop it altogether. There was a time when I wanted to pursue holistic medicine as a career. I'd always done well in the sciences and left school with a string of A's at O and A level. But in the end I got sidetracked.' Celia shrugged philosophically. 'Life never unravels quite as you imagine.'

It did if you wanted something badly enough. Martin wondered what had stopped her? What had turned a bright young girl into this lovely, intelligent, serious woman who was trying so hard to keep the world at arm's length?

'I see you like music,' she said, turning to look at his

CD collection. 'Jazz in particular.' His saxophone, which he'd left out of its case – a brass Yamaha he'd picked up in a pawnshop – was propped against the wall. She ran her fingers over it approvingly. 'Do you play?'

'A little,' he said modestly. 'Someone put a saxophone in my hands when I was about ten and I've been an addict ever since. A few of my mates and I get together every now and then and strum out a few tunes.'

'Sounds like fun. Perhaps one day I'll get the chance to hear you play.' She sounded as if she meant it too.

After she left, he took the newspaper into the bathroom and read it in the bath. He thumbed through all the messages for Mothering Sunday in the centre pages and, with a sinking heart, realised that for yet another year he had forgotten to send Irene a card.

NINE

On Monday morning Martin felt strong enough to return to work. Everyone seemed pleased to have him back although he suspected this had much to do with them hitting a busy spell, and because for three days they had been two people short. Roger kept winking and giving him loaded looks whenever Celia happened to cross his vision which Martin found intensely irritating. Of Oliver, there was still no sign, though he did overhear Hammers leaving two messages on his answering machine. Eve seemed tired, which was unusual for her. Even more of a rarity was the hangover she complained of having.

'Old age,' Roger had said. 'In the end it gets us all.'

Or too many late nights with Piers, Martin thought dolefully.

It appeared – astonishingly – that during his illness no one had been round to the Fitzherberts'. Just once did he dare to mention the maisonette; a remark made in passing, testingly, casually dropped into the conversation to veil his wary interest, but as none of the others picked up on it and as nothing further was said, his worry began to ease. The longer the gap, the less likely he was of being found out.

As he had a backlog of paperwork, he tried to concentrate on catching up, but all morning there were constant interruptions from Tracy who hovered round him, bringing endless cups of tea and plates of chocolate biscuits, as if she was afraid he might fade away. 'You must eat,' she would say, squeezing his hand and sounding like Irene. After a while it became embarrassing.

'I had a migraine, Tracy,' he finally said in exasperation. 'Not heart surgery.'

At lunch-time Oliver returned to work. He appeared out of the blue – Eve throwing her arms around him in delight, Roger rolling his eyes heavenwards in a gesture which said, oh, here we go – offering no explanation for where he had been or what he had done, treating his absence as no more than if he had just popped out for some milk. A curt nod from Hammers and the two men disappeared into the financial room 'to have a chat', but it was evident from their relaxed faces when they resurfaced half an hour later, that they had been able to patch things up.

Martin slipped out to see his bank manager. Although he was hoping to have his overdraft extended, he had gone prepared to have his request turned down – he had already far exceeded his existing limit. But to his surprise (and relief) the bank agreed to loan him an additional five thousand pounds. His mood, on his return to work, was buoyant and acting on impulse he made a quick detour to a local newsagents and bought ten pounds' worth of lottery tickets.

Celia was in reception as he entered the empty office and he was about to suggest taking her to see a movie –

to celebrate – when he noticed her looking at him worriedly.

'What's up?' he asked, shrugging off his coat.

She drew him to one side, away from Tracy who was on the phone at the receptionist's desk. 'Nick wants to see you in the financial room.'

'Don't tell me?' he said, grinning. 'Mrs Helman again?'

Mrs Helman was the purchaser of a flat he had recently sold – a woman with very grand ideas. Earlier she had rung asking him to pick up her furniture as she was *frantically busy* and couldn't possibly cope with her in-laws *and* a move. When he had suggested – without sarcasm – that she hire a removal firm, she had thrown a fit and demanded to speak to the manager. Hammers was out of the office at the time so she had slammed the phone down on him. But he hadn't expected her to leave it there. She wasn't the type.

'No,' Celia said, 'I don't think so. He's got two men with him. They're policemen.'

His smile faded. 'What's going on?'

'Nick wouldn't say. Only that they were asking for you.'

'You're kidding.' Now he was deeply worried.

Celia looked uncomfortable. 'They want to interview all of us. They've already talked to Nick and Roger, but your name was mentioned specifically. Have you any idea why?'

He shook his head. 'I've no idea. But I can't think it's anything to be concerned about.' *They're on to me.*

'I wouldn't bank on it,' said Tracy, coming off the phone – that girl's hearing was more powerful than a satellite dish. 'I happened to catch some of what they were saying when I took in Hammers' coffee. Apparently,' her voice dropped to a dramatic whisper, 'they're following up a murder.'

'Come in.'

Martin opened the door, his heart pumping like a

steam train. Hammers, looking uncharacteristically sombre, was sitting at the desk, his linked fingers supporting his chin. Opposite him were two strangers. All three men rose as Martin stepped into the room.

'Well,' said Hammers, after the introductions had been made, 'I should be getting back to work so I'll leave you to get on with it. Unless, Detective Sergeant, there was anything else?' He looked questioningly at the shorter of the two men.

'Not for the moment, Mr Hammerton. We appreciate your co-operation.'

The detective sergeant had a soft, pleasing voice and looked a bit like Mike Dixon from *Brookside*. Martin tried to hold on to the image.

'So, what's all this about?' he asked, with only slightly more bravado than he felt as Hammers – who at this moment seemed to be his lifeline – left the room.

'We're carrying out an investigation into a recent incident – a very serious one.'

'I see.' Martin glanced nervously at the constable who was wearing a slate-grey suit and looked like he worked out regularly. 'How can I help?'

'We'd like to ask you a few questions, if you don't mind.'

'Of course not.' He lowered himself carefully into a chair.

'You're familiar with the Fitzherberts' property in Arundel Gardens?'

He felt the hairs on the back of his neck rise. 'Yes. We're representing the sale.'

'Indeed. Can you remember the last time you took someone round to view it?'

Martin frowned, his head spinning. 'I'm not sure,' he said slowly, 'I'd need to check the diary.'

'So it wasn't recently?'

'No. It . . . er . . . went under offer last December and only came back on to the market a few days ago. The sale fell through.' He gazed at the sergeant's tie: navy-blue background patterned with gold clocks.

'I only ask because we were hoping you might be able to give us some information.'

The sergeant pursed his lips.

'Look,' Martin said edgily, 'what is all this? What's happened?'

'The Fitzherberts' son has been found murdered.'

He almost laughed. 'What?' A silence. 'You're not serious.' He looked at the two solemn faces, waiting for one of them to grin suddenly, point a finger and say, 'Had you for a moment, didn't I?' But they just stared at him.

'My God, you *are*!' His eyes bulged. 'Christ, that's awful. When did it happen?'

'Last Thursday, we believe, but the body wasn't discovered until Saturday afternoon so it had –' the man paused tactfully '– deteriorated somewhat. As you can appreciate, we're very keen to find whoever was responsible.'

Saturday? He blinked. The Fitzherberts weren't due back from their holiday until mid-week. They must have come home early and found the body.

'Did you know they had a son?'

He didn't react immediately to the constable's question. 'What? Oh, yes. At least I guessed as much. There were family photographs throughout the flat and the third bedroom was full of typical boys' stuff – cricket bat, guitar, the usual signs.' He stopped himself. Last Thursday. Shit, he thought. Oh, shit.

'You have a good memory for detail, Martin.'

He gave a small, nervous laugh but neither man joined in. 'How did he die?' He asked not out of curiosity, but to stall them, buy himself a little time. For the first time since his discovery of the burglary, he digested the full implications of his situation. His client had failed to materialise and the appointment hadn't been entered into the agency diary so he had no way of proving that his trip round there had been a legitimate one. Now he'd gone and told the police he hadn't even been there that day.

What if they found out he was lying? Like a pupil whose name had been read out at assembly for shaming the school, he felt his cheeks warm with remorse.

The sergeant scratched his nose. 'He died from three blows to the head – so severe that the force took out half his brains.' Martin winced. 'Yes indeed. Very unpleasant. A young lad too. Not much older than you. What are you – twenty-five?'

'Twenty-six.' Martin slumped against the back of his seat, conscious of the cylindrical metal bars pressing against his spine. In spite of the heating, the room felt suddenly cold.

'Can you recall your movements last Thursday, Martin?'

He noticed the sergeant's eyes stray to his hands, fidgeting unconsciously on his lap. Instinctively, Martin forced them to be still. 'Nerves,' he admitted.

The sergeant nodded. 'That's quite understandable. Take all the time you need.'

'Last Thursday?' Why couldn't he get his brain into gear? 'I worked until about six. Then I had a dental appointment. After that I went home. I didn't feel very well.'

The sergeant threw a significant look at the constable. 'Can you tell me which properties you visited and with whom on that day?'

'You can't seriously expect me to remember that far back? I do countless viewings and see dozens of faces every day. I'd have to check the office diary which is next door.' He hesitated for a moment. 'Do you want me to get it?' he offered, in a blatant attempt at escape.

'Not to worry, Martin.' The constable took out a notebook and started making notes. 'We can do that later.'

'I had a migraine. I get them occasionally.'

'So you went straight home after your dental appointment?'

'That's right.'

'And you didn't see anyone else that evening?'

'No, I felt sick and went straight to bed.' He rubbed clammy hands down the side of his trousers. All this interrogation was making him very nervous.

'Why are you asking me all these questions?'

'It's all right, Martin, we're not accusing you of anything. We're simply trying to eliminate you and all your colleagues from our enquiries. It's just possible you may remember something unusual about that day, a client acting strangely perhaps?'

'No,' Martin said. 'Nothing springs to mind.'

Martin's nerves were in shreds when he left the cramped, airless room. The others, who were all at their desks, looked up as he opened the door with varying degrees of interest and alarm. It was clear from their faces that they were as stunned as he was. There was a moment of silence, then everyone began speaking at the same time.

'What did they say in there?' queried a frowning Eve.

'Do they have any leads?' probed Roger. 'Was it suicide?'

Then Celia's sympathetic, 'Are you all right?'

And Hammers, 'Did they say how long they would be?'

Martin ran a hand through his hair, unable to answer any of their questions. 'Look,' he said to Eve, 'all I know is that they want to see you next.'

'Oh.' She rose nervously from her desk.

'Don't worry,' he reassured her. 'It's only routine stuff.'

Later, when the police had gone and he had tried to pick up the threads of his work, he thought of the dead young man. Only a few months separated them in age, yet one life was still to be lived, the other had been abruptly cut short. Martin pictured him lying in a room somewhere in the silent maisonette, his head face-down in a pool of thick, glossy blood, while his parents, miles away in Meribel, flew down the snow-encrusted slopes, arms outstretched with a carefree abandon they would never again know.

TEN

Through the large window beyond his office desk, Martin could see the skinny emerald-green front of the old Pie shop, squeezed forlornly between an optician's and a phone shop. It was Friday morning and four kids sat on the pavement smoking cigarettes and chatting. He envied them. It wasn't a day for being stuck inside. With the arrival of April, the weather had turned unseasonably fine, making everyone restless. The sky was of the softest blue and the sun smiled down on Notting Hill with all the energy and heat of July.

Since no more had been heard from the police, Martin had begun to think he was in the clear. The murder had made headlines in the local press – mostly due to the father of the deceased being a government minister and, out of morbid curiosity, he kept some of the more enlightening articles: pictures of a distraught Mrs Fitzherbert walking out to her car; another of her husband leaving Parliament with a stony look on his face; and underneath, a blurred photograph of their son taken – according to the report – a mere three weeks before his death.

It had been four days since Martin had been interviewed and, although he continued to scour the newspapers, the first flurry of excitement and media interest waned as other, bigger stories began to emerge. Lying awake two nights previously he recalled showing a young man around the Fitzherberts' property in the first week of December. He remembered him because there had been something faintly suspicious about his manner – well, he was so young for a start, although Martin was careful not to judge clients by their appearance. But all those questions about security and alarms while hardly giving the rooms a second glance; well, it smacked of something untoward. Now he wondered if there might be a connection with the incident and made a mental note to investigate further. The next day he managed to find the man's telephone number in the office diary and dialled it, only to be told by the person at the other end that he had been working in Cape Town for the last six weeks. So much for that theory.

Then, yesterday, the window cleaner he had seen working across the road from the maisonette was arrested and brought in for questioning after valuable stolen property taken from an address in the same area was found at his home in West London. The murder weapon had yet to be discovered, but he had a known history of drug abuse and the pathologist who searched the maisonette found a large amount of cocaine residue. It was thought the suspect may have wanted the money to purchase drugs.

Martin read that it was while flat-sitting for his parents that the Fitzherberts' only son had apparently stumbled across the thief and, in the struggle to apprehend him, had paid with his life. When he failed to respond to their numerous calls, his parents had grown worried and flown home. Martin pictured them at the kitchen table, eating a bleak, wordless supper, the sound of cutlery scraping against crockery. They would have had to call their daughter at her public school, somehow tell her what had happened to her brother, arrange for her to take time out for the funeral. Then the weeping would have started: first the mother, her body convulsed with the sobs she could no longer hold back, the silent and proud father following soon after, saltwater tears running down his cheeks.

Martin thought back to the day he had been at their maisonette and stumbled on an uneasy thought: had the ringing phone, which had thrown him into such a panic, been the Fitzherberts trying to get in touch with their son? His body had been found in the upstairs bathroom –

the one room Martin hadn't investigated. The realisation that the victim had been lying in such close proximity all the time made him feel rather ill. Suppose his death had not been instantaneous? The sergeant said he had bled to death. What if – and here was a horrifying possibility – he had been alive while Martin was there? If he had only explored a little further, he might have been able to have helped him, perhaps even to have saved his life? The ramifications were too awful to contemplate.

One Sunday Martin drove up to Bury St Edmunds to see Irene. Since his move from Ipswich to London five years previously, he had pushed her to the back of his mind, phone calls and visits home becoming increasingly sporadic. There was a time when to let more than a week go by without contacting her would have seemed inconceivable. Yet now when he went back – he couldn't think of the humble Lego-land council house she had moved to as home – he felt the gulf of time and experience that separated them. It was as if he had climbed to the top of a large mountain and could enjoy panoramic views which she could not share because she had elected to wait for him at the bottom. As on so many of his visits, Irene had prepared all his favourite dishes for lunch, and he ate with an uneasy mixture of pleasure and guilt: pleasure because he knew no one who could match his mother's cooking, guilt because it was a feeling inextricably linked with his love for her.

Before setting off back to London, he stopped off at one of his old haunts, the Inkerman, a warm beery environment which he used to frequent as a teenager. The pub was full when he arrived. He stood at the bar, pint in hand, looking round at the flushed and animated faces. In the far corner he spotted Kevin Gosling, a boy he had gone to school with. He decided to make himself known. After all, they had once been friends. A cry of recognition greeted him as he approached the table and, before long, the pints were flowing. Kevin talked nostalgically about the old days, and he responded, touched by Kevin's pleasure at seeing him and eager to hear news of friends he had all but lost touch with.

Kevin was one of those people with great ideas but forlornly bad at making them happen. When Martin had seen him last he was still living at his mum's, unemployed, sustained by dreams of cruising round the world on his beloved Suzuki 1000, and harbouring some daft plan about building his own casino. By all accounts, however, things had considerably improved since then. He had spruced up his appearance with a suit and a decent haircut, and talked proudly about the large flat he now owned. But when Martin tried to pin down what Kevin actually did, his friend grew vague.

'Oh, you know,' he said cagily, 'house clearances, removals. That sort of thing.' He drained his glass. 'D'you want another of those?'

Martin, who'd already had two halves and faced a long drive, shook his head. 'Better stick to something soft. But hang on. I think it's my round.'

'Put your money away, mate. These are on me,' Kevin insisted. And grabbing the empties, he pushed his way to the bar.

'House clearances?' Martin said dubiously on his return. How was it that Kevin, reckless, compulsive, shopaholic Kevin who had never saved so much as a bean in his life, could afford a two-bedroom garden flat in the smartest part of town? 'What kind exactly?'

Kevin set down two pint glasses, one filled with bitter, the other lemonade. 'The kind where you don't ask too many questions, if you catch my drift.'

'I see.' Martin was beginning to understand. 'This your venture?'

His friend gave a snort of laughter. 'Fuck me, no. I wouldn't know the first thing about running one business let alone four. The boss handles that side of things. He's the brains and the balls. Won't take any shit neither. I just do what I'm paid for and enjoy the spoils.'

Martin pulled on his lemonade. 'Doesn't sound like the sort of bloke you want to get on the wrong side of.'

'He gets wound up now and again,' Kevin admitted. 'His is a stressful job. But the bloke's sound. He took care of things when all that business with Tiff blew up. I mean, I knew something was going on, she was acting so strange and that, I just couldn't prove it. The boss sorted it out. Used his surveillance outfit to get a whole pile of dirt on her.'

Kevin had told him earlier about his brief marriage to nineteen-year-old Tiffany, which had ended when she was found in bed with one of the local constabulary. A week later the policeman's house was burned down. No one ever found out how the fire started. They moved on from Kevin's employment – it was clear that he was reluctant to discuss it in greater detail – and talked instead about school. Slug's name was mentioned – Kevin and Slug had lived in the same street and used to go on spray-painting jaunts round the back of the council estate. Martin asked what he was up to now.

'Still ducking and diving, you know Slug, but doing well out of it. I sometimes catch him in town, driving around in one of those big Mercedes. You know he's got a son now?'

'No,' said Martin, remembering Slug as a muscly youth getting stoned behind the school shed, and his own first taste of a joint – limbs like jelly, unco-ordinated – the helpless, rapturous hysterics which followed. 'We lost touch years ago.'

His last thought, just before he set off back to London, was how strange it seemed to have such a craving to be accepted by a boy he hadn't even liked.

The following Wednesday, he arrived at the office at midday and found Eve on her own. She was having a heated exchange with someone on the phone. After removing his jacket, he sat down at his desk trying not to eavesdrop but picking up strands of the conversation – something about a party she had been to which had upset the person on the other end of the line. It wasn't long before he discovered who she was talking to.

'Who suggested it in the first place? You honestly expect me to believe ... Oh, that's rich coming from you.' She listened for a moment, breathing hard, the tension in her face all too apparent.

Uneasily, Martin edged open a drawer and began rooting round inside for a pencil sharpener.

In a tired voice now, 'I really don't know. You'd have to ask her that ... Next week, who knows ... Well, that's too bad because I'm going with someone else –' She looked across at Martin. 'Martin's taking me ... Martin,' she repeated. 'You know, *office* Martin.' She threw him a quick, guilty look.

From a drawer she pulled out her cigarette pack, and lit one, inhaling deeply as if she was drawing strength from the nicotine. Martin's eyes darted towards the front door. Hammers would go spare if he were to catch her smoking in the office.

'The truth is everything always has to be on your terms, Piers, and it *really* pisses me off.' Agitated, she tapped ash from her cigarette. 'Anyway I can't discuss this now,' she said, her voice politely formal – Martin too had seen a man peering through the agency window as if he was contemplating coming in. 'I'm afraid you'll just have to make your own arrangements.'

Eve hung up, hastily stubbing out her cigarette, and frowned unseeingly at the stack of things on her desk. Martin waited. She drummed irritated fingers next to the empty Coke can she was using as an ashtray. Ter-rum, ter-rum, like the far-off sound of a galloping horse. For a moment he thought she'd forgotten that he was there. Then, just as the man outside opened the office door, she looked up at Martin, the fog clearing from her face. 'You *do* play cricket, don't you?'

ELEVEN

She had a silver Saab, and they drove all the way to Bath with the top down. It was a beautiful evening, the air warm and sweet with early summery smells. Once past Junction 3, they left the choking Friday rush hour and flew along the fast lane of the M4. Eve seemed happy to talk – mostly about work, and her planned summer holiday in the sun – but she smoked incessantly and would sometimes break off from what she was saying, her face growing pensive. It made Martin wonder if she was thinking about Piers. After all, it should have been him not Martin at her side.

The noise of the engine and whistling air made it difficult for their voices to be heard, and after a long hard week they were content to relax and listen to music, the evening wind playing havoc with their hair. For Martin, the fact that they were going away together still hadn't quite sunk in: the two of them at her parents' house near Bath. The bank holiday weekend appeared before him like a reward, a soft hammock roped between two arduous weeks. He tried not to read too much into it. After all, it had only been an argument. She and Piers were still engaged. But a crack had emerged, they weren't as idyllically happy as he'd first feared, and the flutter of joy he felt was hard to suppress. It was like a dream come true.

'It would be lovely if you could come, but if you're busy,' she had said at the office, 'just say. I don't want to drag you away from something important.' What could be more important than spending time with Eve? There would be other people there; by all accounts a great many of them – Eve's younger brother William, who played county cricket for Somerset, had organised a match for

Saturday, in which (she had explained somewhat apologetically) he would be expected to take part. Would he mind? Would he mind, hell! Cricket and Eve all in one weekend. Yes, he thought. *Yes!* And grinned at his reflection in the car window.

They arrived just before nine. Eve turned into a winding drive, the car headlights illuminating heavy undergrowth and the girths of sturdy trees. Several cars were already there: a Jaguar, two Volvos, and a gleaming Bentley. Eve pulled up alongside and switched off the ignition. For a moment everything was quiet.

'Welcome to Partridge Manor.' She turned in her seat and smiled at him. 'What do you think?'

He looked at the house and stared. Most of the evening light had drained from the sky, but there was still enough left for him to make out its shadowy form. The small Georgian mansion was straight out of a fairy tale; impossibly romantic with a tangle of roses fighting to gain entry through the elegant windows, the Ionic porch almost hidden by swathes of wisteria and honeysuckle.

'It's incredible,' he sighed, getting out of the car.

She came to stand beside him and sniffed at the air. 'I love coming back here,' she said, her voice soft and milky. 'Of course, you can't get a very good idea of it at night, but the house is surrounded by over twelve acres of protected land, so there isn't a neighbour in sight. Beats London, don't you think? If there's time in the morning I'll give you a tour.'

In the hall a maid took their coats. 'Hello, Rosie.' Eve gave her reflection one quick check in the mirror. 'Where is everyone – in the dining room?'

'Drawing room, Miss Eve, along with your parents and the Kings. They've been here since lunch, but everyone else is expected in the morning.'

Tennis racquets were stacked against one wall, along with several pairs of green wellingtons. Barbours and flat caps hung from pegs. A large, leather-bound visitors' book lay open on a table. Martin caught sight of one of the signatures. How many homes could boast a royal visitor?

Eve was still talking to Rosie. 'And Will?'

'You just missed him. He went out to some party with Miss Tara and that friend of his from Wales.'

'You mean Giles? Oh, well, if Giles is with them, then it's bound to be a late one.' Eve gave Martin a resigned shrug, 'Guess you'll just have to settle for me and the old fogies tonight.'

They went into a large crimson drawing room, formal and full of beautiful things. Two dogs lay before the fire in contented slumber. One of them raised its head briefly, gave a low woof, then closed its eyes and returned to the arduous task of sleep.

'Ah,' said a man, rising from his chair, a cigarette burning in one hand, 'you made it. We weren't sure if you'd brave the traffic. Apparently it's bloody awful.'

Eve gave a squeak of joy and, as the man engulfed her with a hug, she kissed him affectionately on the mouth. 'We avoided the worst of it. How was your trip?'

A look passed fleetingly between them. He winked at her. 'I'd say we're on the home stretch.'

'Really?' Eve cried, 'Oh, Daddy, that's *brilliant* news.' She said it with such excitement and relief in her voice that Martin turned to her in surprise. But he wasn't given time to think why because she linked an arm through his. 'Daddy,' she said happily, 'meet Martin.'

Howard Scott must once have been devastatingly handsome, Martin thought. Tall and broad-shouldered, his hair was streaked with grey, but it was thick and strong with tight curls crowning his head. Hard green eyes met Martin's as they shook hands.

'Piers not with you?'

Eve, to her credit, didn't miss a beat. 'He's making his own way down in the morning.'

Howard grunted. 'Hope he knows we're depending on him to knock up a few runs.'

'You could always use Martin,' suggested Eve. 'He's very good.'

Uneasy with the compliment, he started to protest – he hadn't picked up a bat for four years – but Howard interrupted him. 'Piers is our number three, and I believe Will's got a full side already.'

Martin hid his disappointment. 'It's no problem,' he said quickly.

'Darling, sort it out in the morning, when everyone's here,' called a blonde woman in a shrill voice, standing by the mantelpiece. 'How are you, Eve? You look a bit peaky. I expect it's all that hard work you do.'

'This is Arabella. My *step*mother,' said Eve, with a slight edge to her voice. Martin suppressed his surprise. He hadn't realised her parents were divorced.

Arabella appeared to be a good few years younger than her husband, and was as blonde as Eve, but there the similarities between the two women ended. Whereas Eve seemed comfortably down to earth about her looks, Martin noticed a contrived falsity about Arabella's every move. The two dogs had roused themselves and approached Martin, drooling at the mouth. One of them pawed at his knee, its eyes soft yolks of curiosity.

'Hello fella,' he said, rubbing his ear. 'What's your name?'

'Ambrose,' said Howard. 'The other one's Marshall.'

'After the West Indian bowlers?'

Howard raised an almost respectful eyebrow. 'I see you know your cricket.'

Arabella, who had joined them, took Martin's hand and gave him a dazzling smile. 'You must both be hungry after your long drive. We've already eaten but I'm sure Cook can rustle up some spaghetti or something.'

'Don't worry,' Eve lit a cigarette. 'We can fend for ourselves.'

'Darling, have you met Michael and Priscilla King?' said Howard, turning to the couple on a fat, faded, royal blue-upholstered sofa. The table in front of them held a tray of tiny coffee cups and a plate of petit fours. The elegantly dressed woman was on the plump side and exuded an earthy sexuality. A black cat slept on her lap.

'Michael and I shared an office in Hong Kong a few years ago.'

'I certainly remember you,' said Michael King who, except for a thin crescent of hair around his ears and at the back of his neck, was as bald as an egg. He struggled to his feet and gave Eve an affectionate kiss. 'You get more like your beautiful mother every day.'

Arabella, who appeared to dislike any mention of the first Mrs Scott, turned brightly to Martin. 'I gather you and Eve work together? Do you sell *lots* of houses?'

'It depends on what the market's doing.'

'Oh, heavens. You sound just like William.'

'My brother Will's a City man,' Eve explained.

Martin wondered how long it would be before they could escape. Mikel, on one of his drinking binges, had kept him up most of the previous night and the effects were now catching up on him. He felt dog-tired.

'So, Eve,' Arabella asked slyly, 'what's this I hear about you and Piers having had a bit of a tiff?'

Howard shot his daughter a look of concern. 'This true, darling?'

Eve glared at Arabella. 'Piers had to work late tonight which is the only reason he isn't here now. I don't know where you get your information from, Arabella, but your sources can't be very reliable.'

'I'm sure Arabella didn't mean anything by it,' Howard said, rebuking his daughter gently.

Arabella's thick gold bracelets tinkled around her wrist. 'Darling, do get us all another drink.'

'What'll you two have?' Howard stubbed out his cigarette and glanced at the new arrivals.

'I think we'll pass, Daddy,' said Eve, much to Martin's relief. 'We haven't had anything to eat since lunch so we might go and raid the fridge.'

'Help yourself,' said Howard. 'There's plenty there. Oh, and no rush in the morning. Play won't get under way until eleven.'

'I get the feeling you and Arabella don't get on,' Martin probed, once they had left the room.

'We agreed to hate each other years ago,' she said with feeling. 'I truly believe that if that woman and her awful daughter hadn't come along, my parents would have worked through their problems. Come on, I'll show you where you're sleeping.'

Of all Eve's family Martin had been most looking forward to meeting her mother. It hadn't even crossed his mind that she might not be here. He had always envisaged Eve's parents as happily married. Shaking off a pinprick of disappointment, he followed her up two flights of stairs past several rooms – a sage-green bedroom with a mahogany four-poster, another which contained a profusion of flowered chintz strewn over curtains, rugs, cushions – rooms he wanted to linger in but only got glimpses of, along a dim, book-crammed passage to his, which was decorated in cream and rose, and full of solid old furniture. Matching fabric hung from the window and made a stiff petticoat for the dressing table, on to which someone had put a tiny jug of flowers.

'I'm afraid the light's not very good.' Eve drew the floral curtains. 'But you can always borrow one of the lamps in my room if you want to read. I'm just down the hall.'

Was that an invitation? 'Eve,' Martin fingered the edge of the quilt on his bed, 'did you mean what you said downstairs – about Piers having to work late?'

She looked almost – he couldn't be sure – contrite, only curiously enough not for herself but for him.

'If you don't mind,' she said softly, 'I'd rather not talk about it.'

When later, after a light supper and a brief amble outside, they parted for the night, Martin's fatigue vanished. For a long time he lay naked and wide-eyed in the dark, warm air, listening to the foreign sounds of the house. He imagined Eve walking into his bedroom and undressing slowly before him. In his mind he could see her hands reach behind her back, her breasts dropping forward as the lacy, uplifting bra came loose and freed them, then turning from him, provocatively, teasingly, bending as she slipped her hands inside her knickers and pulled them down so that he could see the dark opening between her legs. He came in his hand, closing his eyes as the waves of pleasure swept over him, but sleep remained elusive. All the time he was achingly aware of her sleeping just three doors away.

He was woken the next morning by someone snoring against his ear. Wondering if he was still dreaming, he opened his eyes, turned his head and found fur. Ambrose. At some stage during the night, the dog must have crept into his room. Long fingers of light seeped through the curtains. He yawned and looked at his watch. Nine thirty! Shit. He hadn't meant to sleep for so long. After a quick bath, he pulled on some clothes and went downstairs, where he found Eve in the kitchen having breakfast with two girls he didn't know.

'Morning,' she said brightly, and introduced him in a happy, offhand manner which implied that they were much closer than was the case. Tara, the pretty brunette, was Will's girlfriend who worked in public relations. The rather vacuous-looking blonde turned out to be Venetia, Eve's step-sister. She was a typical Sloane who had just completed a secretarial course and was hoping to get a job in London. Whenever he happened to look at her she would smile shyly and avert her eyes.

'Where is everyone?' he asked Eve, helping himself to a small triangle of toast. On the table were a lot of used breakfast cups and plates.

'Daddy wanted to get down to the clubhouse early, so they left together.'

Somewhere a door slammed and soon afterwards two young men sauntered into the room. There was no mistaking for an instant who one of them was; heavy blond hair, the same intelligent green eyes. The likeness to Eve was uncanny. They might have been twins.

'You haven't got a cig, have you?' the other man asked. He was looking a bit grey. 'Only I've left mine at the hotel.' Eve handed him her pack. With a trembling hand he lit one. 'God, I needed that. Slightly overdid the boozing last night.'

'Not like you, Giles,' she said with irony. 'Have you met Martin?'

'Good to meet you.'

'So you're Martin.' The tall blond figure, speaking for the first time, stepped forward. William Scott and Martin shook hands. 'I gather Dad confused things by telling you last night that you wouldn't be needed to play.'

'I don't mind,' Martin said diplomatically.

'Only Giles here is short of one man for his team. We were wondering if you could play after all?'

His heart leapt. 'Certainly.'

'What do you do?' Giles asked him.

'A bit of both – but mainly bowling.'

'Well, we already have a few bowlers in the team but I'll try and squeeze you in for a couple of overs.'

'Thanks,' Martin said gratefully. 'I'll grab my kit.'

He climbed the stairs towards his room with a racing heart. Already, he could feel a combination of excitement and fear racing through his veins at the prospect of playing again. Excitement because it was what he loved best; fear, because he didn't want to let the side down. On the first-floor landing, a crack of light caught his eye. The door to the Scotts' bedroom had been left ajar and, like a child drawn towards wrapped presents round the Christmas tree, he found himself unable to resist having a look inside. Surely no one would mind? For a moment he paused on the landing, his hand hovering on the door knob, but conscious that Howard and his party had already left, he decided to be bold.

The room surprised him, not least because it had been so clearly designed for a man. He had expected Arabella to have made more of an impression on the bedroom if not elsewhere in the house, but the fat glass bowl of pink roses by the bed, and a gauzy nightgown carelessly strewn over the Regency day-bed, were the only feminine touches on display. Opposite the main door, where he stood, a lovely trio of arched windows opened out to a breathtaking view of the rolling countryside and a small lake. Intrigued, he crossed the mahogany floor, his eyes devouring every detail: the green-and-cream antique stripe fabric, the architectural studies, a pair of eighteenth-century globes resting on a library table, and on further investigation, the door to a dressing room concealed behind a cream panelled wall.

'So this is where you've got to.'

He swung round to find Eve standing in the doorframe. Guilt flooded his face. 'Couldn't resist taking a look.' He was mortified to have been caught in her father's bedroom.

Unperturbed, Eve joined him. 'Pretty, aren't they?' She glanced up at a set of silk prints on the wall.

'Very,' said Martin, looking at her. Standing there in an oblong of sunlight, she had never looked lovelier.

'They were an anniversary gift for Dad and Arabella. From Piers's shop in Bath. He has some beautiful pieces. You should see the stuff he had shipped back from India. Last week he sold a Hindu figurine for thirty thousand pounds.'

'Really.' He glanced at the prints, less impressed with them now than he had been a few minutes ago. 'I take it these are reproductions?'

She appeared mildly offended. 'Piers only buys originals.'

'Of course he does.' Stupid question really.

The room had grown warm. He was increasingly aware of it as he watched Eve draw scoops of hair on to her head as though she wanted to cool her neck. She held it there for a few moments then let it drop heavily down her back like some wonderful piece of fabric. A sort of vitality seemed to radiate from her, something which he caught, became intoxicated by. She was close enough for him to smell her hot, sharp scent, too close for comfort. He could feel his erection straining against his flies.

'Anyway,' she sighed, 'I didn't come looking for you in order to have a history of art discussion.'

'Then pick another subject.' He inched closer, drawn irresistibly to her mouth. 'I'm *very* flexible.'

'Ah, but have you a good eye?'

'Piers isn't the only one who can spot an original.'

She giggled, clearly flattered by his attention. 'Aren't you forgetting something?'

'What?' he murmured. Their mouths were almost touching.

'You're playing cricket in twenty minutes.'

The match! Christ. Eve's presence had pushed it from his mind.

'Come on.' She walked back to the door. 'I promised Will I'd have you down there no later than ten thirty.' She glanced at her Cartier watch, 'They'll be wondering what's taken us so long.'

'I'm looking forward to this,' he said, after a detour to his room. He played an imaginary swing in the air. 'I haven't picked up a bat in years but it'll be great to be out on a pitch again.'

She hesitated at the top of the stairs as if something had just occurred to her. She turned to face him. 'Look,' she said. 'About the match today. The boys tend to take their cricket very seriously and it can get a bit competitive. But you mustn't let that throw you. No one's expecting you to perform miracles.'

'No,' said Martin, wrong-footed again. Obviously not.

TWELVE

It was a glorious, blazing day, the Avon sky a faultless blue with no more than the faintest of breezes wrinkling the players' shirts. Pale undulating fields stretched beyond the village boundaries like a patchwork quilt. The sun winked off the whitewashed pavilion where the two teams had been marshalled together, while, all around the cricket field, small parties of spectators gathered, waiting for the match to begin – the Scotts' annual match was a big event for the villagers. To Martin, listening to the nearby chiming of a church bell, it was impossible to imagine a more idyllic scene, yet his mood was far from settled. At fourteen he had been the best cricketing player of his school year, but that was when he had been fit and played every day. What if he no longer had the touch?

His misgivings weren't assuaged by the arrival of Piers Hunt. A small part of him had been hoping the man wouldn't turn up at all. But there he was, his rival, the threat to his happiness, devastating in white flannels, the sleeves of his silk shirt rolled up to show off his deep tan, and talking to Howard with all the confidence and ease of a future son-in-law. Martin – who would rather die than admit it – had gone to the public library and looked Piers up in *Who's Who*. To his dismay, almost half a page had been devoted to his family, details of a distinguished line of aristocracy that could be traced all the way back to Charles 1.

When, five minutes later, the two men's paths crossed, they greeted each other politely but said little. Though it galled Martin to admit it, everything about Piers intimidated him. His status, his height and build, the clipped aristocratic voice, the way he had of not looking at you when he spoke. The bastard!

Giles's team, the South Wales Exiles, won the toss and he sent in his opening pair to bat. Martin had been put quite far down in the batting order so the immediate pressure was off, and he was able to join the rest of his team-mates (a likeable crowd) on the pavilion's veranda. The two batsmen got off to a good start. Time and again they drove the ball smartly towards the boundary line where spectators sat on rugs together with plastic jugs of Pimm's and the weekend papers. Before long, the plucky duo had knocked up an impressive score of sixty runs for nought.

'Run 'em up,' came the encouraging cries of their watching team-mates.

'The man's got no style,' Giles said of his opening batsman, 'but a bloody brilliant eye. Could club the ball all day.'

But his words were ill-timed. The partnership, which had started off so promisingly, came to an abrupt end when the opening batsman took the full brunt of a full pitch in the knee and had to retire from the field.

'Shit,' muttered Giles, a half-pint in his hand. 'All right, mate,' he instructed his number four, 'you'd better pad up.'

The next batsman, the Reverend Digby-Smith, a massive figure with a forest of a beard, marched on to the field as if he were going into battle, the bat hanging from his Goliath hand resembling a toothpick. He clocked up a further eighty magnificent runs for his side but not, unfortunately, before Giles had seen the demise of four more members of his team: three catches and one LBW. Will's side were fielding brilliantly.

After lunch two more wickets fell very quickly and suddenly it was Martin's turn. The South Wales Exiles were now 192 for 7. If they were to present any real challenge to the other side, they were going to need more runs. As the last two men in after him were bowlers, he knew the responsibility must fall to him. He walked out on to the field with grim seriousness, conscious of Eve's gaze following him. Now was his chance, he told himself. All he had to do was keep his head.

He played and missed the first ball, which unsettled him, and left the second which screamed past his ear into the wicket-keeper's gloves. The third ball, bowled by a cunning spinner, made contact with his bat and gave him one run. Relieved to be off the mark, he waited at the non-striker's end, his heart beating as the other batsman, the son of a cabinet minister, took his turn and lashed out at the ball.

'Yes!' he yelled to Martin, as the ball rolled along the ground towards the score box.

Martin followed the line of the ball. 'No, hang on,' he cautioned.

'Run!'

Martin sprang forward obediently and was almost halfway down the pitch when there was a hideous shriek, and Will shot out of nowhere and seized the ball.

'No, wait!' shouted Martin's team-mate who had panicked and scrambled back to the safety of his crease. 'Get back!'

Quick as a flash Martin saw the danger and, turning, hurled himself and his outstretched bat wildly back towards his line. But it was too late. Will had brought up his throwing arm and slung the ball unerringly to knock the bails clean off the stumps.

A thunderous cheer of victory rang out from Will's team, cries of owzat! as the umpire – wearing flip-flops, ill-fitting shorts and a white doctor's coat – nodded solemnly and gave the out sign by raising his stubby index finger.

There was nothing Martin could do but swallow his frustration and with as much dignity as he could muster, make the long, agonising walk back to the pavilion. He had been playing for precisely five minutes.

'Bad luck, Martin,' called the other members of his team. The fault lay with the other batsman, but he still felt he had let them down, and their sympathy only made him feel worse. He should have stuck to his guns. He'd had a chance to play himself into the game, and he had blown it.

At three o'clock, about the time Giles had expected to declare, the last member of his team was given out. Their total was 211.

'They're going to cream us,' said the cabinet minister's son, who, as the seventh batsman, had been expected to get more than twelve runs. 'We've got more chance of getting the Germans to buy our beef!'

'Where's your fighting spirit, son?' the Reverend Digby-Smith said crossly, grass marks spoiling the effect of his cream trousers. 'You've got to have more faith.'

'Oh, I've plenty of that,' came the dry reply. 'It's just that it's with the other side.'

The Scotts' openers, Howard and a thickset bull of a man who, Martin was told, owned three London restaurants, stalked to the wicket looking determined and confident. And why not? Martin thought. They were playing in front of their home crowd and had an easy score to beat.

For the next hour and a half the pair batted without inhibition, notching up a hundred runs without loss, until the restaurateur grew complacent and played a rather casual shot into the air which was caught by Giles. The next batsman in was Piers. Looking as though he was born to play, he gave a casual, disdaining glance round the field, and struck the first ball over the clubhouse into an adjoining field. The ball was retrieved by one of the village boys who threw it back to the bowler, only for it to be sent over the fence again when, minutes later, Piers hit another six.

'Fucking great!' snapped the frustrated third man ten minutes later as Piers continued to cause havoc with the fielding. 'We've got a bloody Tonker!'

'Don't worry,' replied Giles, who was at deep mid-wicket and trying to keep up the team morale. 'Rudders has worked out a game plan.'

Indeed, their best spin bowler may well have figured a way of ousting the seemingly indomitable Piers but he wasn't given the chance because, in the next over, eyes cast upwards while running to catch a ball, he cannoned into a tree and knocked himself out. With one bowler down, the Reverend Digby-Smith exhausted from being overused, and a third man taken off after three catastrophic overs, a despondent Giles chucked the ball to Martin.

'No one else has had much joy, mate. You might as well have a go.'

Martin, who had been stuck out at long leg, uttered a silent prayer of thanks. At last, an opportunity to do something. Don't balls it up this time, he told himself firmly, feeling all eyes on him. He rubbed the ball along the side of his trousers and walked away from the pitch, giving himself plenty of room for his run-up.

Piers, with forty-three runs, faced him with a wicked smile. Martin took a deep breath, tried to psych himself up, and launched forward. Suddenly Piers threw up a hand and stepped to one side.

'Dirt in my eye,' he called out.

Unsettled, Martin returned to his mark and waited until Piers was ready. The bastard's enjoying this, he thought angrily, and spat into his hand.

The first ball he bowled was a full toss which Piers, with arrogant ease, sent over the boundary. It came to a halt a few feet away from Eve, instantly recognisable in her bold, floral dress. Charmingly, she picked it up and, with a sleepy smile, threw it back again.

'Four runs,' signalled the umpire, with a flutter of his hand.

'Not turning out to be your day, is it?' Piers called out, his eyes blue as ballpoint pens. Martin ignored the jibe.

Next, he bowled a yorker and Piers swept his bat elegantly forward in defence. But instead of sailing towards the sight-screen as Piers had intended it to, the ball found a gap and knocked the bail clean off the stumps, cartwheeling it backwards into the air. There was a moment of stunned silence.

'He's bowled him!' the wicket-keeper shrieked, jumping up and down. 'He's bloody bowled him!'

Piers looked around in disbelief at the off-stump lying on the ground. Out for 47, just three runs short of his half-century and the last over before tea. With a furious glance in Martin's direction, he returned to the pavilion, shaking his head as if he had been the victim of some appalling miscarriage of justice. There was a spatter of applause as he stormed up to the clubhouse, throwing his bat down in disgust.

Ten minutes later, Martin had taken his second wicket of the day – and, along with the rest of the players, sauntered back towards the pavilion for tea with an immense feeling of elation.

'Should have put you in right from the start,' said Giles, patting him cheerfully on the back as they queued up for sandwiches. 'Bloody well done, mate. Bloody well done.'

'It was probably just a fluke,' Martin demurred.

'Come off it. One, maybe, but *two* wickets in as many overs smacks of talent to me. Speaking of wickets,' Giles lowered his voice slightly, 'don't look now, but one of your casualties in the corner over there's looking a touch unhappy.' He popped a sandwich into his mouth. 'Bad luck, Piers,' he called out cheerfully across the room. 'Happens to the best of us.'

There were a few snorts of laughter as Piers looked up, saw who Giles was with, and looked away again.

The pavilion filled quickly with hungry people so Martin carried his plate of sandwiches and cup of tea outside and sat down on one of the hard benches. He raised his face to the hot sun and closed his eyes. He couldn't remember a time when he had felt this happy.

'You know, everyone's talking about you,' said a voice, minutes later. It was Eve eating a chocolate roll. She sat down next to him on the bench. 'Mrs King's been saying that if you can sell houses as well as you bowl, she's going to switch from Chestertons to Carlyle. Piers is notoriously hard to get out.'

He could feel the warm brush of pleasure on his skin.

'You're much better than I thought you'd be.' Her voice was light and flirtatious.

He choked on his tea. '*Thanks*. So why did you tell your father last night how good I was?'

'That was for your benefit. I didn't want you to feel intimidated by Daddy. He can be a bit fierce.'

He looked at her. 'You're very close to your father, aren't you?'

She nodded, eyes inscrutable behind her sunglasses, and lit a cigarette. 'He's the most brilliant man I know and I absolutely adore him. I just wish he was at home more. We see so little of each other. His work frequently takes him abroad so he doesn't have much time for the family.' Martin had learned during their drive down that Howard was a senior partner in an impressive architectural firm specialising in industrial design.

'It's odd.' She sighed pensively. 'I don't usually count myself as sentimental but Daddy brings out the protector in me. He's the one person in this world I couldn't bear to lose. I suppose you must feel that way about your mother.' She didn't give him time to respond. 'I think I'd kill anyone was tried to hurt him.'

Oh, for her to feel the same way about him! 'Where has he just come back from?'

'The Middle East. He's been working on a submission for a client out there for months now.'

'Sounds big.'

'Bigger than you can imagine. In fact, I'm not even supposed to talk about it, not until the contract's been signed. There aren't many architectural firms in the UK able to cope with a project of this size so most of the competition has come from America. But negotiations are so close to being tied up that I can't imagine there's any harm in mentioning it to you now.'

Martin stretched his legs, anticipating the moment when he could remove his shoes. His feet, confined for so long, had started to burn in the heat.

She brought her cigarette to her mouth and inhaled deeply. 'He deserves to get it.' She exhaled wisps of curling smoke from her nose. 'He's worked so hard, so diligently. If only he'd let go sometimes, give himself a break. Recently, he's only been home long enough to get his clothes washed and repacked again.'

'At least I know where you get your energy from.'

She smiled ruefully. 'It's not just me. We're all pretty manic in this family. God knows how Arabella puts up with it.' He raised an eyebrow. She grinned wickedly. 'That woman deserves everything she gets.'

'Have you spoken to Piers yet?'

'We had words,' she said, her fair eyebrows snapping together. 'You probably saw he's not in the best of moods.'

Martin looked down at his cup. 'Don't suppose I'm helping the situation much. I don't want to cause any friction.' Liar, accused a voice in his head.

'I wouldn't worry about Piers,' she said firmly. 'You just leave him to me.'

After Eve had slipped off to greet some late arrivals, Martin carried his used cup and plate back into the pavilion which was now almost deserted. On his way out, Piers loomed in front of him.

'This yours?' he asked abruptly, holding up a brown wallet, the leather faded and lined with age.

Martin looked at his wallet in astonishment. He was sure he had left it with his clothes in the locker room. 'Where did you get that?'

'One of the staff found it on the floor of the Gents and handed it over to me. Naturally enough, I had a look inside and found your business card. The money's there so I don't think anything's been stolen.'

'Thanks,' said Martin, unsure how to take this unexpected gesture of goodwill.

'Incidentally, on my way over here this fell out.' From his other hand Piers revealed a damp photograph. He was holding it in such a way that Martin couldn't see what it was of. 'I'm afraid it fell into the sink by mistake. I hope it's not your only copy?'

'It can't be –' Martin stopped as Piers turned the picture round. Oh, God! He gazed at the image. It was of Mrs Fitzherbert, the one he'd taken from the flat last November in Arundel Gardens.

'It can't be what?' Piers repeated, looking at him oddly.

'I was going to say it can't be mine because I don't carry many photographs, except that one, of course.'

'Your mother?'

With difficulty, Martin nodded. Christ. Eve had heard Oliver describe Irene and she must have met Mrs Fitzherbert at least once while dealing with the sale of her maisonette. What if she had been with Piers and seen the photo? He swallowed.

'Attractive woman.' Piers examined the picture. He said it as though this surprised him; as though he couldn't imagine Martin being associated with anyone remotely appealing. But Martin wasn't offended by the tone. He was too busy acknowledging a sense of knee-weakening relief. It appeared that Piers really didn't know who Mrs Fitzherbert was.

To hide his consternation, he asked for both things back. It was with some difficulty that he resisted the impulse to snatch.

'Well, they're yours, aren't they?' said Piers, handing them over. 'I'd just be a bit more careful where you leave your wallet in future. Next time you might not be so lucky.'

Out on the pitch Howard Scott survived just long enough to get his half-century before being stumped. With four wickets in the bag, the South Wales Exiles sensed possible victory for the first time. Then Will came out and shattered any illusions. Disaster followed disaster. Two catches were dropped, the cabinet minister's son, presented with an easy chance of a run-out, made a wild throw and gave the opposition an extra four runs, and all the time, Will, with his steady, sensible game, kept on finding the gaps with his beautifully timed shots.

When the score reached 170 with the loss of no further wickets, Giles began to sweat. The Scotts' team only needed another 42 runs to win. He took Martin to one side. 'I know Will,' he said gravely. 'In this form he'll keep driving all night if he has to.'

'Then we must concentrate on their weak spot,' Martin said firmly, 'and target the other man.'

His plan worked. Keeping Will at the non-strikers' end, the pressure on his other team-mates began to tell and, twenty minutes later, Martin had unnerved four batsmen – clean bowled three of them and broken a stump. The score stood at 209 for nine wickets. The situation had become gripping. Just one wicket to go, but all Will's side needed was three runs to win. Like hounds closing in for the kill Giles had brought his fielders into a defensive position and several of them crouched menacingly close to the batsman.

The moment of truth had arrived. Conscious of a highly charged atmosphere, Martin gathered his wits and, with a deep intake of breath, made his run up and bowled a fast half-volley. The batsman, a tall, lanky youth with pink cheeks and a nervous smile, thrust out his chin in false bravado and struck wildly at the ball. By a sheer stroke of luck, he sent it flying into the air. But what he gained in height he lacked in depth and, seconds later, the ball fell like a stone into Martin's hand.

The team scattered in confetti-like excitement around him. 'Christ, what a finish!' crowed a euphoric Giles. 'I'm going to buy you a bloody large drink!'

'Nice touch.' Sportingly William shook Martin's hand. 'Come back next year and play for our side.'

And then, from nowhere, a golden figure pushing her way through the crowd, leaning up to kiss his mouth. Eve. His Eve. 'Well done, friend,' she whispered tenderly.

Had it not been for the elation of his cricketing triumph, and the amount of alcohol subsequently consumed which put him on such a high, Martin might have been rather more intimidated by the Scotts' dinner-party that evening. They sat down at a table that could easily have accommodated twenty-four. He felt a bit like a pawn, borrowed to make up the numbers on an elaborate chessboard carved out of ivory. He found himself seated between Venetia Palmer-Jones, Arabella's truculent daughter, and Hilary Wick, a novelist who wrote thrillers and took almost an hour to describe the story of her rise to apparent world fame – Martin had never heard of her. Venetia was slim as a blade with dirty-blonde hair, purple fingernails, purple lips and her mother's sharp features. She smoked throughout dinner, picked at her food, and talked obsessively about what she wanted to do with her life. Martin suspected the attraction London held was as much to do with getting away from her mother and Bath as anything else.

Opposite him, half-hidden behind a rather vulgar flower arrangement, was Eve. She looked breathtaking in a strappy hot-orange dress which clung to her like a second skin and revealed a great deal of her legs and her fantastic tits. He felt a pang of jealousy when Piers sat down beside her, but drew comfort from the fact that neither spoke more than two words to each other. Piers spent most of the evening drinking and flirting with the pretty redhead on his other side, much to the consternation of the cabinet minister's son who was going out with her. Only once did he witness anything intimate pass between them. Eve was trying to light a cigarette but her match wouldn't strike. Piers took the box from her and struck it firmly on one side; the flame flared up bright and strong as their eyes met, and she leaned towards it, one hand holding the cigarette to her mouth, the other resting gently on his wrist.

The guests were an imposing lot and the air was thick with conversation about things of which Martin knew very little. Howard, his mood distracted, had to leave the table to take work-related calls twice, but he returned noticeably more relaxed after the second call and began talking about a house he was doing up for a client. Martin's interest was finally stirred.

'Don't you find it much more of a production working on a house in a foreign city like Hong Kong?' asked Hilary Wick, whose strident voice carried down the table like that of a football coach. 'I mean, getting planning permission and that sort of thing. I researched one of my books out there and found the Chinese a very awkward bunch.'

'Not once you've done the initial groundwork and built up contacts,' said Howard. 'In fact, in some ways I prefer working out there. Architecturally speaking, Hong Kong is an incredible city.'

'My wife has always been frightfully keen on interior decorating,' said the Reverend Digby-Smith.

Howard smiled drily. 'That's rather different to interior design which is an aspect of what I do. An interior decorator concentrates on the cosmetic aspect, whereas design leans more towards the spiritual value relating to the inhabitants.'

'I see,' said the Reverend, though it was clear he didn't.

Martin leaned forward. 'Rather like putting a Jacobean chest next to an art deco table lamp and knowing instinctively whether or not they'd work together?'

'Precisely.' Howard seemed pleased with Martin's remark and filled his empty glass with more wine. 'Are you a connoisseur of antiques yourself?'

'No,' Martin answered honestly. 'But I like beautiful things.' And in spite of himself he glanced across the table at Eve.

'Howard,' cut in Piers, 'I must remember to show you that pair of Louis XVI *bras de lumière* I was telling you about. They're rather special.'

'Yes, of course. I'm keen to see those. Tell me,' he said, turning his attention back to Martin, 'where did you learn to bowl like that? It was impressive stuff.'

'School and university mostly. But I was always fooling around with a ball as a boy.' He could feel Piers's X-ray vision boring into his mind.

'Were you at Oxford with Piers?' asked Arabella, passing round the cheese board.

Howard lit a cigar and puffed on it meditatively.

'No,' said Martin. 'Aberystwyth.'

'*Where?*' Arabella looked as if he'd spoken in Arabic.

'That's Mid Wales, I believe,' said Giles, winking at him.

'I must say this is an excellent goat.' The Reverend Digby-Smith turned to Arabella, smearing crumbly white cheese on to another cracker. 'And the venison – splendid.' He smacked his lips appreciatively. 'One of your own, I take it? For how long is it normally hung?'

'Depends what crime it committed,' said Will. Eve giggled.

The venison was certainly delicious, one of the many things about the weekend Martin was savouring. It seemed to him that life could be pretty bloody wonderful.

All this, he thought, surveying first the Limoges porcelain thin as paper, the gleaming silver cutlery marked with a royal crest, then, beyond the window, the dying sky streaked with thin strips of salmon pink. He had once shared a room at college with a boy from Llandrindod Wells whose parents owned a large hotel. Four sisters, one brother, with horses and tennis racquets at their disposal and summers spent in the South of France by the sea; it was the sort of upbringing he had coveted. He had a taste of that greedy envy again, only this time he was a part of it; this time it was real.

He was brought back to earth by Howard who tapped the end of his cigar against the edge of an ashtray. 'Tell me about your father, Martin. Is he a property man?'

Perhaps if it had been just the two of them alone together, Martin might have told the truth. After all, there was nothing shameful about running a newsagents. But, at that moment, all other conversation around the table chose to cease and he found himself the focus of attention. He thought of an article he had read recently about manor houses that had been turned into successful hotels and restaurants. Suddenly inspired, he said, 'A few years back he bought a hotel.'

'What fun. Michael and I are always looking for new places to stay,' Priscilla King interjected. 'You must tell us where it is and we'll look it up.'

'On the West Sussex coast. Er – it's a bit off the beaten track so you probably won't have heard of it.'

'Try me.' Piers leaned forward with sudden interest. 'I have some relatives there so I'm *very* familiar with that area.'

I'll bet you are, thought Martin. It was clear that Piers had taken his earlier dismissal very personally indeed. He gave him the name of the only one he could immediately recall.

'Ah,' Piers pounced. 'So you know Whitelock?'

Martin's hands dampened. 'What?'

'George Whitelock. He runs Tuften Hall just outside Climping. Old friend of my sister's. See a lot of each other, Whitelock and I. In fact I ran into him only the other day.'

'Really?' Martin helped himself to some cheese, hoping that by not saying much Piers would lose interest in the conversation.

'Of course you must know George too.'

'Vaguely,' Martin answered carefully. 'I don't get down as much as I'd like.'

'Odd that I've never heard him mention anything about a Frank Leak – that is your father's name, isn't it?' Piers reached for his glass without taking his eyes off his prey.

Howard was looking at him too. His expression was that of pity, almost disappointment; a look which reminded Martin of the one Frank had given him the night he'd lied about the cause of his fractured arm.

He cleared his throat. 'Yes,' he said. How did Piers know? How could he possibly know about Frank unless Eve had picked up something from Oliver and told him.

'Been there long?' Piers asked pleasantly.

'A while.'

'What,' he said helpfully, 'five, ten – fifteen –?'

'Twelve years.'

'A long time. I'm just trying to work this out. You don't have any French connections, do you?'

Martin shook his head. He could see the Reverend Digby-Stewart out of the corner of one eye. He seemed to have found an invisible but absorbing object on the tip of his chin.

'Are you quite sure?' Piers's voice was incredulous and insulting.

Eve looked stricken. Martin put down his cheese knife abruptly and met his gaze. 'I just said so.'

'Quite. And you would know. After all, it belongs to your parents. Only I seem to remember George telling me that the Manor had been bought out by a gay French hotelier two years ago? It was in all the papers and caused quite a stir with the locals, as you can imagine.'

A pause. 'Which makes me wonder,' he pushed on

mercilessly, his eyes glancing around to see if any of the other guests mirrored his disbelief, 'why George would have made a thing like that up?'

Martin hesitated, a moment too long. Nobody spoke. It was as if the room's temperature had plummeted to zero. Piers's eyes remained fixed on him: cruel and hard with triumph. He was revelling in every squirming moment of his humiliation.

Suddenly, Martin remembered who it was Piers reminded him of. Slug. They both derived the same pleasure from hurting others. Once Slug had strung up a neighbour's cat and, just to see what would happen, poured lighter fluid over its tail. Even now, Martin could recall the crazed wail as the animal's fur ignited. What had started as a boyish prank, had become something altogether more sinister. He should have put a stop to it – had wanted to – but one warning glance from Slug and his courage had deserted him. With a sickening complicity he had stood by, choking back the tears, the need to throw up, and watched without saying a word. For years afterwards, he hated himself for his weakness, for not standing up to a bully. He wasn't about to let the same thing happen to him now. He looked Piers squarely in the eye. 'The hotel's sale came about as a result of my father's death.'

There was an embarrassed silence, then someone coughed and the conversation resumed. Eve, smiling faintly, turned her back on Piers and began peeling a grape.

'Don't pay any attention to him,' said a voice in his ear. It was Venetia. She leaned closer to him and whispered, 'Piers is a pig! Actually, I thought you handled that rather well. He's probably still mad about the way you bowled him out this afternoon. I thought you were marvellous.'

'Glad I've made somebody happy.' Martin reached for his wineglass with a not-too-steady hand. 'So, what did he do to rattle your cage?'

'Let's just say I know what it's like to be on the receiving end of his malicious games.' She removed a cigarette from her bag which he lit for her. She looked at him sideways as if she were assessing him for the first time. 'How long are you staying?'

'Until tomorrow night.'

'Good. Then I'm going to steal you away from the others. You don't mind, do you? Only we can bunk off the morning service which is horribly dull and go swimming in the lake instead.

'Just the two of us?'

She grinned. 'Just you and me.'

'Sure,' said Martin. 'Why not?'

Later, after a highly competitive game of Trivial Pursuit, Piers sloped off with some of the men to the snooker room. Others, exhausted by sun and alcohol, drifted off to bed or to their respective homes. Alone at last with Eve, Martin rested his head on the back of the sofa and gave a contented sigh. 'What a day!'

'It certainly has been for you. Do you always win at everything you play?'

'No. But I notice you don't like to lose either.'

'What's the point in coming second?' She suppressed a yawn with one hand. 'It's supposed to be lovely tomorrow. Why don't we go on a dawn ride? I promised you a tour of the estate. It'll mean getting up early but the views will be worth it.'

'I'd love that.'

They were sitting together in the nursery, a large blue room with pretty sash windows at either end open to the warm evening, on the sort of big comfy armchairs which, like a bed, compelled you to drop off to sleep. Along one wall was a piano on top of which was a stack of old sheet music. Against another, a battered-looking rocking horse, shelves of much-read novels, a writing desk. A tray of coffee things and a bottle of champagne were parked on the table in front of them: their prize for winning

Trivial Pursuit. Ambrose and Marshall lay at their feet twitching and sighing in dog-slumber.

Martin's coffee was still too hot and the cup burned his fingertips. Setting it down on the table, he cast a contented eye at his surroundings and at Eve next to him – preoccupied, smoking a cigarette. He would always remember this day, this time he'd had with her. Even if it didn't hold quite the same meaning for her, even if it was only ... but he wasn't going to dwell on that now. He had imagined doing this: sitting beside her, finally with the opportunity to tell her how he felt. But things were different now. He could feel it. Eve had invited him to stay with her father, someone she thought the world of – surely a point in <u>his</u> favour? And the way she had rushed to his side after the match, her eyes glowing with pride. He couldn't have misconstrued the affection in her expression. It seemed impossible that he could ever tire of her small, perfect face, the beautiful mouth which only a few hours ago, and for a second time, had been pressed against his.

He gazed at her longingly. 'Eve?'

'Mmm?'

'Why did you invite me down this weekend?'

She looked at him with a puzzled smile. 'Haven't you been having a good time?'

'You know I have.'

'Then why the look of worry?'

He relaxed his features. 'I thought it might be to spite Piers.'

Her mouth tightened into a horizontal bracket. 'The best thing is to ignore Piers when he's like this. He's just cross because for once he's not the centre of attention. Today you earned that right.'

They sat in silence, then Eve spoke again, her voice soft once more. 'It's funny. We've worked together all these months and yet in the last twenty-four hours I feel as though I've discovered a whole new person.' She took his hand in hers. 'Can't make you out, Martin. But I like you more and more. I'm so glad we're friends.'

He threw caution to the wind. 'You must know that my feelings for you run a lot deeper than just friendship.'

'Martin. I don't know what to say. I – I had no idea.'

'I think you did. I think it's clear as daylight how I feel about you. Oh, come on, Eve,' he said in a rush. 'All this is driving me crazy.'

There was a loud clatter outside the door, followed by angry cursing from a familiar voice. Piers.

'Oh, dear,' said Eve, 'I expect he's looking for me.'

'Don't say anything,' Martin pleaded. Don't let him spoil things, he almost added.

'I can't go on avoiding him indefinitely. He's been intolerable all weekend. Even Daddy's noticed. We're in here, Piers,' she called.

The door opened. Piers hovered dangerously, filling the frame. 'So this is where you've been hiding yourself.' His tie was loosened and his hair was dishevelled. It was obvious that he had been drinking.

'I missed you, baby. I thought you'd gone up to bed.' His mouth curved into a half-smile, then he saw who she was with. 'Ah! I see Romeo's still following you around,' he said rudely, his eyes coasting the table in front of them. 'Champagne too.' He turned to Martin, examining him closely as if he was something he had just stepped in. 'What does it feel like to have a reason to celebrate? Can't imagine it happens often.'

Eve shot him a look of warning. 'If you're going to be vile you can go elsewhere.'

Piers moved further into the room and sat down in one of the chairs. It was quite obvious he was there to stay. 'This is cosy.' He smiled at Martin.

'We were just talking, Piers,' Eve said scoldingly.

'It's what you were *thinking* that worries me.'

Martin put down his glass and cleared his throat. 'It's been a long day,' he said to Eve, standing up. 'I think I'll head on up to bed.'

'Don't go on my account.' Piers reached for the champagne bottle and poured himself a glass.

Martin felt a pang of hatred. One day, matey, he thought darkly, one day I'll wipe that smug fucking grin off your face for ever. Deliberately, he directed his gaze at Eve. 'Are we still on for tomorrow?'

'Of course.'

'Got something nice planned?' Piers asked.

Martin ignored him. 'About six then?'

She winked conspiratorially. 'Six is fine.'

Martin was too wound up to sleep so he went for a walk. It was a beautiful night, the air still and balmy, sweetly perfumed like a woman anticipating the arrival of her lover. But he wasn't in an appreciative mood. He felt confused and unsure what to do next. If Piers had not appeared at that particular moment he might have found out what Eve's feelings for him really were.

Upstairs in his room, he found a hastily scrawled note on the floor, the contents of which made his heart race. It must have been slipped under the door.

There is no contest. You're twice the man Piers is and I'm so glad you're here to brighten this dreary place up. Can't wait to be shot of the others. See you in the morning. Sweet dreams.

There was no signature. But that didn't matter. Only one person could have written it.

Despite not getting to bed until the early hours, Martin was woken at five thirty by sun which streamed through the windows and lay in gold-yellow pools on the oak floor. With a sense of unreality, he went over the events of yesterday: his cricketing victory, the Scotts' acceptance of him, Eve's note that had left him wanting to jump for joy. Of course, he wasn't stupid enough to think that Piers would just disappear – he wasn't the type to give up easily – but Martin was convinced that after the way he had behaved, Eve would see him for the shit he really was and call off their engagement.

He leapt out of bed and threw on a pair of jeans. Then he went downstairs and made his way to the kitchen. He popped his head round the door and found the room empty, but some early bird – the housekeeper perhaps – had already laid the table for breakfast. He was about to make himself some coffee when it occurred to him that, with a sleeping household, this was an opportune moment to have a snoop round.

He had seen the south-facing drawing room on the night they had arrived, but there were two further formal rooms: the first, a reading room, determinedly masculine, full of books and, bronze statues and with panelled walls. The second by contrast was a palate of muted pastel shades, flooded with light and enhanced with mirrors and fine antiques. Most of the doors to the rooms, as he explored, had been left partially open, but one door, away from the heart of the house, was closed. There was little chance of there being anyone inside, but just to make sure he knocked. No response. Hoping it wouldn't turn out to be someone's bedroom, he twisted the handle and opened the door a crack.

It was a study, but one such as he had never seen before. There were wooden shelves in horizontal and vertical lines everywhere. Some were stacked with over-sized, heavily bound books, others held complex archi-tectural plans and sketches. In one corner was a three-panelled screen behind which a small basin and a kettle was concealed. There was an L-shaped desk by the window weighed down by sophisticated computer hard-ware – a monitor and colour printer which must have cost a bomb. There were portraits on the walls and, intriguingly, a rolling filing cabinet on wheels. But most impressive of all was a conference-sized table in the centre of the room, on which were two powerful spotlights and a fantastic model of a skyscraper. He bent his head in admiration and allowed his eye to run over the intricately detailed forty-storey block no more than a foot high. To start off with so small an object and have it evolve into a landmark was some achievement!

He was about to abandon his exploration when he heard someone approaching the study. Apprehensive about being caught in a room so clearly meant for private use, he shrank away from the door and did the first thing that sprang to mind: hid behind the screen. As he'd feared, the door to the study opened. Martin bit his lip as he heard it very gently close again not moving a muscle as the footsteps moved towards him. There was a moment of stillness, then he heard something ping, something tinny-sounding, mechanical, quickly followed by a flutter and a whine. There was a gap between each of the panels in the screen just wide enough to see through. Martin put his eye up against it, his eyelashes grazing the edge, and blinked. What was Piers doing in Howard's study at such an early hour? He risked a glance at his watch. It was still only five forty-five.

From where he crouched, he had an unimpeded view of the back of the monitor and Piers's head which was facing in his direction. He could hear the stop-start tapping of his fingers on the keyboard, and see the look of intense concentration on his face as Piers scanned whatever was on the screen. What was going on? Had Howard asked Piers to do some work for him? Was it a project of his own and, if so, why the apparent urgency? Piers seemed to be deep in thought. Twice he swore under his breath as he clicked away with the mouse. 'Come on, come on,' he kept muttering until finally his expression cleared. 'Got it!' he hissed victoriously, and from the back pocket of his jeans withdrew – at first Martin couldn't quite see what – a floppy disk. Working with speed, Piers slipped the disk into the A-drive and hit a button on the keyboard. While he waited for the machine, he walked to the window and looked out at the terrace. He stood there for some moments then turned around suddenly. He seemed to be staring straight through the panel. Martin kept perfectly still, trying to slow the panicky pounding of his heart.

As soon as the computer stopped grumbling, Piers switched off the machine, ejected the floppy disk and left the room.

Martin waited until he was absolutely sure Piers wasn't going to make a last-minute return before surfacing from behind the screen. Stealthily he made his way over to the computer and switched it back on. He knew he was taking a terrible risk in doing this, but there was something he *had* to find out. With a quick glance over his shoulder towards the door, he clicked into the main menu and instructed the machine to go into the last opened document. It appeared instantly which surprised him as he'd anticipated it asking him for a password. His eyes widened in surprise. As he scrolled through the architectural plans, the schedule, the financial outlines and figures, page after page of meticulously drawn designs, it became clear that he was looking at Howard's proposal for the project in the Middle East. When Eve had hinted at the size of the scheme, he'd had no idea quite how big she had meant. The skyscraper – planned for the city of Muscat – was going to cost someone two hundred and sixty million in sterling, of which four and a half per cent would go to Howard's firm for their part in the project. Shit! No wonder Howard wanted things kept quiet until the deal had been firmed up. This would make his firm a fortune. Just one thing bothered Martin. What exactly was Piers's involvement?

Five minutes later, he returned to the kitchen and read yesterday's paper until the grandfather clock in the hall chimed six. When, at six thirty, there was still no sign of Eve, he climbed the stairs and tiptoed along the corridor to her room, carefully avoiding the creaking floorboards. He was about to give Eve's door a gentle tap when it opened slightly. Hand poised in mid-air, he listened for signs of movement but could hear nothing from within. Perhaps she had already left for the stables, or simply overslept? The gap was wide enough for him to see through and, unable to help himself, he peered into the bedroom. Then wished he hadn't.

Eve was in bed lying on her back, magnificent breasts exposed, one arm flung out in sleep, with the body of a man – Piers – next to her on his stomach, an arm and leg wrapped across her body, territorial even in sleep. The sheets, which must have been kicked off during the night, lay strewn on the floor next to the same pair of jeans Martin had seen him wearing less than an hour ago. Her face was turned towards Piers, and his hand tenderly cupped one of her breasts. Martin stood there, stunned, unable to tear his gaze away from the scene. They looked so utterly perfect together, like a Titian painting, Eve's porcelain skin startling against the fudge brown of Piers's tanned, muscular limbs. An empty bottle of champagne – no doubt the one from last night – sat propped on the window seat alongside a bottle of wine. Most disturbing was the sight of a black stocking tied to the end of each bedpost.

Then Piers opened an eye and saw him standing in the doorway. The corners of his mouth widened triumphantly into a fuck-you kind of smile at which Martin turned on his heels and marched angrily back along the corridor. Bastard! Fucking, fucking bastard! Fists clenched, blood pounding in his ears, he felt so angry that he made no effort to tread quietly and, when he stumbled on the Scotts' cat, Delilah, snoozing on the landing, he gave it a savage kick.

Downstairs he found Giles loading luggage into the boot of his car.

'I thought you'd still be asleep,' he said cheerfully, 'dreaming about your moment of glory in yesterday's match.'

'The light woke me. You're not going back to London by any chance?'

'As it happens I am. My sister's flying in from Munich and I said I'd meet her at Heathrow. Everything all right? You're as white as this car.'

'I'm fine,' Martin said shortly. 'Any chance of a lift?'

'But I thought you were driving back with Eve tonight?'

'There's been a change of plan. A small domestic crisis.'

'In which case,' said Giles, 'I'd be glad of the company.'

His mind in turmoil, Martin flung what little he had brought with him into a bag, then scribbled a letter of excuse to the Scotts with a message for Venetia. What he wrote to Eve took longer. He couldn't get out of his mind the stockings tied to the ends of the bed. He saw them everywhere he looked: the cord holding back the curtains in his room; Marshall's lead hanging from a hook in the kitchen; and they enraged him. He felt used, humiliated. Just what the fuck had last night's note been about? Letting him believe that she was serious about him, when all along she planned to slink off to bed with that rat? Perhaps his weekend invitation had been nothing more than an elaborate plan to rile Piers. If so, Eve had got what she wanted. No doubt the pair of them were having a good laugh about it now – Piers would surely have told her about him coming to her room. Fool, he told himself, stupid bloody fool!

He zipped up his holdall and cast one quick glance around the room to see if he'd forgotten anything. He knew he was taking the easy way out by leaving, but he simply couldn't have stomached seeing them together a moment longer. On the one hand he felt so let down by Eve that he wished never to see her again; yet, on the other, a despairing voice in his head kept asking her: *Why?*

When he climbed into the car next to Giles he mulled over the irony that, yet again, Sunday had ended on a note of foreboding. He kept his eyes resolutely on the open gates ahead but, as they pulled away along the gravelled drive, he couldn't resist turning for a final glimpse of the Scotts' manor with its elegant Georgian lines, the ivy glimmering like fish scales in the morning light. It was the sort of place he had always dreamed of owning one day. He knew now that he would never see it again.

THIRTEEN

Martin was in no mood for socialising and couldn't be persuaded to join Giles and his sister for lunch on the Fulham Road. Instead he went for a long walk, stopping off for a pint on the way home. By the time he got back to his flat, it was five. Almost every envelope waiting in his letterbox was marked Private, Confidential or Personal and each contained junk mail. One sought to grab his attention by claiming his name had been chosen to be eligible for a huge cash prize, but he threw it into the bin, along with the rest. No sooner had he closed the door to his flat when the phone began ringing. Unable to curb the sudden hope that it might be Eve, he pounced on it. But it was only Venetia hoping to meet up with him mid-week. There was a lot of noise in the background, a stereo playing or television – he wasn't sure.

'We're just down for one night. Mummy's got to go to some dreary dinner party, so I thought I'd take you up on that offer of a drink.'

If memory served him right, *she* had done the inviting. 'I probably won't be able to get away much before nine,' he said, hoping to put her off.

'Nine's fine. I'll come and pick you up from the office.' For an eighteen-year-old she was certainly pushy.

Monday was a bank holiday so he had to wait until Tuesday to see Eve. He had planned on being distant but it was still a shock when she breezed in on a scented wave of jasmine, hair swinging from her shoulders and wearing a charming little suit he hadn't seen before. Her face had caught the sun so that her normally pale green eyes had darkened to the colour of greengages. His first reaction was one of heart-stopping pleasure. Then, almost immediately, he felt the poisonous episode with Piers come crashing down on him.

She tackled him as soon as the morning meeting was over. 'What happened to you on Sunday? You just disappeared.'

'I thought it best under the circumstances,' he responded coolly.

She regarded him under sooty lashes, the face that only forty-eight hours ago had promised so much now deep in speculation. 'You're angry.'

'I'm not.'

'You don't seem very pleased to see me.'

'I've got a lot on my mind.' He hated the sound of his voice, yet was unable to control the haughty, injured tone. 'It has nothing to do with you.'

A worried frown appeared on her forehead. 'Has Piers said something?'

'I'm not remotely interested in anything Piers has got to say. I've got better things to do with my time.' He reached across his desk to pick up a bunch of keys. 'Look, can we do this later? I've got to go.'

As Martin stepped out into the warm day he silently cursed himself, angry that the hurt look on her face should have made him feel so guilty.

'Isn't this great!' Venetia Palmer-Jones shouted at him over the music. They were in Kensington, at some party she had overheard a friend of hers mention. Red table lamps lit the room and there was a strong smell of grass. Venetia, wearing a silver miniskirt, didn't appear to know a soul, but they found themselves a drink and edged their way round the bodies thrusting wildly on the makeshift dance floor. The music was insanely loud and already the drinks table was littered with empty wine bottles and crushed beer cans. Venetia was swaying to the music, her heavily made-up eyes starry with excitement. She had taken a great deal of trouble over her appearance, but Martin thought she had looked more attractive at Partridge Manor when she had been herself.

She brought her mouth up and cupped a hand to his ear. 'Do you want a cigarette?'

'I don't smoke.'

'Me neither – except at parties. Can you get one for me?'

There was a packet of Rothmans on a nearby table. He didn't know who they belonged to but removed one from the box and lit it for her.

'Thanks.' She inhaled deeply and smiled at him. 'I always feel like I come into my own when I'm in London. I mean, Bath's such a drag, don't you think? There's never anything to do.'

'If you feel that way then why don't you move up here?'

She pulled a face. 'Mummy doesn't like the idea of me living on my own. She thinks I'll get in with the wrong sort. I keep trying to convince her I'm old enough to know the difference, but she won't listen.'

'At least she cares.' He grabbed himself another beer. It was only his third but already his fatigue had been replaced by a pleasant daze.

'My best friend's got this eating disorder. It's no secret – she's had it for years. It's not when you sick up all your food, but when you don't eat at all.'

'Anorexia.' He'd once had a friend with the same problem; the relationship hadn't lasted long.

'She was living with her boyfriend in London. About a year ago she very nearly died. Her weight had dropped to four stone. Mummy came with me to see her in hospital and completely freaked out. She's over it now, back to her normal weight, but I think Mummy still worries I could end up the same way. As if!'

Martin's mind started to wander. The room was hot and he was regretting not having gone home first to change. He decided that after one more drink they would leave.

Venetia appraised him thoughtfully. 'Eve's talked to you about me, I suppose?'

'No.' Not that they had discussed much of anything since their weekend together, he thought morosely.

'It's all right. I won't be offended if she has. She usually relishes the opportunity of telling people how she stole Piers from under my nose.'

He paused, the beer bottle at his lips. 'You went out with Piers?' he asked incredulously.

'You don't believe me.' Her mouth took on an antagonistic slant.

'I didn't say that.'

'You think I'd make a thing like that up?'

'Not at all. Why should I?'

'Because she likes you.' She was having to shout again to compete with the music. 'And you can't help but be flattered by that.'

'Venetia, I think you're letting your imagination run a little wild this evening.'

'She's never bloody well liked me,' she complained, her voice young and huffy. 'Right from Mummy and Howard's wedding day, she's treated me like a second-class citizen. Couldn't bear the idea of sharing her precious father, you see. But I've always got on swimmingly with Howard. As stepfathers go he's been really nice and Eve's hated that. She thinks that he's her exclusive territory. You know, she tried to turn him against me and when that didn't work she set her sights on Piers. Knowing what she was like, I'd worried about inviting him down for the weekend – we hadn't been going out for very long – but even I didn't think she'd sink that low. She turned him against me and then she made a play for him herself. And anything Eve wants,' she added, blowing smoke in an angry whoosh towards the ceiling, 'Eve bloody well gets.'

Martin set down his beer bottle. 'From the little I've picked up about Piers, I'd say Eve did you a favour.'

But Venetia was frowning. 'You don't know her like I do. She's a cow and I loathe her.'

He was trying to think of some way to respond, when she grabbed his arm. 'Come on!' she yelled, pulling him towards the bopping throng. 'I'm mad for this song.'

For a while he danced with her, but he didn't like the mindless stuff they were playing, and it was clear that Venetia needed no partner. Eyes shut, head thrown back, she gyrated her hips and twisted her arms in curious little movements, lost in her own inner world. From where he stood he could see through the glass doors leading on to a balcony, a small group quietly getting stoned. Had Venetia taken something herself? It wouldn't have surprised him. For all her efforts to appear tough and independent, there seemed to be a transparent vulnerability about her. It was easy to see how she might slip down the dissolute road her mother was so anxious for her to avoid.

By the time they left the party it was past midnight. In the fresh night air, their clothes reeked of smoke. Venetia was very drunk and had to be supported as they made their way back to her car. She was in no fit state to drive so Martin took the wheel. When he pulled up outside the Scotts' flat in Thurloe Square, she shifted in her seat to look at him. 'You know all that stuff I told you earlier about Piers?' she said in a breathy voice. 'It doesn't mean anything. Not now. I meant what I said in my note.'

'Note?'

'The one I left under your door, silly.'

'Under my door?'

'At Partridge Manor.' She looked at him oddly. 'And I thought I was the drunk one.'

Oh, God! The note hadn't been from Eve at all. This put an entirely different slant on the weekend. He wanted to kick himself. What a prat he'd been, behaving like some kind of scorned lover, allowing himself to believe that Eve would sabotage her relationship with Piers when, in less than three months, they were going to tie the knot. What was it they said about setting your sights too high, he thought with sudden sobriety, and the subsequent, inevitable fall?

Venetia leaned towards him and drawled, 'You can fuck me if you want to.'

His heart sank. He had been anticipating something like this all evening. 'Venetia –'

'I want you to. I've thought of nothing else all night.' Through the car window she glanced up at the darkened building. 'No one's home,' she coaxed, placing his hand firmly, deliberately, inside her short skirt. She was wearing no knickers; he could feel the silky wetness between her legs. Gently, he pulled his hand away.

'I could sneak you into my room without anyone knowing – or,' she added, a rushed, panicky sound in her voice as she foresaw the imminent rejection, 'we could go back to your place.'

Light from a street lamp illuminated the hope in her young face. She was trying so hard. He grappled for something to say that would let her down gently, but there was no easy way of doing it. 'Venetia, don't do this. You'll only regret it in the morning.'

She must have seen the pity in his face because she shrank back into her seat. 'Bastard,' she spat. From the glove compartment she removed a packet of cigarettes and lit one, her hand trembling slightly.

'We both know this isn't to do with me,' he said after a long silence. 'It's about Eve, about pay-back, about revenge. You think that by sleeping with me it will even the score. But you're wrong, Venetia. The only person you'd end up hurting is yourself.'

Angrily, she turned on him tearful pale blue eyes. 'I get enough lectures from my mother, I'm not about to start taking them from some common salesman.'

He winced. 'You don't mean that.'

She gave him a hard look. 'Well, isn't that what you are – someone who *sells* things for a living?' The way she said it made him sound like some seedy dope dealer trying to get kids hooked on heroin. 'Get out of my car.'

Reluctantly, he opened the door and stepped on to the pavement. In a flash she had moved across to the driver's seat. The door next to her was still ajar. He kept it open with one hand and squatted down next to her, resting on his haunches. 'You won't do anything stupid, will you?' he said in a measured voice. 'Because you're way over the limit and if the police were to stop you . . .'

'As if you care.' She gunned the car into life. 'I'm off to find a real man – someone who recognises a good thing when he sees it.' And with that, she slammed the door shut, revved the engine and screamed off down the road.

He got a taxi home. While he was paying for the fare he noticed Mikel, his mad Polish neighbour, standing at the front of the house.

'Hello, my lovely friend. I didn't see you for a long time.'

'Been on another drinking spree, have we, Mikel?' He walked tiredly through the gate.

Mikel rubbed his massive gnarled hands in anticipation – Martin was the only one who would talk to him. 'Oh, you.' He smiled delightedly. 'You so sweet I could *squeeze* you like a biscuit.' He probably could too. The old boy used to box and still possessed a formidable strength. 'Come here, my friend, and talk a while.'

'Not tonight, Mikel. It's been a long day.'

Mikel's voice took on a more urgent tone as Martin rummaged in his trouser pocket for his key. 'You know something? No, please, come here. Don't run away. I tell you this man who do cleaning windows, he bad man. Yes! Very bad!' He was excited now. 'Listen, my friend, you don't want to have these bloody people in your life. I'm old man. But I know these things. They no good –'

Martin closed the door on his ramblings and felt for the hall switch. A dim bulb came on above his head lighting the way up the stairs. Mikel was harmless enough, he thought as he climbed. Loneliness probably drove him to drink, but right now he simply didn't have the energy for it. Once Mikel got hold of you, he would have you out there talking all night.

As he stepped into his flat, a small feathery explosion went off in his face. At first he didn't know what had hit him and his right arm lashed out in self-defence, the other raised to protect his eyes. His fist caught the edge of something soft. He could hear an erratic whirling, a crazed whooshing around his head. Then he saw it: a small speckled bird fluttering wildly about the hall. It was flying about like a frenzied squash ball, backwards and forwards, bashing its body against first one wall then another, scattering a confetti of tiny grey-white feathers. He blinked. What the –? How on earth had it got inside? The bird careened from the ceiling, swooping towards him, then whirled away into the sitting room. Martin followed it, waving his hands to try and guide the terrified creature through the open window but his actions only seemed to panic it even more. It kept hitting the window-panel – thwack, thwack – in a confused and helpless state, then flying off to the other side of the room which proved equally as unyielding. The window – from which it must have got in – was only ajar by about three inches, but he was certain he had shut it before leaving for work that morning. Reaching up, he used both hands to yank it further up, then waited a few feet away to see what the bird would do. It shat twice; a thin stream of Tippex-white shit oozing first down the back of the sofa, then on to the television as it made three more abortive attempts to escape. Finally, it shot through the open space and was swallowed up by the night.

It wasn't until Martin had relatched the window that he was alerted to the fact that something was wrong. On the floor beneath the window were scattered bits of newspaper: the articles on the Fitzherbert murder he had cut out and saved. How, he wondered with a growing sense of unease as he bent to pick them up, had they got there? Had they been blown there by a breeze from the window, or – more worryingly – had someone disturbed them?

FOURTEEN

Martin was on his way back to the office in the Golf the next day, contemplating what he was going to have for lunch as he snailed along the traffic-ridden Holland Park towards Notting Hill, when a call came through on his mobile. With a practised hand, he reached for the tiny receiver on the passenger seat without taking his eye off the road, and pressed the on-button.

'Yes?'

The voice at the other end – male – was unfamiliar. 'Am I speaking to Martin Leak?'

'Who is this?'

It was a bad connection. There was crackling on the line. 'I'm calling from Addenbrooks Hospitals. Mrs Irene Leak – your mother, I believe – was admitted to Casualty about an hour ago.'

Martin took his foot off the accelerator. *Irene!* 'Oh my God. What's happened?'

'She's been involved in a car collision. It happened on the A45 just outside Cambridge. The driver of the car is going to be all right. He got away with a few cuts and bruises, but I'm afraid your mother hasn't been so lucky. We tried to contact her sister in Bury St Edmunds but there was no answer.'

There was some more interference, a mechanical spitting sound, and he had difficulty catching what the man said next. The line kept hiccuping, the voice sounding tinny as if he was talking from a cheap speaker phone.

'– Mercedes hit the passenger side of the car which

meant she took the full brunt of the impact. They've got her in surgery now.'

He gazed at the Land-Rover Discovery pulling out into the road in front of him. *An accident . . . in surgery?* He couldn't be hearing this. It wasn't true. Not Irene. 'How bad is it?'

There was a slight hesitation on the line. 'We don't want to take any chances. I think you should come right away.'

He drove like a madman, tearing along the M40 with his accelerator foot to the floor until he reached the M25 – mercifully clear – intent on one thing only: to get to Irene with as much speed as his little Golf could muster. He took stupid risks, weaving in and out of lanes, angering other motorists as he flashed them out of the way with his headlights, using intimidating tactics by getting too close to the tails of cars in the fast lane. He was heedless to everything but the grey, tarmacked road he was chasing. All he kept seeing as he sped northwards along the M11 was an image of Irene shielding her eyes, a tiny, frightened gasp escaping her lips as the powerful Mercedes ploughed into the side of the car, leaving her body trapped and damaged in a mangled box of metal. What had she been doing going to Cambridge? And who was the stupid sod who had driven her there? The man on the phone wouldn't reveal the extent of her injuries, only that they were serious. How serious was serious? Contained, critical, life-threatening? Oh, God – if there was one listening – let her be unharmed. Help her pull through this. The thought that he might lose her was almost too much to bear and he sat forward, leaning over the steering wheel as if sheer willpower could add speed to the car.

Fortunately he found the hospital with relative ease and, with a screech of brakes, came to a halt outside the main doors of Casualty. Ignoring the shouts of an orderly pushing an empty wheelchair up on to the pavement, 'Oy, sonny, you can't leave your motor there. You'll get *towed*', he bolted through the automatic doors, and ran to Reception. In a breathless voice he asked the woman behind the desk where he could find Irene Leak.

With infuriating laziness, the woman tapped the details into a computer and scanned the screen. After a few moments, she looked up. 'How do you spell Leak?'

He told her. The woman, who was startlingly large, nodded as if she had got it right the first time and resumed her search, but it was clear from her face – downy and overfed like a chipmunk – that she was having no luck in tracing Irene.

'Look,' he explained, with increasing desperation, 'she was in surgery only a couple of hours ago. You must have a record for her somewhere.' 'Hang on,' she said, 'I'll try them upstairs.' She picked up the receiver on her desk and punched in a three-digit extension number. When she got a connection she repeated everything Martin had told her. Then put her hand over the mouthpiece and said deferentially, 'Someone's going to find out for me.'

They didn't keep her hanging on for long, but for Martin the wait seemed interminable, and he drummed agitated fingers on the desk. He was filled with a horrible dread. It was Frank all over again: the call to tell him about the heart attack; Irene trying to camouflage the fear which gripped her – for his sake – but not succeeding; the desperate rush from his university in Wales to the hospital in Ipswich, only to learn on his arrival that he was too late, that Frank had taken his last breath shortly after the call was made. Now he was going to have to face the same ordeal with Irene. I can't take this, he thought. She's dead but they're trying to hide it from me. He knew this to be true with a terrible certainty. It explained the confusion, why things were taking so long. Right now they were probably trying to find someone suitable to tell him the bad news, let him down gently. He had just about convinced himself of this awful probability when the receptionist lowered the phone back into its cradle.

'I don't know where you got your information from,'

she said, 'but I'm afraid we have no one by that name registered here. Nor have we seen anyone today involved in a road accident. There's obviously been some kind of mix-up.' She looked at him rather sternly.

He blinked at her. 'But that's just not *possible*. Someone phoned to tell me she was here, *here*,' he stabbed the desk with his finger. 'They specifically said they were calling from this hospital. You must have it wrong.' The woman looked undecided. 'For God's sake,' he added passionately. 'Do you honestly think I'd make something like that up?'

A phone on her desk began ringing. 'I understand you're upset but if no one has heard of your mother there's not much I can do. Can you give me the name of the person you spoke to?'

He raked a confused hand through his hair, scraping it off his forehead. This was bloody madness. 'No,' he said despairingly, 'I didn't think to ask.'

'Excuse me,' she picked up the shrieking phone, 'I must take this call.'

Martin, his head full of questions, each one straining to be answered, slumped on one of the orange plastic chairs in the waiting area. What reason could the hospital have for making up a story like that? And if it had been a mix-up, as the receptionist had suggested, then how had they accessed Irene's name and his mobile number? None of it made any sense, unless – a horrible thought suddenly struck him: What if he had misheard the man? What if he'd come to the wrong hospital? How long would it take him to track the right one down – hours perhaps?

The obvious thing to do first was to try his Aunt Pauline. The caller had said they'd had no luck in reaching her number, but she might be home now. He reached for his mobile only to find that in his haste he'd left it in the car. 'Is there somewhere I can make a call?' he asked the elderly man with a hacking cough sitting next to him.

The man, clutching a grubby, well-used handkerchief to his mouth, indicated a nearby corridor running off the lobby area. About halfway down on the left was a public phone box. He rushed over to the booth, rummaging in his pocket for change, fed two coins into the slot and, after failing to get through to Pauline, dialled Irene's number. To his astonishment she answered it.

'Martin!' she said delightedly. 'What a nice surprise. A bit of a coincidence you calling now. Fiona Hodge has stopped by to have a cup of tea and –'

He interrupted her. 'Are you all right?'

'Yes, I'm fine.'

'You haven't been to Cambridge today?'

'Cambridge?' She sounded puzzled. 'Whatever for?'

He had wondered the same thing. Through the hospital window he could see the back of his car and remembered the warning the orderly had given him when he'd arrived. He would be wise to go and rescue it while he still had the chance. He didn't fancy having to cough up for the towing fee. 'Look,' he said, his mind whirling. 'It doesn't matter. I've obviously got my wires crossed. I'm just glad you're OK. I'll call you another time when you're not so busy.'

'But don't you want to say a word to Fiona before you go? She's been asking all about you.'

He groaned. Fiona Hodge was a girl he'd gone out with when he was seventeen. She lived in a nearby village and was now married with three little monsters who screamed a lot and generally caused havoc, but she continued to pay Irene frequent visits and, from what he could gather, they spent most of their time talking about him.

'Er, I'd love to, Mum, but it's going to have to be another time. I've got to run.'

It occurred to him, as he hung up, that he hadn't let anyone at work know where he was. He glanced at his watch, then remembered that he hadn't been able to find it that morning. Come to think of it, he hadn't seen it since yesterday. His eye caught the clock on the wall. Three thirty-five. Fuck! It would be five at the earliest before he made it back.

Back at the car he tried to call the office on his mobile, but the battery was flat. No sooner had he connected it to the cigarette lighter, when it sprang back into life. The call was from Hammers. He sounded very cross.

'Where the bloody hell are you?' he demanded. 'I've had two calls from Jerry Smith wondering why you haven't made your three o'clock. He's been waiting almost half an hour.'

Oh, shit. The appointment arranged last week had completely slipped his mind. Martin tried to support the phone between his shoulder and ear as he changed down a gear and pulled on to the ring road. 'I – er – ran into a few problems.'

'Dazzle me with a good one, chum, you've been gone for hours.'

'Hammers, listen,' he was suddenly inspired. 'I've got a bite on Abbotsbury. A client called earlier wanting to discuss a possible deal over lunch. We've talked through the survey and I think we've ironed out the main concerns.'

He sensed Hammers' sudden interest. 'Has he made an offer?'

Martin stalled. 'He's giving it serious consideration.'

The house in Abbotsbury Road, four storeys high with six bedrooms, four bathrooms, a heated swimming pool, and twelve front-facing sash windows which looked directly on to Holland Park, had been on Carlyle's books for months. Ordinarily, it was the sort of dream property agents itched to get their hands on, slicing their rate of commission by half to secure sole rights. Unfortunately the house had proved problematic. They couldn't shift it because it was riddled with structural problems. Every time an offer was made, one look at the thirty-six-page survey had clients retreating with indecent speed. Martin really had been involved in a number of discussions with a property dealer who was considering its purchase, and he now waved this dealer in front of Hammers like a white flag.

'I take it we're paying?' Hammers grumbled, his mood slightly improved.

'A smart move under the circumstances, don't you think?' Up ahead, he could see a blue sign to the motorway.

'Where have you taken him?'

Martin thought rapidly. 'Kensington Place.' The restaurant was a little too close to the office for comfort, but he had no reason to suspect that Hammers would check up on him. He put on his right indicator, hoping Hammers would mistake the noise of the car for a busy restaurant.

'OK,' Hammers conceded. 'Keep him happy, give him what he wants – buy him champagne if you have to. But get him to commit to the purchase.'

As soon as their conversation had ended, Martin called the property dealer's number. He wasn't at home, but fortunately he tracked him down on his mobile.

'How's it going, Martin? Got anything of interest for me to see?'

'Well, actually, I was wondering if you'd had any more thoughts about Abbotsbury?'

There was a moment's silence at the other end of the phone. 'Ah, that.'

Martin registered the sinking feeling he got when he was about to hear something he wouldn't like.

'It's just that I've had a chance to go over the figures. Frankly, the profit margin's too slim to be worth my while.'

'I thought the house had great potential,' Martin pushed desperately.

'So did I, initially. But it's a question of cost. Whoever takes it on, is in for a lot of work and hassle with not much to show when they're done. No, mate, I'm afraid you're going to have to count me out on this one.'

Martin hung up and threw the phone on to the passenger seat. 'Shit,' he said, banging the steering wheel with his hands. 'Shit!'

*

The following evening he met Eve for a drink after work – his instigation. Since Venetia had admitted to being the author of the note found under his bedroom door, he had been feeling rather foolish about his behaviour, both at Partridge Manor and then at the office. He arrived at the pub late – he had been stuck for almost two hours in a building of tenanted flats which a client wanted to convert back into a house – and found her waiting for him at a table near the window.

'I didn't think you'd come,' she said, once he had brought over their drinks; a Guinness for him, whisky rye for her.

'Got waylaid by a builder. I came as soon as I could.'

'It doesn't matter. Besides, I'm the one who should be doing the apologising.' She gazed uncertainly at him from under thick eyelashes. 'For last weekend – for the way Piers behaved.'

'Forget it.'

'But I feel terrible about what happened.'

'In your position I'd feel flattered.'

Her expression was watchful.

'Look, Eve,' he said, treading carefully, 'I can't claim to like the bloke, but to some extent I understand the way he reacted. He was just protecting his territory.'

'I thought you'd still be angry with me.'

'Then you don't know me very well.'

'I don't, do I?' And all at once she smiled, her face bursting into a glowing bloom. 'You know, Ollie said something today which reminded me of the time he had to babysit that vast family of Iranians, do you remember? All those men in tents ordering their wives to wait in the limousine while they looked round each property, only to make him go through the whole rigmarole again for the women once they had finished.'

They both laughed. 'God, they had so much money though. They could have afforded half of Knightsbridge. Speaking of which, I don't suppose you've heard about Mr Ash's place? No, of course you won't have. You were out at the time.'

She meant the flat with the Kama Sutra chess set, the place in which he had spent half an hour hiding in a cupboard. Because no offers had been forthcoming – as Martin had predicted – the value of the flat had been dropped by fifteen thousand and it had been put on the market with a multiple agency. Ironically Carlyle's main competitor, Fairfax Hill, had got the full asking price for it just days before the bank holiday weekend.

'It's been broken in to.' She nodded, as Martin's jaw dropped. 'Awful, isn't it? I couldn't believe it either when I heard – especially following the Fitzherbert fiasco. I mean, what's going on? A number of things have been found missing and Mr Ash is trying to lay the blame on us. Says we're at fault for not having been more careful with keys and security. Whoever got in had access to the alarm code but Hammers thinks he's just trying it on because he's not insured. We've denied all responsibility and I know Hammers has been in touch with Fairfax. Apparently Mr Ash has made the same accusations to them.'

Martin frowned as Eve drew on the remains of her cigarette. 'Anything valuable taken?' His voice was guarded.

She nodded. 'A saxophone. You probably won't remember seeing it, but he kept it in the back room.' Near the fireplace. Martin remembered it well.

'How much is it worth?'

'About thirty thousand pounds. Apparently it's very rare.'

That it was valuable didn't surprise him. It was a beautiful piece, probably used by Coltrane for years. All the same he balked at the amount. Thirty grand was a lot to say goodbye to.

Eve took a sip from her glass. 'Hammers has already spoken to the police. I expect he'll ask if you remember anything unusual the last time you were there.'

'Do they know when the break-in occurred?'

'Yesterday,' she said, stubbing out her cigarette. 'But Mr Ash was in Paris looking at fabric samples or something and didn't get back until this afternoon. He was in a terrible state about it.'

'I can imagine.'

'I wonder if there might be a connection with what happened at the Fitzherberts'?' she said presently.

Martin blinked. 'How d'you mean?'

She leaned towards him, dropping her voice. 'Whoever got into the flat knew how to deactivate the alarm because it didn't go off – in either property – which means we're not talking about your run-of-the-mill kid out for whatever he can snatch. And they managed to open the safe.'

He interrupted her. 'What safe?'

'The one belonging to the Fitzherberts. Six thousand in cash was found missing – I thought you knew all this? These people knew what to look for and where to find it, and I think they had inside information.'

He glanced up, startled to hear his own disturbing thoughts being echoed.

'Think about it,' she went on. 'They could have been using estate agents to gain access to properties on the pretext of buying, when their real intention was to have a good snoop round and check out the security. Simple enough.'

'This all looks very chummy,' said a voice. 'Hello, Eve. I must say you're looking very fetching this evening.'

Martin raised his eyes. The man was tall and heavy-set, with a square jaw and coarse, pale skin. Handsome in that cheery, sloppy blond sort of way, he was holding a pint precariously in one hand. From the look of him he'd been drinking steadily all evening. Some of the beer slopped on to the carpet as he lurched towards them, and for one awful moment Martin feared he might sit down, but he merely rested his free hand on the table to steady himself.

'Harry.' Eve lit another cigarette, ignoring the compliment. 'I thought you were in Paris for the summer.'

'Got back last month. I had to be in London for Jimbo's stag-do.'

'I didn't know he was getting married.'

'Tied the knot two weeks ago. To a girl he grew up with in the same village. Not much up top but quite a pretty little thing and not afraid to wear a dress, if you know what I mean.' Martin winced as Harry laughed. Or coughed. He couldn't tell. 'I'm surprised Piers didn't tell you. It was quite a night. The boys have got a bet on to see how quickly Jimbo gets her preggers.' He cast a curious eye in Martin's direction but as Eve made no effort to introduce him, he asked her, 'Speaking of weddings, have you set a date for yours?'

'Last weekend in August. The invites have just gone out.'

'I shall look forward to getting mine,' he said, a hint of slurring in his voice. Eve murmured noncommittally.

'Got anywhere in mind for the honeymoon?'

'Piers has booked us a suite at the Cipriani,' she said, in a manner which conveyed it was none of his business.

The irony in her voice was lost on Harry who raised an appreciative eyebrow. 'Venice. Very nice too. Don't suppose you need someone to carry the bags?'

She gave him the faintest of smiles and Harry took a nervous swig from his glass. Martin noticed that the top half of one of his fingers was missing. 'Always worth a try,' Harry shrugged. 'So where *is* your lucky intended tonight?'

'Having dinner at his father's club. I expect he'll stop by later at the flat.'

'Well, give the old dog my best.' Harry threw Martin another glance. 'Tell him I'll try and track him down from the office some time this week. I promised him some tickets to the Grand Prix.'

'Lying toad,' she hissed, after he had trotted back to the bar. 'If he has got tickets, which I doubt, then you can be sure it will be Piers who ends up paying for them. He always does.'

Martin eyed Harry curiously. 'I don't sense any love lost between you.'

'Harry Forbes is one of Piers's cronies,' she explained

scathingly. 'We've never seen eye to eye, but he and Piers are practically joined at the hip. He seems to like having Harry around, but I can't understand it. He's such a ludicrous excuse of a man. Spends most of his time drinking and when he's not doing that he's looking for handouts, usually from Piers.'

She threw a rather savage look across the room to where Harry was standing by the bar. 'He's a child walking around in grown-up's clothes. He had to go for this blood test recently and, apparently, he cried like a baby for almost half an hour before he'd let them give him the shot. Has a thing about needles.'

'How did he lose the finger?'

'Oh, that. It happened at a zoo when he was eleven. Got it bitten off after sticking his hand inside the lion's cage, silly idiot. But then that's Harry all over. Act first, think later. He lives practically rent free in a flat Piers owns on Battersea Park Road. I keep telling Piers he should kick Harry out, make him stand on his own two feet, but he won't have it. Says Harry's useful to him. Shit,' she murmured, lighting another cigarette. 'I told Piers I was seeing a girlfriend tonight. If I know Harry, he's bound to tell him he saw me with you.'

'We're just having a drink and I've got both hands on the table. Look.' Martin waved his hands in mock surrender.

That made her smile, but twenty minutes later she brought their cosy drink à deux to an end. She said it was because she was tired and wanted an early night, but he saw right through the excuse. The fear of what Piers might think if Harry mentioned having seen them together had sent her scuttling out of the pub to safety.

'You don't have to do this.' His voice took on an urgent quality as she rose from their table. 'Just because you go out with him doesn't give him exclusive rights.'

'It will when I'm his wife.'

Her remark had struck home, hurt him, but he wasn't going to give up. 'Do you ever think about not going through with it?' he asked her.

She paused, put her glass down and looked at him. 'No,' she said gently. Soon afterwards, she left.

He drained his glass, cross with himself for letting her go like that. No doubt she was now on her way home dreaming up an excuse. He couldn't blame her for doing so, for limiting their evening to one innocuous drink when he had hoped for so much more. He just wished it hadn't left him with such a bitter taste in his mouth.

He took his empty glass to the crowded bar and, having nothing to rush home for, decided to order another. By the time he had paid, his table next to the window had been appropriated by a group of office suits, so he parked himself on a vacant stool near by. For a while he pondered over what Eve had told him. Some bastard had walked off with Mr Ash's saxophone, thirty grand's worth. No wonder the man was looking for blood. Though to be honest, with both agencies accused of negligence, it would be nigh on impossible to make the charge stick. The fact that the flat had been on as a multiple in recent weeks meant that at least ten brokers from two different agencies with three sets of keys had been showing it. Add to the equation all the clients and surveyors traipsing in and out and you were left with an awful lot of suspects. On the other hand, Eve's hypothesis that the break-in might be connected with the Arundel Gardens murder had more than a hint of logic to it.

He became aware of the clang of glasses, the drone of voices around him. Out of the din he heard a tone he recognised. '– it's on me. Least I can do.'

'Feeling flush tonight, hey, Harry? Not like you to be so free with the readies. Get your leg over, you old dog, did you? Is that what's put you in such a generous mood?'

A roar of delighted, self-indulgent laughter followed. With a quick, surreptitious glance over his shoulder, Martin identified the unmistakable figure of Harry chuckling on a stool which didn't look capable of supporting his weight. The man with him was a stranger.

Harry leaned forward and took a messy sip of his pint.

'I've had a good month, that's all,' he said thickly. 'Can't a chap share his good fortune with his friends?' Beads of sweat stood out on his forehead. His eyes were glazed and his mouth slightly open.

There was a crash from behind the bar – a dropped bottle of beer, mild apologies from the publican – which meant Martin missed what was said next.

'What did he do? Put a few tips your way?'

Harry took another swig of his pint and burped. 'In a manner of speaking.'

'You've got the luck of the devil, Harry. With your sort of contacts you'll probably never have to worry about money again. Tell me something, how much do you suppose the old boy's worth? Ten million? Twenty?'

Harry didn't answer. Studying the side of his face, Martin could see the glaze in his eyes as he stared morosely at the beermat in front of him, a forgotten cigarette burning in one hand. All of a sudden, he cleared his throat. 'He's not what you think he is, you know.'

'I don't follow.'

'I mean that he's not what you think,' repeated Harry, more forcibly this time. 'You spend years believing you know someone when really you know nothing about them at all. I should never have got involved. Now it's too fucking late.'

His companion looked uncertain. 'Have you and Piers had some kind of falling-out?'

Harry leaned forward, his face thoughtful and almost transparently frank. Martin thought he was going to blurt out the truth but instead he drained his glass and pushed it away. 'Get me another one of these, will you?' he said, stumbling from his stool. 'I'll be back in a jiffy.' He walked unsteadily towards the Gents, his feet at odds with one another as if they were obeying different orders from his legs.

Martin was mulling over what he had heard when, seconds later, he saw Tracy arrive with a girlfriend in tow. They had taken a great deal of trouble with their appearance, and seemed to be looking for a little male company. Afraid that he might be roped into going to one of the obscure clubs Tracy frequented – and God knows what else – Martin grabbed his jacket, cautiously made his way to the door and slipped out unobserved into the darkened street.

FIFTEEN

The following Monday a policeman stopped by at the Carlyle office. The young man's uniform caused Martin a moment of panic. His first thought was that he'd come about the Fitzherbert case, but it turned out that he was making routine enquiries about Mr Ash's burglary.

With Hammers' permission, they were interviewed separately in the financial room. Martin was the first to go in and was relieved to find himself asked a few rudimentary questions – nothing he hadn't already anticipated, or that gave him reason for concern. However, there was a nasty moment after Oliver came out and Martin was asked to step back into the room.

'Sorry to drag you in here again, Mr Leak. I know you've got work to get on with, but this Mr Lindsey you mentioned. Had you come across him before?'

Martin licked his lips nervously. 'No. He was a new applicant. He said he liked the flat but that he would have to go away and think about it. That was the last time I heard from him.' In fact, Mr Lindsey was nothing more than a figment of his imagination. After the scare with Ollie outside Mr Ash's flat, he had rushed back to the agency and scribbled the name in the office diary to cover himself.

'And you're quite sure this is the number he gave you?' The office diary, which was open at the date in question, faced the policeman on the desk.

'Yes.' He'd made that up too. 'Is there a problem?'

The young officer looked at him and smiled. 'No problem. We just like to have everything clear. Thank you for your time.'

'Ollie,' Martin said, his voice low as he caught his colleague on his own upstairs. 'You didn't say anything in there, did you? About what happened?'

'Asking awkward questions, was he?'

Martin tried not to look as worried as he felt. 'Ollie, just tell me you kept your trap shut? I need to know.'

'Fear not. Your secret's safe with me. Mind you,' he said, lowering his voice to a whisper, 'I always think it's a good idea to keep investments topped up. You never know when the market might fall – if you catch my meaning.'

Since the day when he had heard that the Fitzherberts' son was found murdered, Martin had been haunted – during his waking hours and in his sleep – by shifting images of the victim: the body rotting away in the upstairs bathroom already starting to smell; or, more horrifically, the young man with one side of his head missing – clawing his way across the blood-smeared floor, an outstretched hand pleading for help. Martin couldn't get him out of his mind because he couldn't think of him as a stranger. Damn it, he had read the man's letter to his mother, seen him grow from child to adult in a series of framed photos, hung around his bedroom like a mate over for the afternoon. Because Martin had imagined what it was like being Charles he felt he had come to know him. And it was this insatiable curiosity, coupled with his guilty preoccupation that maybe – just maybe – he could have saved his life, that caused him to dwell on his death incessantly.

Martin often cut through Arundel Gardens on his way back to the office, but as he drove past the house this time, a warm wind blowing in through the car window, his eye caught the agency board outside. Interesting. Which of the three maisonettes was up for sale? Without quite knowing why, he pulled up alongside the house and dug out his mobile. He dialled the number on the board and was put through quickly to a female broker. To his amazement, the maisonette for sale *was* the Fitzherberts'. In a panicky reflex he nearly hung up when she asked him if he wanted to view it. Then he changed his mind. Why not? The agency handling the sale was a new, independent set-up, so it was unlikely that any of the negotiators would know him. And masquerading as a potential buyer would provide him with the ideal cover to allow him access. Perhaps by going back there, he could put an end to his awful dreams.

They met after lunch. She was standing in front of the house waiting for him in the heat. A pretty woman whom he judged to be in her mid-twenties, she looked tidy and wholesome, the sort who would have been head girl at school. She wore a red silk scarf around her neck and matching red shoes. He could tell within minutes of being in her company that she was new to the job, her ill-informed responses to his questions naïve and unrehearsed. Why, he wondered idly as she fumbled with the lock, hadn't the agency sent along a more senior negotiator, as would normally be the case when dealing with a property of this value?

'Sorry,' Red Scarf apologised, as a series of abortive attempts to open the door failed. 'It seems to be stuck. I must have brought out the wrong key.'

'Shall I have a go?' he offered, knowing full well she hadn't.

With a dubious shrug of her shoulders, she handed them over. 'You're welcome to try.'

He slipped the key two-thirds of the way into the mortise lock as he had done on so many previous occasions, gently jiggled it until he felt the tension give, then turned the key to the right. Instantly, the door sprang open.

The negotiator looked relieved. 'You must have a knack,' she said, stepping into the hall.

'How long have you had this place on your books?' he enquired, as she opened the internal door to the flat and immediately consulted her notepad to code in the alarm – he almost made the mistake of telling her the number. Even now he knew it by memory. The door, he noted, had been repainted and fixed to look good as new.

'Only a week. But it's already attracted a great deal of interest. This is a very popular road.'

The implication being that if he wanted the maisonette, he would have to move pretty fast; how many times had he used the same line himself? She handed him the details – a glossy colour photocopy of the façade stuck to the front, and he saw that the price was significantly lower than it had been with Carlyle.

It seemed strange to be inside again, to see the flat restored to a clean and dignified order. He reacted to it as he would have done to an old friend. But there were subtle changes which were, at least to him, immediately apparent. The smell was the first thing he registered. A musty, unlived-in sort of staleness, as if the windows hadn't been opened for some time. He recognised much of the furniture but a new Sony television stood in the place of the old one, and many of the personal artefacts which had breathed life into the rooms were now missing. Gone were the family photographs secure in their metal frames, as were the books and the porcelain figurines that had once graced the mantelpiece alongside an ever-increasing array of gold-edged invitations.

As Martin walked through into the back drawing room, his eyes flew to the wall where the little Burne-Jones miniatures had once hung, now replaced with a series of uninspired prints. He felt a strong desire to loiter and browse, but was conscious of the negotiator hovering close by, mobile and keys in her hand, keen, no doubt, to get back to the office. He tried not to show his irritation, but wished she would show some of the tact he himself accorded clients, and not stand over him like a jailer.

'If I wanted to move quickly, would that pose a problem for the vendors?' he was aware that she would be expecting him to ask some questions.

Red Scarf shook her head. 'They've moved down to the

country and only use the maisonette as an occasional pied-à-terre.'

'Do you know why they're selling?'

'Personal reasons, I believe,' was her cagey response. He wondered if she knew about the maisonette's recent, turbulent history but could think of no way of broaching the subject without giving himself away.

'Would you like me to show you upstairs? The master bedroom's ensuite and there's a study at the back which could easily be turned into a fourth bedroom.'

He followed Red Scarf upstairs past the bathroom – a brief glimpse with his head round the door. He didn't want to linger, but there wasn't a trace of the violent act which had taken place, no lingering bloodstains, no chalk marks outlining the body's form where it had fallen. As he entered the main bedroom a picture of the soiled bed, the carpet littered with debris, the used syringe, welled up in his mind. For a moment he shut his eyes then opened them again to find the negotiator standing by the window. Sun streamed through, catching the colours in her hair like a kind of halo; copper, chestnut, henna.

She turned around and gazed at him, her professional manner slipping slightly. 'I've always wanted something like this for myself.'

Yes, he thought, with a pang of regret. Me too.

Curiosity overcame caution as he stepped into the third bedroom, which had once belonged to Charles Fitzherbert, and he remembered the letter he had found addressed to Charles's mother. *And to think I had once thought of him as a friend. How wrong I was, how horribly misguided I was about him* . . . There was a half-full box on the floor into which someone had begun packing the books. On the bed were three black bin bags that had been tied at the neck – full of clothes, he guessed. The guitar was still propped up against the wall but the signed cricket bat had gone, presumably one of the many reminders too painful to live with.

Before they left the maisonette, Martin turned for one final look, knowing that he would never return. He could not explain his curious attachment to the place, to the family who had lived there, or why he mourned the removal of so many possessions. Perhaps it was that while there was evidence of people living there, the maisonette, albeit briefly, fraudulently, had allowed him to reinvent his past, and to claim the person he wanted to be: a nephew, a son, a brother, who could take his home and his history for granted.

He drove towards his three o'clock appointment, beads of sweat dampening the back of his shirt. The traffic was slow, and as he stopped at some lights he yawned and looked with soporific pleasure at the overhanging green branches of trees and bright fingers of light seeping through. There were no free spaces when he arrived, so he double-parked the car with the hazard lights flashing – with a bit of luck the viewing wouldn't take more than a few minutes. He had just climbed the steps at the side of the house which gave access to the flat for sale, when the man who had been waiting for him came into view. Piers Hunt. He looked cool and unaffected by the heat.

'Thought we might have a little chat,' said Piers. In one part of his mind Martin registered a passing car, the throbbing beat of reggae music vibrating from its metallic blue body. 'There are a few things we need to iron out.'

Martin shrugged, feigning nonchalance. 'What's on your mind?'

'Oh, I think you know. I want you to keep away from Eve.'

Now there was a surprise. 'And how am I supposed to do that, given that we work in the same office?'

Piers folded his arms. 'You're obviously even more stupid than I had first thought.'

Martin started to walk away. 'I'm going back to work.'

'Not until I've finished.' Piers blocked his path.

'Then we have a conflict of interests.' Martin put on a brave face, but he didn't feel like playing games with Piers at all.

Very briefly Piers glanced along either side of the empty road. Then he stood aggressively close to Martin so that their faces were almost touching.

'The only conflict I have,' sneered Piers, 'is with you. You're deluding yourself if you think you have any chance with Eve. She's only using you to get at me.'

His words stung. 'That's what you'd like to think.'

'Go near her again and you'll have me to answer for.'

'Save your idle threats, Piers. I'm not someone you can kick around.'

Piers edged closer. 'You'd be well advised to take what I say very seriously. I happen to know you lied about your father.' He watched the shifting range of emotions cross Martin's face. 'Didn't think I'd find out, did you? But the truth has a nasty way of rearing its head when you least expect it and it was obvious you were faking it. A hotel in Sussex!' He gave a derisory snort, his rich, chocolatey voice dripping scorn. 'The only thing your old man ever ran was some crummy little newsagents. No wonder you wanted to keep that quiet.'

Martin flushed. How the hell did he know? He lashed out angrily. 'I took you for many things, Piers, but not a bigoted, stuck-up snob.'

Piers's face darkened and his considerable arm muscles quivered beneath his shirt. Martin stepped back, startled by the scowling face before him. But help was on hand. It came in the form of a young man who bounded up the steps. He was in shorts and wearing a baseball cap the wrong way round. A sweater was tied like an apron round his waist and in one hand he held a tennis racquet.

'Looking for anyone in particular?' he asked in a neighbourly tone.

'We've just been to view the flat,' Martin explained. The look of menace on Piers's face had been replaced with one of polite indifference.

'Ah,' said the stranger. 'The one on the top floor. I've always wondered what it was like inside. Don't suppose there's any chance of a quick peek while you're here?'

'Actually, we're in a bit of a hurry,' Piers interjected

before Martin could respond. Pointedly, he looked at his watch.

'If you call Carlyle and make an appointment,' Martin said, handing him a card, 'I'd be happy to show you round another time.'

'Sure,' said the young man, sizing up Piers with a glance. 'Well, good luck.' He disappeared into the house.

As soon as the door was closed Piers turned on Martin. 'The problem with you, Martin, is that you judge everyone by your own pathetic standards, but the fact is you know *nothing* about Eve, and even less about me.'

He started down the steps, his black hair gleaming like polished metal under the sun, then turned back. Before Martin had time to register what he was doing, he had grabbed hold of Martin's tie, green-bronze with orange flying pigs – the one Irene had given him – and read the Marks & Spencer label on the underside. The corner of his beautiful mouth curled into an impudent smile.

'It's what I like about you, Martin,' he said nastily, letting the synthetic fabric slide from his hand. 'Your sense of style.'

Martin reached home shortly before nine and parked in a nearby side-street. Still smarting from his earlier exchange with Piers, he was making his way to the house, paying little attention to the traffic noise around him, when a man, the size and build of Ian Botham, stepped out of a parked car and approached him. Martin thought he was going to ask him for the time, or for directions.

'Are you Martin?' the stranger asked.

Martin stopped accommodatingly. 'Yes I am.'

'Martin *Leak*?'

'That's right. What can I do for you?'

To his utter astonishment, the man punched him in the face – catching the corner of his eye – sending him flying backwards through the air. Martin landed awkwardly and gasped as the man yanked him up on to his feet again and hit him a second time. The blow caught him on the chin and something cracked. Dazedly he wondered whether a tooth had been broken.

'Keep your hands off her, you bastard!' the stranger was yelling at him, shaking his fist in rage. 'I'm warning you – touch Venetia again and you won't just be worrying about a bruised jaw. I'll rip your bloody throat out.'

Too stunned to reply, Martin stared at the man – whom he had never seen before – and watched him slam the car door and screech off down the road. Across the road, a mother with two young children were staring open-mouthed.

He struggled to his feet, gingerly touching the part of his face which had received the blows, and got himself upstairs to his flat. The first thing he did was check the damage. Fortunately, all his teeth were intact, but his jacket was covered in dust, his cheek was grazed, and the area around his left eye socket was already displaying the rich, moody colouring of an A1 black eye. Well, he thought dolefully as he gazed at his almost comic reflection in the bathroom mirror, don't think you're going to win any popularity contests today.

'Celia?'
'Who is this?
'It's Martin.'
'Martin? I didn't recognise your voice.'
'Sorry. I know it's a bit late. Did I wake you?'
'No.' A pause. 'Is everything all right?'
'Never better.' He hiccuped, glancing at the row of empty beer bottles lined up in front of him – nine of them – and contemplated going out for fresh supplies.
'You don't sound it. What's wrong?'
He was touched by her concern. 'Today's been . . . Oh, I don't know.' He sighed heavily and glanced up at a daddy-long-legs dancing on the ceiling, 'I just wanted to talk to someone.'
'Where are you now?'

'At home. I was thinking of taking a walk – along the river.'

'Give me ten minutes,' she said gamely, 'and I'll be with you.'

'Oh, Martin,' Celia exclaimed when she arrived at his flat. 'Your *face*! You look terrible.'

'I thought you'd come to cheer me up.'

She eyed him reproachfully. 'Are you going to tell me what happened?'

'Let me get you a drink first.' He swayed as he walked towards the kitchen but, as he passed her, she caught his hand and steadied him.

'Never mind the drink,' she said gently. 'How about that walk I was promised?'

They parked her car in Pall Mall and headed along Piccadilly towards Green Park. It was a warm night, with only the slightest hint of a breeze, patches of clouds crowding in on the half-moon. In spite of it being almost eleven, there were a great many people about, with heavy traffic passing on both sides of the road. To get away from the noise they cut through the park, dark, frothy trees towering above their heads, and only a dim butter-yellow light from the Victorian lamps to guide them. With anyone else, he would have been too embarrassed to admit the circumstances of his black eye, but he found Celia so easy to talk to and, in his inebriated state, the truth – slightly edited – slipped off his tongue.

'Is that why you're so upset?' she asked, when he had finished.

'A bruised ego is the least of my troubles,' he mumbled thinking of Piers's earlier threat, Eve's impending wedding, the insistent worry about the police finding out the truth.

'Do you want to sit down for a bit?' She was looking at him with concern. 'You've gone a bit green.'

He shook his head firmly. 'No. I'd rather push on. The walk's doing me good.'

They wandered into St James's Park and grew silent,

captivated by the romantic scene before them: swathes of floodlit trees surrounded the lake and a bridge – also floodlit – rose in a graceful arch and gazed at its reflection in the water. A swan glided by in motionless splendour in the gloom. Insects, driven into a frenzy by light rising from the lamps beneath the trees, swam around in the air like shoals of tiny fish. Soon they had reached Big Ben and cut down along the Embankment where the traffic eased and the warm late-evening air seemed suddenly peaceful and still.

Celia gave a pleasurable sigh. 'London transforms into something quite beautiful at night, don't you think?'

'When I first moved up here I shared a flat with two blokes just a few streets away. During the summer months I used to do this walk almost every night.'

'Do you miss home?'

'Home?' He felt as if his tongue was experimenting with a new word. 'Home is where you make it.'

'But what about your family?'

He shrugged. 'There's only my mother left.'

Perhaps it was her air of calm acceptance – he felt as if she had known him all her life – or the fact that he was safely removed from the threat of mocking retribution, or simply that he'd had a great deal to drink, that led him to admit something about himself he had never imagined he would. It came out quite suddenly while she was talking about her desire for a brother.

'At school during my early teens,' she said, 'some of the boys used to bully me. They could be pretty cruel – far more spiteful than the girls. I longed to have an older brother, someone who would look out for me, be my protector –' She broke off suddenly as if she was afraid of sounding silly.

'And then?'

She threw him a resigned look. 'Then I grew up. What about you?'

'What about me?'

'Didn't you ever long to be part of something bigger?'

'To long for something and to have it are two entirely separate things.'

Celia's neat eyebrows met in confusion. 'I don't follow.'

'I'm adopted.' He gave a short snort of a laugh and slapped his head. 'My God! I can't believe I just said that. You're the first person I've admitted that to.'

'It isn't anything to be ashamed of.'

'You mean the bit about my parents not wanting me?'

'You know that's not what I meant.' Celia looked hurt and for a moment they walked in awkward silence. 'They say,' she said after a while, 'that adopted children have unique talents.'

'In fairy tales perhaps.'

She smiled, her eyes friendly and curious. 'Were you ever able to find out what happened to your natural parents?'

His face closed. 'I met them once,' he said, looking out across the Thames. 'But the meeting wasn't what you'd call a success. After I'd seen them – well, I gave it some thought, and in the end decided not to further the relationship.'

'Why?'

'There didn't seem much point. We didn't find we had much in common.' He spoke flatly, already backtracking, already regretting the words.

A vehicle honking loudly summoned their attention and they both turned towards the road. The driver of a Ford Escort – changing lanes without indicating – had narrowly missed a motor bike approaching from the rear. The Ford came to a halt at some traffic lights. As it did so, the man on the bike pulled up alongside the car, took off his crash-helmet and swung it forcefully against the passenger window as if he wanted to smash it, angrily shaking his fists at the startled face inside, and Martin thought: *He died from three blows to the head – so severe that the force took out half his brains.*

Celia laid a hand on his arm. 'It can't have been easy keeping something like that to yourself.'

He gave a sigh, warm air dancing over his bare arms as a breeze stirred. 'Look,' he said, suddenly feeling overwhelmingly tired, 'do you mind if we drop the subject?'

Sixteen

His black eye, already a spectacular range of colours, was the source of much interest at the office the following morning. Roger, who was a terrible hypochondriac, hung on to every word as Martin told them all how he had fought off five black thugs carrying baseball bats who were trying to steal his car. When he finished, he was bombarded with questions. Oliver and Celia were finding it difficult to conceal their amusement and Martin would have played along with the game a little longer, were it not for a sudden, rude interruption.

The office door burst open and two men in dove-grey suits walked in and asked to speak to the manager. The taller of the men, carrying a cheap-looking briefcase, was a stranger to Martin but he remembered the constable – the other man – from when he had been interviewed. He watched nervously as they approached Hammers' desk.

Hammers lost none of his composure.

'How can I help?' he asked pleasantly.

The stranger reached into his breast pocket and pulled out his ID card. 'I'm sorry to trouble you again, Mr Hammerton, but could we have a moment of your time?'

'By all means. Why don't you both pull up a chair.'

'We'd prefer it if we could do this in private.'

Martin, Roger, Oliver, Celia, and Tracy who had just emerged from the basement, looked at each other with concern.

'The financial room's free if you want to use that,' Tracy suggested, casting her mistrust of the police aside in a gesture of professionalism.

'The financial room will do nicely,' the officer replied, throwing a brief glance of interest in Martin's direction.

Hammers rose from his chair. 'Follow me,' he said.

The officers resurfaced half an hour later and left – Martin noted worriedly – armed with a stack of files, clients' index cards and the office appointment book.

'What do they want with all that paperwork?' Celia enquired, once Hammers had seen the two men out.

Hammers blinked thoughtfully. 'They've found something which links Mr Ash's burglary with the Fitzherbert murder investigation,' he said. 'And, as acting agent for both properties, we've been asked – voluntarily – to have our fingerprints taken –'

'This is a wind-up,' snorted Roger.

'– to eliminate us from their enquiries. I'm told it only takes a matter of minutes so it shouldn't cause too much inconvenience.'

Martin cleared his throat. 'Do we have to go down to the station?'

Hammers nodded. 'Today if possible.'

'How tedious,' sighed Oliver, snatching up his car keys. 'Well, as I'm heading in that direction, I might as well get it out of the way.'

Martin awaited his return in a state of agitation, prowling back and forth on the office floor like a restless cat. He was terrified that Oliver would tell the police about his illicit visit to Mr Ash's basement flat.

When a subdued Oliver did reappear, Martin sought him out in the kitchen. Roger, who had also been down to the station, was with him.

Oliver held up a hand as he walked into the room. 'Not a word,' he said, before Martin had a chance to say anything. 'I've just had an earful from Inspector Morse and his sidekick, and I'm not in the mood for any more questions.' He yawned and scratched his head. 'Don't suppose either of you have a cigarette? I seem to have run out.'

'What's that on your hand?' Martin asked.

Oliver held his palms out in front of him and inspected each one in turn: they were marked with some kind of black dye. 'Oh, yes. Hope this stuff comes off with soap.'

Martin sat down. 'What did you have to do?'

Oliver shrugged and wandered across to the sink. 'Not much,' he said, turning on the taps. 'Answered a few pointless questions like: what I was wearing the day of the murder; the type of car I drove; what brand of cigarette I smoked. I was expecting to see some action, but it was all a bit of a drag.'

'I didn't have to answer any questions.' Roger sounded miffed.

Martin stared at Oliver's back as he washed his hands. 'Why do you think they were so interested in you?'

A fleeting look of doubt crossed Oliver's face as he reached for a cleanish tea towel to wipe his hands which Martin, positioned at a more advantageous viewing point than Roger caught. 'Perhaps they think I have a closer association with the case than the rest of you.'

But before Roger or Martin could ask him what he meant, Oliver threw down the tea towel. 'Before I die from withdrawal symptoms, I'm going out to buy some fags.'

It was Eve's birthday and the office – marshalled by Martin – had all clubbed together to buy her the pair of leopard-print gloves she had been hankering after. She was thrilled with her gift and by way of a thank-you, came back after lunch armed with a bottle of wine.

'Be discreet with that,' Hammers warned, on his way out. 'And don't let the clients catch you drinking it either.'

'What has Piers got lined up for tonight?' asked Oliver, once he had gone.

Her eyes shone with excited anticipation. 'I don't know. He won't tell me.'

By late afternoon, however, some of her happiness had dimmed. It had faded completely when, at about six o'clock, she received the call she has been waiting for from Piers.

'Problems?' enquired Martin as she slowly hung up.

She gave a little sigh of disappointment and gazed at the phone as if she couldn't believe what it had just told her. 'I've been stood up.'

'What!' Oliver and Martin exclaimed in unison.

'Piers says he can't make tonight,' she told them, her voice dumbstruck.

Martin was appalled. 'But it's your *birthday*. Why can't he make it?' The sod. How could he have let her down?

'Something to do with work apparently. He's got to drive to Devon and won't be back until the morning.'

'Can't he postpone it?'

'Apparently not.' She shrugged and fingered the phone receiver. 'It's too late to arrange anything now. Oh, well. I expect I'll rent out a video.'

'You'll do no such bloody thing,' Martin snapped.

She threw him a wavering smile. 'I don't mind.'

Thinking rapidly, he stood up. 'Don't even think about moving from that chair.'

'Where are you going?'

'Won't be long,' he called over his shoulder.

He took her to the Belvedere, a light, elegant restaurant set in the summer ballroom of the old Holland House in Holland Park. He had had to do some swift talking on the phone in order to secure a table on the small roof-terrace, and the meal – champagne, melting salmon croquettes with coriander, lobster pasta, and a hastily-put-together birthday cake by the chef which was presented to her over coffee – cost him an arm and a leg. But, God, it was worth every penny just to see the smile back on her face. They didn't talk about Piers and, for a few hours, Martin was able to put recent events to one side, so elated was his mood at having Eve to himself.

By the time they drew up outside her flat it was after midnight. For a while they sat in silence, and he wrestled over whether to invite himself up for coffee. He thought he had never seen anyone so beautiful as she was at that moment. All his carefully rehearsed plans to tell her how he felt dried up, so loud was the pounding in his ears. All he could think about was what it would be like to remove her clothes and take her to bed. He could feel his erection respond to the thought.

'You left the lights on,' he said, blinking stupidly up at her window.

Eve arched her neck so that she could see the windows of the flat and her face fell. Abruptly, she slumped back into her seat. 'I left for work at eight this morning. If there's a light on it means someone is up there.'

'Who –?'

'It's Piers. He must have changed his plans, or come back early – I don't know – and let himself in with the spare key.'

He felt concerned about her. 'Do you want me to come up?'

She shook her head. 'I'll handle it.'

'It's no problem.'

'Thanks, Martin, but there's no need.' She glanced back up at the illuminated room with a faraway look on her face. 'He won't do anything.'

She turned up for work wearing dark glasses. That in itself wasn't strange. Sunglasses were as much an accessory to her wardrobe as her Cartier watch and the little Gucci handbag she took with her everywhere. But she drew attention to herself when she refused to take them off.

'Light too bright for you, angel?' said Oliver, fishing.

'No.'

'So what's with the shades?'

'I've got a slight infection and the light aggravates it, all right?' There was a challenging tone to her voice and the subject was dropped. Soon after, she went out on a viewing.

She was gone for ages. The next time Martin saw her was shortly before lunch. With Roger and Hammers covering the office, he had slipped downstairs to the kitchen to get himself some food. He found her sitting with her back to the door, a cigarette burning moodily in the ashtray. He thought he heard her give a little sniff.

'Eve?'

She swivelled round, exposing her wet, swollen eyes, then quickly turned away again.

'Eve?' Real concern now. 'What's going on?'

'It's all right,' she mumbled in a cracked voice, 'I just need a minute alone.'

Martin sat down next to her. She looked as if she had been up all night crying; her eyes – still lovely – were puffy and red. On the table next to the glasses she'd been wearing, was a packet of cigarettes. With a pang he saw they were Marlboro, Piers's brand. She was playing with a line of loo-roll, wringing it to shreds with her hands.

'Eve,' he said gently.

'Please –'

'You don't have to talk, but I'm not going anywhere while you're in this state.'

Eve raised her mint-green eyes, attempted a smile, then burst into tears and threw herself into his arms. 'Oh, Martin. My life is such a mess.'

'Hey, hey. What's brought this on?' He held her as she struggled to control her tears. 'Nothing's *that* bad – is it?' Then he pulled back, afraid she would feel his heart which had begun to beat quite wildly.

'I think I've made a terrible mistake.'

His voice hardened. 'What's he done to you?'

'We had a blazing row.' She sniffed. 'About you.' His heart leapt. So Piers was feeling threatened. 'After you dropped me off last night, Piers was waiting for me. He'd been drinking and was in a foul mood. Oh, Martin, I feel so guilty.'

'You've got nothing to feel guilty about.'

'But you don't understand. There I was thinking he couldn't be bothered to make an effort for my birthday, when all along he'd been planning a surprise party at La Caprice. Can you imagine the awfulness of it – my friends, my brother waiting there all evening with gifts and champagne? He came round to the office to pick me up only to be told that I'd already left with you. When I got home he flew into this terrible rage. I've never seen him so angry.'

Martin digested this information with mixed feelings.

'It's been building up for some time,' she continued. 'Ever since the weekend you came to stay at Partridge Manor. He was pretty wound up about you and I driving down together. Then all that business with the cricket – he can't bear to lose at anything. And now this.' Eve looked at him through wet, spiky eyelashes. 'I think he thought there was something going on between us. And on top of everything else, he found out from Harry that I'd met up with you for a drink – you can always rely on that creep to go running to Piers with his little tales.'

'Did he hurt you?'

Eve looked startled. 'Oh, no. Piers abhors violence. He would never raise a hand to me.'

'But you just said –'

'All I said was that he was angry and upset, but I was just as much to blame for that as he was.' Martin was surprised – how quickly she leapt to Piers's defence.

She seemed to be searching for the right words. 'You've only ever seen him at his worst, but I know him better than anybody in the world and it's just because he's been under a lot of pressure lately that he's tended to be a bit –' she searched for an appropriate adjective '– irrational.'

Martin folded his arms. This wasn't what he wanted to hear.

'Recently, he's been working very long hours – coming home late at night, up again at the crack of dawn. He hasn't been sleeping well at all. It's as if there was something on his mind. I'm worried about him, Martin.

I –' She paused as if weighing up whether or not to confide in him. 'He lost his mother two years ago in a freak riding accident. They were terribly close. Piers simply adored her and the news hit him very hard. Even now he won't talk about it, yet I know he's still struggling to come to terms with what happened.'

Martin registered the peculiar sensation of finding himself suddenly identifying with Piers. He felt a reluctant sympathy for the man he was so jealous of.

Eve took another cigarette and allowed him to light it for her. 'There's something else I should tell you. Since the weekend at Partridge Manor, Piers has been acting suspicious and mistrustful. All this business about my birthday has only made things worse. He's convinced something's going on between us so to put him off the scent I said you had no interest in me because you were seeing someone else.' She caught his look of surprise. 'I'm sorry, but it was all I could think of.'

'Anyone I know?'

'I told him you were seeing Celia.'

'What!'

'Partly to get him off my back. I'm not sure he believed me but at least he calmed down,' she broke off. 'Anyway, I thought it was true.'

'Whatever gave you that idea?'

'Roger told me.'

That time he had rung the flat. Nice to know where Roger's loyalties lay.

'Eve, there's absolutely nothing going on between Celia and I.'

'Really?' She sounded almost hopeful.

'You know what Roger's like – always jumping to the wrong conclusions. He makes an occupation out of it.'

She wiped her eyes and an expression of something very like tenderness spread across her face – a face smudged with mascara. There was a heart-stopping pinprick of a mole just beneath her right eye. She looked like an angel.

'Why are you so good to me?' Her voice was a soft caress.

'Eve –' Oh, shit. His self-control could only last so long.

She put a hand to his mouth. 'Don't. Don't say it.'

'Sorry,' said a voice from the doorway. 'Didn't mean to interrupt. I'll come back later.' Martin just caught Celia's flaming face before she turned away.

'Oh, dear.' Eve sounded almost chirpy. 'I think I've just upset someone. I wonder how much of that she heard?'

With his eyes still fastened to the door, Martin was wondering the same thing.

SEVENTEEN

Martin's quarterly review with Hammers on Friday evening went better than expected. His occasional tardiness in the mornings was still a bone of contention, but Hammers seemed happy with his work which, based on exchanges and sales arranged over the last three months, had brought in forty-five thousand pounds' worth of revenue for the company. After locking up the office, the two men ambled down to the Duke of Norfolk for a drink. The pub was packed with Friday-night drinkers so they carried their pints to a vacant bench outside and sat back in the soupy heat of the evening.

Although his mood was convivial, Hammers looked tired at the end of a week of complicated deals. Beads of sweat appeared on his brow and periodically he would sleeve them off. Other than drinking, Martin wondered what he did to wind down from the exceptionally long hours he worked. Of all the men in the office, he felt most at ease with Hammers. Impulsive and generous, he expected a great deal of his staff but was refreshingly honest about his own shortcomings and would often joke that no woman should be expected to put up with him. At the moment he was seeing a very pretty aerobics instructor – the Spaniard hadn't lasted – but she had been offered a job on a cruise ship and was thinking of taking it.

They had only meant to have one drink, but that soon led to another. Hammers was engaged on a nostalgic and amusing stroll back to his army days when suddenly the publican was shouting for everyone's glasses and dimming the lights because it was closing time. Hammers was well over the limit so he hailed a cab. Martin, who fancied a walk, set off on foot back to the agency to collect his car.

Two couples swung out gaily in front of him. Their movements were reckless, and they wandered off, shouting and singing. Because that was the direction in which Martin was going, he followed them down the darkened street. The row of shops mostly sold antiques – well beyond his price range, but it didn't stop him taking a look in passing. In one of the windows was a display of glass canisters, heavily ornate candle holders made out of silver, a collection of pocket watches. He was reminded of his own watch which had so mysteriously disappeared almost a week ago. Not that it was worth much – the strap he'd recently replaced probably cost more than the watch itself – but Frank had bought it for his twenty-first birthday so it held great sentimental value.

Martin walked on, his thoughts inevitably straying to Eve. Since their exchange in the office kitchen, he had battled with his confusing feelings about her. He felt as if he was being pulled towards something he had no right to, yet he was as powerless to fight the lure as he was the undercurrent of wild waters. And then there was the mystery surrounding her father's Middle East contract. What part had Piers played in it? He couldn't quite put his finger on it but there was something decidedly suspicious about the early hour he had chosen to visit Howard's study and tap into his computer.

Ahead of him the two drunken couples found the entrance to a bar shut. They rattled the door, grumbling to one another, then turned away and disappeared into the night. He had reached the entrance to a small mews and was just about to pass it when a movement caught his attention. At first he thought the hunched figure was a tramp bedding down for the night, but as his eyes adjusted to the dark, he saw that it was a woman. She was sitting on the ground, propped against a garage door, her head buried against her knees, and she was rocking back and forth as though she had hurt herself. He wondered if perhaps she was a drinking casualty and went over to investigate. As he grew closer, he could hear a gasping sound. 'You all right?' he asked in concern, his hand lightly touching her shoulder. She recoiled as if bitten and as she looked up, he gasped. 'Celia!'

She made a small animal sound. Her mouth moved as if to speak but instead, out of it came a sudden thin stream of blood. Martin dropped to his knees beside her. '*Jesus*, Celia. What happened to you?'

Her dress was badly torn to reveal lacerations on her arms and legs as if she had fought with a bramble bush, her lip was split, and she had somehow lost her shoes. He took her trembling body into his arms and held her, shushing and rocking her as she mumbled incoherently against his chest. When, after a while, she began to calm down, he released her.

'Do you think you could manage to stand?' She gave an almost inaudible assent. Gently, he helped her to her feet. 'That's it,' he said, as her grip tightened on his arm. 'Nice and easy.'

There was no way she was capable of making the distance back to his car, but as luck would have it a vacant taxi appeared and he quickly flagged it down. He gave the driver her address but when she protested that she didn't want to go back there, he redirected him to Kensal Rise. In the back of the cab Celia clung fiercely to him, as if afraid that he might abandon her at any moment, but by the time they reached his flat less than ten minutes later, her mood had changed from one of fear to apathy. Her face had become expressionless and she moved like a sleepwalker so that he had to hold her firmly round the waist – then finally carry her – as they mounted the flight of stairs.

The untidy state in which he had left his flat reminded him of the time she had come round when he had been ill and transformed it into a sparkling haven, but on this occasion she seemed not to notice her surroundings. In the living room he helped her on to the sofa, adjusting the cushions behind her head and covering her with a rug when he discovered how cold her hands were. Then he went into the kitchen and poured her a stiff whisky.

'Drink this.' He was alarmed by her ash-white colour.

She murmured something, shifting her head to one side and closing her eyes. 'Celia,' he coaxed, 'you must drink this. It'll help.'

Outside in the road, there was a sudden noise, a sharp crack as if a gun had just gone off. Celia's eyes flew to the window. She looked terrified.

'It's all right, sweetheart,' Martin said soothingly. 'You're safe now. It was only a car back-firing.'

He handed her the whisky. Obediently she brought the glass to her lips, and took a sip. Then she took another, wincing slightly as she swallowed the fiery liquid. After about five minutes she had finished it all.

'Good girl. How do you feel now?'

'I –' her voice was hoarse; she cleared her throat, then raised a hand to her head. 'I must have whacked it when I fell. Have you got an aspirin?'

He brought her two soluble paracetamol and was relieved to see her breathing more steadily, and that some colour had returned to her cheeks, after she had drained the glass.

'Do you want me to call a doctor?'

She shook her head, managing a weak smile. 'Just let me stay for a little while. I feel safe here.'

'You can stay as long as you want.' He sat down beside her on the sofa and took her hand. 'Who did this to you?'

She closed her eyes. 'I don't want to talk about it.'

'It might help.'

'I can't,' she whispered. And then suddenly it all came pouring out.

'I left my car at the back of Holland Park and took the Tube into town to meet a friend for supper,' she began, hesitantly. 'When I returned to the car I found that my two rear tyres had been slashed – some mindless act done for a laugh, no doubt. Stupidly I'd forgotten to renew my RAC policy, so I decided to leave the car where it was and sort it out in the morning from the office. All I wanted to do was get to bed. There were no taxis in sight but it was a really warm night and there were lots of people about so I set off in the general direction of home. At some point I left the main road and took a short cut through the back-streets. I must have been walking for about five minutes when I heard the footsteps. At first I didn't pay much attention but they began to get louder and I got it into my head that someone was following me. Then I thought I heard the sound of a match striking but when I turned round to see who was behind me the road was deserted. So I told myself I was just being irrational and walked on.'

Martin nodded thoughtfully. 'Go on.'

She clutched the empty glass in her hands and gazed blindly at him.

'I had crossed into Chepstow Villas when I heard the footsteps again. There was something not quite right about them. It's hard to explain why but they had a cautious ring about them, almost as if the person was expecting me to turn and confront him. I glanced over my shoulder and saw the orange glow of a cigarette, but then it went out. At that point I can remember feeling the hairs stir on the back of my neck.' She paused, frowning. 'I knew something was wrong but by then it was too late to retrace my steps to the police station, so I pushed on, walking with as much confidence and speed as I could muster.'

'And all this time you didn't see a single cab?'

'Oh, plenty,' she said, dolefully, 'but they were all taken. I had no choice but to keep going. Anyway, as the footsteps closed in on me, I panicked and cut into Ledbury Road. I looked over my shoulder – by then I was almost running – but to my intense relief I saw that whoever was behind me had continued on down Chepstow Villas. I walked on more slowly and soon found myself outside Beach Blanket Babylon. It was absolutely packed and I crossed the road to avoid the noise and cigarette smoke. I was thinking about that evening you took me there for a drink after my first day at Carlyle, the time I managed to spill your beer all down my skirt.' She sighed. 'And that was when he made his move.

'At first I thought something from one of the roofs must have fallen on top of me. This great weight crashed into me and as I tumbled forward, my head caught the kerb. Then I felt this sharp, digging pressure under my arms as I was lifted and dragged face down into the dark mews.' Her eyes were full of terror as she looked up at him. 'I thought he was going to kill me, Martin. I really thought: this is it.'

'Did you get a look at his face?'

Vehemently, she shook her head. 'It all happened so fast. All I could see were his shoes. Loafers; the tongues crested in gold. He must have stumbled because I heard him swear and then felt this terrible pressure digging against my stomach. He flung me against a wall, winding me, and when I struggled to turn round, he pinned me against his body. I can remember pleading with him not to hurt me but it was useless. I could feel him easing my dress up the back of my legs, a ripping sound, then –' She closed her eyes and shuddered, fighting the awful memory. 'He put his fingers inside my underwear and touched me.'

She swallowed. 'I began to scream really loudly but he clamped my mouth with his hand, still using his body-weight to hold me down. His penis was stiff and wet against my thigh. He tried to –' Again she paused, screwing up her face in anguish. 'I swear I did everything in my power to stop him. I kicked him with my feet, tried to wriggle an arm free, managed to sink my teeth into his hand, but nothing I did made any difference. The more I struggled, the tighter the clamp. I was powerless. I couldn't breathe. The smell of his skin was disgusting and I thought I might be sick. I can remember the moment when I gave in to this awful, mindless panic, just shut my eyes to what he was about to do and let my body go limp.

'And then the weight was suddenly lifted from my body. I could hear sounds of approaching footsteps, a tin can being kicked along the pavement, people talking and laughing. I held my breath, hardly daring to look. I lay there without moving until they had passed and when I finally opened my eyes I was alone. He had gone. You found me a few minutes later.'

In his mind Martin returned to the darkened mews, the forlorn shape of Celia hugging her knees, the ripped flap of her dress discarded nearby like a piece of litter. If he and Hammers had left the pub ten minutes earlier, he might have caught the bastard responsible.

'We must go to the police,' he insisted, swallowing anger.

She shook her head. 'No.' She looked shattered.

'But he almost raped you, Celia. Who's to say he won't try it again on someone else? The only chance you have of stopping him is if you report it.'

'I'm sorry, but the very thought of all those questions, making me relive what happened over and over, I couldn't handle that. Not now. Please,' she begged, 'understand. I just want to forget it ever happened.'

He studied her reflectively. She looked done in. 'OK,' he finally relented. 'Just try and get some sleep. You're exhausted.'

He tucked her up in his bed, clad in one of his office shirts, with her wounds washed and treated with antiseptic, and stayed with her until she was asleep. Then he wandered back into the living room and phoned the one person he knew he could trust, an old friend who wouldn't ask any questions.

EIGHTEEN

'Where are we going?' Celia asked listlessly. They were in Martin's car, steaming along the A12 in the baking heat with all the windows rolled down. Oasis sang from the radio.

'To stay with some friends of mine. They live just outside Frinton-on-Sea.'

'But that's on the Essex coast.'

'You wanted to get away.'

'What about the office? I'm supposed to be working a half-shift today.'

'Don't worry. I've sorted things out with Hammers.'

Well, not sorted exactly, but he had rung Hammers at home to say that Celia wouldn't be in to work. 'Honestly, chum,' the big man had sighed, 'it just isn't good enough, absconding with my staff like this.'

'It's not what you think. Give us until Monday. I'll explain everything then.'

'And the cats?' Celia said now. 'Who's going to feed them?'

'Your neighbour has a spare key, doesn't he? Give him a call on my mobile and ask him to keep an eye on them while you're away.'

Celia was watching him. 'These friends of yours?'

'He runs a hotel. She designs costumes. You'll like them. Everyone does.'

The dark grey Golf hurtled into deep country. While Celia dozed he concentrated on the narrowing road which twisted along for miles past villages, farmland, rolling meadows and fields, the rich beauty of East Anglia all around. Finally, he drew up in front of a rambling but charming cottage. Almost at once a man appeared at the front gate. He was wearing swimming trunks and a straw hat.

'That was quick,' he said cheerfully, slapping Martin on the back. 'Still breaking the speed barriers, eh Martin?'

'Celia this is Graham,' said Martin. 'Take everything he says very loosely.' The two men grinned at each other.

'Good to see you both. Come on round the back and get a drink. You must be flagging in this heat.'

They followed Graham along the side of the house to a picturesque garden. A bikini-clad woman was drying herself beside a kidney-shaped swimming pool and came forward to greet them.

'I expect you'd both like a plunge after being stuck for hours in the car. It's so hot I'm averaging a dip an hour.' She directed her gaze at Celia, 'Did you bring a costume?'

'I'm afraid not.'

'Not to worry. You can borrow one of mine.'

Celia collapsed on to one of the recliners at the edge of the pool, her face aimed at the sun, Martin into a chair.

'So, how's life in the fast lane of property?' Graham asked, after they had all been given drinks. 'Looks like you've put on a few pounds.'

'Which suits you,' added Suzanne.

'Yes, you old hound,' Graham agreed, 'you're looking well.'

'Thanks. Although I'm not so sure about you. I detect a few grey hairs. What have you been doing to him, Suzanne?'

She laughed. 'Martin, don't get him started. We'll be here all night.'

Celia, who up until then had hardly said a word, looked at both the men. 'You two obviously go back a long way.'

'We were at university together. I worked extremely hard whereas Graham here wasted most of his time playing snooker at the pub.'

'Not much has changed,' Suzanne teased, giving Celia a sideways glance. Martin had noticed her doing this a few times since they had arrived.

'Ah, but which of us came out with a double first?'

'Yes,' Martin said with a sudden touch of melancholy. 'You surprised us all.'

Graham looked contrite. 'Me and my big mouth. That was a stupid thing to say.'

Suzanne turned to Celia. 'Have we met before?'

'I'd have remembered you if we had.'

'You don't know Tom Amberley, the painter? I thought perhaps I might have seen you at one of his exhibitions – I often help out. No?'

Celia was emphatic. 'I'm afraid not.'

Graham grinned. 'That's what working in the film business does to you – you think you know everyone.'

Celia shrugged. 'Maybe I just have one of those faces.'

They ate a candlelit supper in the garden with nothing but the sound of cutlery on china, and their own animated voices, punctuating the still, warm night. After a delicious meal of rainbow trout, French cheeses and vanilla soufflé, they settled back in their chairs with coffee and brandy.

'It defeats me how you manage to pluck a meal like that out of thin air on top of all your other commitments, Suzanne,' said Martin, pleasurably smacking his lips.

'Did she tell you about her latest venture?' said Graham proudly. 'Ridley Scott's signed her up for his next film.'

'Most of which will be shot on location in Vienna and Prague. Can't believe my luck,' she sighed contentedly. 'I'm having such an amazing year.'

'Who's going to be in it?' said Martin.

'One of my all-time favourites: Rory Calf.'

Celia choked on her coffee.

'Now *he* is the one man besides Paul Newman that I'd contemplate having an affair with,' Suzanne continued, eyeing Celia briefly. She glanced lovingly at her husband.

'Which would mean, darling, that I'd allow you to sleep with Goldie Hawn.'

Celia was still coughing. 'Are you all right?' Martin patted her on the back. The other two looked on in concern.

'I'm fine,' she stammered, red in the face, 'Just went down the wrong way. If you don't mind I think I'll turn in for the night. I'm pretty whacked. It was a lovely supper, Suzanne. Goodnight everyone.'

'You're wearing that thoughtful look of yours, darling,' Graham said, after Celia had gone. 'What are you plotting?'

'I've just twigged where I've seen her before.'

'Who?' said Martin. 'Celia?'

'It must have been a good four years ago, and she had long hair then – that's what fooled me initially, but I remember that slightly haunting quality in her eyes. We met at a film premier. I was there with my mother and she was with Rory Calf.'

Resolutely, Martin shook his head. 'No, no. You must be confusing her with someone else. Celia doesn't have friends like that.'

'Oh, she wasn't a friend. She was his wife!'

Martin knocked on the door of Celia's bedroom. 'It's me. Can I come in?'

She was sitting in a chair by the open window, gazing out into the night. He came and sat down beside her.

'Suzanne's remembered, hasn't she? She knows who I am.'

'Yes,' he said. 'But what I don't understand is why you felt the need to keep quiet about it.' Even as he said the words he regretted them. If anyone understood the value of secrecy, it was him.

A sound came from her, a cough or a laugh, he wasn't sure. She was looking, not at him, but at her hands in her lap, inspecting her nails. 'Have you ever lived with anyone famous?' He shook his head. 'When I first met

Rory I thought he was the most beautiful man I'd ever seen. He was already courting fame so when he started asking me out I couldn't believe my luck. I was plain, gawky and taller than any of the other girls of my age and felt incredibly lucky to get him. Most of the socialising I'd done had been through the church so, at twenty-three, I was emotionally still quite naïve. Rory was from another world. He seemed to exude an exotic glamour, a lifestyle full of colour and freedom.'

'Go on,' Martin urged.

'My parents strongly disapproved, of course. They had in mind someone who had been to bible college and showed leadership direction in the Evangelical Church. But by then I was quite sure it wasn't what I wanted for myself and even more certain when I met Rory. At the time I thought myself deeply in love. I'd have gone anywhere with him.'

She paused and they could hear Graham and Suzanne's muffled voices as they moved about in the bedroom next door. A moth fluttered into the room, attracted by the light, and began battering its tiny body against the ceiling.

'At first we were so happy. Then Rory's career took off and suddenly offers from Hollywood came pouring in. Overnight he made this incredible leap from small-time actor doing fringe theatre to international stardom. He loved all of it, including the money. I, on the other hand hated the invasion into our private lives. We couldn't go down to the local shop without half a dozen journalists poking their cameras in our faces. Eventually we moved to LA. Then the affairs began.' She looked at him with an embarrassed, fierce smile. 'A long, steady stream of them. Perhaps they'd always been going on, I don't know, but I hated myself for staying with him and yet I lived for the times when we were together. I was like someone with a terrible sickness who doesn't want to get better. It was awful. But Rory had this knack of turning things round so that I ended up feeling it was my fault, and I'd been raised to believe that you married for life. I couldn't just walk out.'

'Was he responsible for the scar on your face?'

She bit her lip, obviously shocked by the baldness of the question. 'Rory had a much more dangerous and subtle form of violence. I think he resented his dependency on the female sex. He tried to destroy every woman he got involved with in a way a man with fists never could. No, I got this in a riding accident when I was thirteen.' Her finger unconsciously traced the thin, centipede-shaped scar along her cheek. She tilted her head and watched the desperate fluttering of the moth now trapped inside a lampshade. 'Actually, that was one of things I first loved about Rory. To him, my scar just didn't matter.'

'I don't think it matters either.'

She laughed softly and blushed. 'The year after we got married,' she continued, 'Rory was involved in a sex scandal. He was accused of having intercourse with two underaged girls. He swore it wasn't true but the case made headlines. Then someone found out about his other affairs and the press started snooping into my background. "Sex maniac's wife in missionary position" – you can imagine the sort of cheap things they wrote. Some of it filtered back to my parents' church and they were put through hell. Even after it was discovered Rory had been set up, the ill-feeling against my poor parents continued. The scandal almost destroyed my father's career.'

She looked at Martin, trying to make him understand. 'Don't you see, if I were to go to the police and tell them about what happened to me on Friday it would only be a matter of time before someone made the connection with Rory and the whole thing would blow up again. I couldn't put my parents through that.'

He chose his words carefully. 'You wouldn't have to,' he said gently. 'The police have a duty to protect your identity from the press. No one need find out anything. Look, I know this isn't what you want to hear, but could you really live with yourself if another woman was attacked and you'd done nothing to prevent it?'

They locked eyes, hers brimming with tears. 'No,' she said faintly, 'I couldn't.'

It was almost eleven by the time Martin surfaced the following morning, yawning but restored after his lie-in. While he dressed, he mulled over the things Celia had told him. At least now he could understand why she had behaved in the way she had. Married to Rory Calf, one of a long string of headline-grabbing Englishmen to rock Hollywood. Little wonder he had changed his name to Rory Calf. Richard Catford wasn't exactly glamorous.

Downstairs he found a note from Graham to say that there had been a crisis at the hotel but that they should make themselves at home. The Sunday papers had been left on the kitchen table. Idly, Martin skimmed through the sports section as he waited for the kettle to boil. He was about to read an article on Michael Atherton when Celia appeared. She was carrying a copy of *Oscar and Lucinda*.

'On your own?'

He nodded. 'The others should be back for lunch. How did you sleep?'

'Like a baby. I'd forgotten the stillness of the countryside. It's a lovely house. You're lucky to have such nice friends. I thought I'd catch a bit of sun and do some reading.'

'It's a good book.'

'Oh.' She looked at the paperback in her hand. 'Yes. I've got a copy at home but never had time to get into the story.' She pulled up a chair and sat down. 'I've been thinking about what you said last night. As soon as we're back in London I'm going to go straight to the police and tell them what happened. I feel ashamed I didn't have the courage to do it straight away.'

He put a hand on her arm. 'You're doing the right thing.'

Later they went for a walk. The day felt as if it held the

final moments of summer, provoking in Martin a sudden, reckless yearning to cry out and shatter the shimmering hush with the sound of his voice. He had forgotten how much he loved the country. At the Scotts' it had been different. There he had been so caught up in his rivalry with Piers that there had been little time for his surroundings. But here, away from the recent pressures, he felt strangely free. The air smelt of sweet earth, mid-summer. The light on the surrounding fields was electric and exposed a scene reminiscent of a Ford Madox Brown painting. He could see his friend's cottage on the horizon. The idea of living here, of not having to go back to the bituminous air, the cloying traffic, or his small shabby flat, was so appealing that he almost believed it could be made to happen.

Ahead of him Celia walked slenderly erect. She was wearing a pair of blue shorts with white polka-dots and her long legs, exposed to the sun, had turned a pale coffee colour. He wondered what turbulent thoughts were going through her mind. Since their conversation last night she had said very little, and he was sensitive enough to give her the space he knew she needed.

When he caught up with her, she asked, 'What was all that about last night between you and Graham?' He frowned, not understanding. 'When he was talking about his university degree. It seemed to upset you.'

'You don't miss much.'

'Well, it's just that you rarely talk about yourself. I wondered if it was a competitive thing – a case of him being better than you?'

He laughed. 'No one was ever in any doubt about that. Graham has an amazing mind. As for me, I'll never know how far I might have gone. My father had a fatal heart attack while I was at Aberystwyth. I had to cut short my last year.'

'That must have been difficult for you.'

He shrugged, thinking back to those first few weeks at college – the happiest he could remember. He had thrown himself into his work, eager to be accepted and to do well. His tutors were encouraging. They urged him on like spectators at an Olympic final and the competitor in him responded. Then, out of the blue, came the phone call that brought his student life to an abrupt end.

'That's the way it goes sometimes,' he said. 'Until my father's death my parents had run a small newsagents. As it was their only source of income, my mother tried to soldier on but it was pretty obvious she couldn't possibly manage by herself.' He tore a leaf from a bush.

'So, you left university to help?'

'It was that or seeing her lose everything they had worked for. I kept things going for a few months but I never really settled to it – you can't go back in life, I discovered, it never works. When the lease came up for renewal we sold the shop as a going concern.'

They crossed a stile and followed a path along the side of a hardened ploughed field. She kicked a small ball of soil in front of her. Her hair which, until now, had always seemed so dark to him, looked almost red in the midday sun.

'A perfect day for cricket,' he said wistfully. 'I wonder how our boys are doing in the Ashes?'

'Why is Test match cricket called that?'

'The name came into use some time towards the end of the last century when England burned the stumps and sent the ashes in a jar to the Australian side. We normally get thrashed, but this year we've already beaten them in the one-day international and –'

Celia suddenly swung round to face him. She had gone very pale. 'What did you just say?'

'We beat them three matches in a row.'

'No, before that. You said they *burned* the stumps.'

'*Ye*-es,' said Martin, not understanding.

'Well, that made me think of fires and then I remembered what he said to me. He said: "This will teach him to play with fire."' It took Martin a moment to work out who Celia was talking about.

'It's all starting to come back. The loafers he was wearing, some kind of a crest on them. I'd know them if I saw them again. They were very distinctive.' Her eyes narrowed against the sun's brightness. '"This will teach him to play with fire,"' she repeated. 'Now, why would he say "him" and not you – meaning me?'

'Perhaps he was referring to someone else?'

'Precisely.'

'– which would mean –' Martin tried to follow her alarming thought pattern.

'– whoever attacked me,' she finished glumly, 'is probably someone I know.'

NINETEEN

In spite of the seriousness of all that had happened, their mood had lightened by the time they drove back to London and they almost had fun on the journey, with Celia telling him stories and feeding him Liquorice Allsorts they'd bought at a petrol station. They discovered shared interests: a yearning to travel, a fondness for home-made pasta and Cuban music, a desire to move out of the city one day and have kids. Perhaps it was because she no longer had anything to hide, coupled with the effects of the country air, but she seemed to have relaxed into someone softer and warmer – funny too. Martin looked at her giggling like a girl who hasn't laughed for a long time, and was struck by the realisation that she kept on surprising him. Other facets about her emerged: that she hadn't been on a horse since the accident to her face, that she practised yoga every morning, could speak French and that after separating from Rory, all her hair had fallen out.

By the time he pulled up outside her flat the dying

embers of the sky were glowing softly. He could feel the skin of his face tightening from the hours in the sun.

'Looks like it's going to be another scorcher tomorrow.' She arched her neck to admire the sunset through the open roof and he remembered the photograph of her as a teenager with a lustrous mane of hair. Then she looked at him, her gaze serious once more. 'What am I going to tell Hammers?'

'That's for me to worry about. I said I'd handle it and I will. I'll make sure I'm in early so that I can get him on his own. What about you?'

'I'll go to the police first thing tomorrow. There's probably not much they can do now but at least they will have been alerted.' She picked up her bag and got out of the car. Before she went into the house, she came round to his side and dipped her head to his level.

'Martin, I probably won't get a chance to say this tomorrow, but thank you. For being *so* kind – everything. I don't think I could have coped if you hadn't been around.'

Impulsively, she bent forward to kiss his cheek, and when he took her hand, he felt the quick pulse of her slender wrist beneath his thumb.

'See you tomorrow,' she called, as he slipped the car into gear. And as he pulled back out into the road towards home, he began whistling softly to himself.

He woke early to find his duvet kicked to the foot of the bed and the sun pouring through the window. For a moment he lay very still, then gradually the weekend's events came back to him. With a stretch, he roused himself from bed and opened the window, letting the dull roar of traffic into the room, before going into the kitchen to put the kettle on. It was still only seven so when he had made the tea he returned to his room and lay back down on the bed with closed eyes, feeling warm syrupy fingers of light stroking his face.

He had only meant to rest his eyes, but woke with a start to find the tea stone cold and the clock now reading five past eight. He flew out of his flat doing up shirt buttons, hastily wiping sleep from his eyes. On the way to the office the flashing fuel light on the panel of his dashboard forced him to stop off for petrol, which further delayed him, but for once luck was on his side. Hammers hadn't yet arrived. The others were downstairs in the kitchen having an early smoke. From the hall he could hear their indistinct conversation but when he opened the door they all fell quiet and looked at him. No one said anything for a moment.

Oliver cast an appraising eye over his dishevelled appearance. 'Someone dressed in a bit of a hurry this morning,' he said sardonically.

'Yeah, you look shafted, mate.' Roger's voice was a curious mixture of sympathy and laddish amusement. 'Bit of a late one, was it?'

Eve, looking fresh and beautiful, and spooning sugar into her mug, frowned at him and said nothing. If he hadn't known better he could have sworn her look was accusatory.

'It was too hot,' he said, taking the coffee Roger handed to him. 'I couldn't sleep.'

Roger looked mischievous. 'I bet you couldn't.' Now what the hell did that mean?

The clock on the wall registered eight thirty-five. Anxious not to miss his opportunity to grab Hammers when he arrived, Martin – coffee in hand, headed back upstairs. On the way up he was stopped by Oliver who must have followed him out.

'I'm curious, Leak,' he said catching up, 'about what's going on with you and Celia?'

He turned round. 'Who told you that?'

'Just someone asking questions. I said I didn't know, although,' he paused thoughtfully, 'I've had my suspicions.'

Martin managed a smile. 'Well, whatever you've heard it isn't true.'

'I believe you,' Oliver said innocently, 'But you know how tongues will wag.'

*

Hammers was ten minutes late for the morning meeting. He arrived muttering crossly to himself, having been pulled over and issued a ticket for driving down a bus lane. Martin managed to steal a private moment with him to explain what had happened on Friday. He told him that Celia's spinster aunt in Frinton-on-Sea had been broken into over the weekend and had rung her in a state of hysteria, and that Celia had turned to him for help. It was the best he could come up with, and a preoccupied Hammers seemed to accept its authenticity. In fact he looked quite concerned.

A shriek from the basement interrupted them. For a split second Martin looked at Hammers, then they both rushed downstairs to see what had happened. They found Tracy screaming at her reflection in the loo mirror, fingers tearing frantically at her eyelashes.

'Get it out! Get it out!' she wailed as Oliver then Eve crowded into the tiny room.

'OK, OK,' said Hammers gently. 'Just let me have a look.'

But Tracy continued to scream and it wasn't until Oliver slapped her – none too gently – that they found out just what had happened. Tracy, suffering from an eye infection, had squeezed what she thought was eye-drops into her left eye, only to discover that she had inadvertently used nail glue.

'How the *fuck* do you make a mistake like that?' Oliver mumbled with his usual sensitivity.

Roger shot him a thin smile. 'Ever thought of a career in counselling?'

'Come on,' Hammers coaxed, guiding the trembling girl out of the room, 'Let's get you to the hospital.' Then to Martin, 'You'd better bring my car round to the front. The keys are on my desk.'

Martin was just helping Hammers to get Tracy into the passenger seat, when a police car pulled up behind the BMW. Three men – two in uniform – stepped out and approached them.

'Are you Martin Leak?' one of them asked curtly.

His heart gave a thud. 'Yes?'

The man held out his badge. 'You're under arrest.'

TWENTY

They drove him to an entrance at the back of the police station, handcuffed to a strapping young lad who wouldn't answer any of his questions, who didn't say much either to his two colleagues sitting in the front of the car, and who escorted him inside in the same taciturn manner. In a daze he listened to the man who'd arrested him give the custody officer a short explanation of the facts – that he – Martin Leak – was suspected of being involved in the murder of Charles Fitzherbert. They signed him in, took down all his details, then read him his rights and asked if he wanted a solicitor to be present. Martin shook his head dumbly, barely grasping what was happening. No, he didn't want a solicitor. He hadn't done anything wrong; to ask for one would surely have been construed as an admission of guilt. And that's when they told him they had a warrant to search his flat. He thought of saying that he'd left his set of keys back at the office, but there didn't seem to be much point in lying; besides, the custody officer looked quite capable of breaking the door down. So he dug into his pocket and, with a sick feeling of dread, handed over the keys; they would find the newspaper cuttings he had kept on the Arundel Gardens case.

Then the custody sergeant led him down a corridor into a narrow cell and asked him to undress. Martin looked at him in disbelief: he thought he was joking, but another man appeared carrying some white overalls with a zip up the front and a pair of white plimsolls which were handed to him. The second man recorded each item as he took it off and placed the clothes in an over-sized brown paper bag. They allowed him to keep his shirt, socks and underwear, then they left him alone, the cell door clanging shut with an ominous finality. He eyed the single bed with suspicion but as there was nowhere else to sit, he lowered himself on to the thin plastic mattress and gazed morosely at his surroundings: custard-yellow walls, an emergency bell above his head, strip lighting, a loo sectioned off from the bed by a waist-high partition wall. The window was too far up to see out of – even with his arm outstretched he couldn't reach it. And why was the ceiling so high? To stop prisoners from hanging themselves? He swallowed nervously. What crime did they think he'd committed? All right, he'd done some stupid things in his time but for God's sake, he wasn't a *murderer*. He kept asking himself what they hoped to find in his flat. Were they there now, prying amongst his personal stuff while he sat here powerless to do anything about it? And what about his clothes – his shoes? *They can lift perfect footprints from a carpet*, Roger had told him. He put his head in his hands. Oh, God, please tell me this isn't happening.

He was left to sweat it out for almost three hours before they came to get him. The custody sergeant showed him into a small, windowless room which accommodated a table, four wooden chairs and a double tape deck. He was asked if he wanted a cup of tea, which he gratefully accepted – and just for a moment the friendly gesture made everything feel normal again – but then two more men entered the room and one look at their expressions communicated the seriousness of the situation. He was in for a rough ride.

'How long have you worked at Carlyle, Martin?'
    'About a year.'
    'Do you like your job?'
    'I enjoy meeting new people, the challenge of a sale.'
    The Detective Inspector, who had steely-blue eyes and a reddish moustache, looked at him and smiled. They had been questioning him for about half an hour, mostly

concerning his background and previous employment. But he knew that the sympathetic approach would not last long: he had seen how they worked on *The Bill*. At some stage they were going to throw the subject of the Fitzherberts at him, and he steeled himself for that moment.

'What were you doing on the eighth of May?'

Martin frowned. 'The eighth of May?' he repeated, counting back the days in his mind to that abortive journey he had made to see Irene in Cambridge. 'I was at work.'

'Let me be more specific. What were you doing between the hours of 1pm and 5pm on that day?'

'I really couldn't say without checking the diary.'

The inspector folded his arms. 'Perhaps I can help you. Did you meet up with anyone called Mr Hollioake?'

A spider of anxiety crawled up the back of Martin's spine. Mr Hollioake was the property dealer he had lied to Hammers about seeing, the one he had said was interested in purchasing the house in Abbotsbury. Should he come clean and admit that some joker had thought it amusing to send him rushing to his dying mother's bedside in a hospital eighty miles out of London, only to find that the whole thing had been nothing more than a hoax. Oh, sure. He could imagine all too well how funny these blokes would find it.

'Er – yes,' he lied. 'Yes, I did.'

'Where did you go?'

'We had lunch together – to discuss a possible sale.'

'I see. And you went to a restaurant?'

'Yes,' he said, sticking to the story he'd fed Hammers. 'Kensington Place. It's in –'

The inspector, his jaw gently working a piece of gum, interrupted him. 'That's all right. We know where it is. I'm told the food's very good there. How much was the meal, do you remember?'

Martin made an educated guess. 'About sixty pounds.'

'You told Nick Hammerton that Carlyle were going to pay for the meal, yet you never submitted a claim for expenses. Why was that?'

He shrugged. 'Sometimes I save up my expense receipts and hand them in at the end of the month.'

A spark of encouragement from the inspector. 'So you have a receipt?'

Shit. 'No, not on me. It'll probably be amongst my papers at home.'

'I'm afraid that's already been checked,' the inspector said. 'Think again.'

Martin swallowed, his suspicions confirmed. They had already been to his flat. 'Guess I must have mislaid it.'

'You *mislaid* the receipt. Surely you have some record of the meal somewhere, a credit card statement at least?' he said reasonably.

He felt the sweat begin to collect under his armpits. 'No. In fact, now I come to think of it I remember I paid in cash.'

'Sixty pounds. Always carry that amount of cash around, do you?'

He cleared his throat, his discomfiture evident. 'Not always, no.'

'And you're absolutely certain it was the Kensington Place you went to?'

'Positive. Just what are you getting at?'

'I'm not really getting at anything. It's just that the restaurant has no record of your having been there. Nor, in fact, does Mr Hollioake recollect any lunch meeting. He claims he was in Birmingham that day – for a funeral.'

Martin reddened, but before he was given a chance to say anything, the inspector turned his head. 'Sergeant, can I –?' he said, gesturing to something.

The sergeant took a piece of paper from a file in front of him and handed it to the inspector, who placed it in front of Martin. 'Any idea what these are?'

On the paper, scribbled in ink, were two sets of four

numbers, one under the other and circled. He recognised the first set of numbers immediately: 8434. It was the Fitzherberts' security code. The second one took a little longer to recall, but it soon came to him: he had used it to access Mr Ash's flat.

'None whatsoever,' he said, staring at the scrap of paper sealed in a small plastic bag, his heart hammering away. And he thought: It's coming.

'So that isn't your handwriting?'

'No. Never seen it before.'

'OK then. Tell me about your visit with Mr Lindsey to Mr Ash's basement flat.'

Mr Lindsey. The name registered faintly in the back of his mind. Then it clicked. The client he had made up that Sunday Oliver had met him leaving the flat. Oh, no, Ollie. Don't say you went and actually told them.

'Did you for any reason go into the cupboard in the hall?' prompted the inspector.

He could see where this was leading and decided to brazen it out. 'I might have popped my head inside. Clients generally like to see what's behind a closed door.' He hadn't meant to sound sarcastic, but the interrogation was getting on his nerves.

'Did you touch anything in the cupboard?'

'Not that I recall.' Ollie and his big mouth – the stupid sod.

The inspector nodded slowly, his gaze abstracted as if he had suddenly lost interest in the conversation. Martin generally relied on an intuitive sixth sense about people, but he couldn't tell whether or not the man believed anything he'd told him. Then, out of the blue, the inspector suddenly asked, 'Have you got the time on you?'

The question caught him by surprise. Automatically, he glanced down at the pale strip of skin on his wrist where his watch was usually fastened, then remembered that he didn't have it. The sergeant held something up in his hand. 'This what you're looking for?' he asked.

Martin gazed at his missing watch in astonishment. 'I don't understand? Where did you find it?'

Both men watched him carefully. 'We thought you might know the answer to that.'

'It disappeared a few days ago, that's all I can tell you.' His brow creased in confusion. He had turned the flat upside down only the previous day in his search for Frank's twenty-first birthday present. 'I thought I'd lost it.'

'Do you remember where?' Martin shook his head. Didn't the guy have ears? 'Could you have accidentally dropped it in Mr Ash's bedroom while you were stealing his things, including a rare saxophone?'

Martin's eyes widened. '*No,*' he protested hotly. 'That's absurd. Look, you've got to believe me. You've made a mistake. I had nothing to do with that theft.'

The inspector made an indistinct noise in the back of his throat and looked significantly at the sergeant. 'All right, Mr Leak,' he said, with ominous lightness. 'If you say so.'

Bewildered, he sat there thinking. It had been weeks since he had last been to Mr Ash's place, yet his watch had only disappeared a few days ago. What the hell was going on?

'Let's go over your last visit to Mr Fitzherbert's maisonette.' The inspector consulted the open file in front of him. 'According to these records, you were last there about two weeks before Christmas, is that right?' Martin nodded slowly. 'For the benefit of the tape Mr Leak is nodding his head,' he said, and Martin's eyes slid towards the moving spools of the cassette deck, reminding him that everything he said was being recorded. 'You didn't go round there again for any reason?'

Martin sighed. 'Why do you keep asking me that? We've already been over it three times. Can't we just get on with whatever it is that you want from me, so I can go back to work?'

'All in good time, Martin. I don't like to rush things.'

'Look, Inspector,' he said reasonably, trying to appeal

to the DI's better nature, 'I can't explain how my watch ended up in Mr Ash's flat. I'll admit it does seem a little odd, but I'm an estate agent, I meet a lot of people and take on new instructions all the time, and yes, part of my job is to go round properties, accompanied or otherwise, but come on,' he entreated them with a wavering smile, 'that doesn't make me a killer, does it?'

The inspector had clearly forgotten his sense of humour that morning. 'You still haven't answered my question.'

'Which was?'

'That the last time you were at the Fitzherberts' home was two weeks before Christmas?'

'*Yes,*' exasperated now. 'How many times do I have to tell you?'

The inspector nodded as he looked in seeming puzzlement at the document – half a dozen sheets of A4 – laid out before him. 'Funny thing is, our lab reports show that you *were* there on the day of the murder.' He looked up, his blue eyes unwavering, frank. 'And we can prove it.'

Martin felt a horrible chill rush through him. He had a strong desire to run from the room, but suppressed the urge. How could they know? For one insane moment he suspected this was an attempt to call his bluff, but then they told him about the mug of whisky with his fingerprints all over it and that shut him up. His mouth, parched like the Sahara Desert, went even drier when the inspector unearthed a third plastic bag because he could see what was inside: the press cuttings of the murder and Mrs Fitzherbert's smiling image, frozen in a camera's eye.

'Know who this is?' Martin bit his lip as the inspector held up the photograph of Mrs Fitzherbert. 'Mr Fitzherbert certainly does. Last time he saw it, it was on the desk in his study.' His palms were sweating. The room seemed unbearably close and stuffy. He could hear the loudness of his breathing and tried to control the rhythm, but it was no use.

'Perhaps,' the inspector suggested, after an agonising

pause, 'you can explain what these items were doing in a box under your bed?'

Martin was silent. Shit, he thought. Shit. Shit.

The inspector leaned forward and eyeballed him. 'Let me explain the situation to you, Martin,' he began in the tone of an authoritative parent. 'You're in this up to your neck and unless you start co-operating with me, I'm going to make sure we keep you here for a very long time, do you understand me?'

He came clean and told them, with difficulty – well, it wasn't the sort of thing that was easily explained – about his preoccupation with other people's lifestyles. They didn't seem to give his gibbering much credence. Even to his own ears it sounded feeble, but he could feel the inspector giving him peculiar looks now and again as if he found his story too preposterous not to be taken seriously. If anything, the DI looked a little put out, as if what Martin was telling him undermined their line of questioning. You're in a responsible job, they told him, people put their trust in you. How do you think they'd feel if they knew what you really got up to in their homes? His sojourn in Mr Ash's cupboard didn't go down too well either and brought an amused sneer from the sergeant, so he glossed over that bit and moved swiftly on to Arundel Gardens, about how he had come to be there that fateful morning; the decision to wait in the warmth for the client who never turned up, his shocked response to what he had found inside. And then the questioning resumed again, on and on, chipping away at each tiny detail, until he thought he couldn't stand it any more.

They kept on asking him why he hadn't called the police when he found the maisonette turned upside down, why he'd felt it necessary to hang around for so long. Did he usually make a habit of drinking whisky alone in the middle of the afternoon, or had someone else been there with him? Did he remember talking to anyone while he was there? Before he could think about it he said no, and so they told him that the little old lady on the first floor – tracked down in Florida – had given them a description of him over the phone, and then, as more tea was brought in, they changed the subject again and asked him how much he was paid, whether he had any financial problems. And while he was pondering the significance of this, they showed him a copy of his credit card and bank statement – almost four grand in arrears. The damning evidence against him continued to mount and all the time alarm bells were ringing louder and louder in his ears: *six thousand pounds missing from the safe*. Then they decided to introduce a little light entertainment and it got really ugly. He was shown the forensic photographs of Charles Fitzherbert: Charlie with his brains splashed all over the bathroom floor, his head – what was left of it – lying at a grotesque angle from his twisted body, and they asked him why he hadn't gone into the upstairs bathroom. Why was it the *one* room he had avoided? Hadn't he wondered if the burglar was still there? Or had he not bothered because he already knew what lay behind the door?

After it was all over, they returned him to his cell where he was allowed to change back into his own clothes. Dazed and shattered by his ordeal, he lay on the plastic mattress for an hour and gazed disbelievingly up at the high ceiling, wondering if he would ever again know the taste of freedom. He was trying to rid his mind of the image of Charlie Fitzherbert's dead body when he heard a key in the lock and the door suddenly opened. In stepped the custody officer.

'We're letting you go,' he said shortly.

Martin sat up, blinking. 'But I thought –?'

'Our enquiries aren't complete, so for the meantime you're free to leave.'

'You mean I'm no longer under arrest?'

'You catch on quick. I'll need you to sign a bail form

before you go. The DI wants you to report back here in two weeks,' he cautioned, 'but in the meantime . . .'

They gave him a lift back to the office. The station's clock was nudging five and he could have gone straight home – a bath and a hot meal seemed a very attractive prospect – but he was anxious to put in an appearance at work, just to show the others that he had nothing to hide.

Hammers wasn't in the office when he got there, and Tracy had been sent home with a bandaged eye, but Roger, Oliver and Eve were at their desks.

'We've been worried about you, Martin,' said Roger, hanging up quickly when he saw him. 'I was about to ring the station. What did they want with you? We heard you were arrested?'

'I wasn't arrested. Just a few matters to sort out.'

The look of disappointment in Roger's expression was so transparent that Martin said, 'But I'll show you the burn marks if you like.'

'Come on,' urged Eve, after a moment's pause. 'Don't keep us in suspense. What happened?'

He gave a shrug, a casual gesture meant to dampen their curiosity. 'Apparently they thought I could give them some information.'

'What about?'

'An old applicant of mine,' he said, reciting the story he'd concocted on the way. 'They think he might be connected with the murder, but I shouldn't think it will lead anywhere.'

Oliver didn't say anything for a moment. Then, 'So why did they hold you there for so long?'

'I had a lot of people to talk to,' Martin responded, a trifle sharply. He did not feel like discussing the finer details of his ordeal with Oliver. He sat down at his desk and began sifting through his messages.

'Were they nice to you?' asked Eve gently.

'Not particularly,' he admitted, then quickly added, 'But then policemen aren't paid to be nice.'

'Sounds to me like they're clutching at straws,' decided Roger. 'I mean, if all they can do is to keep dragging us back into the picture, then they can't be very close to catching their man.'

'I agree,' said Eve and, with a smile, held out a packet of chocolate fingers to Martin. 'Have a biscuit?'

'If you don't mind me saying so,' Oliver remarked a little later, out of earshot from the others, 'you're looking a little bit on the rough side.'

Martin smiled acidly. 'Yes, well, it'll be no thanks to you if I am.'

'Oh,' said Oliver, understanding. He had the decency to look embarrassed. 'I swear it wasn't my fault. But that time I had my fingerprints taken they asked a lot of questions and, well, they were very persistent. They knew something fishy had gone on at Mr Ash's and I think they thought I'd had something to do with it. Frankly, Leak, when push came to shove I wasn't going to put my neck on the chopping board – not for you or anyone else.'

'Thanks. I'll remember that when you want a favour.'

Oliver looked at him curiously. 'Did they really put you through it?'

Martin sighed, suddenly relieved that it was all over. 'Let's just say I don't want a repeat performance.'

Back at his flat, drained and confused, he wanted more than anything to draw the curtains and sink into oblivion on his bed. It seemed the answer to all his problems but sleep was impossible. Questions that he himself wanted the answers to kept whirling round in his brain like snowflakes in a storm. He felt curiously vulnerable and exposed with the lights on, but he didn't want to turn them off, so he went around the flat systematically drawing all the curtains. At one point he laughed at himself. Stupid and irrational to be so paranoid, but if the events of the day had taught him anything, it was to display a little caution. Someone – he didn't know who – was trying to set him up; he was quite sure of it.

Now that he'd had time to think about it, too many

things didn't add up; the matter of his watch, for instance. Oliver had caught him outside Mr Ash's flat in early December, since when he hadn't returned. So how was it possible that his watch, which went astray a little over two weeks ago, had ended up in the hands of the police? Could they have been trying to trick him, some conspiracy theory they'd dreamt up to get him to talk? He digested this unlikely scenario with another, more probable one: Had someone planted his watch there? He recalled the evening he had come home and found his front window open – a window he unfailingly locked when leaving the flat – and Mikel's insistence that someone had been snooping around. Then there was the bogus phone call to tell him about Irene's accident. It was obvious now that it had been nothing more than a ploy to get him out of the way for a few hours – enough time to break into Mr Ash's flat and make it look as if Martin had done it. But *who* had done all this, he asked himself again, and again, and *why*?

Every now and then he walked over to the living-room window and peered out into the semi-darkness as if, somewhere out there, a pair of eyes was looking back at him. He tried to think of all the people he might have upset in the past, vengeful clients whose sales had fallen through and who felt he was to blame, but it was Oliver's name that he kept coming back to. Only Oliver had known about his solitary visit to Mr Ash's flat. Only Oliver, of the Carlyle staff, had met Irene. It would have been easy to find out where she lived, what her movements tended to be, when he had coaxed her into conversation that day she had called at the office. And with access to Mr Ash's flat Oliver could easily have planted his watch there, then called Martin on his mobile. No one could deny that the two of them hadn't had their share of quarrels, and, God knows, the man could be intensely annoying, but what was his motive? Martin sensed that Ollie was too much of a coward to involve himself in anything as risky as a murder. It would be entirely out of character, yet what other explanation could there be?

TWENTY-ONE

During a busy period the next day, a DHL delivery man handed Martin a small brown package. It was addressed to Eve and marked 'personal' in heavy black capitals but as she was out with a client he signed on her behalf. Noticing that it came from Avon he wondered briefly if it was from her father, then deposited the parcel on her desk and thought no more about it. Until later, when Eve returned and, in a brief lull during the mad rush of the afternoon when she, Roger and Martin were the only ones left in the office, set about opening it.

'Another admirer?' Roger suggested, after she had pulled out a slick-looking silver Walkman with headphones.

She was rummaging through the packaging, trying vainly to find an accompanying note. 'I can't think who could have sent it.'

Roger leaned forward curiously and inspected the Walkman, his jaws working a piece of chewing gum which made tiny popping sounds as it collected pockets of air. 'Must have cost a bit.' It was rumoured that an ex-boyfriend had once remarked on his bad breath and Roger, taking the comment to heart, had let gum-chewing grow into an obsession.

Eve pushed the eject button. 'Ah,' she said victoriously. There was a tape inside which must have had something written on it, because her eyes flickered across it. Martin looked on, intrigued.

She slotted the cassette back into the Walkman and secured the headphones over her ears. Then she pressed play and sat back to listen. Almost at once her face darkened. She frowned in irritation and appeared to be about to turn the machine off but, as she contemplated the sounds in her ear, she let the Walkman drop into her lap. She relaxed back in her chair and, as she listened, the tightness around her mouth began to ease. Her expression shifted to one of amusement. A couple of times she giggled quietly, then settled down with a dreamy, faraway look in her eyes. What kind of music evoked such fluctuating emotions in her? Martin wondered, observing Eve with practised discretion. And then it occurred to him: perhaps it wasn't music she was listening to, but a voice.

He picked up an incoming call and spoke briskly without losing her from his vision. By the time he had hung up Eve had finished listening to the tape.

Roger's mouth tugged on a plastic bottle of Fanta. 'Well?'

She hesitated fractionally before speaking. 'It's from my uncle in Manhattan. He's a journalist and I lent him my Walkman while he was staying with us last Christmas. Only it was ruined after he left it outside overnight when it rained. He promised to send me another one when he got home, but that was months ago. I'd forgotten all about it.'

Martin didn't know what he expected to hear by way of explanation, but this wasn't it. 'I thought it had been sent from Avon?' he said suspiciously.

'Dad's just returned from the States and he always sees my uncle even if it's just for lunch. He must have brought it back with him.'

Martin didn't know why he knew she was lying, or why she would feel the need to. But for the rest of the afternoon he was aware of her restlessness and several times caught her glancing at her watch.

She left the office punctually at six and as she slipped hurriedly into the street, Martin adjusted the angle of his chair so that he could watch her. Quickly, she was swallowed up by the stream of passing commuters and he felt the disappointment of losing her – even for a few hours – nibble at him like a fish. It was a fine evening with the sun giving everything a muted, hazy look: ideal weather for a barbecue. He was about to get back to work when he spotted her again, the light catching the autumn-leaf yellow of her hair. She was standing near the edge of the pavement and seemed to be looking for something – or someone. Suddenly, with an impatient glance at the traffic, she skipped across the road. On the other side, waiting for her, hands in pockets and wearing a careful smile, was Piers.

It seemed that they gazed at one another for some moments without speaking. Then Piers began to talk. Eve had her arms crossed as she listened, her eyes directed at the ground or at the stream of passing pedestrians. After a while, however, they drew closer together and her gaze kept returning to Piers's face, almost as if she couldn't help herself. Martin sat watching them, unaware that he was holding his breath: Piers leaning forward to extract something that had flown into her eye, his free hand cupping her cheek tenderly, and, in response, Eve tilting her head trustingly. When he kissed her, it was on the mouth, a long, slow, greedy kiss, his left hand moving from her chin to her neck, his fingers finding their way inside her collar. Other people's intimacies usually fascinated Martin but at this he found he had to look away. When he returned his gaze they had linked hands and were disappearing up Campden Hill Street.

He had to wait almost an hour, suppressing a burning curiosity, before he found himself alone in the office. But when the opportunity presented itself, he approached Eve's desk with an almost reluctant apprehension. It was as if he didn't want to be proved right. On the other hand he would get no sleep tonight unless he satisfied his curiosity. He opened the drawer. It was crammed with things – office stationery, biros, Tampax, a Dicta-phone, a roll of film, loose change, yesterday's *Mail*, the rather startling sight of an unopened box of condoms. The Walkman had been tucked along the side. Having eased it out, he wound the tape back to the start and brought one of the head speakers to his ear. He listened to it for about four minutes and, when he could endure it no further, switched the machine off and shut the drawer.

On the way home that night, the traffic heavy and slow because of roadworks near Shepherds Bush roundabout, he carried a vivid picture of Eve's expression of thoughtful happiness. But it was the warm, insidious, sensuous voice of Piers which swamped his mind, like the persistent, seemingly innocent lapping of waves along a shoreline.

On Friday – a day he would later wish he had never woken up to – the atmosphere in the office was tense and businesslike. With his mind split in a hundred directions, Martin picked up an envelope addressed to him which had been left on his desk and opened it. As he did so, a folded piece of paper fluttered to the floor. Eve, who was passing, bent down to pick it up and handed it to him with a stomach-turning smile.

'Thanks,' he said bleakly.

'My pleasure,' she said, turning away, unaware of his gaze trailing her.

He couldn't rid himself of the grim realisation that she was back with Piers. It enraged him to think of them together again, making it necessary to maintain a cheerful disposition and pretend he wasn't affected by her presence, yet all the time miserably aware of who was responsible for her radiant mood.

One of the lines on his desk was flashing. He picked it up and had just said 'Carlyle' when he cast a look at the slip of paper in his hand. As soon as he saw what it was he turned cold.

'Hello? Hello?' A voice buzzed in his ear. 'Is anyone there?'

'I'll have to call you back,' he stammered, dry-mouthed. The phone slipped from his hand into its cradle as he fought off a rush of panic. Everything around him became too bright, dazzling, white around the edges, as a sudden wave of dizziness gripped him. He thought he might faint and held on to the desk to prevent himself from falling.

'Bad news?' Celia was looking at him with concern.

'What?' He gradually began to register his surroundings, the sudden hush, the four pairs of eyes now fastened on him.

'Your letter. You turned white as a sheet when you opened it.'

He mumbled an excuse as he rushed down to the loo. With an unsteady hand he locked the door and collapsed on the lavatory seat. A horrible, painful knot had formed in his gut. He could feel himself breaking out in a clammy sweat as he looked again at the piece of paper. It was a press cutting, withered and aged, dated almost twenty-seven years previously. No accompanying letter, no signature or clue to show who had sent it, but he knew exactly where it had come from: from a cardboard box he kept under his bed along with letters and photographs. So this is what had been taken. Not money or furniture. Something far more valuable: his past. The tiny room was boiling. He freed himself from his jacket, fingers grappling with the top button of his collar which threatened to choke him. He could feel his sides drenched in sweat. What is the matter with me? he thought. You're being ridiculous. There's nothing to be afraid of. But he couldn't stop trembling and, Jesus Christ, it was happening all over again: the floor opening up and this horrible, shameful sensation taking him back to the time when he was just a ten-year-old boy.

LIFE BEGINS FOR BABY FOUND IN TESCO'S CARRIER
Only the sternest of hearts could fail to be touched by the story of the three-week-old baby found abandoned outside a newsagent in Ipswich yesterday. Hungry and cold, the $10\frac{1}{2}$ lb boy was discovered inside a Tesco's carrier bag among the Sunday papers by proprietor, Mr Frank Leak. A sign around the infant's neck read: 'Forgive me. He's a good baby. Please look after him.' It was Mr Leak

who heard the infant's faint cries shortly after waking at 5am. 'I was on my way down to sort out the papers and heard this wailing sound. Couldn't believe my eyes when I saw what was making it.' The baby was immediately given some warm milk. 'Whoever has done this must have been in a real state,' said Mrs Irene Leak, who runs the small newsagent with her husband. The local authorities have been alerted and a search is now under way for the mother of the baby boy, who police believe may be in need of urgent medical attention. For the moment the mystery baby will remain with the Leaks.

They had never mentioned it to him. Not once in all these years. It was as if, after his entry into their lives, Martin had become something they were ashamed of, something to be kept hidden, away from the prying eyes of neighbours. Even now he could still feel the shame, the devastation, as the secure and comfortable world he had known collapsed around him. He had been ten years old and was rummaging round in the kitchen drawer for the toy gun Frank had confiscated and, in his haste, had sliced his finger on the large meat-knife that had been put there for safe-keeping. The shock of finding those press cuttings – a small piece of history Irene had been unable to throw away – was to colour the rest of his life. Because of what had been shut away in that drawer, and his deep-rooted fear that he must have done something monstrous for his real parents not to want him, he too had kept it a secret, afraid to bring himself to reveal to his adopted parents what he had found.

He couldn't stay in the office. Not the way he was feeling. As he resurfaced from the basement the curiosity of the others was almost tangible. He knew they would start asking questions if he remained and, in his scrambled state of mind, he would be unable to deflect them.

'I'm going out,' he said, snatching keys from his desk.

Hammers looked up, startled. 'When will you be back?'

'Not sure.'

He started walking towards Kensington Gardens. It was a very hot day, the sky a canvas of flawless blue which brought a sharp clarity to the outlines of buildings. The park was awash with activity: unleashed dogs in a fury of excitement, Frisbees wafting through the still air like tiny fluorescent spaceships, people sunbathing, large Middle Eastern families taking a lazy stroll from their homes in Bayswater and Lancaster Gate, teenagers demonstrating their roller-blade skills.

The fresh air helped to clear his head. He found himself a spot on the grass near the Orangery – a magnificent greenhouse with citrus trees framing the long sash windows – and sat down, gazing unseeingly about him. He couldn't shake off the forensic photographs the police had shown him, the victim's mouth half-open as if trying to say something, perhaps a desperate, last-minute plea for his life before being fatally struck down. God knows how long he had taken to die, but someone had left him there to rot, Martin thought, staring with a sick feeling into the distance. Now that same person was out there somewhere trying to pin the blame on him. He suspected everyone – colleagues, friends, even people he hardly knew – and his paranoia was driving him mad.

Who had got into his flat? Who was walking around armed with the secret of his past, and why were they trying to destroy him? The police had been forced to let him go because they had no forensic evidence against him, but this didn't provide him with any comfort. He knew they were watching his every move, waiting for him to stumble and fall. He felt strangled by the tension surrounding him, trapped and helpless like a fly caught in a massive web of fear. When he did manage to drift off to sleep at night, it was never for long. Nightmares of being stalked by a faceless figure, the terror of a sledgehammer raised threateningly, then the hideous slap of impact as the weapon made contact with flesh, left him trembling and drenched in sweat. And what made it worse was that it wasn't his flesh that was pulverised, but someone else's. It was him holding the sledgehammer.

He had lied to Celia when he had told her he had been to see his natural parents. The real truth was that he didn't even know if they were still alive. For years he had toyed with the idea of tracing them but two things stopped him: fear that he might not like what he found and a desire to protect the feelings of Irene and Frank. As a boy, Frank's first heart attack had affected him deeply. Having already lost two parents, the thought of losing another made him grow up very quickly. Through a sense of loyalty and fear he learned to shoulder the responsibility for his adoption alone, but after Frank's death the desire to find his real roots had taken on a new urgency.

Following an abortive trip to Somerset House, he got in touch with the Social Services. In an anonymous room, he sat with his life in a file on his lap and waited almost half an hour before opening it. Inside were the few details recorded after he had been examined in hospital when he was just three weeks old. The smattering of information might have appeared insignificant to others but to Martin it was like stumbling across a treasure trove; his thick crop of hair, the slight cough he had picked up, the size of his hands . . . Amongst the paperwork was a newspaper article about his abandonment identical to the one he had discovered in Irene's kitchen drawer. Even the cardboard note tied round his neck had been saved. The handwriting, almost a direct copy of his own, gave him a shock, as if someone had crept up from behind and thrown iced water over him. Which of them had written it – his mother or his father? All at once, the terrible sense of anger he had for so long harboured, gave way to a feeling of profound sadness. Perhaps his mother had run away and left him because she had been in trouble. Perhaps she had died during labour and his father simply couldn't cope with the screams of a tiny infant.

The counsellor told him that unless his natural parents wanted to be found, there was nothing that could be done to help him. When it became clear that tracing them was as improbable as time standing still, the full implication of his abandonment struck him as forcibly as a bomb exploding in his face. He would never know his real birthday, his medical history, the colour of his mother's hair, the sound of her voice. For the rest of his life he would wonder if he had siblings, where his parents had come from, how his father made his living, whether they would have liked each other. His past haunted him even more intensely than before. He looked for characteristics he recognised in himself in the people he passed in the street, in the clients that walked through the doors of Carlyle: a mole on the side of a cheek, the sound of a voice, lips that formed a wide, generous smile, an infectious laugh, a left-handed man or woman. Not knowing where he came from sometimes enabled Martin to fabricate new and far more satisfying roots than the ones Frank and Irene had given him. At times his fictitious parents – an adoring mother, exquisite-looking with soft hands and a musical laugh, her husband, a charming diplomat with friends across the globe – almost eclipsed the more probable reality, one blighted by poverty and wretchedness.

TWENTY-TWO

Hammers had asked Martin to view a handsome maisonette taken on earlier that day in Powis Square. Oliver – who had been delegated to go with him – was in a vile mood and Martin was anything but pleased about being stuck in a car with him. He made no attempt to ask Martin sitting next to him in the passenger seat whether he minded him smoking but merely unwound his window and, mimicking Martin, leaned his elbow outside.

Martin's own mood was pensive. Last night he was

convinced someone had been following him. On his way home he had stopped off at Sainsbury's to buy some food and noticed a man standing near the entrance, with his right shoulder leaning against a wall. The man, tall and well-built, wearing a loose coat and with a hat pulled down over his face, wasn't looking at him, but Martin had an uncanny sense that he was being watched. When he came out of the store, twenty minutes later, the man was still there. He tried to rid himself of his paranoia, but as he made his way back to the car he noted that the man walked quickly over to a parked Rover and got into it. In his rear mirror he saw the car pull out and follow him to the exit. It might just have been coincidental, but instead of turning left into the Harrow Road, he took the long way home, weaving in and out of the back-streets, making sudden turns, until he was absolutely convinced he had lost his pursuer. It therefore came as a shock to find the Rover – apparently empty – parked outside his flat on arrival. For the rest of the evening he kept a watchful eye from the front window, certain now that his movements were being tracked. But it wasn't until after midnight that he saw the man again, leaning against the car bonnet smoking a cigarette. A few minutes later he flicked the stub into the road, got into the car and drove off. When he was sure the man wasn't coming back he switched off all the lights in the flat. His heart was jumping like a kid on a trampoline. All night he sat up in the dark, thinking.

Oliver had turned right into Portobello Road only to find his path blocked by an industrial refuse truck. Two men in blue-grey overalls were throwing boxes of rotten fruit and vegetables from the market stalls that lined the street into the back of the truck. Every so often the machine's iron teeth ground the contents together. Oliver impatiently sounded the horn.

One of the men threw him a withering look, then resumed working, his movements now elaborately slow. From the side of a fruit stall, his colleague dragged four bulging plastic bags, one of them leaking liquid like a snail's trail.

'Oh, come on,' he snapped, kneading the steering wheel with his hands. A queue of traffic, including a bus and a police car, had formed behind them. 'Can't the fool see he's holding everyone up.'

'Just give him a minute,' Martin said shortly. Oliver's tone annoyed him.

It took a lot more impatient hooting from Oliver before the refuse truck finally eased away from the road. Oliver found a gap and sailed magisterially past, ignoring the driver's angry gesticulations. 'Congenital morons!' he muttered, the odour of smouldering rubber on the road behind them.

'What's bugging you today?' Martin asked tersely.

'Having to put up with imbeciles like that. I'm not surprised they collect rubbish. It's about all their pig-brains can manage.'

One of these days his rash comments were going to land him in trouble. Martin knew that he had planned to take his producer girlfriend away to Devon for the weekend but that at the last minute she had pulled out because of work commitments. This wasn't the first time it had happened – they both worked long, unsociable hours which put additional strain on a relationship that seemed to be going nowhere. But Martin sensed that today the cause of his colleague's irritation stemmed from something else.

'Don't suppose you could lend me a few quid?' Oliver said after a pause, eyeing him shrewdly. 'Just enough to tide me over until tomorrow. Tracy's promised me a sub.'

'How much?' Martin still hadn't been paid back for the last twenty he had lent him.

'Fifteen should see me.' Resentfully, Martin handed over the notes. 'Good man. I tried asking Roger, but the sod's tighter than a Swiss bank. I'll pay you back before the end of the week.'

'Sure,' Martin smiled coldly. They both knew he would never see that money again. There was a silence. Oliver shifted in his seat as if he found the sudden hiccup in the conversation uncomfortable.

'I see you're wearing a new watch.' He glanced at the cheap Seiko on Martin's wrist. 'What happened to the old one?'

Martin looked sharply at him. 'Why do you ask?'

'No particular reason. I just noticed, that's all.'

They stopped at some traffic lights. Oliver took a pull at his smouldering cigarette then returned his hand to the gear stick. Martin sat stewing; had the remark about his watch really been an innocent one, or was something more sinister at play? If Oliver was behind this vendetta against him, he might have mentioned the watch in order to find out how he was handling the pressure. Martin threw his colleague a cautious glance, hoping to catch him in an unguarded moment, seeking confirmation of what he feared. But Oliver looked the same as he always did; bored and slightly contemptuous of the world around him. He did not look like a killer.

A wailing car alarm drew their attention to the other side of the road. They watched a bullish-looking man in mirrored shades that glinted against the sun, step out of a puce-red Lamborghini and gloat as a couple of leggy girls, half his age, sauntered by.

Oliver laughed cynically. 'Someone ought to tell him he's lost most of his hair.'

The man sat down at an empty table outside a café and Oliver's eyes followed him, coming to rest on a striking couple at a nearby table. 'Well, well,' he said incredulously, 'if it isn't old Uggers. Now there's a turn-up for the cards. Thought he'd slunk off back to Brussels. And if I'm not very much mistaken that's Francesca Dell'Andrea with him,' the foreign name rolled off his tongue with surprising fluency. 'I wonder when they became an item?' He whistled admiringly. 'Lucky fucking dog.'

Martin gazed blankly at the olive-skinned beauty talking to a waiter. 'Someone you know?' he asked casually.

'*That* vision of loveliness, believe it or not, is Eve's

predecessor. While it lasted, at least. Her relationship with Piers didn't endure for very long. Quite frankly,' he added mysteriously, 'it should never have happened in the first place.' At the mention of Eve's name Martin felt himself tense. 'Francesca's father owns half of Italy. I remember him throwing this amazing bash in Venice for her twenty-first. This was before she knew Piers, you understand. All the right people were invited. Charlie was one of the guests and when someone introduced him to Francesca the attraction was instant. I've never seen two people so mad for each other. It took him less than a week to persuade her to move in with him.

'They'd been together for about a year when Charlie asked her to marry him. Of course she said yes and they planned this fantastically elaborate wedding in Paris,' he chuckled. 'Charlie was unable to believe his luck that such a gorgeous creature had agreed to be his wife. We were all green with envy.'

He slipped the car into gear as the lights turned to green and Martin took a last curious look as they sped forward and the couple disappeared from view. Charlie. Charlie. The name buzzed away in his brain but he couldn't place it. 'Were you invited to the wedding?'

Oliver made a curious sucking sound with his lips. 'Unfortunately not,' his voice was laced with a touch of drama. 'The event was cancelled at the last minute. Charlie came home one day and found Piers and Francesca fucking their brains out over the kitchen sink.

'Charlie and Piers were at Eton together and great friends,' he said, warming to his story. 'In many ways they were quite similar; wealthy backgrounds, keen on sport and travel, an eye for making money, popular with the girls. They liked Charlie because he was self-deprecating, had this knack of making people laugh, putting them at ease. Piers – well, he didn't have to make an effort at all. You don't when you have his kind of looks.'

And money, Martin thought, with a touch of savagery.

'Then Francesca appeared on the scene, hanging on Charlie's every word, and I think Piers must have made up his mind to have her, come what may. That's the kind of person he is. Francesca was pregnant at the time – with Charlie's baby – so when he kicked her out she was devastated. I think she knew her mistake right away but at that point Charlie was too angry to see reason. What choice did she have? She couldn't very well go back to Italy, being a good Catholic girl – her father would have hit the roof – so she moved in with Piers. A week later she got rid of the baby.'

Oliver scratched his head. 'As friends go Piers is only loyal up to a point. What you've got to understand about him is that he's a control freak. He has to have things on his terms. With Francesca it wasn't a case of him wanting to split them up, more that he had to prove to himself he could have her.' He shrugged. 'I like Piers but get too close to him and you'll get your fingers burnt.'

'What happened to Charlie?'

'He went off the rails for a while, drinking heavily, dabbling in drugs – the serious kind. He was really cut up over what had happened, refused to see any of his friends. His parents got quite worried about him. The irony was that Francesca continued to beg him to take her back, but Charlie had made up his mind. Perhaps if she'd kept the baby he might have –' he sighed, 'well, who knows? Anyway, he eventually got his act together and took this job working for an American television company – by all accounts doing well out of it, which only makes what happened all the more tragic.' His voice trailed off rather wistfully as he flicked his cigarette stub out of the window.

'What do you mean?'

Oliver threw him a surprised glance. 'Oh, shit, I keep forgetting you didn't know him. Charlie was the Fitzherberts' son, the one who was killed.'

Martin was too shocked to speak. 'You *knew* him?' he said, after a stunned silence.

Another sheepish glance from Oliver. 'Quite well, actually. Mind you, we're talking years ago. Eve's the only one from the office who knows about the connection.'

Instantly, in his imagination, Martin was back at the Arundel Gardens maisonette. He could see the tall, lanky, good-looking youth scowling from within the silver frame, his signed cricket bat, the bag of prescribed drugs, the letter to his mother full of the suffering he had endured – obviously a reference to his doomed affair with Francesca.

Oliver extracted another cigarette from his packet which he lit and drew on heavily. 'Actually, I did see him one last time back in April – at a friend's stag party. Piers was also there although I don't think he realised Charlie had been invited – and vice-versa – or they probably wouldn't have come. Oh, they both put on a decent enough show for the groom, but you were aware of the tension between them. Anyway, we'd arranged to go paint-balling in this forest just outside London. Ever tried it?'

'Er, no.' Martin shook his head. He was still trying to get his head round the idea that Oliver and Charlie had been friends.

'It's quite a hoot. Except that Charlie took it far too seriously. In fact, by the way he was acting you'd have thought he was fighting a real war. In the middle of the game Piers got his gun jammed or something, but Charlie kept firing these yellow pellets, shot after shot at him like he wanted to kill him. Fortunately, we were all wearing visors or Piers might have lost an eye. I guess Charlie felt it was his due. There was certainly no love lost between him and Piers.'

Martin listened in a state of bewilderment.

'We went on to this Mexican bar. As you might imagine the margaritas were soon flowing and we all got pretty plastered. After my sixth, the evening started to get a little fuzzy, but I do recall one incident. Charlie was doing impressions of Desmond Lynam and Richie Benaud, giving Rory Bremner a run for his money – he always was good at voices. In the middle of all this, Piers

228

went to the loo and while he was gone his mobile rang – he'd left it on the table. For a laugh, Charlie decided to answer it in Piers's voice. It was a brilliant impersonation. You honestly couldn't tell them apart. There was Charlie keeping the charade up with whoever was on the other end for quite some time. He'd just hung up when Piers came back, wanting to know who he'd been talking to, only Charlie never got a chance to tell him because the stripper arrived and the evening got rapidly out of hand.'

He slowed down at a zebra crossing to let a pedestrian pass and glanced at Martin. 'You realise that's why the police started sniffing around that day. Somehow they'd found out about my connection with Charlie and thought I was mixed up in what happened. Oh, I don't mean they thought I might actually have killed him, only that I was holding back information – which incidentally isn't true. It seems that someone visited the Fitzherberts' place on the morning of the murder, but they don't know who. Your name came up in the conversation.'

Martin could feel blood pumping around his temples. 'What did they mention my name for?'

Oliver looked baffled. 'It was the oddest thing. They asked me if you smoked.' He grew pensive again. 'One of the first things Charlie and I ever did was share a smoke.'

He pulled the car up beside a cream stuccoed mansion in Powis Square. Black kids were playing football in a fenced-off recreation area. A traffic warden slapped a ticket on to the screen of a green Volvo, eyes watchful, as if fearing the driver might at any moment reappear and cause a scene. They both got out of the car, Oliver jangling a bunch of keys in his hand, Martin still deep in thought.

'Funny,' said Oliver, mounting the front steps. 'Mother of a friend of mine used to live in this house.'

Martin's head jerked round. The word *mother* reverberated in his brain. He went cold as a shocking thought dawned on him. As a close friend of Charlie's, Piers would undoubtedly have met both his parents, perhaps even knew them well. When Piers had found his wallet containing the photograph of Mrs Fitzherbert, and Martin had told him that she was his mother, Piers must have known he'd been lying all along!

TWENTY-THREE

The following day they all arrived for work tired and out of sorts. Oliver, who opened up the office, had a hangover the size of a football pitch and was nursing a headache. Roger's neck had come out in a rash, which, he claimed, was an allergic reaction caused by some prawns he had eaten. Even Hammers, who could usually be relied on to bring an air of jocularity into the office, seemed uncharacteristically withdrawn. Of Eve there was no sign.

On the phone Martin was listening to the complaints of a man who was fed up with the three Carlyle 'sold' signs in his road – which had been on display for two months. Martin's attention had wandered to the street outside, where a convertible forest-green Jaguar XK8 – his dream car – had drawn up outside the office. Lucky sod, he thought, gazing at the sleek, cigar-shaped lines with longing. Then he noticed who was inside. Eve, with a smile loaded with desire, reached across to the driver's side and gave Piers a kiss which lasted too long for comfort, then got out of the car.

'Can't you do something about it?' the man on the phone was saying. 'They're a real eyesore.'

'New toy?' Oliver enquired as Eve breezed into the office and put down her bag. She was wearing one of her little pastel suits and had fastened back her blonde hair with a green velvet clasp. Her face still held the remnants of sleep.

'Yes,' she cooed – a little smugly, Martin thought. 'Nice, isn't it?'

'When did he pick that up?'

'Yesterday. It drives like an absolute dream.'

Oliver sighed wistfully. 'Must have been worth waiting for.'

She looked at him, a little surprised. 'Oh, honestly, Ollie, you know Piers never waits for anything. It was one of those spur-of-the-moment decisions.'

Martin turned his head to get another look at the car but it had already disappeared.

'I don't care if the car has wings,' called Hammers, eyeing Eve sternly over the rim of his steel-framed glasses. 'It still got you here half an hour late.'

She threw him a charming smile. 'Sorry. Piers had to drop off something important for his father. It couldn't wait.'

'I dare say,' came the dry response, 'but I expect you to do it in your own time not mine.'

'Hammers is a bit grumpy today,' Martin later overheard her complaining to Oliver. 'Probably wishes he owned a car like that himself.'

Yes, Martin thought. Don't we all.

It had been a quiet morning and, with Hammers out meeting solicitors, Eve had spent the past hour on the phone trying to sort out her wedding arrangements. All of a sudden she hung up and glared at the receiver. 'I *wish* he wouldn't do things without checking with me first,' she said crossly. Oliver raised an enquiring eyebrow. 'Piers has invited bloody Harry Forbes to the wedding after I'd expressly asked him not to. He knows I can't bear that sexist pig.'

Martin recalled the loutish, thickset individual who had stopped to talk to Eve that night they had gone for a drink.

Oliver flicked a trailing blond lock from his brow. 'So what? Your guest-list's large enough to swallow even the likes of big Harry.' He leaned back in his chair and linked his hands behind his head. 'I wonder if I should get married?'

Oliver was the only one from Carlyle who had been sent an invitation, but none of the others were supposed to know this. Martin had only found out because during a moment alone in the office, he had been rummaging through the drawers of Oliver's desk looking for sellotape. And there it was, shoved carelessly back into its envelope with the top half sticking out.

> *Howard and Vivienne Scott*
> *are pleased to announce*
> *the forthcoming marriage*
> *of their daughter*
> *Evelyn Scott*
> *to*
> *the Honourable Piers Hunt.*
> *The service will be held –*

There wasn't time to read it all, but to have what he already knew, feared, spelt out for him in black and white, left a sickening ball of dismay in Martin's throat.

That evening he and Eve were the last ones in the office so it was left to them to make sure that everything was switched off and locked up. He had just opened the front door for her when she suddenly turned. 'Hang on,' she said, slipping past him back into the office, 'I've left something in the kitchen. Will you wait for me?'

It felt as if he had been doing that all his life and yet she seemed further away from him now than she had ever been. He watched her disappear downstairs, then shifted his gaze to her desk where she had left her bag. Without thinking, he walked over to it and slipped his hand inside. There was the usual eclectic jumble: make-up, pens, money, a Mars bar, a squashed box of cigarettes. An address book. And it was then that he had an inspiration. He picked it up, turned the pages quickly to H and scanned down the column: Herringbone, Hornby, Hatfield, Hunt. Ah. There it was. He made a mental note of the address and was hurriedly shoving the little book back inside the bag when he heard her footsteps on the stairs.

'Ready?' she said, walking towards him.

He rearranged his face and smiled. 'Ready,' he replied brightly. 'Don't forget your bag.'

It was almost ten by the time he got there. In the soft evening light, Piers's building, tucked away in an exclusive corner of Chelsea, looked deserted, and his car was neither in the drive nor anywhere in the road that he could see. The chances were that he had already gone out for the evening but as Martin didn't have anything better to do, he decided to sit it out for a while. It wasn't just idle curiosity – to see where his rival lived – which had brought him there, but a number of niggling questions festering in his mind, not least about Piers's latest acquisition. A coveted car like the XK8 cost about £60,000 with a six-month waiting-list. How had he managed to jump the queue? Martin wanted to get at the truth and there was only one way to do so.

He had been waiting for about half an hour when, as luck would have it, the Jaguar suddenly roared into sight and came to a stop almost directly opposite him on the other side of the road. Instead of pulling into the drive, Piers, emerging from the car alone, left it double-parked as if in a hurry and skipped smartly up the front steps, disappearing inside the building. From his viewpoint Martin, who had slithered down in his seat to avoid being detected, was unable to make out the number-plate, so he risked getting out of the car to take a closer look. Thirty seconds later he was safely back in the driver's seat and searching for his mobile.

'Hi, Kevin?'

'Who is it?' Suspicion.

'It's Martin.'

'Oh, Martin,' warmer now. 'How's it going, mate?'

'Aside from a chronic need for more money and a bit more time off work, life couldn't be rosier.'

Kevin laughed. 'You and us all, mate. What's up? I haven't heard from you since Christmas.'

'I know. It's me being slack.' He kept an eye out for Piers. 'Look, I need a favour – some information on a car, an XK8. Can you get it for me?'

'No sweat. I've a good mate who works for the Vehicle Registration Department. What's the number?' Martin told him. 'Give me a couple of days and I'll get back to you.'

He had just hung up when Piers re-emerged from the building. Martin thought there was an urgency about his movements. He seemed flustered, edgy, as if he were the recipient of bad news – or so it appeared. Certainly something had happened to make him lose his usual implacable composure. Intrigued, and acting on impulse, Martin switched on the ignition and pulled out into the road. But instead of heading home, he followed the Jaguar at a prudent distance. The car turned into the Old Brompton Road and headed east with some speed towards South Kensington. From there it carried on up through the wide, grey streets of Knightsbridge, mercifully clear, and had just passed Harrods when a woman, who hadn't been looking where she was going, suddenly stepped out in front of Martin, forcing him to slam on the breaks. The Jag was disappearing ahead of him, but he caught up with it and followed the car to the Marble Arch roundabout where it cut back on itself, sailing along Park Lane until it came to a stop outside a gaming club.

He tempered his speed as he glanced up at the casino's sign. Whatever he had been expecting it wasn't this. As Piers stepped out on to the street a uniformed man rushed over to the driver's side, doffing his hat in a gesture of recognition. Piers handed him the keys and quickly entered the club. Martin, denied any such privilege, spent ten frantic minutes driving around in circles until he eventually found a parking space.

Allowing no time to question his actions, he quickly made his way back to the club, determined not to lose sight of Piers. He could see the doorman holding open the

234

front door to a smartly dressed couple as he approached, and began to think that there might be something wrong with his plan. For a start he had never been inside a casino before and had absolutely no idea how they operated. He didn't have much money on him either and there was a good chance they wouldn't take plastic, especially for a new customer. About the only thing in his favour was that he was correctly attired. He glanced down at the suit he'd worn for work – a little crumpled but sufficiently conservative not to attract any unwanted attention.

'Can I help you, sir?' The doorman stood solidly between him and the entrance.

'Yes, er – Any chance of getting in?'

The doorman eyed him with scepticism. 'Are you a member?'

'No. Unfortunately not. Is that a problem?'

'I'm afraid only members and their guests are allowed into the club.'

'I see.' Martin felt for the five-pound note in his pocket, the only cash he had, and wondered if he dared risk a small bribe. 'I don't suppose an exception could be made –?' he tried, holding out the note so that there could be no doubt about his intentions. The doorman looked at it with contempt and Martin quickly put it away. Obviously not. Oh, well. It had been worth a try.

He was hovering on the pavement debating what to do next, when a taxi pulled up and out stepped the portly figure of a man. He was wearing bifocals and an ill-fitting suit, an unexpected two-inch gap of sockless ankle exposed below the trouser hem. Working on a hunch, Martin decided to approach him.

'I don't suppose you're a club member?' he asked.

The man, brandishing a fat cigar, looked at him shrewdly. 'Won't let you in, eh?'

'Afraid not. And I was really hoping to play.'

'Feeling lucky tonight, are you? I could use a bit of that. Last night I lost a bloody fortune on the tables. Still,' he said, his small brown eyes twinkling with the prospect of a more fortuitous evening ahead, 'always room for improvement, I like to think.' He popped the cigar in his mouth and patted Martin's shoulder. 'Come on,' he said decisively. 'You can be my guest. Maybe a little of that luck of yours will rub off on me.'

The doorman glared at Martin as they stepped into the building, 'What's your name, squire?' the man asked him in a loud whisper, handing his membership card to the girl behind the desk who swiped it on a machine. 'I'll need to sign you in.' One quick flourish in the guest book and they were through.

The plush and opulent room upstairs was decorated with chandeliers and a great deal of glitter. Around the gambling tables men in dinner-jackets sat on high chairs like Wimbledon umpires keeping a watchful eye over the proceedings. In spite of there being so many people the room exuded an atmosphere of quiet and calm almost like that found in a library. The vast majority of the customers were dressed for a long night in comfortable rather than formal clothes, and sat with their eyes fastened to the tables. The air was heavy with cigarette smoke.

Until now, Martin's only impression of the inside of a casino was what he had seen in films: an impossibly glamorous world, full of restrained passion and absurdly beautiful characters. But the customers around him were, he had to admit, a pretty unsavoury-looking bunch. Not wanting to appear conspicuous Martin suggested to his companion that they get a drink at the bar. But the man, eyeing the main area of the room where all the action seemed to be, evidently had other plans and suggested they meet up later.

Martin ordered himself a beer and nervously downed half of it. At any moment he expected to feel a hand on his shoulder and to be escorted from the premises for being there under false pretences. The bar gave him a clear view of the room and it was while he was searching for Piers that his eyes picked out his new friend at one of the roulette tables. He seemed to be enjoying himself although it was hard to tell if he was enjoying better luck. And it was then that he spotted Piers. He was at the far end of the table, facing in Martin's direction with a stack of oversized chips in front of him. Martin soon realised that he was worrying unnecessarily about being seen. It seemed to him that Piers only had eyes for the spinning roulette wheel.

'You look like you're new to this,' said a voice. Startled, Martin turned to find that a Chinese man had taken the stool next to him.

'Is it that obvious?' he asked ruefully.

'Only to me. But then I'm paid to be observant. I'm a journalist, covering a story about gambling. Cigarette?'

'No, thanks,' said Martin. 'So you're not a player yourself?'

'Good grief, no. Watching a little ball play pick a number all night long isn't my idea of fun.' He smiled with derision and clicked shut his lighter. 'The game is for losers. Believe me. Sit here long enough and you see it all happen.'

'But people must win otherwise they wouldn't bother to play in the first place.'

'Sure, but you'd be astonished how desperate they are to come back and spend it all again. The odds always favour the club but their greatest advantage is the punter's greed. They come with only one thing on their mind. Take him, for example,'

As he spoke he nodded towards the green baize roulette table where Piers was sitting, wreathed in smoke, but it was a moment before Martin realised that it was actually Piers he was talking about.

'I've been watching him and the signs are all there. He's been in four nights in a row. Turned up here about half an hour ago and ordered himself a meal. But when it arrived, he didn't touch a thing. Too keyed up. All he wanted to do was get to the tables.'

Fascinated, Martin's gaze fastened on Piers. His face

was deadpan but he was watching every move the croupier made with hawk-like intensity, his hands resting on a stack of coloured chips. The only sign of tension was his ceaseless smoking, sometimes taking no more than a couple of puffs from a cigarette before mashing it out and lighting another.

'He never plays for small stakes, always high. Seems to be on a running streak at the moment, I'd say he's up about fifty grand.' Martin's mouth dropped. 'That's about how much he lost last night. Now, if he was smart he'd quit while he's up but he won't because he's a fool. If I had to bet on anything tonight, it's that he carries on to the bitter end. Real gamblers like him need to lose.'

Fifty thousand pounds in one night? Martin was having trouble taking it in. Jesus *Christ*. Who in their right mind frittered away that much money? He knew Piers was well off, but this kind of spending was of a different order. It was more than foolhardy, it was sheer bloody folly.

The croupier at Piers's table called out 'New colour', then handed Piers a mountain of coloured chips. The table was covered in small towers of circular bits of plastic, each placed as a bet against any one of the thirty-seven numbers. It was hard to believe they were playing with real money – hundreds and thousands of pounds being risked against the turn of a ball. The staggering sums being squandered sickened Martin, but even so he found himself compelled to watch. A small part of him, the part that queued up for Lottery tickets and tuned in for the results on Saturday nights, understood the compulsion.

There was tension in the air. Martin could feel it. He forgot the time, where he was. Because suddenly Piers wasn't winning any more, and the intolerable strain he was under was beginning to show. Twice he asked for the croupier to be changed, irritated apparently with the speed at which the wheel was being spun. On another occasion he asked to speak to one of the inspectors – the suits in the high chairs whose job it was to keep everything running smoothly – and changed to another table. He still smoked incessantly but now he was making marks on a score card as the numbers on the table came up. It was as if he believed he saw a pattern and was betting on probabilities. But whatever system he was following, the magic touch of previous evenings was no longer there; he was in serious trouble.

Piers was staring at the chips in front of him being hoovered up by the croupier. The vitality seemed to have drained out of him, his tan rapidly fading. He looked like a man who had just lost everything and as he brought his hand up to light another cigarette, the silver lighter winking, Martin found he couldn't bear to watch any more. He shouldn't have come. He didn't belong in a place like this. At that moment Piers got up from his stool and turned towards the bar. Martin quickly turned his back, ducking his head down for fear of being seen. But when he looked up he saw Piers disappearing into the loo. He also noticed that Piers had left his cigarettes and lighter on the roulette table. On an impulse, he walked towards it, one eye on the door to the Gents, until he was close enough to see the lighter properly. He paused by the chair in which Piers had been sitting only for a split second but it was all the time he needed. The initials, engraved in silver, appeared to glare at him accusingly, C.F.H., and he knew chillingly, where he had seen the lighter before.

In the underwear drawer of Charlie Fitzherbert's bedroom.

With haste he returned to the bar, aware that at any moment Piers might return. He knew that he had to get out of the club – and quickly.

The journalist held out a fresh beer. 'I ordered you another drink,' he said amiably.

But Martin had seen enough. He declined politely, thanked the man for his time, then made his way towards the exit sign and slipped outside, the sound of metal coins

vomiting from a machine behind him. He left as anonymously as he had arrived, yet he felt contaminated by
what he had seen, unable to shake off the gaunt,
despairing look in Piers's eyes.

TWENTY-FOUR

Martin's heart was thumping so wildly as he made the
journey home, he thought it would burst. There was
something not quite real about what he had seen tonight.
He felt that at any moment he might be jolted awake, his
head in his folded arms, and discover it had been nothing
more than a dream.

Although it was very late, he found that he couldn't
stay in the flat. He felt stretched, pulled tight like a rope,
and decided the only solution was to go for a walk. God
knows, he needed some air. He tried not to think, but all
sorts of things – and in no particular order – began to
occur to him. For instance: the old lady who had caught
him coming out of the Fitzherberts' maisonette had
mentioned seeing another man arrive, who claimed he
was a negotiator, yet no one from the office had been
round that day and Carlyle had had sole agency. Could it
have been the murderer she had spoken to? At first he'd
suspected Oliver, believing him to have lied about his
cancelled appointment in order to cover himself, but after
their conversation in the car he had discarded that
theory. Then there was the night he had gone for a drink
with Eve. He recalled overhearing a conversation
between Piers's friend Harry and the gaunt man who
bore a close resemblance to an undertaker. At the time he
had assumed that Harry's reticence about the size of
Piers's inheritance was to do with his long-term friendship with him. Now he realised that this was not due to
loyalty, but out of fear. He could still remember the look

of glazed apprehension in the big man's eyes as he'd hugged his pint: *He's not what you think he is*, he'd said. *You spend years believing you know someone when really you know nothing about them at all.* Did he know something about Piers that no one else did? *I should never have got involved. Now it's too fucking late.* The words of a drunk man perhaps, but to Martin they had sounded worryingly heartfelt. Oh, God, he thought with a quickening dread, this was leading him to some dark and sinister place he wanted nothing to do with, but he pushed on regardless. He had the feeling that he was getting somewhere. Like a computer screen that had been unscrambled, all the black lines suddenly began to form shapes – shapes that he could read.

It was a hot, balmy night and above him, a full, creamy moon gleamed in the sky. The street was empty yet it seemed as if the city moved around him, whispering secrets. As he stepped out to avoid some dog excrement he thought he saw a man with a pulled-down hat and loose coat standing further up by the railings, but it must have been the moonlight playing tricks on him. He turned into another road, came to a set of traffic lights and, waiting for them to change, watched the steady stream of traffic whooshing past, red streamers of tail-lights trailing behind. Piers struck him as the restless and hungry sort, a man made vulnerable by his need to control, but dangerous too, like a time bomb waiting to explode. *Found them fucking their brains out over the kitchen sink.* Just how far would he go if pushed? He slowed his pace, his mind racing as urgent questions kept presenting themselves.

What you've got to understand about Piers is that he has to have things on his terms. Oliver's words. And Oliver knew him better than most. Suppose they'd had another argument? Suppose Charlie had done something to make Piers really angry – lose control? But why, then, did Piers have his lighter? Given the circumstances of their relationship Charlie would hardly have made him a gift of it. Was it possible – the thought crawled over Martin like a clammy, feverish sweat – that Piers had killed his friend to silence him?

Everything began to rush at him then; the press cutting of his infancy, Oliver's hands covered in black dye after being printed, his confession to Celia about his adoption, playing the piano at Arundel Gardens, the photograph of Mrs Fitzherbert – Martin stopped dead. Wait a minute. Wait a fucking minute. It was like a grain of sand that had been rolling round in the oyster-shell of his mind, growing bigger and bigger until he could see the pearl inside. Piers had said nothing about the photograph when he'd handed it back to him, even though he knew perfectly well that it was not of Martin's mother. Yesterday, when Martin had learned of Piers's friendship with Charlie, he had kept wondering why Piers would let an opportunity to humiliate him slip by. It was obvious now that his decision to keep quiet about the photo was a calculated move on Piers's part, ammunition to be stored up for future use against him. It came as a shock to Martin to find himself on the receiving end of so much black hate.

He turned south and headed down Scrubs Lane, blind to the lampless, murky gloom around him as he continued to speculate. There was still the question of Mr Ash's flat and his now recovered watch. If Piers had been responsible for planting it he must have known about his Sunday-morning vist there and that wasn't possible . . . And that's when it dawned on him that Oliver must have told him. Of course. Probably just slipped out, said as a bit of harmless fun (*I'll be able to dine out on this for a week*). The burglary at Mr Ash's flat must have been engineered as part of the set-up. Piers could have planted his watch there after he'd stolen it from his flat – along with the press cutting of his abandonment – to keep the police away from his own door. That still didn't explain how he'd accessed Mr Ash's security code. According to Eve, the doors and windows to the flat had been left undisturbed. So had someone at the office tipped him off? Eve perhaps? In a flash he recalled Piers lounging at his desk last November, the spilt glass of champagne, the particulars of Mr Ash's basement flat lying in front of him. In all the confusion of Piers's arrival Eve must have left them there by mistake. He remembered now that she was late for a viewing and that they had miraculously turned up in Piers's hand. *These what you're looking for?* He knew the alarm code because Martin – stupidly showing off his memory for numbers – had actually recited it.

A shiver of fear ran down his spine as he realised that Piers must have intended, all along, to make him the scapegoat. And he had made it so easy for him. All the petty insults and unavenged humiliations which he had endured now rose to the surface and tipped the balance of fear towards anger. Martin's thoughts boiled. Fuck him! Piers had been on the warpath for weeks now, letting off small explosions. It was time to lay a few land-mines of his own.

Burlington's Café was reached along a gravel-laid avenue through Chiswick Park. Martin had discovered it one day when a sudden shower interrupted his walk there and sent him scuttling for cover. Today, couples sat outside at wooden tables in the sunshine, prams and pushchairs parked within arm's reach. One sturdy-looking man carried his son on his shoulders and he was reminded of childhood walks with Frank. Just the two of them – man to man, as Frank was fond of saying – out into the flat countryside from where, on a clear day, the land and sky touched and you could see to the end of the world.

His thoughts were interrupted by Celia, sitting opposite him who, like Martin, was on her day off. 'What's absorbing you?'

'A century ago this whole area would have been green fields.' He sighed. 'It frustrates me to think of all our beautiful countryside being eaten up with yet more roads.'

She watched the kids playing. 'I'd love to own enough land so that from where I lived, I wouldn't be able to see a single main road or a car.

When he asked, referring to her recent ordeal, if she had heard any more from the police, she began to fiddle with his sunglasses which were lying on the table.

'No leads yet. They did call to go over my statement, but I really don't think they're all that hopeful of finding him.' She smiled at him. 'To be honest I just want to put it behind me. In the past I've let too many negative influences shape my life. It's time to move on.'

He guessed she was referring to Rory. 'I think you've been handling it incredibly well,' he said, taking her hand and gently squeezing it. 'It takes guts to bounce back so quickly from something so frightening.'

She blushed as if his praise meant a great deal to her. 'It's either that or making myself a prisoner in my own home. Besides – and don't ask me to explain why – I have a feeling he won't try it again.'

But for the shrill beeping of his mobile, Martin might have been tempted to press her for an explanation. The caller was his friend Kevin.

'Sorry I couldn't get back to you before, mate,' he said. 'It's been sodding bedlam here.'

'Any luck?' Martin asked eagerly.

'The car belongs to some geezer named Piers Hunt but until a week ago it was registered under the name of Steve McInerney. Paid for it in cash. That's all I've got. Any use to you?'

'Not sure.' Steve McInerney. He'd heard that name somewhere before. 'Thanks, Kevin. I owe you one.'

'You know there's a rumour going round about you and me,' Celia said after he'd hung up. She giggled, as if the idea rather appealed to her.

'I had heard.'

'Do you think they found out about us going away together?'

He shook his head. 'Hammers won't have said anything. He's pretty good like that. But I think our friend Ollie might be at the bottom of it.'

'Why?'

He looked at her, at the warm column of her neck caught in the sun, and tried to think of a way of avoiding the truth. 'I expect he got it from Piers – who may have heard it from Eve. He has it in his head that there's something going on between Eve and I –' if she only knew the half of it – 'all rubbish, of course, but I'm afraid your name was used as a decoy.'

'I see.' She seemed depressed suddenly. 'You do realise they're getting married in a matter of weeks?'

As if he could forget. It seemed as if every magazine he picked up these days had an article about the impending wedding. He couldn't get away from the damned thing.

'Will you be going?'

He gave a snort of derision. 'I'd rather choke,' he said carelessly.

She threw him a shrewd glance. '*Is* there something between you and Eve?'

'What do you mean?'

'That day in the kitchen when I found you together –'

Now it was Martin's turn to play with the sunglasses. 'I – er – I was just trying to comfort the poor girl. She was very distressed.'

Celia blew on her coffee, studying him with her enormous grey eyes. 'You're deluding yourself, Martin. It's glaringly obvious that you're in love with her.'

He averted his gaze, uncomfortable about having his feelings aired. 'I just want Eve to be happy.'

'Perhaps she's happy with Piers. Have you thought of that?'

He shook his head determinedly, thinking not only about the disturbing scene he'd witnessed in the casino, but of the other dark things he had pieced together about Piers. A kind of burning began in the pit of his stomach as he said, 'She'd be a bloody fool to go through with it.'

Celia's mouth formed a semblance of a smile but the

glow died in her eyes as she said, 'Then for your sake I just hope she comes to her senses in time.'

TWENTY-FIVE

For many, the weekend started at six o'clock on a Friday evening but this was not the case for the negotiators at Carlyle whose doors remained open until eight and who worked weekend shifts on a rota basis.

At five thirty Hammers went out on an appointment leaving Eve, Martin and Celia in the office. Celia took an incoming call. 'It's for you,' she said to Eve who was eating a Bounty bar.

Eve picked up. 'Hello? Oh, *hi*, darling. I hoped it might be you. What? You haven't! Front row?' she gave a squeal of delight. 'I thought it had been a sell-out ... God, yes, I'd love to. When for?'

'I'll be downstairs if you need me,' Martin curtly told Celia. He knew who Eve was speaking to and couldn't face hearing another sugary exchange.

The fax machine had run out of paper so he made a detour to the stationery cupboard to get fresh supplies. Back upstairs he found Eve reading something on his desk. When she realised he was there, she threw him a charming little smile.

'Martin,' she said in the voice she used when she wanted something, 'I need to beg a favour. Piers has managed to get tickets to see the premier of *Lord of the Dance* – tonight. Only I've got a viewing at seven forty-five and I can't get hold of the guy to cancel. I wouldn't normally ask, but I've been wanting to see this show for weeks.'

Piers. Always Piers. He was sick to death of hearing that name and the power it wielded. The man seemed to have some kind of Midas touch. Concerts, film premiers, meals at five-star restaurants. Enjoy it while it lasts, he thought angrily, because I'm going to get your boyfriend.

'I've checked your diary,' Eve said hurriedly, 'and you haven't got anything planned for tonight. You'd be doing me the most enormous favour.'

He had been about to say yes, but as he opened his mouth he caught Celia's eye. Whether it was the idea of Piers scoring yet another point, or his sudden irritation at Eve's assumption that he would do as he was asked, he wasn't sure, but something made him change his mind.

'Sorry, Eve,' he said firmly, 'but despite what the diary says I'm afraid I do have prior commitments.'

'I see.' She made little attempt to hide her displeasure. Her gaze slid over to Celia who was packing up her things, but instead of trying her luck with her she walked to the back of the office and slipped into the financial room – to call Piers back, no doubt, he thought dourly.

Celia waited for the door to close before she spoke.

'If you *weren't* doing anything tonight,' she said gently, 'you could always come and have some supper with me. I make a mean pasta.'

His eyes shifted from Celia to the closed door, then slowly back to Celia again. 'Pasta, you say?' And in spite of the way he was feeling, he grinned. 'What time do we eat?'

'How was Friday night?' Martin manoeuvred his Golf round three double-parked cars. Eve was sitting next to him in the passenger seat, scribbling notes in her Filofax. It was Monday afternoon and Hammers had asked him to accompany her to an important meeting with a surveyor on behalf of some German clients. She looked at him blankly. 'The show you saw?'

'We didn't go in the end,' her voice sounded flat and dull. She had seemed preoccupied all day – as if she had something on her mind.

He felt a pang of guilt. 'What happened? Your client keep you long?'

'Oh, no. I managed to get hold of him in the end and changed the appointment.'

'Then why didn't you go?'

She eyed him sharply. 'It was personal.'

An orderly row of pock-marked terraced houses greeted them, each front door painted a different colour. They found the right number and rang the bell before using the key. Inside, a Persian cat greeted them. Eve had been warned in advance not to let it out, as friends would be calling later to collect it. 'Go on,' she snapped, shooing the animal away. 'Scat.'

The interior was unexpected. A far cry from the Laura Ashley-style house Martin was trying to sell six doors along. The first thing to hit him was the colour of the walls; a vivid pink with lime-green ceilings. It was full of time-warped ephemera, ranging from 1950s to the 1970s: the leopard print curtains, a row of Barbie dolls, the red sofa reminiscent of a diner booth, lurid gold cherubs on the wall.

'She's an artist,' Eve explained, 'and by her own admission a compulsive hoarder. Says she can't go out of the house without bringing something back.'

Martin raised an eyebrow. 'I can see that. What does this woman eat – cocaine?'

The surveyor was late. Eve complained of hunger and found a tin of biscuits in the overcrowded kitchen. The room was a mess, dirty dishes and wineglasses stacked carelessly to one side as if the owners had left in a hurry. Eve extracted two biscuits and held out the tin to Martin who was leaning against the fridge, but he declined. A child's set of building blocks added to the clutter on the wooden floor. Eve bent to pick up a brick and weighed it thoughtfully in her hand.

'Do you want to talk about it?' he finally asked.

She gave a little stir. 'I was just thinking about how quickly life can change.'

He frowned. 'In general or specifically?'

She seemed not to hear him. 'Did you know I was born in Partridge Manor?'

'I didn't, no.'

'I always saw it as a place that would be there for me no matter what. A bit like the way I viewed my father as a child.' She put the building brick back in the box and began opening doors until she found what she was looking for: a drinks cabinet. He watched her take a bottle of whisky out of a cupboard and splash some into two glasses, wondering where this was leading. Then she opened the window and lit a cigarette. 'I don't know about you,' she sighed, handing him a glass, 'but I need this.' Her smile was bright but he wasn't fooled by it.

'What's upset you?'

She blew smoke towards the ceiling. 'It's OK. I'm not going to fall apart. It's just the uncertainty, the not knowing what's going to happen that's getting to me.'

He was completely baffled. 'What uncertainty?'

'Daddy's contract – the one I told you about – he's lost out to another firm. One of his competitors came through with a better quote.'

Martin's mind flashed back to the incident he'd witnessed in Howard's study. Could there be any connection between that and Piers's recent heavy gambling? 'Poor Daddy.' Her voice wobbled. 'What's going to happen to him?'

He offered a comforting arm. 'There'll be other jobs – other contracts.'

She raised her eyes to him in despair. 'But you don't understand. *Everything* depended on this one deal. There's a strong possibility that we might lose the house.' Surely not, he thought. 'His company has been experiencing difficulties for months. Things got so bad Daddy had to take out a mortgage on the manor to help keep the business afloat. Then the Middle East contract came up and Daddy threw himself into the project, investing a great deal of time and money. But now –' she mashed her cigarette out in the ashtray, '– if he doesn't find something else, this could mean our ruin.'

He could hardly believe his ears. 'Things can't have got that serious.'

She looked at him hard. 'Martin, it's about as serious as it can get.'

They drifted back into the living room and surveyed the unashamedly gaudy decor. The cat had followed them in, its tail a bushy question mark as the animal rubbed itself sensuously against Eve's leg. She picked it up by the scruff of its neck and shut it in the kitchen. To take her mind off her father, Martin told her about the film he had been to see with Celia. They had decided to go after their coffee at Burlington's, but it was a very bad film and they had left giggling halfway through.

He felt Eve's scrutiny as he fell silent. 'You and Celia,' she said, draining her glass, 'I suppose you've slept with her?' When he didn't answer, she added, 'Or isn't that any of my business?'

'You're right. It isn't. But since you ask, we've become quite close.'

'You don't find her a bit – I don't know, dull?'

'Not at all. She's fun to be with.'

'Meaning that I'm not?'

He gave her a sideways glance. Last Friday all she could talk about was Piers. Why the interest in him all of a sudden?

'You know what I think of you,' he said after a moment had passed.

'Yes.' A little shamefaced she looked down at her hands. 'I like Celia, it's just that I used to think you and I were good friends too. Lately, I've noticed you pulling away from me. Which is a pity because I miss what we had.' She raised her eyes. 'Have I done something?'

It took Martin a moment to react to this declaration. It was a new situation for him: Eve making conciliatory overtones. Just now she had sounded so sincere, gazing at him so steadfastly, but a cautionary voice reminded him that Eve had often raised his hopes before and dashed them just as quickly.

'Eve, you've made your choice and we both have to live by it.'

'Does that mean we can't still be friends?' She touched

him, the merest brush of her fingertips against his hand. It was like a mild electric shock.

He swallowed. 'I'm handling it the only way I know how.'

She was near enough for him to count her freckles. 'It doesn't have to be like that.' Something in her voice put him on alert. 'I mean,' she murmured, closing in on him, 'that there is a way for us to be together – here. Now.'

She brought a hand up to the nape of his neck, the other cupped his face. Adrenalin ran through his veins, he felt light-headed, giddy.

'Eve,' he said faintly, confused by the sudden turn of events. 'Jesus. What are you doing?'

'What you've always wanted me to do. This,' she purred, touching her lips to his, 'and this,' she nibbled his ear. 'I'm taking advantage of you, Martin.'

He felt all the strength ebbing from his body but his mind hung on to the fact that the surveyor might arrive at any moment. 'Christ, Eve, we can't.' His prick was already hard, straining to be liberated, as she tugged at his zip.

Green eyes gazed at him boldly, her lips like strawberries, and she whispered, 'Where's your sense of adventure?'

His control snapped. He had dreamed about this moment for so long that he let himself forget about the imminent arrival of the surveyor. Nothing was going to stop him from claiming her.

He was already groping for the clasp of her bra, casting aside her skirt as they fell to the tigerskin rug, a mounting friction of heat and flesh, their limbs intertwined in a strange ritual, like a dance. The walls vibrated as a heavy goods vehicle drove past outside, but all he could hear were their gasps, the quiet clicking of their lips as he slid his tongue into her mouth, his hands flying wildly – frantically – all over her body as if he didn't know which bit of her to touch first.

He was on his back now, Eve straddling him. He could feel her soft mouth tracing the indent of his sternum, following the line down to the dark mound of hair between his legs, his erection rampant and angry, ready to explode as her hands dug into his buttocks for leverage. She began to lick him with her tongue, teasingly. I'm in heaven, he thought, there's no place to go after this, and groaned at the delicious frustration of it all, thrusting his pelvis upwards at an imaginary womb – wanting to be inside her – as the light friction of her tongue hardened, increased more and more until finally she took his engorged cock in her mouth.

'Shall I go on?' she asked huskily after a few minutes.

'God, Eve,' he muttered, stroking her hair which had made a blonde fan across his belly. 'Stop now and I'll die.'

She took him in her mouth again, skilfully playing with her lips and tongue, and he knew that if he could keep on feeling this exquisite pleasure, he would never again know a moment of unhappiness. He was on the edge of an orgasm when there was a ringing in his ear – thin and high-pitched. Eve broke away. 'Shit.'

'What –?'

'My mobile.'

He cursed the bloody fool who had invented portable phones. 'Leave it,' he croaked, sensing her withdrawing.

'I can't. It might be Hammers.'

For a few moments he lay there catching his breath while she spoke into the machine. When it became obvious that she wasn't going to finish the call in a hurry, Martin stood up and fastened his trousers. The magic they'd shared a moment ago had evaporated.

'That was the surveyor,' she said, pressing the off-button on her phone. 'He's on his way over now.'

He inhaled frustration. 'Left it a bit bloody late, hasn't he?'

'Says he got held up in traffic. Look, why don't you get off? I'm sure I can handle him on my own.'

He thought wildly. 'Later then. We could meet up at your place.'

'Not tonight.'

'But this is important –' He stopped himself. 'Oh.' He stiffened. 'I see.'

'Now, don't go jumping to conclusions. It's not what you think. His parents had arranged this dinner weeks ago. I can't very well cancel at this late hour. I'm expected there in forty-five minutes.'

'But you didn't think to mention it twenty minutes ago. What did you bloody well expect – a quick appetiser with me then straight on for the main course with Piers? *Jesus*, Eve. You can't play games with me like that,' he said furiously. 'I'm not a toy you can pick up and put down on a whim.'

As he scowled at her he told himself he was a fool for still being here, yet all the time he kept thinking how sensational she looked. Even now, despite the turmoil of anger in his gut, he found her irresistible.

'Don't,' she begged, jumping on his indecision. 'I don't want you to leave like this.'

'You should have thought about that before.' He had already gathered together his things, propelled by the need to escape from this crazy house and his unmanageable feelings. He grabbed his jacket from a chair and flung it over one shoulder.

'Enjoy your dinner,' was his parting shot. Angrily, he slammed the front door behind him.

TWENTY-SIX

Early the following evening it rained. Suddenly there was a chill in the breeze and light from the sky seemed literally to drain away with the rainwater. People hurrying home from work regarded the menacing clouds with indignation. Within minutes they had scattered like flustered pigeons, flying towards shop awnings as the explosive downpour drenched them. Martin, on his way back from Faron Sutaria where he had dropped off some keys, skipped hurriedly through the small pools of rain, using his jacket as a makeshift umbrella.

'This is soaked!' He shouldered off his coat and held up the offensive article to Celia at her desk. The others were all out on appointments.

She laughed. 'You look as if you've just swum the English channel. Do you still insist on public transport tonight?'

'No,' he grinned ruefully, wiping rain from his face. 'We're definitely taking the car.' Celia had been given two front stalls tickets to a West End show by an actress friend of hers who was in it, and had invited him to join her. 'I'll just take this downstairs to dry. Do you fancy one of your herbal teas?'

She winked at him. 'Now there's an offer a girl can't refuse.'

While he was waiting for the kettle to boil – his jacket hanging over a kitchen chair – he picked up the newspaper one of the others had left and skimmed through it. In his haste to get to the sports page he very nearly missed the article tucked away in the business section. But, like fate, his eye was caught by one small headline.

MCINERNEY'S MIDAS TOUCH DOES IT AGAIN
Steve McInerney, 49, one of America's leading architects, has secured a substantial contract to design a revolutionary new hotel in the Middle East. He founded his own firm in 1977 and designs high-quality buildings around the world. McInerney owns 75% of McInerney Rock Holdings, his parent company, which is worth more than $80m, and he has a stake in GFI, the British property group, worth $21m. Howard Scott, a partner with Spencer, Bell, Scott Associates, who lost out on the planned hotel in the city of Muscat, was not available for comment.

It was the photograph of Steve McInerney that finally made the name click. So that was where he had first heard the name. He has read about the millionaire's lavish wedding at Lambton Place Health Club. More interestingly, he remembered that one of the guests had been Piers Hunt. The jigsaw was finally coming together; he had found the connection.

He heard the door to the office upstairs open briefly then close again. The indistinct tones of a man carried down to the basement. As he poured boiling water into two cups – English breakfast for him, strawberry and vanilla for Celia – he could hear her clear, high decibels saying, 'I'm afraid she's not in right now.'

Somebody obviously looking for Eve, Martin thought as he ventured back upstairs careful not to spill the tea. She had left with a client at tea-time, some two hours ago, and had yet to return. He was beginning to think she was avoiding him.

At the top of the stairs, Martin stopped and drew in a sharp intake of breath. Piers Hunt, looking every bit a man in control, was leaning across Celia's desk at the back of the office, his hands spread apart like tent pegs to support his weight. His appearance, as always, was one of studied casualness: double-breasted blazer, Gucci jeans, a Jermyn Street shirt with three buttons undone at the neck. Only a smattering of rain glimmered against the black mass of his hair.

'As I say, you're welcome to wait for her. Or I can take a message.' He could tell by the tone of her voice that Celia wasn't enjoying Piers moving beyond the boundaries of professional acquaintance.

He walked towards them, a kind of panic spreading through his body, pressing against the inside wall of his skin, and said with as much casualness as he could muster, 'Looking for Eve?'

Piers regarded him with cordial distaste. 'Ah, Martin, I thought you'd be prowling about somewhere. Where is she? I should have picked her up at six – we have a meeting with the vicar.'

'Why don't I get her to meet you somewhere – save you

having to hang around,' Martin suggested, wanting him out of the office – the sooner the better.

Piers looked at Celia. 'No. I rather think I'll wait here.'

A brown leather sports bag lay on the floor by her desk, suggesting that Piers had come straight from the gym. He took a seat and began to flick restlessly through property magazines. From time to time he turned his attention to the window and gazed through the rainswept glass. Celia caught Martin's eye and, when she was certain they weren't being observed, gave a complicitous shrug.

Piers seemed determined to sit it out. Eventually, Martin started to make some follow-up calls, but he found it impossible to concentrate and, as the minutes ticked by and there was still no sign of Eve, he noticed Piers become increasingly fidgety. Bored with waiting and with the limited choice of reading material, Piers cast the magazines aside and began to pace up and down the office like a caged panther. Eventually he stopped at Celia's desk and, perching a muscular buttock on one corner, began to pick up objects, inspecting them with the careful interest of an archaeologist. 'Busy?' he said, conversationally.

She looked at the framed photograph in his hands. 'I am, rather.'

'Yours?' The picture was of a two-year-old girl.

'No,' she said shortly. 'My cousin's.'

He ran a manicured thumb over the glass surface. 'Pretty creature. She looks like a little doll. Girls that age are quite flawless, don't you think?'

Celia's response was cagey. For once Piers's way with the opposite sex seemed to be failing him. She answered all his questions in monosyllables, making it clear that she found his presence unwelcome. Martin, watching the exchange, could have hugged her. Her rejection of Piers felt like a personal triumph and for a moment the threat the man posed vanished from his mind altogether. But it wasn't a feeling which lasted for long.

'Tell me,' Piers said to Celia, casually folding his

powerful arms, 'is it all work or do you get to spend time with the boyfriend?'

She raised her large grey eyes. They were cool. 'I don't think that's any of your business.'

Piers laughed and said to Martin, 'I think I've just hit a nerve.'

'Cut it out, Piers. Can't you see she's trying to work?' It was an effort to keep his voice down but he was conscious that they were in an office – at any moment someone could walk through the door.

Piers grinned, obviously enjoying the tension he was creating. 'What's the matter, Martin? Am I treading on your turf?' Then he moved his attention back to Celia. Before she realised what he was doing, he had put a hand to one side of her hair and pushed it aside so that he could see her face better. Almost sensuously, he ran a finger along the line of her damaged cheek.

'That's quite a scar,' he said. 'I expect men find it rather a turn-on in a kinky sort of way.'

Celia had gone white and she was staring at his hand – the hand he had just touched her with – in utter horror.

Martin stood up abruptly. 'That's it,' he snapped at Piers. 'Get out!'

Piers turned on him. 'As if I'm going to take orders from you.'

'She doesn't have to put up with this crap,' Martin said angrily, forgetting himself suddenly. 'Get out before I do something I regret.'

Piers winked at Celia. 'I don't think our friend here's very happy with me.'

Something about the way Piers spoke told Martin that it was too late to back down now. He could feel the words pushing against the back of his throat, clamouring to be spoken. 'I know all about your involvement with Steve McInerney. He paid you a back-hander to pass on files belonging to Howard Scott, information which enabled him to secure the building contract in the Middle East. I know about the car too.'

'That's quite a fanciful mind you have, but then I'm

forgetting how often your *inventiveness* comes into play.' Piers's voice was saturated with scorn. 'You'd just love to be able to pin something on me. Anything that would make this – crush you have for Eve easier to bear. But all this nonsense you've drummed up about the XK8 is about as pathetic as the tale you spun about your father. Can't bear it, can you, to see others prospering? You're nothing more than a social climbing parasite with small-minded aspirations.'

Martin's stomach tightened. 'I never mentioned anything about the car being an XK8.' A flicker of doubt crossed Piers's face. Martin pushed home his advantage. 'What you did was illegal. You could be put away.'

'Martin,' Celia cautioned nervously.

'Oh, don't stop him,' Piers grinned, quickly recovering his composure. 'This is getting interesting.'

But Celia's voice had had a sobering effect on Martin's temper. Who knew where his rash comments might lead? He couldn't actually prove anything – not without incriminating himself at the same time. 'Forget it,' he said, backing down.

'Come on, Martin, tell me what it is you think you know.'

'I was there in Howard's study, Piers,' he said, dimly aware of the rain beating down outside. 'I saw what you accessed.'

Piers shrugged. 'You're clutching at straws.'

'Am I? Then tell me, how do you think your future father-in-law would feel if he knew you had made a copy of his proposal and handed confidential information over to McInerney, his direct competitor?'

'Howard Scott wouldn't know a business proposition if it was shoved up his backside. The man's a jerk.'

Martin was taken aback by the vicious malice in Pier's voice – he'd always thought the two men had got on so well.

'And Eve? What about her? Did you stop for one minute to consider her feelings when you signed away her

258

family home, her father's career? *Jesus*, don't tell me you did it for a lousy car? Even you wouldn't stoop that low.'

Piers's jaw tightened. 'Eve will never have to worry about money again,' he said in a measured voice. 'She has me to take care of her now.'

'Oh, you've made quite sure of that. But you're not going to get away with it.'

Piers grinned. There wasn't a trace of culpability on his face. 'I don't think so,' he said insultingly. 'Frankly, Martin, you haven't got the balls.'

What followed next happened in a whirl. He heard a noise and, as he span round to identify the source, fearing it might be a customer, everything else around him faded into a grey fog. For there, in the doorway, stood Eve, still as a statue, gazing at Piers, her eyes the startling green of an angry cat ready to claw. Water dripped from her soaked dress and a puddle had collected around her shoes. How long she had been there listening to them arguing, Martin couldn't be sure, but from the look on her face it was plain that she had heard enough.

Piers walked towards her. 'What kept you?' he said with studied lightness. 'You're late.'

'Oh, I think I arrived just in time.' If looks could kill, thought Martin, a hushed spectator in a spellbinding play.

'Now, hang on a minute.'

'Tell me,' she interjected, her mouth drawn tight, her eyes accusing. 'Do you speak about me behind my back in the same complimentary way as you speak about my father, or is it just him you despise?'

'You misunderstood –'

'Spare me the lies, Piers. I might have forgiven you for making a fool of me, but I could kill you for what you've done to my father. You've completely destroyed his career.'

'Eve.' A hint of desperation leaked into Piers's voice for the first time, 'The man's *lying*.'

She looked at Martin and he wondered if she was thinking about last night and what so nearly happened.

'He's not the one with his hand in the till.' Piers flinched as she brought her face back to him. 'And the fact that you're not even prepared to admit it to my face only makes me despise you more.'

With the cool precision of a surgeon, she removed the diamond-studded ring from her engagement finger.

'What the hell do you think you're doing?' Piers's voice was dangerously soft as she set the ring down on a nearby desk

'It's over, Piers. I can't marry a liar, let alone a cheat. I'll pack what things you've left at my place and have them sent over in the morning.'

'You'll do no such bloody thing. You and I are going to have this thing out – somewhere,' he glared across the room at Martin, his eyes blue bullets, 'with a little privacy.'

The engagement ring winked extravagantly under the office lights. Piers picked it up and grabbed her hand as if he intended to haul her out of the office, but Eve began to struggle. 'I'm not going with you,' she hissed. 'Piers, don't! You're hurting me.'

Martin stepped forward and caught hold of his sleeve. 'Let her go.'

Piers threw him a cautionary look. 'Keep the hell out of this.'

But Martin yanked more firmly. 'I said take your hands *off* her!'

Piers fractionally relaxed his grip on Eve but in doing so – Martin was momentarily distracted by her little cry as she whacked her freed hand against the door – the man whirled round, swinging his arm hard, and his fist connected with Martin's cheekbone. Something crashed into Martin from the side – he had fallen against a desk. He reeled back more surprised than hurt, and Piers lunged at him again, this time to grab him by the collar. He gasped – Celia's shocked, white face looming into his vision – as Piers slammed him against the wall.

'Listen, you little shit. I've had just about all I'm going to take from you,' he snarled. 'You've already been warned not to interfere. One more step and it won't just be the police you'll have to worry about.' Martin could feel himself choking as Piers twisted his shirt collar in his hands. 'I could bury you so fucking deep in dirt they'd have you locked away for the next ten years. So don't threaten me.'

'It *was* you,' Martin gasped, finding it difficult to speak. 'You set me up.' There was a weird roaring noise in his head and he began to grow dizzy from the lack of oxygen to his brain.

'Piers,' Eve warned, her voice curiously far away.

The hands tightened as Piers brought his face closer. The back of his eyeballs felt ready to burst but he let his body go limp and stared unblinkingly at Piers.

'Stop it!' Celia screamed, throwing herself at Piers. 'Stop it now! Can't you see you're choking him to death.'

'It's no more than he deserves,' Piers muttered, but very gradually Martin felt the grip loosen around his neck.

Piers ran a hand through his hair and straightened his jacket. Then he lit a cigarette, clicking shut the lid of Charlie's silver lighter with a flick of his hand. He cast one brief glance at Eve who stood frozen between the two men, then, with a terrible composure, he brushed past her through the office door and out into the rain.

'You're bleeding,' Celia said to Martin, thunder rumbling outside. 'Let me get you something for it.'

He touched the side of his face, and briefly examined the traces of blood on his index finger. But it was Eve who held his attention. She hadn't flinched as Piers closed the door behind him. Now she looked small and frightened suddenly. He wanted to reach out and fold her into his arms. Then she dropped her bag and he didn't get a chance to think about anything because, with a little cry which sounded like a wounded cat, she flew past a startled Celia into his arms.

'Take me away,' she begged, sobbing against his chest as blood trickled down his forehead. 'Please, Martin, take me somewhere where I'll never have to see him again.'

TWENTY-SEVEN

His affair with Eve began that evening and they spent their first night together at her place. So intent was she on putting distance between Piers and herself that she insisted he take her away somewhere immediately. For Martin, who had begun to despair of ever having her, the prospect of the two of them spending the weekend together was irresistible and he booked them on a flight leaving for Italy the following morning. Very early he dragged himself from her warm, sleepy kisses, knowing he wouldn't be gone for long, and drove over to his flat to pack some things: he left Eve soaking in the bath with a promise to have a taxi waiting on his return.

His flat greeted him with its usual chaos but today he just ignored it. Grabbing a suitcase from the top of his wardrobe he hastily walked from room to room collecting items from cupboards and drawers: lightweight clothing, swimming trunks, washing things, passport, his driver's licence, and threw them roughly into the case. There was a new John Grisham novel next to his bed. His hand flickered over the cover and for a moment he thought about taking it. But with Eve around, he doubted he'd be doing any reading.

Having done his packing so quickly and feeling ravenous, he went into the kitchen and fixed himself a bowl of cereal and some strong black coffee. It was as he was lowering himself into a chair in the sitting room to watch breakfast TV that something in the corner of the room, next to a small, cluttered lamp table, caught his eye. He knew then with a horrible sense of foreboding that Piers *had* been in his flat on the day of the bird incident. He had also been back for a second visit – some time last night presumably – looking for revenge. He knew this because of what was sitting on the table.

Mr Ash's missing saxophone.

He sat very still, trying not to panic. He was waiting for the frantic beating of his heart to slow down, for the tension exploding in his head to ease up. Only it didn't. It just got worse. His eyes travelled back to where Mr Ash's saxophone lay. In a matter of seconds it seemed to have grown in size. Its very presence so dominated the room that he couldn't tear his gaze away from it.

Kneading his brow with his fingers, conscious of the early signs of a headache beginning to set in, he tried to figure out a plan. He couldn't very well leave the saxophone where it was. He would have to ditch it. Easy enough to do. Find a half-empty skip in some gloomy, residential street on the other side of London, and casually drop it in. Most people would still be in bed so the likelihood of someone seeing him was slim. But could he really bring himself to throw away such a valuable and coveted instrument? Once used by the great John Coltrane? He realised that he didn't have any choice. Holding on to it was too risky. He picked up the phone and dialled Eve's number to tell her he would be a little later than planned, but the line was engaged.

He was standing by the window in the front room with his coffee cup in his hand when he saw a car coming down the empty road, but growing larger by the moment. He lowered his cup on to a nearby table without taking his eyes off the vehicle, as it slowed down and finally came to a halt in the road directly below him. 'Oh, Jesus,' he murmured, as three plain-clothed officers stepped out of the police car. His gaze flew to Mr Ash's saxophone. He heard the slamming of car doors and watched as the men quickly made their way to the front door – of *his* building, his heart hammering inside his ribcage like a tiny pneumatic drill. So that was why Piers had done it. He must have been waiting for him to come home and then tipped off the police. The doorbell rang. He froze. If I let them in now, he thought, I'm done for. They'll lock me away and never let me out again. It was too late to do anything about the saxophone but he couldn't let them find him there. Whatever happened, he *had* to make that plane to Italy. He needed distance, space, time to think through this bloody mess.

The doorbell rang again, prolonged and more insistent this time. He let it ring. Mind racing, he bolted into the hall and snatched up his house keys, his mobile – which he'd had the foresight to recharge – then rushed back to his viewpoint at the front window. Warily, cautiously, he glanced down in time to see one of the officers back off from the house, his neck craning up towards Martin's window. In a wild, panicky reflex, he ducked back down. He would just wait for them to go. They weren't going to stay out there all day. They must have many other arrests to make.

Then he heard another bell shrilling through the house, only this time it was coming from Mrs Wingate's flat. She would let them in, he was quite sure of it. Seized by fresh panic, he realised he had to get out – and quickly. His suitcase, with everything he needed inside, was close at hand. Shoving his mobile into a pocket, he grabbed the case then very gently eased open the door to his flat. He could hear voices downstairs on the ground floor, Mrs Wingate's rising above the others. 'The times vary but he doesn't normally leave for another hour. What's all this about, anyway? It's very early to be calling round.'

The door to Mrs Wingate's flat had been left slightly ajar. A radio was playing inside. He tiptoed over to the landing window, listening carefully for any movement on the stairs, and eased open the lower sash. Quiet as a cat, he slipped his suitcase through the gap and stepped out on to the wrought-iron fire escape. Confident that he couldn't be seen, he none the less checked to see that the rear alleyway was empty. Very gently, he closed the window behind him and, suitcase in hand, stole down the steps and across the back garden, vaulting the small wall beyond. To his right the alleyway eventually came to a dead end, but a few feet away to his left was an iron gate. He grappled for the keys in his back pocket. One of them matched the gate's lock – he hoped. There had never been an occasion to use it before but he slipped it into the lock and, to his intense relief, the gate opened. Freedom. He felt like a prisoner who had just escaped from a ten-year prison sentence. He was out. Thanking God for giving him the sense to park his car at the back of the building, he made his way to it quickly and sped off towards central London.

They flew to Pisa and drove on to Lerici in a hired car without a thought for the consequences they would have to face on their return. Martin – who paid for it all on his Visa card – discovered that the bank which issued the card had inexplicably raised his credit limit just days before their departure. His small victory over Piers and the availability of so much money made him reckless and he set about impressing Eve with expensive gifts. The first afternoon he spent six hundred pounds on a tiny pair of antique earrings that had caught her eye. The gesture was made carelessly, as if he were used to spending large amounts of money, but there was also a desire to prove to her that Piers wasn't the only one who could cater to her extravagant lifestyle.

Ever present in the back of his mind was the serious trouble he was in. The police would undoubtedly arrest him on his return to the UK and that would lead to them charging him with Charlie's murder. But fuck it. He had half a mind not to go back at all. Out here, his world had shrunk to their hotel room, the beach, the Mediterranean sun and the azure sea. They could do it – the two of them – build a new life for themselves in Italy. But would Eve give up her life in England for him? It was a desperate solution, yet it felt as if the only reality was the intensity of his relationship with her.

'Kevin. It's Martin.'

'Mate, the line's fucking awful. Where are you calling from?'

'Italy. Look, I need your help.' He kept his eye on the bathroom door where Eve was having a shower. 'I don't have much time. Kevin, it's really important that I talk to your boss.'

'How do you mean?'

'I need to speak to someone in the know. Someone with the right sort of contacts. I'm up to my neck in trouble.'

'What did you do?' Kevin's voice sounded alert suddenly.

'I'm being set up for a murder I didn't commit and I know who it is but the police can't help me, and I've no real proof and –'

'– and you'd like me to arrange a meeting?' Kevin interrupted.

Martin inhaled deeply, like someone surfacing for air. 'Yes.'

'Sorry, mate, but it doesn't work like that.'

'I'm desperate, Kevin. You've got to help me. I've no one else to turn to.'

He could hear Kevin lighting a cigarette, weighing up his request. 'Look,' he pressed, 'I just want to talk to the man. There isn't much time left and he's my only hope. I can't do this alone.'

Keith exhaled. 'Let me put it to him and see what kind of reaction I get. He's a very busy bloke and funny about who he deals with, but I'll see what I can do. Fair enough?'

Martin clasped the receiver, flooded by a wave of relief. Thank God. 'That's all I ask,' he said gratefully.

'I'll be in touch when I have some news.'

'Do that. I'll be back in London late Monday night. But don't try and get me at home. Call me on the mobile – any time. Oh, and Kevin –'

'What?'

'Thanks. I really appreciate this.'

'No promises, mate.'

*

Eve wore the earrings that night as they drank French champagne from the balcony of their hotel room – two bottles of the stuff. She was still wearing them – but nothing else – when they later went for a swim and ended up fucking in the shallow end of the pool. He had been opposed to the idea – not the fucking, which had gone on for almost an hour and with so much intensity they almost made electricity – but her decision to streak from their room to the pool. 'Don't be such a prude,' she'd scoffed drunkenly at his insistence on bringing a towel. 'Everyone's gone to bed. Besides, we're in Italy. Nudity's a way of life here.'

Now, however, out in the inky gloom of the pool – set apart from the hotel by a wall of citrus trees and under the eye of a creamy, perfectly round moon – Martin's inhibitions had evaporated.

'Do you think we'll be sacked?' He was floating on his back gazing up at the galaxy of shimmering stars.

'You worry too much,' she said, kissing him; she knew nothing of his predicament. 'I can handle Hammers.'

She dropped her head back into the water so that her hair was fully submerged. Her breasts loomed up above the surface like a sacrificial offering. He put out a hand to cup one and to his amazement – well, it *had* been an eventful evening – he could feel his cock respond, fattening and stiffening under the water. The tendons in her neck tightened as she pulled herself upright, her hair clinging to her back like the skin of an otter. He wanted to take her again.

'I'm hungry,' she announced. 'What can we eat?'

'You're optimistic if you think we're going to get room service at this time of the morning. Anyway, I need something to whet my appetite first.'

She glanced down at his erection distorted by the water, a wicked smile appearing on her lips. 'I think we could –' she began.

He threw up a cautionary hand, suddenly still. 'Shhh. I could have sworn I heard voices – singing.' He stood up in the water, and looked out across the sweep of citrus trees to the lights of the hotel beyond, trying to locate the sound.

'Don't be so paranoid. There's no one out there.'

He was about to say something in reply when there was a burst of laughter – they both heard it this time. He wheeled round. The noise was coming from the beach. Then it seemed to disappear down the road like the sound of a departing car, only to return again. It was the raucous sound of several inebriated men, no doubt on their way back to the hotel. He eased himself silently out of the pool to get a better look, startling a cicada out of the cracked pavement at the poolside. There were more cheers and the shouting was louder now. He cast a glance over his shoulder at Eve's naked body, milk-white in the moonlight. He could tell that she knew she was by beautiful the way she was looking at him.

'This might be a good time to think about heading back to our room,' he said uneasily.

Now he could see the shadowy forms of the revellers – five of them – bottles of wine and beer swinging from their hands, one of them carrying what looked like – he peered closer – a microwave of all things, as they picked their way none too steadily towards the pool. His eyes flew to their room key sitting on a plastic sun-bed. He bitterly regretted going along with Eve's plan not to bring any towels.

She giggled. 'Sounds like quite a party.' Because she was still in the pool she couldn't see what he saw. 'It might be fun to stay.'

'Christ, Eve. One look at your –' he waved a hand in the general direction of her glorious breasts, the pale pink nipples erect with cold, 'and we'll have a bloody *riot* on our hands.'

'I think I'm capable of handling a bunch of tipsy schoolboys.'

The 'tipsy schoolboys' – army blokes, he guessed if the tattoos and crew-cuts were anything to go by – were only a few yards away now, closing in on the entrance to the pool. One undid his flies and pissed against a tree, another – who he thought he caught saying 'eat shit fuck-face' – struck a wine bottle against a rock, shook it threateningly at one of the men with him, then threw the rest of the glass remains onto the lawn.

Martin grabbed the room key, then pulled Eve from the pool. 'We've got to get out of here,' he whispered.

'How exciting,' she whispered back.

'Come *on*.'

They made it to the edge of the tree enclosure and shrank down behind a hedge just as the youths appeared at the edge of the pool. But when after several minutes it became clear that they were in no hurry to leave – and were stripping off their clothes to swim – Martin and Eve began to tiptoe across the lawn. They had cleared a distance of fifty yards when the first catcall came. Martin cursed. The youths had spotted them – or rather Eve. He had a feeling that she would have liked him to play the macho bit, but he wasn't about to take on those five thugs for anyone, not even to prove himself as tough as Piers.

As they raced back to the hotel, Martin conscious of his cock swinging between his legs, they were pursued by jeers and wolf-whistles. He was amazed to hear Eve behind him laughing quietly in the darkness.

Twenty eight

During the early hours of Monday morning, the Italian sun not yet summoned from sleep, Martin lay gazing up at the shadows on the hotel ceiling in a cold sweat. Eve stirred next to him, her arms thrown out in a careless abandon. The opportunity was there for him to take her, as he had done frequently since their arrival at the hotel, but he decided not to disturb her. He had been dreaming again.

He was in Kensal Rise cemetery standing by his car. In

his hands was Mr Ash's saxophone which had been filled with earth, green shoots sprouting through the crumbly surface. He had just lowered the saxophone into the boot of the car when he became aware of footsteps approaching. With a rush of terror, he realised he must hide the instrument before it was discovered but the top of the boot, when he tried to pull it down, wouldn't budge. Panic-stricken, he struggled to lift the instrument out of the boot, but it was suddenly like handling solid steel and, in his haste to move it, he lost his balance. He reeled backwards and the saxophone slipped from his grasp, cracking in several places as it hit the ground. Hundreds of orange-brown cockroaches crawled amid the strewn earth and broken pieces of metal.

Then someone coughed. He whirled round and found himself facing six police officers. One of them, smoking a cigarette, stepped forward towards him, close, too close.

'I thought I'd find you here,' he said. His blue gaze was steady, slightly mocking in the bright sunlight.

'What do you want?' Martin glanced nervously at the other policemen.

'I hear you're quite an accomplished sportsman.'

He was surprised by the remark. 'From who?'

'A mutual friend told me.' To Martin's horror he bent down and with the lighted end of his cigarette, singed the glossy back of one of the insects. The smell – an evil, acrid smell that turned his stomach – made him gag and woke him up.

A glance at his watch told him it was still only four thirty, but he found it impossible to go back to sleep. Even with his eyes open he could still see the grinning face of the police officer.

It was Charlie Fitzherbert.

The room was airless, and Martin tossed restlessly from side to side, unable to relax. Finally, he got out of bed and dressed in a T-shirt and a pair of swimming trunks. Careful not to wake Eve, he grabbed one of the towels from the bathroom, slipped his feet into a battered pair of loafers and silently made his way down to the pool.

The blue-black water was perfectly still, mirroring the freckled sky of stars, and the moon was half-full like a drowsy, partially closed eye. By noon, the poolside would be chock-a-block with sun-worshipping residents, but for now it was his to enjoy alone. He left his T-shirt, shoes and hotel key on one of the tables and dived gratefully into the cool water. The temperature change brought clarity to his sleep-ridden brain, and he swam for some time, enjoying the coolness against his skin as he lapped back and forth. Out of the corner of his eye he caught a movement, something dark and travelling fast, but when he turned it was gone. Probably a wild animal, he thought.

Eventually he grew tired and came to a stop at the deep end, keeping himself afloat by resting his folded arms on the edge of the pool. He supposed he felt happy, being here with Eve. It was what he'd always wanted; the two of them together at last. He just wished their new relationship felt a little more stable. Oh, the fucking was great. He had no complaints there. But a few niggling questions kept eating away at his thoughts. Take last night, for instance, when they were being chased by those drunken youths. Was she really so naïve as not to have realised the vulnerability of their situation? Or was it more a case of testing him – deliberately courting danger in order to see how well he handled it?

Then there was the speed of her recovery from the break-up with Piers. He had tried several times to get her to talk about it but she always managed to deflect his questions, often with a frosty smile before changing the subject. It was almost as if Piers had never existed. He found himself watching her when she felt herself unobserved, looking for signs of grief, of regret, some sense of loss. But if she felt any pain she kept it well hidden. Only one thing gave her away and that was her incessant smoking. And another thing: he never knew what she was thinking, about him, about their future together. She wouldn't confide in him, so he kept pieces of himself back too. It was disconcerting that sex together could be so intense, so intimate, when they seemed little more than strangers in all other aspects of their relationship. They seemed to speak a different language.

He struck out against the water and swam six lengths in rapid succession then came to a stop again at the deep end of the pool. He tried to picture Eve as she had been on their first night together, but instead an image of Celia drifted into his mind, her features bright and sharply defined, and he felt her absence with a physical force. If ever he had needed someone to talk to it was her. She had a knack of putting things into perspective, of always being able to take the sting out of a situation. He didn't know anyone else with that ability and he realised how badly he needed it now. He missed her company, the smile she had for him each morning she arrived for work, the way she wrinkled up her nose when she laughed. He missed her shrewd, practical mind which so often surprised him, the way she allowed herself to be vulnerable when they were alone together, and he was suddenly overcome with remorse. On Friday evening he had abandoned her without a thought for her welfare. It was she who had taken the main brunt of Piers's anger, Celia who had leapt hotly to his defence when Piers had him pinned to the wall, but all he had been able to think about was protecting Eve. Recalling that they were supposed to have been going to the theatre he chastised himself yet again. She had deserved at least a telephone call by way of explanation. It was a rotten way to treat a friend.

Everything was still and quiet but for the gentle slap, slap of chlorinated water and for a while Martin just listened to its comforting melody, making circles with his legs while his mind was deep in thought. He was hauling himself out – one leg still dangling in the pool – when a pair of Timberlands came into his vision, inches from his hands. Surprised to find he had company, his eyes travelled up towards the stranger's face. The man had his back to the moon so his features were an indistinct blur, but there was no denying the familiar bulk of that body silhouetted against the sky.

'Convenient of you to be alone,' said Piers amiably. 'But then you always did make things easy for me.'

Shivers of apprehension crawled all over Martin's scalp. An alarm bell warned him to do something – quickly, make a move, run, get the hell out of there, but oh Christ, oh Jesus bloody Christ, it was already too late. He didn't see what Piers hit him with: just the upward, blurry swing of his arm. The blow landed above his left temple like an explosion, shuddering his bones, his teeth, and sent him reeling backwards; a blinding flash of magnesium light against a black background. He fell awkwardly, twisting his body so that his chin caught the blunt edge of the pool, cracking his teeth in the process, but it didn't hurt. The surface of the pool gave way to his weight, like an embrace, as he sank back into the water and observed with wonder how the dark sky seemed to ignite and break out into a spray of glittering stars.

He must have briefly lost consciousness because the next thing he became aware of was being dragged by his feet like a sack of grain along the concrete terrace, the soft skin of his cheek scraping against the rough surface. Something was sliding down his face. He tasted it. It was blood. His head felt like a split watermelon, a thousand migraines rolled into one. Fuck, it hurt! In an attempt to stop himself, he tried to grab hold of something but it was all happening so quickly and – funny – why couldn't he move his arms? Then he realised that something was holding them against his waist. He felt himself roughly hoisted up and his head flopped forward awkwardly, as if his neck muscles had become suddenly useless. The blood was running into his eyes but by squinting he could just make out the white outline of a chair and feel something being hastily wound round his chest and secured to it. Then nothing. Not a sound from Piers, which he found more ominous because he couldn't identify where he was. The wrought iron chair suddenly jerked backwards and

in a groggy panic he thought he was going to fall, but
instead realised he was being dragged backwards along
the ground to the edge of the pool – the deep end – and
with a certainty that struck dread in his heart, he knew
what Piers had in store for him.

With his back to the pool, Martin could see through
half-closed eyes that his adversary was working rapidly;
he was fastening the cord that bound his ankles through
the gaps in the chair.

'How did you find us?' he asked weakly, playing for
time.

'Eve left the time and details of your flight next to the
phone by her bed. I still have a key.' Piers's voice was full
of a mixture of triumph and satisfaction.

Martin licked his lips and tasted his own blood. 'You
don't have to do this.'

'Oh, but I've been so looking forward to it. Killing you
is going to be an occasion to savour.'

'Like you did Charlie Fitzherbert? Did you enjoy
killing him too?'

Piers smiled chillingly. It had been a mistake to
provoke him. Christ, he should be trying to talk him out
of it, making him see the error of his ways, not stirring
him up! A dizzy wave of faintness drenched his limbs in a
cold sweat. If only he could think straight. Piers,
watching him struggle feebly against the rope, smiled.

'You're sweating. It's a disagreeable sight. Time to cool
off.'

As he saw Piers's eyes shift to where his foot was
positioned against the leg of the chair, he tried to fight the
awful, weakening terror that flooded over him, his
pounding heart, his bowels threatening to give way. He
knew exactly what the man intended to do and began
thrashing helplessly in his seat but there was no escape.
With almost casual disdain, Piers gave the chair a jerk,
one sharp push, and it toppled backwards into the pool.
Martin snatched a frantic gulp of air through his nose as
he fell, then the surface gobbled him up.

Time lost all meaning the moment he entered the

water. It engulfed him, sucking him down into its dim, silent depths with one greedy swallow as the chair, drifting like debris in space, gently grazed the bottom, ending up on its back. Horizontal, he lay there, eyes blinking myopically against the thick wall of water, and followed the path of air bubbles rising towards the surface. At first he could see nothing but murky shadows. Then the reflected form of Piers which loomed at him from above, wavering and distorted by the rocking waves. He just stood there watching him, like someone peering into a lavatory bowl to make sure that all the shit had been flushed away.

Then suddenly Piers wasn't there any more and he realised that this wasn't some sick game they were playing. No one was going to save him. He had been left to die alone.

A fresh wave of panic caught in his chest until he grew dizzy. Like a deranged being he began to wrestle with the cord which had him trapped, jerking his body from right to left, crazy with fear. Time had stopped with his breath – he had only been in the water for a couple of minutes – but the pain was already starting to eat at his lungs. He could feel his heart pounding from the strain of trying to fight his way out, but yes – already the cord, fastened around his chest and arms with more speed than care, had begun to slacken and within seconds it was loose enough for him to shrug off. Working rapidly he began to attack his bound ankles secured to the chair but no matter how much he twisted and pulled, the knotted cord would not give. He clawed a path across the floor of the pool, dragging the heavy chair behind him, and as he did so his fingers made contact with something sharp. It was the neck of a broken bottle. It must have been cast into the pool by one of the thugs they'd seen the previous night. A chance! His lungs burned for air but he kept his head, fighting against panic as he hacked frantically at the cord with the jagged edge, not caring that he cut deep into his own flesh as he worked. Just as it seemed as if his lungs would explode, the cord gave way, and he shot to the surface like a rocket. In that split second he gasped for air, and hailed the joyous sensation of being alive and able to breathe again.

His euphoria only lasted a moment for he remembered Piers. His head snapped round, water spraying from his hair and rippling the pool's surface, expecting to see a raised arm poised to hit him again. To his astonishment the lone figure hovering nearby on the grassy verge wasn't Piers – but Eve!

'Martin?' Her sleepy voice had a doubtful ring as if she couldn't be sure whom she was addressing. Wearing the hotel's towelling robe she moved closer, a surreal flower against the lightening sky. She seemed to expect some kind of explanation from him but it was costing him dear just keeping himself afloat: speech would have been impossible. His eyes kept darting around, watchful for Piers's return. But they were alone. Eve was peering down at him from the pool's edge, her expression shifting from puzzlement to shock as her eyes got used to the dark and she saw him clearly for the first time. 'My God, Martin,' she gasped. 'What on earth has happened? You're hurt.'

'I'm OK,' he spluttered, paddling weakly towards her. 'But you can hardly keep your head above the water.' She sank to her knees and extended an outstretched arm towards him. 'Here,' she called. 'Grab on to me.'

With Eve's help he was able to haul his weakened body out of the pool and with her arm supporting him he managed to stand. But with legs that seemed to be made of string instead of muscle, it was difficult to remain upright. He tried to shake some of the fuzziness from his head but moving it only made it worse. And there was another pain, like cigarettes being stubbed out against his flesh. He looked down at the blood seeping from the gashes around his ankles.

With Eve taking the brunt of his weight, they had managed to reach his towel which was hanging over a chair when he suddenly doubled over and vomited a spray of watery liquid. Trembling, he sank to his knees and waited for the waves of nausea to pass, ever-fearful of Piers's return while he lay there helpless as a baby. Warm wind blew gently against his skin but he couldn't stop shivering. He could hear the distant sound of waves hitting rocks, someone softly murmuring to him, while above and around, bats banked and rode, black shapes hanging in the air. Blinking water – or was it blood – from his eyes he turned on his side and saw Eve watching him anxiously. Shifting his vision he could see distant trees where Piers might be hiding watching him, waiting for his next move.

'I need to get back to the hotel,' he managed to say. How much had she seen?

'Do you want me to fetch someone?'

'No,' he said quickly, not wanting to be left alone. 'I can make it – with your help.'

She passed him his shoes and T-shirt and helped him to dress. 'Those are going to need attention,' she said, frowning at the angry gashes on his ankles, 'and your head. You're losing quite a bit of blood.'

She debated for a moment, then removing the towelling belt from her dressing gown, used it as a bandage to stem the flow of blood from his head wound. 'How did you know I'd be here?' Martin asked.

'I didn't,' she said, concentrating on the job at hand. 'But when I woke up and found you were gone I decided to come and find you. You weren't in the bar or the lobby so the pool seemed the next obvious place to look. I could see that someone was here and I thought it might be you, but whoever it was took off in a terrible hurry when I called your name. Made straight for those trees.' And she pointed south, towards an area of dense overgrowth. So that was why Piers hadn't stuck around to the bitter end.

Eve suddenly stopped what she was doing and looked at him, curiosity seeming to make her eyes a deeper shade of green. 'Are you going to tell me what's been going on?'

For a second he contemplated telling her the truth but, as he opened his mouth, the words seemed to stick in the back of his throat. Could he take the risk? How honest had she actually been with him where Piers was concerned? He couldn't be sure how she would react, not only to what had just taken place but also to his suspicion of Piers being Charlie Fitzherbert's murderer. How could he even begin to explain that the person she had almost made up her mind to spend her life with, had already killed one man, and had very nearly taken the life of another. Would she believe him? Would she even want to? There was just enough doubt in his mind to keep what he knew to himself. So he told her instead that the thugs had come back. They were drunk, he said, looking for trouble, and outnumbered by five to one he had been an easy target. To his relief she seemed to accept his explanation, more concerned about his injuries than anything else.

A warm wind had built up while they'd been talking. With Martin's head turbaned in white towelling, and hobbling painfully, they made their way back to the hotel. Behind them, in the semi-darkness, the trees seemed to shiver.

TWENTY-NINE

The morning after their return, Martin woke with a sudden start – in Pike's spare bedroom in Acton – to sunlight and the screaming of a car alarm outside. The early light made the small room, which was normally used as a study and smelt musty, look squalid. The contents of his luggage spilled out on to the floor next to the desk. He lay listening to the rhythmic pulse of his breath which reminded him that he was alive and well. Already his near-brush with death seemed to belong to someone else, yet only a few hours had passed since their rushed departure from the hotel. After landing at Heathrow – hidden behind a pair of dark glasses and wearing a ridiculous hat purchased in the duty-free shop – he had packed Eve home in a taxi, then called his old friend to see if he would give him a bed for a couple of nights. The discovery of Mr Ash's saxophone made his own flat too dangerous to return to. Camping out at Eve's place would be no less risky – there was always the threat of Piers turning up unannounced.

Restless and jumpy, a state of mind he was now getting used to, he crept into the living room and pulled on the only clean set of clothes he had with him. Then he let himself quietly out of the flat, keys and mobile in hand, taking care not to wake Pike. The two men had stayed up late into the night sharing a bottle of wine but not once did Pike make him feel that he was owed an explanation. His musician friend could be relied on not to ask awkward questions.

The air was fresh against his sunburnt skin and he inhaled great gulps of it as he strode with purpose through the streets, keeping a watchful eye out for lurking policemen. He couldn't shrug off the feeling of restlessness he had woken up with, the peculiar sensation of wanting to be somewhere specific, yet not knowing what that place was. A hunched woman pulling a supermarket trolley with the hooked end of a walking stick, shuffled by in the opposite direction muttering to herself but she wasn't the only one to attract odd looks. Martin had done what he could to patch up his injuries, but there was no disguising the bruises on his face, or the golf-ball-sized lump above his left temple. The damage to his now bandaged ankles was safely concealed under his socks.

He was about to have some breakfast when his mobile rang. He stopped in a shop doorway to take the call. It had to be Eve: no one else knew of his return. 'I missed you last night,' he said, tenderly.

'How touching,' the familiar scornful tone of Oliver's voice assailed his eardrum. 'I've been trying to get hold of you for days. Where the hell have you been?'

Martin smiled weakly. Some things never changed. 'Taking a well-earned break.'

'With Eve as your little playmate, I hear, you old dog,' his colleague quipped. 'I'm going to have to re-evaluate my opinion of you, Leak. However did you manage such a coup?' His voice sounded almost respectful.

'You're letting your imagination run wild again, Ollie. What do you want?'

'Now, now. Don't be so hasty. I've got information to trade.'

'What information?' He was suddenly fearful. Did it have something to do with the police? Had they been back to Carlyle asking more questions?

'What if I said I sat up with a mutual friend half of Friday night.'

'And which mutual friend would we be talking about?'

'Piers Hunt. He doesn't seem to like you very much.'

Even the mention of the man's name filled Martin with dread. 'What exactly did he say?'

'Asked a number of questions about you – some I have to confess are a little hazy now. We must have consumed over a bottle of whisky.' Martin touched the bump on his head, testingly. He was in need of another painkiller. 'Livid probably best sums up his mood. Not in a shouting, smashing sort of way, more of an icy calm. Quite unnerving actually. It's not a side of Piers I'm particularly fond of, although you did give him good cause. You're fortunate he didn't know where you were, otherwise you'd probably be in intensive care.' Oliver paused. 'He's not going to accept this thing you have with Eve without a fight, you know.'

'I do realise that.' Martin's voice was heavy with irony. 'Don't suppose you know what his movements are?'

'He's down on the family estate. His uncle died suddenly over the weekend, so he plans to stay there until after the funeral. Incidentally,' Oliver asked, 'where *did* you go?'

'Italy. And that's all you're getting.' Martin sighed,

suddenly tired of all the lies and pretence. 'Look, I've got to go, but I'll catch up with you later.'

'You are coming in to work today then?'

'At some stage.'

'Well, good luck with Hammers. You're going to have to spin him a pretty convincing yarn. By the way,' he ended before hanging up, 'don't suppose you remember seeing a brown bag lying around the office by any chance? Only Piers mentioned he might have left it there last Friday.'

'No. Doesn't ring any bells with me.'

He caught the Tube back to Eve's flat where he had left his car, debating what to do next. In spite of what he had said to Oliver it was too risky going into the office. He knew that his job was on the line but it wouldn't take the police long to find him there and then he would be unable to do anything about clearing his name. He had to buy himself as much time as possible until Kevin contacted him. Kevin was his only hope.

His tank was low so he stopped off at a petrol station to fill up the car. At the same time he gave the interior a good clean; empty crisp bags, a mangled A–Z, soft drinks cans, property details, an earring down the back of the passenger seat – a little jade cross framed with a gold scalloped edge – which he recognised immediately as belonging to Celia. As he held the tiny, dazzling jewel in his hand, he recalled her ludicrous formality on her first day at the office. And then, after her attack, carrying her up to his flat, her arms round his neck as if it were the most natural thing in the world to do. Some time during that night a sudden cry had woken him. When he went to investigate he found her mumbling to herself, her eyes squeezed shut. From the doorway of his room, blue-black light pressing against the window pane, he stayed and watched her for almost an hour. One arm carelessly thrust behind her head, fingers caught in the velvet-brown of her hair, the other arm across her breasts as if, even in sleep, she felt the need to protect herself.

Seeing Celia again was about the only good thing about being back.

Kevin's call finally came through while he was having lunch in a brasserie at Strand-on-the Green.

'I haven't much time, mate, so I'll make this quick. He's agreed to see you.'

Martin sat more upright in his chair. 'When?'

'Tomorrow morning. Can you make it down to Ipswich?'

'Just tell me where to go.' Kevin gave him the address and time. 'Oh, and one tip,' he said before ringing off. 'Don't be late. The boss isn't someone you want to keep waiting.'

THIRTY

At first he thought he had come to the wrong place. He looked up at the red-brick building – once a primary school but now all boarded up – and tried the door again. No answer. Perhaps he had misunderstood the instructions? He made an effort to remember what Kevin had told him but the same address kept repeating itself in his mind. This *had* to be it. There wasn't another house for half a mile. He tried the door handle and was surprised to find it yielded instantly. Gingerly, he pushed it open and stepped into the gloomy interior, a briefcase swinging from his left hand. Immediately a bright light came on and, as his eye caught a security camera whirring above the door, he felt a flicker of unease, but he was damned if he'd back down now. There was too much at stake.

Four doors faced him, one of which was open. He passed through it – another light flickering on as he did so and followed the path of the hall as far as it would take him. At the end he was confronted by two more doors. He tried the one on his right first but found the room stacked with wooden crates of méthode champenoise and Martell Taittinger cognac and boxes crammed with cigarette cartons, video games, computer hardware. He whistled quietly as he tried to calculate how much the stuff was worth – must have been an awfully big lorry. He was tempted to look round further but spotting another security camera, quickly left.

The second door took him into an office which he could tell at a glance had no windows – or, if there were, they had been blacked out. A man behind the desk was on the phone but waved him in motioning him to sit down, which he did with relief: his ankles were still causing him considerable discomfort. While he talked, Martin was able to take stock of his surroundings: the raised aquarium full of brightly coloured fish, the row of computers humming in one corner, the room he'd just come from showing on the closed circuit TV monitor. He tried to avoid eye contact with the man on the phone but it was difficult to look elsewhere. He was the size of a small ship; enormously fat and broad with a few tufts of blond hair on his otherwise bald head, and wearing enough jewellery to put Hatton Garden permanently out of business.

Martin was studying a Pirelli calendar with a bikini-clad figure on the front, wondering what it was about the voice that sounded so familiar, when the fat man hung up.

'So.' Kevin's employer sat back in his leather swivel chair and linked his stubby fingers across the vast expanse of his belly. 'I hear you've got some problem you want sorting out.' Obviously not someone who minced his words.

'Yes. I, um –' he cleared his throat, 'I want to put a surveillance on someone.'

The man laughed. 'Pissed you off, have they?'

He flushed, aware that he was handling this badly. 'You could say that.'

'Why come to me?'

'Because you know people,' Martin said carefully, trying to flatter him. 'Because you can make things happen.'

The man reached over to a fridge behind him and pulled out a Diet Coke. Martin declined when he was offered one.

'Can't say I blame you,' the man said. 'I'm supposed to be losing weight.' He grinned ruefully as he clicked open the can. 'They'll probably discover one day that this slimline crap gives you cancer. What'd you do to your face?'

'Someone tried to rearrange it for me.'

'That why you're here?'

'Partly.' Martin gave him a summary of events, up to and including his flight to Italy. 'Right now he probably thinks I'm dead,' he finished, 'but it won't take him long to discover the truth and then he'll come after me again – if the police don't get me first.'

'Why single you out?'

Martin had had time to think about this and answered truthfully, 'I made it easy for him.'

Something electronic crackled on the man's desk. In one surprisingly swift movement, he reached forward and pressed a button, and again Martin was struck by an extraordinary sense of *déjà vu*.

A voice flooded into the room. Martin had thought the grille above the fish tank was for ventilation but it was obviously some kind of intercom. Who else was in the building?

'The shipment's through, boss. Gary said to do like we did before but I wanted to check with you first.'

'Who's got the dough?'

'Pinlock. Fifty K in twenty bills.'

'He doesn't get a penny until that stuff's checked. Tell Gary to get over here as soon as it's done. And get those crates shifted. They've been hanging around for too long – creates the wrong impression.'

'Right, boss.'

The fat man looked across the desk at him as if there

had been no interruption. Did he do all his communicating from the safe confines of this office?

'What you're asking me to do,' he said finally, 'is to break the law.'

'I —' Martin said falteringly, thrown by the sudden moral tone in the man's voice. 'All I want is for you to monitor his movements, find out who he does business with, who his contacts are. He's a desperate man — what happened in Italy only goes to prove it. Sooner or later he's going to slip up and I just want to make sure we're there when it happens.'

'Have you any idea what something like that will cost you?'

'I've got enough money to cover it.'

The man consulted one of the screens on his desk. 'You owe over four grand on your credit card, and you're down to seventy quid in your current account. Pay-day's not for another week and you've just had yourself one expensive weekend in Italy.' He glanced up again. 'Hope she was worth it. What are you going to use for currency — Monopoly money?'

Martin flushed angrily. 'How the hell did you know —?'

'That's why you're here, isn't it? Because of what I have access to.'

The man drained the contents of his Coke can and belched loudly as Martin digested the truth of this remark. What else did he know about him? Had his address come up on the screen — his date of birth, the companies he had worked for, his entire bloody sex life? He was starting to feel really uncomfortable.

'Worked it out yet?'

Martin assumed they were still talking about his finances.

'Oh, come on, Martin. I thought I'd taught you to be quicker than this.'

'Taught me what —?' That was when he noticed the gold crucifix twinkling at the man's throat. He gazed at it open-mouthed. His mind kept telling him one thing but his eyes were telling him another. There had been a time

– long ago – when he had seen a crucifix of a similar kind, only then it was round the neck of a wiry seventeen-year-old with a lot of nerve and a sick sense of humour.

'Slug?' he gasped incredulously.

Slug chuckled. 'S'pose I have thickened out a bit.' He patted the folds of fat that constituted his stomach. 'The hair went four years ago but then who gives a fuck. It's saved me a fortune in haircuts.'

'I don't believe this. Why didn't Kevin tell me it was you?'

'Because he's paid to keep his mouth shut unless I tell him otherwise.' That sounded more like the old Slug. 'And because I wasn't sure whether I was going to like what you'd turned into – I mean an estate agent, for fuck's sake!' He nodded towards Martin's briefcase. 'Look at you, you've even brought along your fucking school satchel.'

Martin flushed. 'It's something I'm good at,' he responded hotly, feeling himself slipping back into his old defensive role.

'No money in it. You should have stuck with me, I'm telling you. I've got three houses all paid for upfront.' He never could resist the opportunity to brag. 'I support two ex-wives, a boy of nine who goes to public school, and I've got more petty cash in this drawer than you'll make in a year.'

Martin glanced at the oversized suit he was wearing which looked as if it had come off the rail at C&A, but which had no doubt cost him an absurd amount of money.

'How'd you get out in the end?' Slug said after a pause. 'I always wondered. Break anything?'

Martin shook his head. 'No thanks to you,' he said drily. 'But I could have. You owe me that much at least.' A note of desperation entered his voice. 'I can't do this alone, Slug. Without your help, I'm a dead man.'

'You should have thought of that before you got involved with that rich bitch of his.'

He reddened. 'All this happened long before Eve and I got involved. She has nothing to do with this.'

'She was his bird, wasn't she? I can tell you now, if you'd run off with my missus, I'd have cut off your balls and posted them back to you.' He sucked in air through his mouth. 'You always were a soft touch when it came to women.'

A small hard pellet of dismay lodged in Martin's throat. He was beginning to realise that his trip down here had been a waste of time.

'This geezer Harry you mentioned,' Slug said suddenly. 'D'you know where he lives?'

'Harry Forbes? He has a flat on Battersea Park Road. I don't know which number but I could get it for you,' Martin said eagerly.

Slug was scribbling something down. 'Don't need it. What about Hunt?' That was easy. Martin recited to him the Chelsea address he'd memorised from Eve's book. 'I'll get Kevin on to it. That's his area,' said Slug mysteriously. 'Don't suppose you have any idea of Hunt's movements?'

Martin nodded and recounted what Oliver had told him the previous day.

Slug interrupted him. 'The estate?'

'In Tetbury. It belongs to the family – worth millions. Piers will inherit it all when his old man dies.' Martin added this unnecessary piece of information knowing that it wouldn't go down too well with Slug.

'Is that right? Well, then he'd better enjoy it while he can.'

Martin looked at his old friend with renewed hope. 'Does this mean you'll help me?'

Slug eyed him slyly. 'Oh, I'll help you all right. But we'll do it my way, not yours. You've got to learn to think big and act fast. Forget all your surveillance shit. That's for kids. I've got a *much* better idea.'

THIRTY-ONE

Visiting Irene hadn't been part of Martin's plan but as he left Slug he had a change of heart. Half an hour wouldn't hurt. He didn't call first to say that he was dropping in. He just took a chance on her being there.

Irene was on good form and as she fixed lunch he sat in the snug kitchen with a cup of coffee in his hand, listening to her recount the small, mundane events of her life, a world that had shrunk so small that it was now no more than the size of the Lego-land village she lived in. Whenever he thought of her, he pictured her in the kitchen like now, plump hands kneading dough, flour powdering her chin, the room fragrant with the smell of newly baked bread.

While he was sitting there watching her work, he thought about the office. By now it would be obvious he wasn't coming in today. He wondered if Eve would be worried about him, whether Oliver would mention their phone conversation. Celia would be there too. What did she think of him after his behaviour the other evening? It was a funny thing about Celia. Whenever he thought about her he felt a sense of incompleteness, as if she should be playing a much bigger role in his life. They had become good friends and he hoped he could still count on her wise and non-judgemental counsel, but there was always this intuitiveness he got when he was around her, of there being more. He remembered her once asking him if he was happy. He must have looked surprised because before he could reply she had smiled and briefly squeezed his arm. 'Forget it. It was a silly question.'

The phone rang. Irene rubbed her hands on a tea towel and took the call in the next room, so he went out into the garden and waited for her there. As he lowered himself into a chair, he felt something slide out of his pocket. His wallet lay open on the grass and as he bent to retrieve it, he saw the press cutting. The horror of that day at the office, when he'd stuffed the clipping inside the flap of his wallet, came flooding over him.

For the last couple of hours he had been studying Irene's appearance. His memory seemed to have played tricks on him. When he thought of his adopted mother he always pictured a stout but vital woman, with flaming red hair and a stubborn will to match. Recently she had let the natural colour grow back and it was as if the greying hair had escalated the ageing process. In the months since he had last seen her she appeared suddenly to have grown old.

It suddenly occurred to Martin that, at sixty-one, she was at an age when she might die and yet one crucial issue remained unresolved between them. This realisation took him over with such force that he'd had to look away in case she read the pain in his eyes.

The lawn was scorched and yellowing, sharp blades of sunlight slanting down between the trees. Irene's voice carried through the open window and he thought he heard his name being mentioned. After all these years he was still trying to come to terms with Frank's death. Maybe it was his recent near-miss with death that had made him more aware of Irene's mortality. He had already lost three parents. Was he really prepared to risk losing Irene too without finally clearing the air? If ever there was a time to do it, surely it was now.

His mood was pensive as she joined him. She was carrying a tray of tea things. 'I stopped off at the shop on my way down,' he said, squinting against the sun as he helped her with the tray.

'At our old place?' She glanced up at him. 'I hear they've made a lot of changes.' He waved away a wasp, and noticed a fleeting expression of regret on her face at the mention of her old home. She resumed pouring. 'Whatever made you go there?'

He shrugged. 'I've been thinking about Dad quite a bit

recently. Maybe it's a seasonal thing, the anniversary of his death coming up. I thought I might visit his grave while I was here.'

Irene looked pleased. 'You could take some flowers from the garden.' She threw him a quizzical glance, trying to gauge his mood. Then they both said together, 'There's something –'

'Martin, is everything –?'

They smiled at each other, Irene indicating that he should go first.

'Mum,' he chose his words carefully. 'I want to talk to you about something that's been bothering me for a long time.' She looked at him expectantly. 'It's about me,' he began, 'I –' Then, realising this was going to be more difficult that he had anticipated, he reached into his pocket and removed the press cutting from his wallet. 'About this.'

She wrestled with the glasses around her neck so that she could see what he had given her. When she saw what it was, the colour of her skin changed rapidly. 'Oh, dear,' she said in a hopeless voice.

For some moments she gazed at the cutting, which lay in her lap like a faded leaf, then she looked sadly away into the distance as if collecting her thoughts. The air burned with tension. Martin's ears hummed. There came a point when he thought he couldn't bear it any longer. Then she suddenly got up and went inside the house. He was just starting to get worried when she reappeared with a packet of Rothmans.

'*Mum!*' said Martin, as he watched her sit down and draw deeply on a cigarette. She coughed a little, carefully blowing the smoke away from his direction. 'I never knew you smoked.' He was shocked. Seeing Irene smoking was like watching her have sex.

'I don't normally. Only in times of emergency.' Her hand shook slightly as she put the matches in her cardigan pocket. 'When – how long have you known?' she said finally.

'Since I was ten.' Her frown deepened. 'That time you

caught me bleeding all over your kitchen floor. Remember how cross you were? I'd just found the cuttings in a drawer.'

'It was because you were always playing with knives,' she said reflectively. 'They seemed to hold a real fascination for you and I fretted all the time that you'd one day do yourself a real injury.' She looked at the newspaper cutting gripped tightly between her thumb and index finger.

'I often wondered if you knew. Some nights when I couldn't sleep I would lie there beside your father and wonder what to do, what was best for us all. Your father was dead against telling you. His way of thinking was why get you all upset when you'd never be able to trace your real parents anyway. What breaks my heart is that we protected you all these years for nothing. You should have come to us. We could have talked about it.' She stubbed the cigarette out, having only taken a few token puffs.

'I never blamed either of you,' insisted Martin.

'Perhaps not. But I can't help blaming myself.' Her voice was sad. 'You never knew this but nine years before we found you, Frank and me had another baby. We called him Colin after Frank's grandad. He was a sweet little thing but ever so frail. Cried all the time. We found out later that he had a rare form of leukaemia – passed on through dormant genes in Frank. The doctors told us his chances of surviving were only small, but you know what your father was like. He just kept believing the leukaemia would go away.'

She had caught hold of his hand and stroked it as if she wanted to provide comfort not for herself but for him.

'We lost Colin three days before his first birthday. It took a long time to get over his death, knowing we couldn't ever have any more. Oh, we coped all right, you have to, don't you? But it was like a light had gone out in Frank. Colin going changed him so much I thought he'd grieve himself away. Then you appeared like the baby

Moses, yelling your tiny heart out like you wanted to wake the whole neighbourhood.'

Her face relaxed and she smiled at the memory. 'You were a gift, Martin. The most wonderful gift. You being found – well, that only made you more special, don't you see?' *They say that adopted children have unique talents*, Celia had once said to him. 'They wanted to take you away, put you in one of those foster homes, but we fought hard to keep you. And Frank,' Irene chuckled, 'you never in your life saw a man so proud. He used to carry you around in his arms with a great smile on his face. His mates at the pub used to tease him about going soft.'

A feeling of gratification spread through Martin, a warm melting sensation, like the hot potatoes Frank used to blow through the T-shirt on his back. 'Did you ever find out who left me there?'

'There were rumours, of course. For weeks the locals talked of little else but nobody ever came forward to claim you. And although I know it isn't a Christian thing to say I thanked God for it every night. The authorities thought your real mother had given birth in secret because of her age and not being married. Back then people weren't too sympathetic towards a young girl bringing up a child on her own.'

'Is that what you think happened?'

'Who can say? All I know is whatever her reasons, she was a silly fool to give you up.'

He looked into her eyes which were brimming with tears and felt his own fill. 'I'm glad we've talked,' he said, his voice not quite steady.

'Me too, pet.' She reached forward and tenderly placed both her palms to his face. 'Sometimes,' she said, 'I feel so much love for you I could weep.'

He was back at Pike's flat by eight, drained both physically and mentally by the events of the day, yet curiously exhilarated. He knew he had found a vital and powerful ally in Slug, someone who was prepared to take on Piers and fight his corner. The plan – well, it was bloody risky, but at least he'd be doing something with a modicum of control, and that in itself made him feel better. His talk with Irene . . . well, that had released feelings of a very different kind: an insurmountable relief mostly, coupled with a measure of inner peace he had never before known. For much of his life fear had prevented him from facing up to the truth. Now, he wondered why he had ever imagined that telling her would be so hard.

He was in the bath when his mobile went off. It had been ringing all day, mostly calls from the office; one from Eve asking why she hadn't heard from him; an increasingly irate Hammers wanting to know why he hadn't returned to work. As there was little Martin could say to assuage his employer's concern, he had let the messages build up. Hauling himself out of the bath, he wrapped a towel around his waist and checked his voicebox, wondering if the call had been from Eve to say she could now make supper after all. To his surprise it was a message from Celia. As he listened to her voice, his breathing quickened and his palms began to sweat. The room seemed close and stuffy in spite of the open window. When he had heard it all, he tried to calm his racing pulse by taking several slow, measured breaths, then he rewound the machine and played it again.

Celia kept her voice unnaturally soft and low as if she was anxious not to be overheard. 'Listen, Martin, I don't want to worry you unnecessarily, but we've had a visit from the police – it's about three o'clock now and they've just left. They've been asking Nick,' she meant Hammers, 'all sorts of questions about you, why you weren't here, where you'd gone, when we expected you back at work. To begin with, I didn't think much about it, but then I found out they'd been in here asking for you on Saturday too – I wasn't working that day. I caught one officer hanging around your desk, going through your drawers. I would have said something, only I was with a client at the time and I think Nick must have told him it was OK to look. Hang on –' Her voice broke off suddenly and he could hear another voice – he thought Roger's – and phones ringing in the background – then she came back. 'Sorry. They took your diary and an old cheque-book you'd left in one of the drawers, and some other stuff too.' There was a pause, rustling. 'Martin,' she said presently, more urgently now, 'I don't know what's going on or why the police seem so interested in you all of a sudden. But I think you're in trouble and if you are, and this has been of any use, then I'm glad I called. I –' she hesitated as if she wanted to say something else. 'Oh, it doesn't matter. I really hope you get this message. 'Bye.'

He called her at home and gave her an abridged version of recent events. He hadn't planned to tell her. It just sort of came out. The need for support, understanding, a friend to talk to. All the time they spoke he was conscious of a sudden, inexplicable barrier between them, erected by Celia – and it bothered him. Before hanging up he said he was coming round to see her and when she started to make excuses – which was unlike her – he brushed them aside. There was something he had to sort out.

She was wearing a floral cotton robe when she opened the door later that evening, her wet hair wound above her head in a turban made out of a towel. 'Come in,' she said, closing the door quickly.

It was still light outside, a beautiful evening, the air sultry and unseasonably warm. The windows in her living room were open and he could hear a dog yapping in the street below. It was strange being back – he hadn't been here since Christmas – yet her flat seemed pleasingly reassuring; the books, the photographs, the warm honey-stain of the furniture, it all had a welcoming feel like coming home after a long absence. Her two cats were asleep on the sofa, their soft, furry limbs interwoven, and he sat down on an adjacent seat, stroking one of them behind its ears. Immediately it began to purr.

'Thanks,' he said, as Celia resurfaced from the kitchen and handed him a drink.

Her brows were drawn together with worry as she sank into a chair. 'Does Eve know what you've told me?'

'No.' He looked into his glass. 'I've still got that thankless task ahead of me.'

'She'll be devastated.'

Yes, he thought, but for whose sake? 'Did she mention anything about her plans for tonight?'

She shook her head. 'Not that I recall. But she was pretty shaken up by the visit from the police and went home soon after so we didn't have a chance to talk. Were they planning to arrest you?'

'Yes,' he said bleakly. 'Which is why I can't come back to work.' Not yet, at least.

'You can't hide for ever, Martin. They'll find you eventually.'

'Not if things go according to plan.'

'Just be careful, please, for my sake,' she said, with sudden emotion. 'I don't want anything bad to happen to you.'

It wasn't what she said but the manner in which she said it that made him look at her. He held her gaze, unable to look away, and something inexplicable passed between them. 'About last Friday,' he said awkwardly, 'the theatre and everything. I feel really bad about letting you down.'

'Oh, that,' she said a little too brightly. 'It wasn't very good.'

'It's just that with what happened –'

'I really don't mind.'

Her being so nice about it was only making him feel worse. 'Incidentally,' he went on, trying to lighten the atmosphere, 'I came across this in my car.' From the breast pocket of his shirt, he pulled out her jade earring. 'It was down the back of the passenger seat.'

For a moment her face lit up. 'It must have been that time we went to Essex – to stay with your friends. Oh, I'm so glad. I've had those dear little earrings since my grandmother's death when I was six. They're the only reminders I have left of her.'

He was pleased by her reaction. 'I meant to tell you earlier only I never got a chance –'

'I know,' she interrupted, her face clouding over again. 'It's a difficult time for us all.'

He frowned. 'Celia,' he said. 'If there's something troubling you – and I can see there is – then for God's sake tell me. I want to help.'

Celia – her face very pale – took another sip of wine then put her glass down with exaggerated care.

'Last Monday Nick asked if anyone had seen a brown sports bag lying around in the office.'

'Belonging to Piers Hunt,' Martin nodded. 'Oliver mentioned it to me. I take it the bag hasn't turned up?'

She shook her head. 'No, and it won't because I took it home with me. No one else knows,' she went on quickly. 'It's just that when I found it I couldn't think what else to do.'

Why did this make him suddenly fear that he was about to hear something very bad? 'What would you want with Piers's sports bag?'

She didn't answer him right away. 'I found a pair of shoes inside.'

'Shoes,' he repeated, not understanding.

'– Identical to the pair I saw the night I was attacked. Oh, I know what you're going to say,' she rushed on, 'but I know I'm right. These were hand-made loafers costing over two hundred pounds.' She looked at him challengingly. 'How many people do you know who can afford to spend that kind of money on a pair of shoes?'

He cleared his throat. 'Celia, what are you trying to tell me?'

She leaned forward in her chair. 'That evening he came to the office, when you and Eve –' she faltered, 'I thought then that there was something familiar about him: his voice, the way he smelt, the scar on his hand . . . At the time I was too worried about what was happening to you to think clearly. But there was something about his physical presence and what it communicated.' She looked at him squarely, 'Well, it frightened me. *Really* frightened me. It reminded me of how I felt the night he . . .'

Martin suddenly recalled her telling him that she had bitten her assailant's hand, hard enough for it to leave a mark. For a moment neither of them spoke. They just looked at each other, appalled by the seriousness of what she had just revealed. The truth – and there was no doubting it – hung between them in the air: a thick and heavy fog.

'I didn't know what to do,' she continued, her face full of anxiety. 'That's why I didn't say anything about the bag. I was afraid no one would believe me. So I took it home and hid it under my bed. I kept expecting Piers to appear looking for it. Every time the agency door opened I thought it would be him. You've no idea how anxious and jumpy that made me feel.'

Her eyes searched Martin's face for reassurance, but he was silent. He was thinking: the bastard, the complete fucking bastard. He'd picked on Celia because he believed – God help you and your big mouth, Ollie – that Celia was his girlfriend and by hurting her, he was getting at him in the most effective way – Jesus! What wouldn't the man resort to? An image of Celia's wild, tear-stained face the night of her attack came into his mind, then of Piers leaning threateningly over her desk, one hand gently caressing her damaged cheek. *I expect men find it rather a turn-on in a kinky sort of way.* I should have been there for her when she'd needed me, he thought, furious with himself. Instead I was off gallivanting in Italy with Eve. 'Is the bag still here?'

She shook her head. 'I threw it away,' she admitted.

'For God's sake, *why*?'

'Because,' she said defensively, 'I wanted to put the whole thing behind me. Not to have to think about it any more.'

Martin heard the old grief constricting her voice and for the first time he felt her resentment. The anger she felt towards Piers for what he had put her through, towards himself for having given her so little in return for her help and understanding.

He almost told her about the plans he and Slug had made for the following day but then changed his mind. Somehow he didn't think she would approve. She looked small and defenceless suddenly in her cotton robe. He badly wanted to take her in his arms and hold her, reassure her that everything was going to be all right.

Instead he said, 'He's not going to get away with this. I promise you that now. I won't let him.'

She gave him a hopeless look. 'But what can you do?'

He compressed his lips into a thin line and, in a savage voice, said, 'Nail the bastard.'

THIRTY-TWO

Martin spent most of that night either tossing restlessly in Pike's camp-bed or wearing down the living-room carpet as he paced back and forth like an expectant father. Since the shock of her disclosure he hadn't been able to get Celia out of his mind – sweet, gentle Celia – *his* Celia – or the fact that that cowardly shit had very nearly raped her. He felt like getting in his car right now, driving down to that vast estate of his and giving him the beating he deserved in front of all the relatives.

When the sun finally came up shortly after five, he was asleep on Pike's sofa, one arm hanging off the edge, dreaming that it was not cushions that supported his weight but the floor of a punt and he was trailing his hand in a warm, moving river. For a while he lay there motionless, trying to remember how he had ended up on the sofa: he could still feel the gentle rocking of his imaginary boat. But then the pleasing sensation of half-sleep, half-wakefulness was abruptly broken when he recalled what faced him.

He left the car outside Pike's flat in Cumberland Park and walked to the North Acton tube. While he was waiting for the train to arrive Kevin called him on the mobile: 'Remind me never to drink tequila slammers again,' he said by way of a good morning. 'I feel like shit.'

A businessman, walking along the platform towards Martin, came to a stop a few feet away and opened up a newspaper.

Martin spoke softly into his mobile. 'How did it go?'

'Piece of cake. I could get inside the Bank of England if you wanted me to.'

'But did you find anything?' The man in the suit was looking at him over the top of his paper. Martin turned away.

'Quite a bit, mate, yeah. This bloke Hunt's in debt all right. His desk was littered with red bills and threatening letters from his bank. Between them and the casinos I'd say he owes something close to four hundred grand.'

Martin whistled, earning himself another look from the suit. Everything's starting to make sense, he thought.

'The place was in a right tip,' said Kevin. 'He can't have been there in days.'

Just then the phone line began to crackle and he could see his train approaching the station. In another few seconds he would lose the connection. He put a hand over his free ear to block the deafening noise and shouted, 'Kevin, my train's here. I'll have to go.'

'OK, mate. Well, good luck. Really hope it works out for you today.'

Throughout the journey he worried about being followed, but at every nervous turn of his head, all he saw was a sea of commuters. Nothing struck him as being out of the ordinary. Then it occurred to him (paranoia again, he thought, I've got to stop this) that maybe the police had found out where he was staying and were having him tailed at a judicious distance.

By the time he reached the South London address Kevin had given him, he still had an hour to kill, so he bought himself a newspaper and sat in a café drinking one cup of coffee after another until his system began to feel overloaded. Although it was still early, it was already hot and his concentration was fragmented and displaced. He barely took in the paper's headlines – it was expected to be one of the hottest Junes ever – but instead gazed out of the window imagining he could see a police officer in every face that passed. He felt keyed up, completely out of his depth. Slug had sworn he had everything covered, but Christ, he was taking a terrible risk. If anything were to go wrong ... Martin wiped the back of his hand to clear the dampness which had formed on his brow, feeling, in spite of himself, the electric pulse of illicit excitement. His senses seemed suddenly fine-tuned, everything around him sharper, more vivid. It was the same buzz he used to get when he went uninvited into a client's home – but, for some inexplicable reason, much more powerful.

At a quarter to nine he settled his bill and set off purposefully up the Wandsworth Road towards the New Covent Garden Market. The address, which wasn't immediately apparent, turned out to be a vast, semi-derelict warehouse containing more than two hundred units. After spending several minutes trying to find the right lift, he got out on the sixth floor, as instructed, and followed the grey corridor (which had a strong odour of paint) until, after several turns, he reached a large, corrugated-iron door with a red light above it.

A quick glance over his shoulder told him that the corridor was empty. He raised a clenched hand – this was it, his last, his only hope – and was about to knock, when a muffled scream rang out from inside. His heart stopped. The sound chilled him; it was the sound of human pain. OK, he thought nervously. Crunch time. He could leave now, walk away and take his chances with the police, or he could see this thing through to the bitter end. It didn't seem like much of a choice. Inhaling deeply, he gave the door a rap. After about a minute, a stranger opened it. He wore his hair closely cropped, with crawling sideburns that drew attention to a long, heavy jaw. Opening the door wider, he nodded curtly for Martin to come in.

The studio – which had so much floor space that it resembled a department store, but was almost entirely devoid of furniture – was shadowy and cool, only a few thin blades of sun infiltrating the room through the covered windows. Sitting with his back to the window, the bald head, the rotund swell of his obscenely large figure unmistakable in the dim light, was Slug. A man sat on a stool in front of him. Both heads turned sharply in Martin's direction as the door behind him clanged shut.

Slug grinned. 'Pull up a chair,' he said, beckoning him forward. 'We were just getting acquainted with your friend.'

Martin looked at the man on the stool, a man he had met only once and never much liked the sound of, but who now evoked in him a feeling of pity. Harry Forbes, naked from the waist down, his face and legs badly lacerated, looked out of his mind with fear. Beads of sweat mingling with blood trickled down his brow and dribbled off the end of his chin. On a table a few feet away was a box of ampoules filled with a milky liquid, and a wicked-looking syringe. Martin, already feeling out of his depth, was alarmed by the size of the needle. Then he noticed another man standing behind Harry, tall and lanky with ginger hair and a large mole above his right eyebrow.

'Cigarette, Harry?' Slug asked courteously. 'Give the man a smoke, Gull. He looks as if he could use it.' Gull, the man who had opened the door, stepped forward and stuck out a packet of Marlboro. Harry took one, keeping the pack Gull had offered him, and lit the end with a trembling hand. 'Why have you brought me here?' he said coarsely, after the first deep inhalation of nicotine hit its mark. 'What am I supposed to have done?' Above his head blue-white smoke curled towards the ceiling like wisps of clouds.

'Feeling guilty about something, Harry?'

He shook his head vehemently. 'Whatever it is you think I've done, I'm innocent!'

'Then you've nothing to worry about.' Slug smiled pleasantly as he sat down in the canvas fold-up chair. 'We just want a little chat about your mate, Piers Hunt. I hear you two see quite a lot of each other.'

Harry immediately looked shifty.

'You've been misinformed. I, er – haven't spoken to him in weeks.'

'You wouldn't happen to know about his recent trip to Italy then?'

Harry's head snapped round. 'What trip? He never mentioned anything about going away.'

'So you *have* spoken to him?'

'No,' said Harry, flustered. 'As I said –'

Slug drew closer, a wolf about to pounce. 'You wouldn't be lying to me, would you, Harry? Because I've got a thing about people lying to me. Brings out a side in me that I don't like very much.'

The man with the ginger hair came up behind Harry unseen and, with a massive hand, sent him a stinging blow on the back of the head. Harry sucked air through his teeth as he recoiled from the impact and gazed warily at the table where the syringe lay.

'Reckon it does look a bit nasty,' said Slug, examining his nails. 'Can't stand needles myself. You never know what you might catch.'

Martin, watching from a distance, wondered if he'd been right to tell Slug about Harry's phobia. *He cried like a baby for almost half an hour before he'd let them give him the shot*, Eve had told him the night they'd met Harry in the pub. Judging by his expression, they had exposed a decidedly vulnerable nerve.

'Consider yourself a bit of a gambler, eh Harry?' Slug asked. 'Well, in case you're wondering what's in the syringe, it's a cocktail. Might just put you to sleep for a few hours. Or –' he folded his chubby arms and smiled thoughtfully, clearly enjoying himself '– it could have a more permanent, more *damaging* effect. Depends how strong the dosage is, but then you'll have to decide on that for yourself.'

Wide-eyed with fear Harry sprang to his feet. There were several livid marks on his right thigh and his left knee bore a nasty gash as if he'd fallen heavily against something. 'You can't treat me like this,' he blustered – it was impossible to maintain even a modicum of dignity with exposed genitals. 'You've picked the wrong bloody man, let me tell you, if you think these idle threats of yours are going to work.'

'I'd sit the fuck down if I were you, Harry,' warned Slug, no longer smiling. 'We didn't bring you here to play musical chairs.' He nodded at the man with ginger hair. 'Do it, Monk.'

The man he called Monk had been staring at Harry lazily from the far side of the room, lifting a hand every now and again to bring the cigarette he was holding to his mouth. Dropping it to the floor, he crushed the stub with his foot and, advancing to the table, picked up the syringe. A strange noise escaped Harry's mouth when he saw him do this. The syringe was the biggest Martin had ever seen; not one of those disposable, plastic things used to take blood, or give a vaccination. This instrument, made of glass and stainless steel, looked more suitable for inseminating cows. Monk broke the glass neck of one of the milky ampoules, angled the bottle and inserted the tip of the syringe needle into the top.

Harry's eyes bulged with fear. 'Please,' he begged, as a small amount of fluid spurted from the tip of the needle into the air. 'Don't –'

Slug shrugged nonchalantly. 'It's your choice, Harry.'

Monk brought the needle inches from Harry's sweating face. 'Make him stop,' moaned Harry in terror. 'For *Christ's* sake. I'll do what you ask, just make him stop.'

Slug waved Monk away. 'OK. Just don't waste my time.'

Harry's body sagged with relief. 'What do you want to know?'

Martin stepped forward so that he was standing directly in front of him. Until then he had been feeling sorry for Harry, remembering what it was like to have three inspectors tongue-lashing him hour after hour until he couldn't think straight. But now he thought of Celia's terror-struck expression in the mews that night, her trembling body as he'd carried her in his arms, and the anger rose in him until his hands shook so hard he had to fist them.

'Tell us about Charlie Fitzherbert,' he said coldly.

Harry looked up sharply, alarmed by the new voice. 'Who have you been talking to?' Close to, Martin could see that his right eye, puffy and swollen, was partially closed.

'Someone who knows an awful lot about you.'

Harry snorted. 'I don't believe a word of it.'

'Your loyalties are misguided, Harry,' Martin said evenly. 'You may not choose to say anything, but they were very keen to tell us about you.' He was bluffing, clutching at straws, but Harry didn't know this.

Harry paled. 'Whatever he's told you, he's lying. I had nothing to do with Charlie's death.'

'Come off it, Harry.' Slug this time, his voice menacing. 'We heard it gave you quite a hard-on.'

Harry was sweating like a pig. 'No! I swear it.'

'Don't lie to me, fuck-wit,' spat Slug.

'It isn't *true*, I tell you.'

Martin could tell he was lying. It was obvious by the shifty way Harry's gaze kept slipping from his. Something in him snapped. He had come here not just for revenge, but for proof. Proof of the crimes that had been committed against him, to clear his name with the police, and Harry held the key. His hand snatched up the syringe on the table, and he lunged at Harry. 'Tell us, you bastard, or I'll stick this in you myself.'

Harry screamed as the tip of the needle nicked the skin of his right arm. 'All *right*!' he cried as Martin took his hand away.

For a moment the room was silent, Harry's sweat-drenched face bleached so pale that his eyes took on a luminous brilliance. Carefully he lit another cigarette with trembling hands, exhaled, and shook out the match.

'I'd known Charlie almost as long as I've known Piers. We'd meet up sometimes for a drink,' he said at last, blowing smoke out of the corner of his mouth. 'That Wednesday – the day before it happened – Charlie called to say he had some Hawaiian pot and did I want to come round and share it with him. His parents had gone away for the week so we knew we'd have the place to ourselves.'

'You went alone?' Martin asked.

Harry nodded. 'We got pretty loaded. Stayed up all night drinking and smoking – it was strong stuff. The next morning neither of us felt like sleeping so we carried on drinking – the old boy stocks an excellent malt whisky.' He blew out a vigorous plume of smoke. 'I was lying on the sofa gazing up at the ceiling in a bit of a stupor when Piers arrived. I could tell Charlie hadn't expected him because he was immediately agitated, nervous and on edge – I thought it must be the effect of the dope. Piers was clearly very angry about something – he didn't exactly look pleased to find me there either, which was strange because we'd shared an amicable lunch only two days previously.'

Slug nodded impatiently. 'Get to the point, Harry.'

'He launched forth about some message from Charlie he'd intercepted by chance on Eve's answering machine. He said that if Charlie had any ideas about trying to wreck his relationship then he could think again. To my surprise Charlie merely threw back his head and laughed. Thought no one knew about your sleazy little sideline with Steve McInerney, he said, but then if you will go leaving your mobile around in public places. Charlie's eyes had this glazed, crazy look as Piers asked him what he meant exactly and Charlie laughed again. Got you worried now, you two-timing bastard, haven't I? And he started ranting on about what McInerney had said to him on Piers's mobile one night – thinking it was Piers on the other end, how he knew about the two hundred thousand Piers had borrowed from him.'

The night of the stag-do, Martin realised, the one Ollie had mentioned. *It was a brilliant impersonation. You honestly couldn't tell them apart.*

'He said that Eve had every right to know what kind of man she was marrying.' Harry dabbed at the corner of his damaged eye which was weeping a yellow discharge. 'I watched Piers's face. It was ashen. His hands were balled into fists and I really thought he might go for Charlie, but he just stood there listening to him angrily raving on until he became quite hysterical. I was feeling very uncomfortable by now, worried about it getting out of hand. Charlie began to shout obscenities at Piers, really laying into him about how he never thought about anyone but himself, that he abused his position, his friendships, to the point where no one felt they could trust him, including his precious family. Then he said that before he was allowed to gamble away the family's entire estate he had half a mind to go down there and tell his father what kind of a son he really had . . . And that was when Piers slapped him.'

Harry looked thoughtfully at the thread of smoke curling from the end of his cigarette. He seemed to have forgotten the circumstances that had brought him here.

'I don't think he meant to hit him as hard as he did, but Charlie just stood there, a large white mark stamped across his cheek, looking rather stunned. I decided to get the hell out of it but as I struggled to my feet the room started to spin and Charlie suddenly ran towards the stairs, shouting hysterically that he was going to let everyone know what Piers had done to Francesca and the baby.

'I heard him running upstairs, still shouting threats, and then a door slammed. I can remember turning to Piers and saying "Let's go, old boy," thinking we'd have a drink some place so that he could cool off. But as I spoke, we heard the ping of the phone coming from an extension upstairs. Then Piers told me to stay where I was and began to head for the door. "What are you going to do?" I asked him in a daze – the walls were still moving and I was beginning to feel distinctly unwell. But he never answered. I suppose I should have tried to stop him from following Charlie upstairs but even I couldn't have imagined what he'd do.' At this point Harry broke off, sweat pouring from his brow.

Martin felt a lump growing in the pit of his stomach. 'What happened next, Harry?' he asked softly.

'For a full minute everything was silent. Almost eerily so. Then I heard this muffled thud coming from above me, as if something heavy had been dropped. I staggered to the door and called out, you have to believe that, I really did try, but the dope – the drink, it –' he faltered, his Adam's apple plunging then rising again.

'Then Piers reappeared. God, I don't think I'll ever forget the look on his face – like a madman – as he came back down the stairs, his hands, his clothes covered in blood. He just looked at me without saying anything and because I couldn't stomach the prospect of being alone with him, I stumbled out of the room. I found Charlie's body in the upstairs bathroom. He was dead. The telephone was hanging off the wall and there was a cricket bat lying by his side, covered in blood and bits of –' he hesitated at this point as if he was picturing the gruesome scene. 'Piers must have hit him over the head with it several times. *Jesus*, I've never seen so much mess, I'd never have imagined –'

With a rush of what was almost like nausea, Martin was overtaken by the feeling that he was being sucked down through the earth by a powerful undercurrent which threatened to engulf him.

'By then I was feeling too ill to even think straight,' Harry continued, his face red and blotchy and streaked with tears of remorse. 'I could feel the bile rising in my throat and ran into the next room and vomited on the bed. I felt dazed, stunned, appalled at what had taken place, but I didn't know what to do. I mean, this was the last situation I thought I'd get myself mixed up in. Eventually Piers came and found me and I **told** him we should call the police but he wouldn't hear of it. He said that what had happened to Charlie was nothing compared to what he'd do to me if I didn't keep my mouth shut. Then he reminded me of our little agreement.' Harry cleared his throat and shifted uneasily. 'I was between jobs at that time and he had lent me some money. I also had the use of his flat, which made my situation a little – well, delicate.' *Lives practically rent-free in a flat Piers owns.* Another awkward pause. 'It was Piers who came up with the idea of making it look like a burglary. He was very convincing, made it all sound so rational, like it was the only choice we had. We couldn't very well get rid of the body, so we had to make it look as if Charlie had stumbled on an intruder.' He gave a shaky laugh. 'The coppers bought it too – for a while.

'Piers found a pair of rubber gloves from under the bathroom sink which he made me put on and used his own leather ones so that we wouldn't leave any trace of fingerprints – he thought of everything. I didn't like wrecking the flat but I was too scared to argue. You weren't there,' he justified. 'You don't know what he was like. He had just killed a man. It might have been me next.'

'What about the money?' Martin asked.

Harry ducked his head and, after a moment, said, 'We found it in the safe. Piers was able to work the combination and got it open. There was a wad of cash inside.'

'How much?'

'About six thousand.' *I've had a good month. Can't a chap share his good fortune with his friends?*

'Did you take anything else?'

'We took the TV and the stereo – we had to take something otherwise no one would have believed it was a robbery – but that was all, I swear.'

'Who messed up Charlie's room?' Martin asked, thinking about the lighter. Harry thought about it, then said, 'Piers did. In fact he was quite insistent about being the one to do it. Anyway, we got bin liners from the kitchen and put Piers's clothes into one – there was blood on everything – and he changed into one of Charlie's suits. We put the cricket bat into another bag along with the gloves and loaded them both into my car. No one saw us leave. Piers didn't like the idea of us driving away separately but we couldn't risk leaving one of our cars behind so we went in convoy, me up front, Piers in the rear.

'As I drove off, my greatest fear was that the police would stop me – one look inside those plastic bags and I'd have been done for. Approaching an amber light, I heard sirens wailing and panicked. The lights had just turned red but I slammed my foot down on the accelerator and jumped them. I knew I had to outrun them. Then in my rear mirror I saw the fire engine – no, two of them – closing in on me. I was forced to keep driving as there was nowhere to pull up. When I checked my mirror again, I could see that Piers was still at the lights. Here was my chance. I had already reached a decision not to go to the police; I hadn't done anything wrong, but who the hell was going to believe my word against his? I needed some insurance. At the next red set of lights, I grabbed the bin liner behind the passenger seat and pulled out the first thing I saw. It was Piers's monogrammed shirt, covered with blood. By the time the lights had turned green, I'd stuffed the shirt inside the glove compartment, retied the bag and shoved it back where I'd found it. Piers caught up with me at the council dump ten minutes later. To my relief he didn't seem to suspect anything, but he kept up the threats.'

'And you got rid of the bags there?' said Martin.

'The pit was the size of a small house. There was no chance of anyone fishing around amongst the rubbish – it smelt awful, so we just threw them inside. Then we waited for a while and watched it being lifted by a crane and taken off to be burned.'

'What did you do with the shirt?' Slug asked.

Harry looked at the floor and received another clout round the ear from Monk. It must have been quite a blow because blood started oozing from his left ear.

'I buried it.'

There was a long silence. Martin's eyes were smarting from the cigarette smoke. 'That everything?' he asked.

Harry nodded dumbly as if recounting the events of the murder had sapped every last bit of his strength. Slug pulled his considerable bulk out of his chair, wiped an invisible piece of dust off his silk shirt, and gave a curt flick of his fingers. Gull stepped forward and dumped Harry's trousers, underpants and shoes at his feet.

'You can get dressed now,' he said sharply.

Harry, disbelieving, looked first at Slug, then at Gull and finally at Martin. Then he hastily began to scramble into his clothes as if afraid that Slug would change his mind. When he had finished tying his shoes, he pulled himself up and said in a cowering voice, 'What happens now?'

'Now?' Slug repeated, taking him by the scruff of the neck and eyeballing him. 'Now, you scummy scab, you piece of turd, now is when you show us where you buried the shirt.'

They were fortunate with the traffic and made the A3 in good time, Gull at the wheel, Slug next to him in the passenger seat, and a doleful Harry squeezed in the back between Martin and Monk. He'd told them that he had taken the shirt to his parents' place in Surrey the day after the murder, and buried it in a nearby wood.

'Will they be at the house?' Martin asked Harry.

He shook his head. 'They're in Wiltshire visiting my sister so it should be empty.'

Martin was relieved. Monk, at his side, was about as chatty as a deaf mute, but he could feel the violence seething within him and dreaded to think what might happen if he unleashed it on a concerned parent asking too many questions.

Gull parked outside the secluded Tudor house and they

all got out. Then Monk disappeared inside a toolshed with Harry and re-emerged minutes later carrying a spade. With Harry in the lead they set off through the garden and followed a path into the woods beyond, ferns and dead wood cracking underfoot. A warm wind blew from the south, gently rustling leaves, and Martin rolled up his sleeves, relieved to be out in the fresh air. They continued through the undergrowth until, after fighting their way through coiling bramble bushes and stumbling over a pile of roughly sawn rotting logs, they reached a clearing under the trees. It was here that Harry suddenly came to a halt. He pointed to a spot where the earth looked fresh and Monk speared into it with the spade. Everyone gathered round and the tension mounted as the hole grew bigger. But they didn't have long to wait. The shirt – pale blue cotton – was in a see-through plastic bag, and although it was scrunched up Martin could see the bloodstains, patchy and dark, by now almost black. Monk handed the bag to Gull who took the shirt out.

Slug said in a quiet aside to Martin, 'That'll convince them if anything will.'

'But is it enough?'

'Are you kidding? It's been practically marinated in the victim's blood.'

'Wait a minute,' said Gull, interrupting them. He'd found something in the breast pocket of the shirt.

Slug moved closer. 'What have you got?'

Gull, shrugging, held a plastic tape in his hand about the size of a matchbox. 'It's a microcassette.'

'Want to explain this, Harry?' asked Slug.

But Harry was looking as surprised as the rest of them. 'I've never seen it before,' he said rather too convincingly.

'Looks to me like the kind used for a Dictaphone,' said Martin, 'or an answering machine.'

He exchanged glances with Slug and knew their thoughts matched.

'Your parents have an answering machine, Harry?'

'Yes,' he said, 'they do.'

Harry, Monk and Gull were instructed to wait in the

car while Slug and Martin made their way to the house. Following Harry's directions they soon came across an old Panasonic in a room off the hall that was crowded with large potted plants, assorted old furniture and fading rugs. Martin slipped the cassette into the machine and pressed the play button.

The voice on the tape was one he had never heard before; the angry and bitter tone of someone who had been betrayed in the most shocking way; who had not only lost the woman he had loved but whose child had been aborted without his consent. *Even now, I can't think of them without feeling a terrible rage, a burning desire to get back at them for what they've done.* It was the voice of a dead man.

The call must have been one of the last Charlie had made before his death. Piers must have removed the cassette from Eve's answering machine before going round to see Charlie. No wonder he had arrived at the Fitzherberts' flat with so much urgency. He stood to lose everything. Not just Eve, but the respect of his peers, his father, his inheritance which represented a small fortune.

Slug slapped him on the shoulder. 'I'd say you've got enough there to get that fucker put away for thirty years.'

They dropped Martin off at Hammersmith Broadway and he got a bus the rest of the way. He was dreading what he had to do next, yet realised that he had no alternative. He got off at Holland Park and, with growing apprehension, made his way down to the police station in Ladbroke Grove. Braced for the worst, he introduced himself to the constable behind the desk, a kindly fellow who took a note of his details and then showed him into a starkly furnished room. After he had been there for a while, he looked at his watch. The constable had been gone for ten minutes and it bothered him. He had told the policeman it was urgent, so why was he taking so long to come back?

In order to kill time, Martin took out the eight scratch cards he'd bought that morning and etched off the silver lining. Not a single number matched. In disgust he threw the cards to the floor. When was he going to learn to stop throwing his money away? he thought mournfully. His eyes grazed the watch on his wrist. Fifteen minutes. He didn't like this at all. He could feel his armpits dampen, a cold sweat trickling down his sides. Was he mad to have come? The plastic carrier containing the shirt and the tape lay in his lap and he gripped it tightly because his future depended on it.

He was reaching a point when he thought he couldn't stand the waiting any longer when the door burst open, and a detective inspector appeared.

'Martin Leak?' he said brusquely, holding open the door which led to another room. Martin stood up, his legs trembling. 'Would you like to step in here.'

THIRTY-THREE

It was raining when Martin left the police station more than four hours later. He raised his face to the heavy drops, warm as bathwater, and let the shower wash over him until he was completely drenched. He felt shattered, as if he had just driven a thousand miles. But he was a free man: the world seemed suddenly fresh and wonderful, and he wanted to embrace it with a new abandon. Triumph at escaping from an imminent catastrophe filled his whole being with spontaneous joy; he had won. He had told the police everything, well, almost everything – editing out Slug's involvement – and had handed over the evidence. He learned that Mrs Wingate *had* let the police into his flat and that Mr Ash's saxophone had been checked for fingerprints before being returned to him. When it was explained that all the charges against Martin had been dropped, that he was free to go, the relief was so enormous that he almost broke down. It was only then that the strain he had been under in recent months finally hit him. Even now, as he sloshed through the puddles back to his flat, two police cars were wending their way back from the Tetbury estate where Piers and a hundred friends of the family had gathered for his uncle's funeral. What a surprise they must have had!

In spite of his weariness, his longing for a bath, a change of clothes, Martin didn't want to go back to his flat or to be alone. The events of the last twenty-four-hours still felt unreal, as if he had watched it all happening to someone else in a darkened cinema and had then stumbled out into brilliant sunlight with the story-line continuing to replay itself in his mind. He wanted to share the moment of triumph with someone, to celebrate his freedom if not his victory over Piers, even though it felt curiously hollow. He thought of Eve, beautiful, dazzling Eve, but he couldn't face her – not yet, not under such circumstances. The truth could wait for a few more hours. There was only one person he felt the need to see, one person who would understand, to whom he owed a debt of gratitude. He waved down a passing cab and, remembering that today was usually her day off, gave the driver Celia's address.

So elated was his mood that it didn't occur to him she might not be at home until he had paid off the taxi and raced up the steps to the front door. But after several rings on her bell it was clear that the flat was empty. Suddenly dispirited, he sat on the steps and gazed out into the road. This must surely be one of the happiest days of his life, he thought. Everything had come right for him. His freedom, the recent breakthrough with his mother, Eve's reciprocal love ... Yet it was Celia, not Eve, he wanted to share his happiness with.

Puzzled by his inner confusion, he flagged down another cab and reluctantly told the driver to take him home. The day was still insistently lovely and he pushed the window down to let in the passing sounds of celebratory music ranging from reggae to rock. Somewhere, in a nearby flat, he could hear the plaintive cry of a hungry baby. He was looking out at the shops, the houses which had become so familiar to him, all rushing by in a kind of daze, thinking of nothing when the taxi braked suddenly. He was jolted forward and, as his hand shot out to stop himself from falling, he could hear the cabby mumbling apologies from the front. He stuck his head out of the window and saw that immediately ahead of them a woman was lying on the road. She must have stumbled in her rush to beat the lights. Two individuals had already rushed to her aid and she appeared unharmed, so he didn't get out to help. Instead his eyes came to rest on a police car drawn up parallel to the cab, just a few feet away, but going in the opposite direction. There was a man in the back. Must be taking some poor bugger back to the station, he thought, remembering that recently that had been him. And then the hairs stood up on the back of his neck and the hot terror of Italy rose like a tidal wave all over again.

It was Piers, sitting between two men and staring stonily ahead, his head strangely motionless as if he was listening to himself think. Yet Martin had the distinct impression that he knew he was being observed, that at any moment he would incline his handsome head towards the window and stare at him. Martin was paralysed with fear. Air caught in his throat, a hot flush ran through his body as he waited, picturing the expression on Piers's face just before he pushed his tied-up body into the pool. But the moment never came. The taxi began to move forward, and Piers disappeared.

Waves of relief swept over Martin. His lungs began to work again and he told himself that he had nothing more to fear, but it took a long time to stop shaking. Weakly, he rested his head on the back seat and closed his eyes.

Oh, Jesus, he thought. It's over. It's finally over.

He had arranged to meet Eve at eight o'clock that night. When he arrived at her flat her mood was stiff and awkward, as if they were strangers meeting under difficult circumstances. She looked lovely and her green

315

eyes, had a luminous bronze tint, but she was not the girl he had been with in Italy, or the person he had said goodbye to at Heathrow two days ago. Something had changed.

'Do you want a glass of champagne?' she offered. 'I've opened a bottle.'

'What are we celebrating?'

'Nothing in particular. I'm just in the mood for a drink. It's been a long day.'

Her flat had pleasing contours, high ceilings, and afforded a good view of the leafy enclosure that backed on to Oxford Gardens, but the rooms looked as if they had been furnished from an Ikea catalogue, randomly and without thought. He had always imagined it to be full of tasteful pieces of furniture such as the ones he remembered seeing at Partridge Manor. A dozen or so novels were stuffed in one corner of the room, but they were all pretty lightweight, the kind of books you read on an aeroplane. Pictures of Piers – disconcertingly – haunted the surface of a table by the window. As he accepted the glass he wondered why she hadn't got around to removing them.

They both sat down. A moment of silence passed before he opened the conversation. 'How is it being back at work? Did you sort things out with Hammers?'

She shrugged. 'I made him a lot of money yesterday and that put him in a more lenient mood. He's pissed off with you, though, for not returning any of his calls.'

'I'll ring him in the morning.'

'I gather you're a free man.'

He paused, the fluted glass at his lips. So the word was out. 'Who told you?'

'Hammers got a call at the office from one of the investigating officers. You must be very relieved.'

She sounded faintly sarcastic and he looked at her, trying to decode the thoughts tripping through her mind. 'You could say that.'

She lit a cigarette and smoked it greedily. 'You might have told me, Martin.'

He looked down at his drink. 'I thought about it – I mean I wanted to.'

'You went to Italy with a murder charge on your head,' she suddenly flared. 'You *knew* the police would be looking for you and that by taking me I'd be incriminated too but you never said a word. Didn't you think I was entitled to the truth?'

'Eve, everything escalated so quickly. All I saw was a chance to get away. I needed time – and space to get my head round what was going on.'

'We spent *three* days and nights together,' she accused, 'and you expect me to believe that in all that time the right opportunity never presented itself?'

'It wasn't that simple,' Martin said defensively.

'You *lied* to me.'

'No,' he responded with feeling, 'I was shielding you.'

She snorted disbelievingly. 'From what exactly?'

He left Piers's name unspoken but it hovered over their conversation like a buzzard circling a carcass. 'I didn't think you were ready to handle the truth.'

She speared him with her green gaze. 'You know what I think,' she said. 'I think you were using me.' Her look was defiant. 'And I'm not the only one who thinks you've treated me badly.'

He looked at her in amazement. 'Who have you been talking too?'

She got up and walked to the window, her cigarette pointing towards the ceiling like a little pistol.

'Eve,' he urged, 'I was being set up. I meant to tell you, in fact I was planning to do so tonight, but at the time I – I couldn't afford to take any risks, can't you see that?'

Quick as a flash she turned on him. 'Then it's true that you didn't trust me.'

'That's not what I said.' For a moment he brooded in his chair. She looked tired and he noticed a small crop of spots which had broken out on her skin. It was an insignificant detail and yet he was struck by an altered perception of her. It was as if he had previously seen her through a mist, a gauze of chiffon, which had now been taken away, revealing imperfections. 'All I'm asking from you is a little understanding,' he said finally.

'Some would say that's more than you deserve.'

'Tell me who you've been talking to. I have a right to know who's been spreading false accusations about me.'

'All right then.' She looked straight at him and said defiantly. 'It was Piers.'

His lips slackened in shock. 'What!'

'He called me.'

Jesus! 'When?'

'The day after we got back from Italy. He wanted to meet me.' Her eyes met his then slid away. 'It was just one drink.'

Martin couldn't believe his ears. '*Christ*, Eve, have you any idea –?'

'At least he had time for me, which is more than can be said for you,' she hurled back. 'What conclusions was I supposed to draw after our holiday? You said you loved me, that I was all that mattered to you, yet no sooner had we landed at Heathrow than you dumped me in a taxi and disappeared for two days. No call to let me know you were all right. No one even knew where to get hold of you.'

'Eve,' he warned, trying to keep a grip on his emotions. His tone was dangerously low.

'You don't own me any more than he does. Who I choose to see is my affair.'

'Even when they've murdered someone?' he said abruptly.

Now it was her turn to look shocked. 'What!'

He sighed, jerking hair off his forehead with an impatient hand. 'They've arrested Piers for the murder of Charlie Fitzherbert.'

Blood drained from her face. 'It isn't true,' she said faintly.

'It is, Eve. And they can prove it. I admit that I lied to you but only about one thing. Those thugs at the hotel pool never beat me up, it was Piers. He hit me over the head, then tied me to a chair and pushed me into the pool. He meant to kill me. Your intervention was what saved me.'

She was very pale. 'You're just saying this because you can't bear the thought of my being with him.'

'I'm telling you,' Martin said, moving towards her and gripping her shoulder in frustrated anger, 'because it's time you knew what kind of monster he really is.'

She pulled away and blocked her ears with her hands like a child. 'Get out,' she spat.

Martin stared at her, stunned, his face reddening with fury. He wanted to hurt her as she had hurt him, but he did nothing. When he finally spoke, his voice was laced with disgust. 'Then perhaps you deserve each other after all.'

She hesitated, fractionally. 'Martin.' She put a hand on his arm. 'I'm sorry.' Her eyes fell on him in a sort of appeal, but for once her beauty failed to move him. He pulled his arm away, his mouth set, his gaze impenetrable.

There was a touch of panic in her eyes as she watched him collect his jacket. 'Where are you going?' she asked as he reached the door, her voice lacking its earlier rancour.

'I'm going home, Eve,' he said, without turning round, 'where I belong.'

Two days later, he was back at Carlyle. At first he wasn't sure he had a job to return to, but Hammers agreed to meet him for a drink after work and the two of them talked it through. To Martin's surprise it transpired that Hammers had been deeply worried on his behalf, and had even contacted the police when he failed to turn up for work. It was strange being back in the office, trying to pick up the pieces, getting embarrassing we-never-doubted-you-for-a-moment slaps on the back from his colleagues – with the notable exception of Eve.

She was sitting in her usual place for the morning's meeting but quickly averted her eyes when she saw him arrive, and Martin took a seat on the other side of the room.

'I start on a rather sad note,' Hammers began, 'when I tell you that Friday was Celia's last day with us.'

A prickle rose on the nape of Martin's neck. 'What did you say?'

Roger turned to him in surprise. 'I thought you knew?'

'I can't say I was happy to let her go,' Hammers sighed. 'She was one of the best senior lettings manager I've ever worked with. But she had her reasons and I have to respect her decision.'

Oliver leaned back in his chair so that the front two legs were off the ground and folded his arms. 'Probably gone to sign up with some ghastly commune.'

'I don't get it.' Martin was struggling to take this in. 'Celia wouldn't just walk out on a job.'

Hammers looked at him. 'Oh, it wasn't sudden, chum. She came to me with her resignation almost two weeks ago, but at the time she asked me not to say anything. I don't think she wanted us to make a fuss.'

'We weren't going to,' said Oliver, winking at Eve, who was sitting in moody contemplation.

'Have we got a replacement yet?' Roger asked. 'Only things got pretty tight after Rupert left us in the lurch last year.'

'Sorted,' Hammers reassured them. 'Judy Deagle's coming over from the Bushell's office in Hammersmith. She starts tomorrow.'

Eve frowned. 'Who is Judy Deagle?'

'Oh, you can't miss her,' mouthed Oliver, widening his arms as far apart as they would go. 'I'm telling you the woman's he-*uge*!'

THIRTY-FOUR

Chiswick was like stepping into a small patch of rural England, Martin decided. Inherently middle class, it was peopled by those who had grown out of Notting Hill with its artfully decorated flats, stripped floors and roof terraces. They came west to settle down, and to structure their lives by starting a family. Martin was well aware that house prices were steep, especially in the much-sought-after Bedford Park, but what might have bought them scruffy rooms in the Gate, would, in Chiswick, afford them a terraced house with a garden of their own.

Martin took the tube to Turnham Green. The Terrace – as it was known – was active with shoppers. There were people with young children everywhere. Women wearing silk head-scarves like the Queen, carried baskets containing organic meat, cheese wrapped in waxed paper, Tarte Tartin and pre-packed meals from Marks and Spencer.

The estate agency was about halfway down on the right-hand side. When Martin found it he didn't immediately go in, pretending to be engrossed in the property details displayed in the window. But it was the office which held his attention. Celia was on the phone, her head tilted to one side in that funny way she had when someone had her full attention. He waited until she hung up then pushed open the door.

The office was busy so she didn't immediately spot him. Three people were waiting to be seen and as there was nowhere for him to sit, he hovered in the doorway. When their eyes met he half-smiled and caught her startled look. Then she swept a hand across her dark helmet of hair and came to meet him. He had been about to speak when a woman, waiting on one of the sofas with her husband, suddenly vacated her seat and approached him somewhat indignantly.

'Excuse me,' she said in a quarrelsome voice, 'but I believe *we* were here first.'

In confusion Celia looked from Martin to the woman. 'Please, come and take a seat at my desk.'

Celia threw him a quick look of apology over her shoulder as the couple picked up their shopping bags and made their way over to her desk.

One of the other negotiators now approached Martin. 'Perhaps I can help you with something?' he said in a Sloane voice, refined and expensive. 'Are you looking to buy?'

Martin's mind raced. 'What are two-bed flats going for in this area?'

He spent ten minutes with the broker looking through particulars, one eye keeping a careful watch on Celia. But because she still seemed to be embroiled in a lengthy discussion with the couple and there was only so much hanging around he could get away with, Martin made some excuse about his pay-and-display ticket running out of time and left.

Back outside, he stuffed the details of half-a-dozen flats into his back pocket, feeling as if fate had deserted him. The pedestrian light turned green and he crossed the road without any particular plan. He contemplated going home and calling her at the flat later, but later seemed a long way off and his thwarted attempt to talk to her had irked him. There must be some way of seeing her. As he walked he felt the weight of his mobile phone in his jacket pocket. He took it out and pressed the memory button which stored important numbers. Good. Celia's mobile was among them. While it rang he took shelter in a doorway.

'It's me,' he said, when she answered.

'You shouldn't have come. It's better if I don't see you.'

He ignored the brush-off. 'I need to talk to you.'

He could hear her thinking. 'It's a bit difficult right now.'

'Look, I'll wait for you somewhere. Just give me ten minutes of your time.' He said this as if everything he was ever going to accomplish in his life turned on how she would respond.

A pause. 'All right,' she sighed, a ringing phone and her name being shouted in the background. 'At the Copper Kettle in half an hour.'

She was late, her face flushed as if she had been

running. 'I can't stay long,' she said, sliding into the seat opposite him.

'What will you have?'

'Camomile tea,' she said to the waitress.

Without realising it, he had been worried that she might change her mind and not turn up. So, seeing her now, a little drawn as if she hadn't been sleeping properly, but with that strange sort of loveliness she had, made his heart give such a glad and violent leap, he thought it might burst.

'How's the new job?'

'It's OK.'

'You don't sound very enthusiastic.'

'Maybe I'm getting a little disenchanted with the industry.' She seemed not to want to talk about herself. 'How are things with you? I heard they dropped the charges.'

'Yes,' he said. 'No more looking over my shoulder.'

'You must be very relieved.'

'I am.'

It was only very slight – her resistance – but it was glaringly obvious to him. Like a turtle she had withdrawn into her shell and was going to take a lot of persuading to come out again. He coughed. 'It's not the same, you know.'

'What isn't?'

'The office,' he said, 'without you.' She looked down and because he could feel her embarrassment, he quickly added, 'You should see who they've got as a replacement. She's had to bring in her own special chair because the existing one can't accommodate her bulk.'

She laughed. 'Judy's all right once you get to know her,' she said, her eyes lighting up briefly, 'and she gets good results. She used to be a physical fitness teacher.'

'Really,' he said doubtfully.

'Actually, I don't think I'll be in this job for long. I'm thinking of leaving property altogether.'

He was alarmed by this unexpected statement. For all he knew she might have met someone – God, had she? –

or be making imminent plans to move abroad, somewhere he wouldn't have access to her. 'To do what?' he asked cautiously. Her hands rested demurely on the table – tantalisingly close to his, but he resisted the urge to reach out and take hold of them.

'Practice holistic medicine. It's something I've always wanted to do. The College of Homeopathy have offered me a place next year and I'm thinking of accepting.'

'Oh,' he said, almost knocked out with relief. 'I think that's a *terrific* idea.'

The pure grey eyes settled on him, evaluating, enquiring. 'Do you?' she said finally, as if she'd expected him to laugh at her suggestion. 'Do you really?'

'*Christ*, yes. No one wants to be stuck selling properties all their life. I envy you having the talent to do other things, especially something you enjoy so much.'

'And you?' she said, uncomfortable under his scrutiny. 'What about your plans, now that it's all over?'

He shrugged. 'Get a place of my own. Find someone to share it with.' You, he thought silently.

'What about Eve?'

He shifted his gaze. He didn't want to talk about Eve. 'She's very independent,' he said, vaguely. 'I don't think she's quite cut out for a life of domesticity.' He looked at her, trying to gauge what was going on in her mind.

'Celia,' he said, reaching for her hand. 'All that business about Piers; I'm *truly* sorry that it happened, that you felt you had to leave your job. I should have been there for you and I wasn't and I feel terrible about it,' he admitted, clearing his throat. 'But I want to put it right. I want things between us to go back to the way they were.'

She smiled sadly at him. 'Martin, it can never be the same again. It's too late for that.'

'Please don't say that.'

'I've got to get on with my own life, move on, don't you see?' No, he didn't. He didn't at all. '– And you, well you've got so much going for you now. Things will look different in a few days.' She glanced at her watch and got up very suddenly. 'I must go or I'll get into trouble.'

A knot tightened in his throat as she reached for her bag. She was slipping away from him and he couldn't think what to do about it. Blind panic filled him.

'Celia,' he beseeched. 'Don't go. Not yet. There's still so much to talk about.' You and me, he thought hopelessly.

'I must. They'll be wondering where I am.'

'Can I see you – at least give you a call – over the weekend?' He felt like the bird he had found trapped in his flat, battering its body against the window-pane in a useless bid for freedom.

She looked at him with her rain-coloured eyes, and even before she spoke he thought: she's abandoning me, closing the door, locking me out of her world.

'We both know that wouldn't be a good idea.' She bent forward, gave him a quick feather-like kiss on his cheek. 'Goodbye, Martin,' she said gently.

He was seized by a desperate urgency. He tried to get his mouth to respond but nothing came out and all he could do was watch her turn and walk out of the café. He had the impression that happiness was beyond him as he watched her skip across the zebra crossing. Then she reached the corner of the road and was no longer in view.

It didn't take long for the details of Piers's fall from grace to spread. On Wednesday the story made headlines.

'Fucking hell,' Oliver's mouth hung open. 'I don't bloody *believe* it. Has anyone seen this?' He held up an open copy of the *Daily Telegraph* where there was a large photograph of a dazed Piers Hunt being escorted away by two plain-clothed officers, under the caption:

Heir to millions arrested for the murder of cabinet minister's son

Hammers, Roger, Judy – Celia's replacement – and

Martin all stared at the headlines in varying degrees of shock and intrigue.

'They had the story on TV this morning,' said Roger, who had never been much of a fan of Piers. 'It certainly spiced up my breakfast.'

Oliver looked at him incredulously, 'How would you like to be in his shoes? He could get life for this.'

'Should have thought of that before he killed him,' Roger said piously.

'Don't let Eve catch you reading that,' warned Hammers. 'She'll be in later. It can't be easy for her right now.' He glanced uneasily at Martin as he said this.

'What's Eve got to do with it?' Judy asked.

'She very nearly married him,' Roger explained.

For once Hammers was taking an interest in the office gossip. 'Is there any mention of when the trial might be?' he asked, hand hovering over the telephone.

Oliver, buried once more in the paper, gave his head an abstracted shake. ' "Hunt, arrested at the family estate in Tetbury during a funeral gathering for his uncle," ' he read out, ' "is being held in police custody after being refused bail. The trial date is thought to be scheduled for some time next month." ' He lowered the paper and whistled. 'They're not going to let him out.'

Roger made a scoffing sound. 'Money can't buy you everything.'

Oliver peered over the top of the paper at Martin. 'You're keeping very quiet about all this, Leak. Of all of us I'd have thought you'd be the most interested.'

Martin got up from his desk and wandered to the top of the stairs. 'Some people,' he said flatly, 'get exactly what they deserve.'

He had a viewing – a new conversion on the Portobello Road – which turned out to be a waste of time. But he didn't care. He was blind to everything around him: the Hockney-blue sky, the smell of exhaust fumes, beautiful dark-skinned girls in butterfly-thin dresses that floated teasingly across their thighs. He had expected to revel in Piers's undoing, savour the sweet, glorious taste of revenge, yet he had never felt so depressed in his life. Since his visit to Turnham Green, a migraine the size of a Trident submarine had grown inside his head. Even now, with powerful drugs to keep the pain at bay, he could feel the grim throbbing of his right temple.

He kept going over the details Oliver had read out to them: Piers's entire business affairs now under investigation; the arrest of Harry who had been found wandering along Chelsea Bridge in a drunken state, the media hovering around the Cotswold estate like a swarm of wasps. He wondered if Eve had heard the news yet – she had been with clients all morning so he hadn't seen her. Would she want consoling? Probably. But that wasn't his job any more. That side of his life was well and truly over.

He should have realised that it was never going to last. Right from the start he had accepted that he was the outsider. Only, he had hoped to find himself on the inside by believing in the dream of Eve. For a while, being with her – having her – had made all things seem possible. He had wanted her in the same way that he had wanted to buy into the Fitzherbert lifestyle; to step into someone else's shoes and draw a veil over his own feelings of inadequacy. Viewed from a distance, the illusion worked. But up close, like coloured light, his fantasies were as insubstantial as a hologram.

On his way back to the office, he stopped in Colville Terrace to buy two lottery tickets and a paper – he wanted to read the details of Piers's arrest later on. As an afterthought, he added a scratch card to his purchases. He was still thinking about Piers as he used a coin to scratch the card as first one, then two five hundred pounds appeared in their little boxes. He smiled ruefully as he attacked the last box. Here we go, he thought resignedly. He ran the coin in zigzag lines along the silver square as first the pound symbol appeared, then a five and a zero – it was obviously going to be a fifty, then the final figure of a – he blinked – another zero. No! His eyes were playing tricks on him. But there it was in black and white: three matching amounts. Jesus wept! He'd just won five hundred bloody pounds. He couldn't stop smiling as the man behind the till counted out his money in fifty bills. Someone up there was smiling on him today.

'What are you going to spend it on?' a black teenage kid was watching with ill-concealed envy.

'Don't know,' Martin answered, in a daze. 'I really don't.'

He went out into the street, pulling sheets of air into his lungs.

Opposite was a flower shop – Harper & Tom's declared the awning – with a stall outside. Even to Martin's untrained eye, the arranged mixed blooms looked lovely. If he was being sensible he should bank the money. But then he thought: hang the overdraft. He had almost decided to reward himself with a visit to the hi-fi shop in Kensington – there was a music system he'd had his eye on. Instead – without knowing why – he found himself drawn inside the florist.

'Can I help you?'

He thought the shop assistant had spoken to him, but an expensively clad woman dragging along a forlorn Jack Russell by its lead, had followed him into the shop, and assumed the question had been directed at her.

'Yes, young man,' she said in response, her vowels loud and condescending. 'I'd like one of those bouquets and I'd like it wrapped in clear cellophane as a gift.'

While the assistant prepared the bouquet and rang the amount on the cash register, Martin began to look around him at the displays.

'How much for these?' He was pointing to some flowers a foot high with fuchsia and bright orange heads.

'The Gerberas are a pound a stem.'

'I'll take all of them,' he said impulsively, as the woman with the Jack Russell brushed past him on her way out.

The man tore off a sheet of paper and began to take out the stems as Martin's gaze flew around the shop to see what else took his fancy. 'What about those tulips – the two toned ones over there?'

'They're Dutch, specially bred, so I'm afraid they don't come cheap.'

'I'll take those too.'

'How many d'you want?'

'All of them.'

The man's jaw dropped. 'The whole bucket?'

'If that's all you have. And the roses,' Martin rushed on with mounting excitement. 'The pink and the red. And those as well, the ones that look like sweet peas – anything with a smell to it.'

Three more people had entered the shop and hovered in the background with varying expressions of amusement, surprise, even resentment, as more and more of the buckets were emptied. 'Is this going to take long?' one of them asked eventually.

Martin grinned ruefully. 'Sorry, but it's for a very good cause.'

'Will-iam,' the assistant shouted through to the back, his arms laden with Martin's flowers; peonies, roses, cornflowers, Ipericums, Lisianthus, giant poppies in cream, hot yellows and oranges, giant irises. 'Give us a hand up here.'

He didn't spend quite all of the five hundred, but the flowers – by the time he had cleared most of the shop's stock, had cost him a considerable chunk of it. He requested that they held off the delivery until after eight o'clock – which they were happy to do – as he wanted to be sure to catch her at home. Then he attached a short accompanying card.

Celia, he scribbled, *I'm having a good – no, I'm having a rather wonderful day, and I wanted you to be part of it. Martin.*

THIRTY-FIVE

A hot July rolled into a boiling August and Martin spent a great deal of his spare time reading on his unmade bed with the windows wide open, or going to see films by himself; he didn't feel much like socialising. He did, however, make the effort to keep up with Pike and the band. They had lost their female vocalist, but they still played occasionally at weekends and Martin would go along, thankful to lose himself in the happy oblivion of music for a few short hours. Mostly he thought about Celia, but sometimes he would catch himself thinking of Eve; she had left the agency a month earlier to help run a new, glitzy set-up in Knightsbridge, but he wasn't sorry to see her go. If she hadn't gone, he would certainly have had to make a move himself. Sometimes he would linger in town for an hour or two over a coffee after work, watching couples holding hands; families sharing a noisy, affectionate meal; teenagers tucked away in corners exchanging kisses with dreamy expressions on their faces. Each scene reinforced in him a hollow feeling of unbelonging. He began to live from day to day, in a temporary hand-to-mouth existence, closing himself off to both the past and the future. This wasn't due to feelings of melodrama or self-pity, but because he had become resigned to the fact that his life was intrinsically flawed.

One afternoon he drove to where Celia worked and sat in his car, waiting for her to finish for the day: countless messages had been left on her answering machine but his calls were never returned. She finally emerged at six, and skipped off up the road towards the Tube as if she was in a hurry. With no plan – only a hopeless, desperate need to see her – he had followed her in the car. Outside the

Tube there was a space between a van and a Peugeot, large enough for him to pull into. He called her name as she crossed the road towards him and when she waved, her face lighting up as if she was genuinely pleased to see him, he felt his spirits soar. But she ran past his car and he realised it wasn't him she was acknowledging after all. It was someone else, waiting for her by the flower stand outside the station. The man was tall and fair and undeniably attractive. Martin tried to convince himself that the man was a client, or a colleague from work, but that illusion was dashed when Celia rushed into the stranger's arms and had the breath half squeezed out of her body. After that he drove home and got throwing-up drunk.

The following week, during a half-hearted attempt to clean his flat, Martin stumbled across the property details he had picked up on the day he had met Celia in the Copper Kettle. His first thought was to throw them away. But perhaps because, somewhere inside his black cloud of confusion, he saw in them a chance for himself, something of which Frank would approve, he took the particulars through to the kitchen and laid them out on the table instead of consigning them to the wastebin. After glancing through them with a professional eye, he reached for the phone and called the acting broker. One of the three flats he had singled out was sold, another was under offer, but the third – situated a minute's walk from the Tube – was still available. Would he like to see it? Acting on a sudden impulse, he went and viewed it that same afternoon.

His intentions – or so he thought – had been no more than to occupy an hour or two of his time, yet from the moment he entered the flat, tucked anonymously behind a short row of shops, he knew he was going to buy it. He didn't care about the mottled carpet, the bathroom window that was sealed tight by a careless lick of paint, the kitchen which, in the near future, would have to be ripped out and replaced. What he saw was the pretty

Victorian fireplace, the high ceilings, the fact that it was peaceful and each room offered space to breathe. Some-one had left the mud-brown curtains in the main living area drawn, but the fabric was insubstantial and sunshine cast butterscotch rays into the room. He threw them open and gazed out on to a garden the size of a small park.

'That's Bedford House,' said the negotiator, who was showing him round. 'Half of Chiswick used to belong to it.'

He could see a child's swing and trees – too many to count – all around him, the bright yellow splash of a laburnum – which obscured his view from the road and neighbouring gardens. It was the sort of view which might inspire novelists to write, artists to paint, idealists to dream of a better world in which to live. 'How long have you had this place on your books?' he asked.

The negotiator's response was vague.

'Any bites?' Martin pushed.

'We did have one very keen buyer but the woman couldn't raise the finances. I think,' he emphasised, taking advantage of Martin's interest, 'that were you to make a decent offer, my client would give it very careful consideration.'

But standing there in that little oasis of calm, Martin didn't need any further encouragement. The flat felt absolutely right. As a first-time buyer and taking full advantage of his close connection with Carlyle's resident financial adviser – along with a generous pay-rise from Hammers – his move to secure a mortgage was a smooth one. There was one nasty moment when the vendor threatened to pull out after the collapse of his own purchase, but that proved a false alarm and a completion date was set for the end of October.

He got some gentle ribbing from Oliver when he found out. Chiswick was for middle-aged harridans and retired brigadiers, he said, but there was no denying his veiled envy of Martin's acquisition. 'Have you heard the news about Eve?' he said to Martin one day when the two of them found themselves alone in the office.

'I haven't spoken to her in weeks,' said Martin, copying his new address into his diary.

'She's back with Piers.'

He glanced up, 'Since when?'

'Around the time she left the agency, so I'm told. She's been going to see him in prison twice a week.'

Martin felt both let down and tremendously sorry for her. Stupid girl, he thought, then realised that he didn't care. The squad of lawyers, retained at an enormous fee to represent Piers, had managed to defer the trial until the new year. The police had warned Martin that he would be needed as a witness and he was only too willing to do whatever it took to put Piers behind bars.

'Her father's business has folded,' said Oliver. 'He's going to have to sell Partridge Manor.'

That beautiful house, Martin thought with regret. He had liked Howard. He certainly didn't deserve the shit Piers had thrown at him.

'Personally I don't see it lasting,' Oliver remarked, quite out of character. 'I think the only reason she's gone back to him is because she's worried about what's going to happen to her now that she doesn't have Daddy to fall back on. But put those two in a domestic routine, without Piers's money, and they'd probably slit each other's throats. In my considered opinion, your exit, Martin, was a very timely one.'

Martin braced himself for Oliver to add some snide comment, but to his utter surprise the look on his colleague's face was one of begrudging admiration. And it suddenly struck him that in all the time they had worked together, this was the first time Oliver had called him by his Christian name.

November, unexpectedly Carlyle's busiest month of the year, unfolded in a frantic blur. Martin, trying to push through four deals before the Christmas break, hardly got a moment to himself and had to put on hold the improvements he wanted to make to his new home. Boxes of clothes, CDs, books and family memorabilia acquired over the years, lay stacked in the spare room until early December, when the scrambling for property relaxed.

It was late one Friday evening and he was trying to fix a cupboard to a wall above the bathroom sink when he was interrupted by the doorbell.

He peered through the spy-hole in the front door and saw Celia, distorted by the lens, standing on the balcony steps outside. His first thought was that she must be an apparition, a figment of his imagination, but when he looked again she was still there. Unexpectedly, he felt a surge of nervousness as he opened the door.

'Hey,' he said. 'What a surprise.' He ran a not-too-steady hand through his hair and beckoned her in. 'A very nice one, I might add.'

'I took a chance,' she said, looking far from confident herself. 'I wasn't sure if you'd be in.'

She looked different somehow. Her hair was longer, it almost reached her shoulders, and she was wearing lipstick, a bold move for her.

'Can I get you something to drink?'

'Why not open this?' She relinquished a bottle of champagne wrapped in blue tissue paper along with a small package. 'Call it a belated house-warming.'

Inside the package was a copy of *The Wizard of Oz*. 'When I saw it in Dillons I thought I must buy it for you,' she said wryly. 'It seemed somehow appropriate.'

He thanked her – struggling at the same time to grasp the fact that she was really here.

'You've got a fire,' she exclaimed delightedly, stepping into the sitting room.

'It throws out some pretty decent heat.'

'They can make all the difference to a room.'

'Yes,' he said, his tone apologetic, noticing for the first time the mess around them, 'I'm hoping to start painting in here over the weekend.'

He wasn't finding the small talk easy so he withdrew to

the kitchen and scoured through cupboards, trying to find two clean glasses. When he returned with the opened champagne, he found Celia with his office keys in her hand. She was examining the leather key-ring, shaped like a saddle with a stirrup buckle on one side.

'Did you get this from Eve?'

He looked at her in surprise. 'How did you know that?'

'You're not very observant. She used to have one exactly the same.'

To cover his confusion he poured out the champagne. 'We've split up, you know.'

'Yes,' she said, sitting down. 'Roger told me.'

'He did?'

'He rang me about a month ago to check on a rental and dropped it casually into the conversation.'

The sly old dog. 'Is that why you came tonight?'

She looked at the drink in her hand, then back to his face, as if checking it against a long-held memory. 'It was part of it,' she admitted. 'When I first discovered that you and Eve had started seeing one another, I was furious with myself for ever having believed otherwise. Right from the start you were so clearly smitten by her, but I kept on hoping you would change your mind. When you took me away that weekend I felt a shift in our relationship. You were so sweet and kind that I began to think we might make a go of it. But then all that stuff emerged about you and Piers and,' she gave a sigh, 'after what happened, I felt –' she stumbled, '– like some sort of scapegoat. You've no idea how angry and upset that made me. I had to put some distance between us.'

Her voice was grave as she spoke. 'I had to decide what I wanted in life. I knew I couldn't continue working with you and Eve and after a while I began to feel that I'd got you out of my system. But when Roger mentioned that Eve was standing by Piers, I realised that nothing had changed.'

'But I thought – ?'

'Don't you see? I had to be sure your coming to see me

wasn't about you being on the rebound, looking for someone to pick up the pieces. I couldn't have faced being used for that purpose. Then your flowers arrived – my God, Martin,' her face lit up suddenly, 'I'd never seen so many flowers in my life! I was completely bowled over.' They both smiled at the inadvertent cricketing pun. 'No one had ever before done anything so – over-the-top for me.'

Her gaze shifted to the curtainless window. In the uppermost pane was the creamy glow of the moon, and beyond, faintly, came the muffled rumble of a passing train.

Martin inhaled nervously, faced with two possibilities. The moment had come when they would either draw together or – and it was too awful to contemplate – she would gather together her things and walk out of his life for ever. Her response to what he said next could tip the balance either way.

'I'm in love with you, Celia.'

She looked at her hands. 'I know.'

'But?' His agony was prolonged by her lapse into silence. 'I mean,' he pushed on desperately, 'is that such an intolerable situation to find yourself in; being loved by me?'

She raised her eyes. 'Love isn't enough on its own, Martin. What if we've left it too late?'

'We won't know without trying.'

'I'm afraid.'

'So am I,' he admitted and opened his arms. 'Now come here.'

Later, lying on the floor together, their skin aglow from making love and the heat of the fire, Martin's thoughts took on a simple, elemental quality. This is it, he realised. This is everything. All we can hope for is the here-and-now. Life cannot be grasped, or manipulated, but only lived. He was comforted by a memory, brief and vibrant like a firework, of something Frank had once said to him: 'I believe that the afterlife is what you leave behind in other people.'

336

Martin knew that he had to accept the facts; that his real parents were lost to him for ever. He would never know what went through his mother's mind when she woke him up, washed and dressed him, placed him inside a supermarket carrier bag and carried him through the hushed, deserted streets of Ipswich one July morning. The truth went with her the moment she turned her back and walked away.

'You're looking very pensive,' Celia said, her voice fragmenting the image of his ghostly mother until it had gone completely from his mind. She gently nuzzled her chin against his neck, sighing contentedly.

'I was just thinking that for the first time in months I feel genuinely happy.' He looked at her and swallowed. 'I think if I were to lose you now –'

She put a finger to his lips. 'Shush,' she said gently. 'You've got me. You've always had me, right from the day I first saw you in the office.'

'That long ago?' He raised an eyebrow. 'Well, it was obviously my irresistible charm.'

She laughed, pinching him gently on his bottom. 'How the male ego swells. That's the last time I confess anything to you.'

'Tell me something,' he said, remembering suddenly. 'I saw you once with a blond man, tall – rather good-looking,' he added begrudgingly. 'Who was he?'

She had to think for a moment. 'I don't know anyone by that description.'

'Yes, you do. You met him one evening a few weeks ago after work – outside Turnham Green Tube.'

Her face suddenly cleared. 'Oh, you must mean Blake.'

'Yes,' he said bleakly. 'Blake.'

'Blake is married to my cousin. The photograph I used to keep on my desk at Carlyle is of his little girl.' She looked at him shrewdly. 'Do you mean to tell me you were spying on me?'

'No,' he said, feeling a little shamefaced but mostly relief. 'Well, at least not intentionally.'

They both smiled. He gazed into the blue-orange heart

of the fire, his face burning, a glow in his belly. One day, he mused, one day soon I will tell her. I will tell her the truth about my abandonment. Because it is part of me, a part of me she must know, and because being honest with one another is the only way this relationship has a chance of working – God knows, I want it to.

Celia shifted herself into a sitting position and filled each of their glasses. 'What shall we drink to?'

'To us?' he said, taking one.

'To your new home, Martin,' she declared, raising her glass to salute him, 'and to it being my best birthday ever.'

He looked at her disbelievingly. 'It's not, is it?'

She nodded.

'Well, in that case,' he said, feeling a lightness float through his veins. 'Happy birthday, beautiful.'

And like the soft contact of mouths meeting for a kiss, they gently clinked their glasses.